...st novel, *Testament*, was published by Macmillan
... g a national competition. She works for the National
... Society and is a member of the Society of Authors and
... Crime Writers' Association. She lives in Coleford, Glos., in
the Forest of Dean.

2 ?

Also by Alis Hawkins

The Teifi Valley Coroner Series

Alis Hawkins

NOT
One
OF US

CANELO

First published in the United Kingdom in 2021 by

Canelo
31 Helen Road
Oxford OX2 0DF
United Kingdom

A CIP catalogue record for this book is available from the British Library.

Print ISBN 978 1 80032 471 8
Ebook ISBN 978 1 80032 470 1

Look for more great books at www.canelo.co

Printed and bound in Great Britain by Clays Ltd, Elcograf S.p.A.

1

For Sam and Nancy

with all my love

Glossary

(terms appear in the order in which they occur in the book)

betgwn – the outer garment of most Cardiganshire working women in the nineteenth century. It featured a tight, low cut bodice and a long back, sometimes gathered up into a 'tail'. It would have been worn over a blouse and petticoats with an apron over the top.

Mic y Porthmon – Mike the drover

'machgen i – my boy (affectionate)

swci lamb – an orphan lamb reared by hand

caseg pen fedi – literally 'the mare at the end of harvest'. The name given to the last sheaf to be tied

merched y gerddi – the garden girls

'ngwas i – (colloquially) my lad

Llwyo – an English equivalent would be something like 'Spoonsy' or 'the Spoonster'

dyn hysbys – cunning man, hedge wizard, white witch, healer

dewin – wizard

fach/bach – term of endearment, literally 'little'

coron fedw – birch crown

Deio'r Gwahoddwr – Deio the Inviter/Bidder-to-come

Wil y Gwahoddwr – Wil the Inviter/Bidder-to-come

crachach – gentry or upper classes (slightly derogatory)

hiraeth – a longing for times or places past

gwas bach – literally 'little servant' – generally reserved for the youngest or most junior servants

caru yn y gwelu – courting in bed, 'bundling' (see historical note)

twpsyn – idiot, stupid person

Harry

When the library door opened and Benton Reckitt was announced, I knew that somebody must be dead. Dr Reckitt did not make spontaneous social calls.

'Probert-Lloyd, I've just— Oh, I'm sorry, I didn't realise you had company.'

My private secretary, Lydia Howell, turned to face him. 'Not company, Dr Reckitt, only me. I take it you need to see Harry urgently?'

It was a reasonable assumption, given the energy with which Reckitt had steamed into the room.

'Somebody's just brought me the most interesting sudden death.'

To most people, sudden death is shocking, troubling, even disturbing, but to Benton Reckitt it was invariably *interesting*. My spirits, very much lowered by a letter from the county magistrates that still lay open on the table next to Lydia, were suddenly lifted.

Lydia rose from her chair. 'Then I shall leave you to it.' She picked up the offending missive and folded it away. If only the magistrates' latest attempt to bring me to heel could be put aside so easily.

'No,' I said, standing to forestall her withdrawal, 'please stay. Another pair of ears can only help.' And eyes, I might have said. Central blindness meant that I saw Reckitt as nothing more than a large figure in riding clothes. The minutiae of his dress, visible only in my peripheral vision, were lost to me, as were his facial expressions.

Lydia sat down again without comment.

I waved Reckitt to a chair and resumed my seat. 'Do go on.'

'I've just received a visit from a farmer's wife from the other side of Eglwyswrw – towards Brynberian. She was away working for a few days when her husband sent somebody to tell her that her eldest daughter was dead.'

Sent somebody. It must say something about relations between man and wife that he had not gone to break the news himself.

'And the *interesting* cause?' I asked.

'Sudden natural death.'

'Natural?'

'Those were the exact words written on the death certificate by the quack who was called to the house.'

I stifled a grin. In Reckitt's opinion, any medical practitioner who did not adhere to his own rigorous scientific standards was unworthy of the title 'doctor'. 'So had she been ill?' I asked. 'How old was she?'

'Pertinent questions. The young woman concerned was nineteen years old, and until she was, apparently, found dead in her bed yesterday morning was in perfect health but for a slight cold a few days ago.'

'Does her mother suspect foul play?' Lydia asked.

Reckitt turned to her. 'She doesn't know what to think. But she *is* convinced that her husband is keeping something from her.'

'She thinks he might have had a hand in his daughter's death?' Lydia persisted.

'What she *suspects*, Miss Howell, is neither here nor there,' Reckitt said. 'The fact is that no satisfactory cause has been given for this apparently healthy young woman's death.'

Unexplained death was a constant affront to Reckitt, and he would do anything in his power to render it explicable.

'I take it that this lady would like me to give my opinion, as coroner?'

'Yours and mine both. She'd heard of my particular expertise in these matters.'

'She's not asked you to perform a post-mortem examination, surely?'

'Not in so many words. But she came to me for my opinion on how her daughter died. It comes to the same thing.'

I put that blatantly self-serving suggestion aside for the time being. 'And where is this lady now?'

'On her way home. If we're quick about it, we'll find her still on the road.'

It was some time since I had heard the hall clock strike three. We would have to hurry if we were to have decent daylight in which to view this unfortunate young woman's body. 'Very well. I'll go and change.'

'Shall I send for Mr Davies?'

I turned back to him, schooling my features into blandness; I did not want Reckitt to think that John Davies's absence represented anything other than a well-deserved holiday. 'I'm afraid you'll have to stand in as my assistant on this occasion, Reckitt – John's not here. He's in London. At the Great Exhibition.'

John

If I'm honest, I hadn't been that fussed on seeing the Great Exhibition. I felt as if I knew everything about it already. Ever since the Queen had opened the Crystal Palace to the public, the illustrated magazines had gone on and on about nothing else. Lavish pictures and gushing descriptions. Endless praise and admiration. The whole thing'd soured on me a bit. And then Lydia Howell had dissected it all for us in minute detail after she'd been up to see it with her friend, Miss Phoebe Gwatkyn. The pair of them'd come back full of it.

But in the end, I went because I needed to get away. Away from Glanteifi. Away from Harry. Away from my boss, Glanteifi's estate steward, Mr Ormiston. And away from myself, too – from the coward I'd turned into since taking on the under-steward's job.

So here I was. Surrounded by the arts and industry and manufacturing and inventions of half the world in a glasshouse that enclosed eighteen acres of Hyde Park. Eighteen acres! That'd be a whole farm at home. The size of it made the two elm trees that'd been left standing inside look like toys.

But it wasn't just the size of the Crystal Palace that took your breath away – it was the colourfulness of it all. I hadn't been expecting that – not in a glasshouse. But the glass was the only colourless thing in the whole place. Even the iron framework was painted, every inch of it, in blue, yellow and red.

That morning, I was standing in front of the 'Trophy Telescope', one of the illustrated magazines' favourite exhibits.

'Does it work?' the boy at my side asked. 'Or is it just a giant model?'

I turned to look at him. Daniel Williams, hall boy to Miss Phoebe Gwatkyn, lady of Alltybela, fancifully known as Lleu after a character in Welsh mythology, was looking quite the young toff. He had a new suit of clothes, and his fair hair was barbered and oiled.

Miss Gwatkyn had asked if I'd mind bringing him with me, and I'd said yes because he was a sparky lad, Lleu. Good company. Then I'd discovered that I was bringing half a dozen other servants with him – the ones who'd been left in charge when Miss Gwatkyn'd taken the rest of her household up to the Exhibition with Lydia Howell.

'You know London, John,' she'd said. 'You know how things work. They won't get lost or come to harm with you.'

That was an exaggeration. I didn't really *know* London at all. I'd been to the city twice before, but at least that meant I knew it enough to get the Alltybela lot to their boarding house without breaking a sweat. And find a hansom cab to take me to the grand house off Ladbroke Street where Harry's friend Gus Gelyot was putting me up.

As it happened, Mr Gelyot'd walked us over to Hyde Park that morning and was standing in front of the Trophy Telescope with us.

'Oh, it's perfectly functional,' he said, in answer to Lleu's question. 'That's the whole point of this vast carnival of industry. That it all works.' He flung out a hand. 'Behold, the wonders of the modern world, courtesy of His Royal Highness Prince Albert, de facto king-emperor of half the globe.'

I caught Lleu's eye and gave him a look. *Don't worry, it's not you, he's always like this.*

'Anyway, gentlemen, delightful as this has been,' Mr Gelyot said, 'I must leave you. I have a luncheon engagement.'

If I'd known him better, I might've teased him, asked if he was meeting a young lady. As it was, I didn't dare. It was less than a year since I'd first stayed at the Gelyots' house when Harry and I'd been working on our first investigation together. On that visit,

Mr Gelyot'd tried to put me in the servants' quarters. Granted, I'd been a solicitor's clerk then, not Harry's under-steward, but I still didn't know Gus Gelyot well enough to risk any kind of familiarity.

I watched him saunter off, swinging his silver-topped cane, immaculate in a dark-blue jacket and trousers, with a sky-blue-and-gold waistcoat. He always dressed like a dandy, but I still thought he was off to meet a woman.

'Shall we have something to eat as well?' I asked Lleu.

He grinned and slapped his pocket. 'Got enough in here to keep me going for now. Not everyone wanted their breakfast.' Which probably meant that the older servants'd been drinking the previous night and had ended up with sore heads this morning after trying London's India pale ales and porters.

'All right then,' I said. 'Now it's just us, let's go and look at the farming machines.'

I wasn't that keen on gawping at mechanical mowers and crop-sowing machines, to be honest, but I knew Harry'd be interested, and telling him about the new machinery would give me an excuse to talk to him – again – about improvements on the estate.

Ever since I'd started working under Mr Ormiston, I'd been trying to work out why Harry didn't get more involved in things, why he never seemed to discuss the business of the estate with his steward. Because it needed discussing – as far as I could see, the whole estate was in danger of going to rack and ruin.

As the summer'd gone on and I'd got more and more worried about the way things were shaping up, I'd dropped I don't know how many hints about the three of us having a discussion about the estate's management. But Harry'd brushed them all off. In the end, I'd decided the only thing for it was to come right out with it and tell him he was going to have to step in and do something. Specifically, to go back to some of his late father's plans for the estate. But he'd just point-blank refused.

'I've told Ormiston what I need from him,' he'd said to me in a tone of voice that wasn't going to be argued with, 'and I'm doing him the courtesy I wish others would allow me. I'm letting him get on with his job without interference.'

So I'd tried – as diplomatically as I could – to raise a few things with Mr Ormiston, but I'd got short shrift from him, too. 'You may feel you know better than me, Mr Davies, because your father was a tenant farmer. But let me tell you, things look very different on the other side of the ledger. You barely knew Mr Probert-Lloyd senior, but I can tell you that though he was a thoroughgoing gentleman of the old school and an exemplary magistrate, he did not have the instincts of a true squire. He was too lax with the tenants. Mr Harry Probert-Lloyd is cut from a different cloth. He understands financial realities.'

That'd made me even more worried. Because as far as I could see, Harry didn't have a clue about financial realities. Not when it came to running an estate. Glanteifi was teetering on the edge of bankruptcy, and tenant's son or not, I could see that if Mr Ormiston carried on the way he was going, we'd be over the edge and ruined before a twelvemonth was out.

Lleu and I made our way to the south-western edge of the Crystal Palace, where the floor plan told us we'd find the agricultural machines. The boy was looking about him in a fashion fit to crick his neck, but still, he was right to try and take it all in, wasn't he? No point being there otherwise.

The trouble was, a lot of the exhibits didn't interest me at all – the kind of decorative items that seemed to be everywhere you looked – and I was so busy trying not to worry about what was going on at home that it was a big effort to pay attention to the more interesting stuff.

I knew everybody else was saying how astonishing it was that such a huge structure could be built out of glass, but the thing that really struck me was the sheer acreage of cloth everywhere. Quite apart from the undyed canvas that covered all the flat bits of roof to stop the sun cooking everybody inside, in the central two storeys of the glasshouse every interior surface seemed to be draped or hung with material. Display stands were covered in red cloth. Vast national flags hung from the upper galleries. Colourful hangings divided different sections of the Exhibition.

Mind, I'm not saying that such an enormous amount of glass *wasn't* astonishing – it was, of course. My job at Glanteifi was educating me in how much it cost to put up even small buildings, so I was in a position to be more impressed than most people by the Crystal Palace. Quite apart from the glass and steel that'd been needed to build it, I didn't know where to start working out what acreage of woodland must've been felled to make the floorboards we were walking on.

Like everything else at the Great Exhibition, the floors'd been designed by somebody who knew exactly what they were doing. There were wide gaps – maybe as much as a third of an inch – between each floorboard on the ground floor so that all the dust and bits that people dropped were just brushed down the cracks by the ladies' dresses whisking over them. No labour needed to sweep the floor clean, so costs were kept down. Of course, on the upper storey, things were different. Up there, the boards'd been fitted closely together, otherwise we'd all have been standing in a gentle rain of dirt.

Lleu and I stepped aside as three young women, arm in arm, came towards us as if we weren't there. I watched them as they swept past. Dainty. Neat. Pretty. Waists nipped in by their ridiculously full-skirted dresses, hair shining and uncovered. They looked totally different from the practically dressed girls at home. From another world.

'Look at that!' Lleu was pointing at a huge steam-powered engine.

'It's one of those new threshing machines,' I said.

'You'd never get that in a threshing barn!'

'You're not supposed to. This is what you have *instead* of a threshing barn.' And instead of all the men whose winter work it was to wield the threshing flails. This kind of machine had caused riots twenty years ago in England for exactly that reason – men out of work, families with no food. So far, I only knew of one steam thresher at home. And that one didn't belong to a farmer, it belonged to a miller.

'Don't get too excited,' I told Lleu. 'Not one in ten of the gentry back home would be able to afford one of those. Not in a month of Sundays.'

Besides, you'd only want one if you needed all your corn threshed at once, to sell on the open market. And Glanteifi wasn't in that league. Not by a long shot. If we'd had that much corn to sell, we wouldn't've been in the financial situation we found ourselves in.

I turned towards a smaller machine for mowing corn or grass and was just asking Lleu whether he thought it would work in the little fields at home when a voice behind us said, in Welsh, 'Well I never! Who'd have thought I'd hear the language of heaven here?'

The accent was like my own and I looked around expecting to see somebody I knew.

But as it turned out, I didn't know him. Not yet, at any rate.

Harry

Making the most of the turnpike road, Reckitt and I cantered up the first half-mile to the junction that would take us south to Cenarth. Then, swinging sharply downhill, we slowed our horses to a walk down the sudden gradient. I had become ever more reliant on my little mare's ability to pick her own way along the sometimes rough and ready parish roads of the Teifi Valley, and now I let her have her head.

The day was sultry, though I knew it might be a different story on the slopes of the Frenni and had brought a coat, which was rolled up with my other things behind my saddle. It was odd not having John at my side as I rode out to a sudden death, and I could almost hear him complaining about the conditions. *Close, isn't it?*

Close was a better word than sultry; the warm air did feel as if it was pressing in about you, like a damp sheet. There was not a breath of wind, and I was glad of the movement of air past my face as the lane flattened out and our horses extended into a trot once more.

I wondered what John's response to the Great Exhibition – the government's hubristic expression of Britain's international significance – would prove to be. Perhaps a spell in London would put him in a better humour than he had been recently, take him out of himself. He had developed something of a fascination for the city and its many faces, and I knew from my own experience that to a man of twenty, London held attractions that provincial life simply could not offer.

At my side, Reckitt seemed uncomfortable. He did not rise to the trot like a man at ease in the saddle but bumped up and down like a green stable boy riding bareback. 'Tell me about the woman who came to fetch you,' I said. 'What was she like?'

He turned towards me. 'What do you mean, what was she *like*?'

Reckitt despised vagueness, but he generally managed to infer the meaning behind such questions well enough; clearly, I had underestimated how onerous he found horsemanship. His usual habit was to hire a trap for his travels, and it was an indication of his haste today that he had chosen to ride instead.

'Age?' I offered as an example. 'General demeanour, level of education or intelligence, ability to take in information offered to her...'

'About forty, I suppose,' he said. 'Aged by hard work, but strong.'

'Physically?'

'And in terms of her character, I should say. As is so often the case in women. One almost never sees a physically large woman who is also meek and biddable.'

Though I had never considered it before, he was right. Men might be described as gentle giants, but large women were always *formidable*.

'I should say she was intelligent rather than educated,' he continued. 'Though we did speak in English.'

The fact that this woman's command of the language was better than Reckitt's Welsh did not necessarily indicate any great fluency on her part. Being physician to the Cardigan Union workhouse, Reckitt had mastered sufficient Welsh to hold a conversation about symptoms and illnesses, but he would not be comfortable holding a long conversation in the language.

'And she told you her husband was hiding something? Did you get the impression that the two of them were at odds? In general, I mean, rather than in this particular case.'

A brief pause ensued. 'How would one tell? She simply told me what had happened and asked me to come and give my opinion as to the cause of her daughter's death.'

Until that point, I had assumed that this lady had knocked at Reckitt's door rather than my own simply because his house, in Cilgerran, was nearer to her own farm than Glanteifi by several miles. However, now it seemed that perhaps it had been his idea, and not hers, to involve me. In which case, my arrival might not be entirely welcome.

'Was there anybody else at home with her husband and the deceased daughter while she was away?' I asked.

'No. Her other two daughters had gone with her.'

'And the reason for the eldest's staying at home?'

'The head cold I mentioned. Didn't fancy half a day's walk and a lot of hard work into the bargain.'

We reached the point where the road was forced steeply up onto the lip of Cenarth gorge and our horses slowed to a strenuous walk.

The few details Reckitt had been able to give me about the dead girl's family were intriguing. The fact that her mother and sisters had been working away from home suggested that the family did not hold much land; it would be beneath the dignity of a substantial farmer's wife, however impecunious, to take up work elsewhere. However, the bereaved woman's apparent demeanour and command of English made it unlikely that she was a labourer's wife.

'I assume the family are smallholders?'

Reckitt seemed to be having some trouble staying upright in the saddle on the steep incline. 'I didn't ask.'

Feeling that it might be both prudent and kind to let him concentrate on keeping his seat, I kept further questions to myself and considered my own position. If Reckitt were to find injuries that had been overlooked by whoever had signed the death certificate, then I would be obliged to have a jury assembled to view the body. If, on the other hand, he found no obvious indications of foul play, or, indeed, an unreported accident, I would have an uncomfortable decision to make. He would, without doubt, want to perform a post-mortem examination so as to be able to rule definitively on cause of death. However, given that a forensic dissection cost two guineas, the county magistrates were not enthusiastic about the procedure being carried out without good reason. And describing exactly what kind of natural death a young woman had succumbed to was not, in their eyes, nearly good enough. Given that I had just received a letter detailing new procedures designed to limit the scope of the coroner's powers, it would be unwise of me to spend public money in a way they would see as profligate.

-

At Cenarth, we rode over the Teifi into Pembrokeshire and trotted up into the Cych valley, crossing the little river then climbing up and heading towards Cilwendeg. I remembered a visit to the mansion there one summer when I was a small boy; somebody had taken me to see a shell grotto in the grounds. Being only four or five and never having been to the seaside, I had not encountered shells before, and the fact that little animals had once lived in what looked like hollow stones had had to be explained to me. Such a thing, I recalled, had seemed scarcely more reasonable than the existence of unicorns.

The memory disturbed me slightly because I had forgotten the visit until now; I had become used to the notion that my widowed father had neither made nor received social calls during my childhood.

I tried to put thoughts of my father aside. Every time I thought of him, I heard again the words of one of our older neighbours at his funeral. 'He had great hopes of you, Henry. I trust you're not going to let him down.' But the fact of the matter was that my father and I had never seen eye to eye and the hopes he had had of me were not those I had nurtured for myself.

As we came to the drovers' road to Cardigan, I stared straight ahead, so that the whirlpool – my name for the patch of grey blindness at the centre of my vision – rested on the ears of my little mare, Sara. Below the blind nothingness, I could see Sara's mane, above it the rounded tops of the Preseli Hills rose in the distance ahead of us.

Would I have known the mountains were there if I had not previously been able to see the vista in front of me? I could not be sure. The eye specialist I had consulted had told me that I must make as much use as I could of what he called *the memory of seeing*, so that I might train myself to interpret what now remained visible to me. But, memory being such a tricksy beast, I sometimes wondered whether I only imagined what I saw, rather than actually seeing it.

After a few minutes, we turned uphill, and I looked about me as the high ground opened out on either side of us. The air smelled different here, the earth more peaty, lacking the undernotes of clay that were ever present down in the valley. Above us, the sky was a vastness of blue and scudding white that stretched out over the whole of the Preselis, and the landscape, visible for miles in every direction, was so different from the confined vistas of the Teifi's tributary valleys that it felt as if I was in a different country.

I had never been to this corner of the Teifi Valley Coroner's purview before; though we were in one of the parishes of the Cardigan Workhouse Union, which marked the southern limit of my jurisdiction, we were well into Pembrokeshire.

At a crossroads where an inn stood ready to greet travellers from every direction, Reckitt chose a road that would take us still further up onto the hilly slopes.

After a few minutes, he pulled up and, standing in his stirrups, called, 'Good day, to you! We're looking for Rhosdywarch.'

On the other side of the hedge, a man straightened from whatever he was doing. 'About Lizzie Rees, is it?'

'Yes. This is Mr Probert-Lloyd, the coroner.'

The figure moved closer to us. 'Sad news, young girl like that, whole life ahead of her—'

'Yes, yes,' Reckitt interrupted. 'Are we near?'

His tone earned him a few seconds' reproachful silence before the man provided directions. 'Rhosdywarch's on your right as you're going back up the hill after the ford,' he concluded. 'You'll know it by the apple trees on the south side.'

We continued, and not five minutes later, after we had splashed through the shallow water of the ford, Reckitt called out once more.

'Mrs Rees!'

As the woman turned in the road at the sound of her name, I could see from the movement of her hands that she was knitting as she walked. I could not see it clearly but I knew that the ball of wool she was using would be hung on a hook from her belt.

'Another minute and I'd have been home before you,' she called, in English, hands still moving as we trotted towards her. 'That's our place up there.'

So this was the dead girl's mother. She would not know it, but Reckitt's remembering her name was an indication of the intensity of his interest in her daughter's death. Obscure Latin terms for fragments of human anatomy tripped lightly off his tongue, but, in general, personal names seemed unable to find a foothold in his capacious memory.

We dismounted and, introductions having been made and condolences offered, walked with Mrs Rees the last fifty yards or so to a small cluster of whitewashed buildings. The hands holding her needles moved backwards and forwards in a movement as rhythmic as her footfall, and I wondered what portion of a stocking – or pair – she had knitted on her journey to and from Reckitt's house. When I was a boy, it had been many a young woman's proud boast that she could make a pair of stockings in a day, given enough time with her needles.

As we turned aside to her house, Mrs Rees pushed her knitting into the bodice of her *betgwn*. 'Welcome to my home, gentlemen. Please, come and tell me what happened to my Lizzie.'

John

The owner of the Welsh voice behind us turned out to be a youngish man called Jem Harborne. And like me and Lleu, he'd come up from the Teifi Valley.

'I'm here for the textile machines,' he told us. 'Want to come and have a look?'

I'd had enough of looking at horse-drawn mowers and steam threshers, so we let him drag us off with him for company.

I never knew there were so many machines involved in making cloth. My understanding of how it was done by hand, from watching my mother spin and sell her yarn, was pretty simple – you carded the wool so the fibres were all straight instead of tangled up, then you spun it and sold it to a weaver, who made cloth out of it. But here, there were rows and rows of machines involved in manufacturing cotton and silk and wool and linen and every one of them looked incredibly complicated.

Mr Harborne used words like 'slubbing' and 'roving' and 'willowing'. He pointed out lace machines that I didn't understand at all, and a machine for printing calicoes that claimed to be able to print eight colours at once and then dry the cloth before rolling it into a bolt. We even walked past one that he called a 'gassing machine'. Apparently it singed away the loose fibre from lace and muslins.

'It's similar to what shearers do when they cut the nap on woollen cloth really fine,' he said. I didn't like to tell him I didn't have a clue what he meant, but he must've seen it in my face. 'It's a skilled job. Makes the cloth finer, smoother.'

A skilled job. So how would a brute-force machine do it? How would it know when to stop singeing? But we'd moved on.

'This is the kind of thing I'm interested in,' Mr Harborne said, stopping alongside a gleaming machine with tightly stretched fabric on it. 'Made in Blackburn – this one here's for weaving very fine woollens, and that one there is for the heavier cloths.'

I looked at the machines. They weren't any bigger than the hand looms I'd seen weavers using at home – smaller, if anything, more compact – but they seemed to have a lot more moving parts. And they were made of iron that gleamed with greasing oil, whereas the looms I was used to were all made of wood.

Because Lleu was a child, he asked the question I'd been too polite to ask. 'Why are you interested in these machines, Mr Harborne? We don't use them at home.'

Harborne looked him in the eye. 'That's *why* I'm interested in them. Because we need to *start* using them at home.' He looked from Lleu to me. 'Why don't we go and have something to eat, and I can tell you all about it? We Teifi boys should stick together.'

My pockets weren't full of food like Lleu's, so I agreed to go with him. But whatever he said and however much he might sound like us, Jem Harborne didn't look like a Teifi boy. He had a kind of restless attractiveness to him, a *glamour*, that I'd only seen in people from away. And then there were his clothes. His shirt and necktie were nothing special – just London fashions – but his suit was a different matter altogether. It was made of a smooth, finely woven fabric that didn't look like either wool or linen.

'Angola,' he said when he caught me staring. 'Silk and wool blend.' He held his arm out for me to feel it.

I kept my hands to myself. I wasn't used to talking about fabrics like a woman, still less feeling one on a stranger. And I'd never heard of a fabric that mixed silk and wool. *Angola*. Another new idea to take home.

'Have you been to Soyer's symposium?' he asked as we walked past displays of fabric towards one of the exits at the western end of the Crystal Palace.

'No, what's it about?'

He grinned. 'It's not that sort of symposium.'

Outside, the sunshine felt fresh after the dead-air heat inside, and even though the crowds were still jostling and jabbering around us, their voices didn't press on your ears the way they did inside the glasshouse. It was a relief to be out in what passed for fresh air in London.

We followed Mr Harborne through the crowds milling in and out of Hyde Park and crossed the road to a grand house that stood behind a wall with two sets of double gates let into it. Between the gates the words 'Soyer's Symposium' were painted.

Something Lydia Howell had said came back to me. 'Hold on,' I said. 'Is this where the biggest dining room in the world is supposed to be?'

'That's it! Soyer got the firm who built that,' Jem Harborne jerked his thumb back over his shoulder at the Crystal Palace, 'to put up a huge glasshouse for him behind Gore House. It can sit hundreds, and he's had the longest tablecloth in the world made for it – over a hundred yards!' He grinned. 'Not much of a feat of weaving, but imagine washing it!'

I smiled, but in truth, I wasn't thinking about his tablecloth. Just the thought of Lydia Howell had knotted my stomach up.

What was Harry getting her to do while I was away? Since she'd come to Glanteifi to work for him, back in the spring, she seemed to have influenced every aspect of life in the mansion. With me away, Harry'd be bound to turn to her even more than usual and I dreaded him comparing the two of us. Lydia's quiet competence made me feel about twelve instead of twenty.

I'd never been able to understand why she wanted to work for Harry. Why she wanted to come back to the Teifi Valley at all, come to that. During the Rebecca tollgate riots, seven or eight years ago, she'd played a very dangerous game. She'd pretended to be somebody she wasn't and she'd been found out – something Harry and I had discovered when we first worked together, investigating the murder of his one-time sweetheart, Margaret Jones.

In Lydia's shoes, I'd have kept well away from the Teifi Valley. For ever. But after we'd found her in Ipswich, she and Harry'd started writing letters to each other, and before we knew it, she'd turned up with her bizarre idea of coming to work for him.

As we walked up to the door of Soyer's Symposium, I hung back, Lleu at my side like an uncertain shadow. We didn't have enough money to eat in this kind of place.

'Come on!' Harborne urged.

I shook my head. 'I don't think...'

'It's not just for toffs, if that's what you're worried about. Come on, I'll show you.'

Whether it was for toffs or not, I still wasn't sure I wanted to go in. How impressive could a massive glass dining room be anyway, after the Crystal Palace?

'Look.' Harborne pointed to a notice above the door that read, *Say how many you are, and at what cost you wish to dine; you need say nothing more, your dinner is settled.*

All very well, but what if you wished to dine at tuppence ha'penny?

That was answered when we were asked for a shilling just to get in – as much as we'd paid to see the whole of the Great Exhibition! I shook my head again. 'Mr Harborne, I don't think—'

'Your shilling partly pays for your dinner,' the money-taker said, as if he'd had to say the same words ten thousand times before.

'Partly?'

Jem Harborne butted in. 'You can dine like a king for two shillings.'

'But—'

'Come on! We've got time to look around before they start taking orders at two.'

Lleu held his hand out. 'Here's my shilling.' He looked over his shoulder at me. 'I may never come to London again, so I'm going to see everything I can while I'm here!'

The two of them disappeared inside and I was left with no choice. If I stayed out here, I'd be a caricature 'Cardi' – a Cardiganshire miser with long pockets and short arms.

An hour later, we were finishing our dinner and I couldn't believe I'd wondered if it'd be worth the money. Alexis Soyer's restaurant was a marvel.

Jem Harborne said Soyer'd called it a 'symposium' because he wanted to educate people while he fed them. And entertain them too. According to Harborne, advertising posters'd gone up all over London calling the symposium a 'Gigantic Dining Encampment of All Nations'. And from what we'd seen, that was no exaggeration.

Before we sat down to eat our dinner in the biggest dining room in the world, we'd walked through smaller rooms in the main house that seemed to represent every country and civilisation on earth, from China to Italy to the frozen north. Every inch of the place was painted with murals and decorated with objects from around the world, and there were technological wonders too – gas lamps whose light was flung about the place by mirrored glass, a gigantic gas-fired apparatus in the outdoor kitchen that was roasting a whole beef carcass, even a glass ceiling filled with water where little goldfish were swimming!

'You should see this place at night,' Harborne said, leaning back in his chair till the front feet were off the ground. 'It's like fairyland – lights everywhere and all the magical effects Soyer's technicians have been able to conjure up. Mind you, with all the gas lamps and candles everywhere, it gets viciously hot. People've been known to faint clean away!'

I nodded. The whole place was astonishing enough by day, but by night I could picture it being like a giant magical box lit up from inside. 'You've visited at night yourself, have you?'

Harborne held his hand up, fingers splayed. 'Five times!' He let his chair tip forward and leaned over the table at me and Lleu. 'I'll tell you one thing. What with this,' he gestured around us, 'and that monstrous glasshouse over there, nobody in future will ever be able to say that something can't be done. If you've got the will, you can do anything, anywhere. And quickly, too. Paxton built the Crystal Palace in *ten months*, and for less than half the cost of the original design. *Less than half!* And look at it – it's a wonder of the age.'

I nodded. It was; no argument about that.

Harborne leaned further over the table. 'The "Crystal Palace". Whoever called it that was a genius! Think about it. People *might've* come to see "the world's biggest glasshouse", but it doesn't sound very exciting, does it? But "the Crystal Palace"?' He began holding up fingers. 'Riches, royalty, magic. Genius!'

We'd had nothing to drink with our dinner, but I began to think Jem Harborne might've been drinking before we met him. He seemed unnaturally enthusiastic about everything.

'So, my Teifi boys, what's caught your eye for the farms back home?'

Lleu looked at me. I rearranged the cutlery on my empty plate. Whatever I thought about the machines we'd seen, Glanteifi didn't have the money to buy a single one. We were in enough debt already. Just the thought of it made me start to sweat. And whatever Harry thought, the way Mr Ormiston was managing the estate would make things worse, not better.

I tried to ignore the prickles of panic up my scalp and took a deep breath. 'Seems to me,' I said, 'that all those mechanical contraptions are designed for a different type of farming.'

Jem Harborne cocked his head, wanting me to explain. But I couldn't tell him that they were just too expensive for our little farms. 'They're built for big, flat, tidy fields,' I said. 'They'd never cope with our slopes. Or the size and odd shapes of the fields.'

'Are you telling me that you haven't seen a single machine that might be applicable back home? What about that sheep-washing contraption?'

'We've got the river.'

'The machine for bruising gorse, then?'

'That's one of the things labourers do in the winter.'

'Labourers? That's the point of machines – to do away with the need for labour!'

'But what would the labourers do if they didn't have the work? Their families'd starve!'

Lleu was watching me and Harborne as if we were the only people in the room. And why wouldn't he? This was his life we were talking about. I knew for a fact that he'd gone to work in Miss Gwatkyn's house because his parents couldn't afford to feed him.

'Machines are coming to the Teifi Valley whatever you think,' Harborne said. 'And the labour will just have to go somewhere else. There's going to be no end of jobs down in the Rhondda mines once they get the pumping systems right. They've got coal measures down there to last a lifetime.'

'But people can't just pack up and go south!'

'Why not?'

I shook my head. Jem Harborne had no idea how the world worked when you were so poor you didn't know where your next mouthful was coming from. 'If you're going to walk to the Rhondda valleys, you need enough food to keep you going on the way there. That's got to be four or five days of walking – a week if you're taking your whole family.'

'Who said anything about walking? I'm talking about the railways!'

'We haven't got any railways at home.'

'*Yet*. But they're coming – fast. And when they get to Llandysul and Newcastle Emlyn and Lampeter and Tregaron, people will get on the train and leave. Imagine it – breakfast in Llandysul, supper in the Rhondda.' Harborne was waiting for me to say something, I could tell. When I didn't, he just smiled. 'They're sinking a new coal pit down there as we speak, gentlemen. *As we speak!*'

He leaned back again. Behind him, through the glass wall, I could see people wandering around outside, gawping at the decorated gardens and Soyer's outdoor kitchen. Was Harborne right? Would the people at home who scratched a living from their smallholdings and laboured for a pittance just move away to find a better life somewhere else? Perhaps. Some people'd already gone further, hadn't they? To America. But they were mostly farmers who'd been able to save money for the passage. Cottagers and labourers would never be able to put enough aside. But if the railways came, like he said...

I didn't want to think about that. Because if there weren't enough labourers, then machines were the only solution and Glanteifi just wouldn't be able to afford them. Not unless our financial situation changed quickly.

The thought made me start worrying about what Mr Ormiston was doing while I was away. Just thinking about his attitude to the kind of smallholders Jem Harborne was talking about put icy fingers around my neck. He'd be very glad to see labourers and cottagers loading their families onto a railway carriage and leaving.

I fixed my eyes on the crowds milling about on the other side of the glass and tried to put Micah Ormiston out of my mind.

There were all sorts out there in the grounds – men and women mingling, some well-dressed and some in working clothes, a few soldiers in uniform, foreigners with their different fashions. Was this the future – nobody staying where they started out, just going off to the next new thing and making a life there?

I knew that in the next week or so we might be forcing people to leave Glanteifi and go somewhere else because we had to deal with all the tenants who were in arrears with their rent. They'd be hoping and praying that Mr Ormiston'd let them have more time, maybe even reduce their rents. But I knew for a fact that he was planning to throw them all off their land. I knew what that would mean for them so I was going to have to do whatever I could to stop him. And I was dreading it.

'Are you something to do with the railways then, Mr Harborne?' Lleu asked.

'Not at all. I'm a textiles man. But you've got to keep abreast of what's going on. It's the only way you'll get ahead. I've been working in Newtown up in Montgomeryshire. They're decades ahead of us in terms of mechanisation. *Decades.*' He leaned over the table again. 'I went up to Yorkshire recently to see some of the mills there. Do you know how many spinning mills there are in Leeds? No, neither do I. But I know how many there are in the Teifi Valley – one.'

That was a surprise to me. I didn't know there were any.

'But that's going to change,' he went on. 'And I'm the one who's going to change it. With the railways coming and markets opening up in the coalfields, the Teifi Valley is going to be the best place in the country to produce textiles. And I'm going to be the first to do it!'

Harry

Drawn by the sound of our voices and the horses' hooves, Mrs Rees's younger daughters and her husband soon joined us in the house. The apples that the girls had been picking were still warm from a whole day's sunshine, and their sweet fragrance mingled with the smell of the wood fire and the astringent smell of a recent coat of limewash. I looked around the kitchen as well as I was able, acutely aware of how much more John would have been able to take in. The thought brought with it an unwelcome reminder of how reserved John had been since our argument over Ormiston's running of the estate. He'd barely spoken to me for the fortnight before he left for London.

'This is my husband, Mic, and my daughters, Ann and Gwen,' Mrs Rees said as the little girls began to take apples from their aprons and place them on the kitchen table.

I inclined my head to the slim figure who had risen from his chair. 'Mr Rees, may I offer my deepest condolences?'

As I did not want to assume that he shared his wife's facility with English, I had addressed him in Welsh, and he responded in the same language. 'Thank you, sir. It's Mic y Porthmon they call me,' he added. 'If you talk about Mic Rees, nobody'll know who you mean.'

So, he was a drover. 'Do you drive cattle still?' I asked.

'No. Not since I met Esther and we settled down here. Would you like some cider?' he asked. 'Or tea? You've come a fair way.'

'Mr Probert-Lloyd isn't here to drink tea,' his wife snapped. 'He's here to see Lizzie.'

'I know. But the least we can do now you've dragged these gentlemen here is offer them something.'

25

Without answering, Mrs Rees pushed him out of the way and bent to pick up a large jug from the hearth. 'Go and fill that,' she thrust it at one of the girls, 'then put the kettle on the fire.' Turning to us, she reverted to English. 'Not to waste your time, Doctor, Mr Probert-Lloyd – will you see my Lizzie before you have your tea?'

'Of course.'

She led us to the bedroom, which was separated from the kitchen by a huge dresser and the back of what I took to be a box bed. As we passed to one side of the dresser, I was pleased to see that windows, front and back, let in a decent amount of light; my partial vision made it almost impossible for me to make out anything that was not well lit.

But it seemed that Elizabeth Rees's body was not in this room. As I took care not to stumble over the rag rugs that lay on the beaten-earth floor, I saw Mrs Rees open a door in the end wall.

'We thought she'd be better in the weaving shed.'

Until a coffin was made, the body would need to be kept at a distance to prevent the house being infected with the smell of putrefaction. However, though the weaving shed's large windows had been covered with white sheeting out of respect to the dead, it was little cooler than the main part of the house.

Reckitt drew back the sheet and revealed Elizabeth's body, clad in her long petticoat. 'Mrs Rees, may I ask you to undress your daughter, please?'

Mic Rees, who had followed us from the kitchen, took a step back, obviously uncomfortable at the thought of his daughter's naked body being exposed before him. Seeing an opportunity to speak to him alone, I indicated that he and I should leave Reckitt and his wife to their business.

Once he had shut the door behind us, I stood beside the bedroom window so that as much light as possible would fall on him. However, I knew that I would be able to see very little that might help me discover the truth of what had happened to Mic y Porthmon's daughter, and once again I felt John's absence keenly. 'When exactly did your daughter die, Mic?'

He cleared his throat. 'This morning. I found her dead in bed.'

'*This* morning? Not yesterday?'

'No. Today.'

In which case, Esther Rees had barely seen her daughter's body and heard her husband's account of what had happened before she had taken to her heels and walked the seven or eight miles to Cilgerran to speak to Reckitt. Her suspicions must have been aroused instantly, and I wondered what it was that had made her so determined that Lizzie had not died a natural death.

Scanning the room, I could see no other beds.

'Your daughters sleep in the loft?' I asked, indicating the ladder that stood in the corner, ready to give access to the loft under the eaves overhead.

'Yes.'

Without John, I would have to rely on Reckitt to examine the bed.

'When did you discover that Lizzie had died?' I asked.

'Well...' Mic Rees hesitated. 'I'm not sure of the time. Not exactly. Lizzie's usually up with the sun – *was*, I mean – and she'd call to wake me. The light doesn't get in to the box bed. But this morning, the cow woke me, shouting to be milked. I knew something wasn't right straight away, because it was properly day and the ladder was still up – Lizzie hadn't come down yet. So I called up to her that the cow'd be in through the door in a minute. But there was no answer.' He fell silent and I did not hurry him. I did not want to embarrass him if he was mastering tears. 'I thought maybe her cold'd turned into a fever,' he said eventually. 'And she was still tired after being away working.'

'Away?'

He took a shuddering breath. 'She'd been down south,' he said, his distress evident in his voice. 'Went for harvest work with some of the other local girls.'

'I see. How long was she away?'

'A month or so.' He cleared his throat. 'They went as soon as the hay was in.'

Had Lizzie caught something worse than a summer chill while she had been away from home?

'Did she already have the cold when she came home?' I asked. 'Yes.'

'And was it just that that was making her feel under the weather, or was there something else?'

'No. Nothing. She said she ached a bit, but I think that was all the work and sleeping under a hedge on the way back. The damp gets to you even if you're young, doesn't it?'

'But it was the cold that stopped her going with your wife and your other daughters, was it?'

With the whirlpool trained on his chest, I saw him nod above it. 'Yes. Generally she'd have been happy to go over to Ffynone with her mother and sisters. It's not all hard work when women get together, is it?'

I wondered what Mrs Rees and her daughters had been doing at the Colbys' mansion. The promise of work must have been substantial, as Ffynone was a good three hours' walk away. 'Was it more harvest work?'

'No. It was one of those big affairs Mr Colby has through the summer. Other businessmen and their families up from Merthyr for a week. Esther's niece is a laundrymaid there. She can always get work for my girls when there's a big party on.'

I wondered if Lizzie Rees had been feeling more unwell than she had admitted. I did not imagine that she had lightly forgone a few days' working holiday with her female relatives.

'Had Lizzie been down south to work on the harvest before?' I asked.

'Yes. Last year. And the year before. It's good money if a girl knows how to work hard.'

'Yes, so I gather.' Farmers' wives and daughters in the 'soft south' of Pembrokeshire, the area sometimes called Little England Beyond Wales, were rumoured to regard fieldwork as beneath them.

'And she'd had no ill effects the previous times?'

'No, none. She's a good worker. Brought back a tidy sum, fair play to her – that's why I didn't let her mother push her to go over to Ffynone. I thought she deserved a day or two to get over her cold.'

As he was speaking, Esther Rees appeared, startling me slightly as I had not heard the door to the weaving shed open. 'I should have made her come with me,' she said, obviously having caught the gist of her husband's last comment. 'But you could never refuse her, could you?'

'What d'you mean by that?' Mic Rees flared.

'You treat the three of them like little *swci* lambs – as if they need nursing by the fire! They've got to learn to make their own living!'

'What was Lizzie doing down south if she wasn't making her own living? It's not me that's too soft, Esther, it's you that's too harsh – you never gave that girl a minute's peace from your nagging. She could never please you!'

I did my best to ignore the tense silence that followed his outburst. 'So,' I said, turning my deficient eyes to Mic Rees, 'last night, was Lizzie late to bed?'

'No.' He sounded chastened. Or perhaps he was just embarrassed by the insults he and his wife had traded. 'We were both busy in the shed till the light went – Lizzie spinning, me on the loom. Then we came in and had supper and went to bed.'

'Who brought the wool?'

Mrs Rees's question surprised me. Her husband seemed equally taken aback. 'What?'

'There wasn't any wool here to spin when I left, so who brought it? Was it him?'

'Dear God, woman! Enough! It doesn't matter who it was now, does it?'

'It does if he was here. If he did something to her!'

'That's enough, I said! Nobody did anything to her.'

Silence fell, and before Mrs Rees could take her chances with her husband's temper once more, Reckitt appeared, notebook in hand. It was his habit to take detailed notes during his examination of a body.

'You said that your daughter had just come back from harvest work,' he said, as if he and Esther Rees were in the middle of a conversation. 'Was she used to hard physical labour?'

'Of course. We all work hard. Before she went down south, she'd been haymaking around the farms with everybody else.'

'With no ill effects?'

'No.'

'Did she ever seem short of breath or struggle to keep up?'

'Never. She was strong; fit.'

'And when she was a small child – did she have any serious illnesses? Fevers? Measles?'

'No. She had colds sometimes, in the winter. And all of the girls had the chickenpox at one time. But that's all.'

'Did she ever seem dizzy, or faint?'

There was a brief silence. 'She did faint every now and then,' Esther Rees admitted. 'But girls do sometimes, don't they?'

'Every now and again?' Reckitt asked. 'Was that every month, every two months…?'

'No, nothing like that. No more than five or six times in her whole life.'

'I see. And your wider family?'

'What do you mean?'

'Are there sickly individuals – anything like this?'

Mrs Rees shook her head, but it seemed her husband could not say. 'I left home at sixteen,' he explained when Reckitt asked him, 'to go on the road with the drovers, and I've never been back.'

'Where are you from?' I asked. His dialect was from further up the Teifi Valley.

'Up towards Llanybydder.'

A wild and thinly populated area. He probably felt at home here on the slopes of the Preselis.

One of the girls suddenly appeared between the box bed and the wall. 'Tea's ready, Mam.'

As we all made to follow her back into the kitchen, Reckitt put a hand on my shoulder. 'A moment, Probert-Lloyd...?'

Mic and Esther Rees hesitated, unsure whether to stay or leave us alone. 'We'll be with you shortly,' I said, settling their dilemma, before turning to Reckitt.

'This cold the girl supposedly had,' he said, his voice pitched for my ears only. 'I see no evidence of it. No reddening or roughening of the skin around her nose and lips as you'd expect. I think there's something else here.'

'Such as?'

'I don't know yet. But give me time and I believe I will.'

John

Late that afternoon, I left Lleu with the rest of the Alltybela lot at the enormous pink glass fountain that was the main meeting place in the Crystal Palace, and made my way back to the Gelyots' house.

My head should have been full of the Exhibition, but it wasn't. It was full of Jem Harborne and all the things he'd been talking about. Railways. People leaving. The coalfields. I couldn't stop thinking about it all. According to Harborne, the railways'd be on our doorstep in five years. And then, everything'd change.

I tried to imagine the farms on the Glanteifi estate without their army of labourers and farm servants. With machines instead. What would happen to farmers helping each other – getting together to cut hay, to shear sheep? If it was all done with machines, everybody'd be on their own, wouldn't they? No community at all. Just every farmer working by himself with his machines. It made me feel cold.

Would farmers back home riot over the use of machines, like they had in England? It wasn't like we never rebelled – we'd done it over tollgates under the Rebeccas. But that hadn't ended well. Nobody'd want to go back to night-time mobs and threatening letters. But did that mean we just had to stand by and let it all happen – let machines drive us off the land?

Jem Harborne hadn't come back to the Exhibition with me and Lleu after our early dinner or huge lunch or whatever that meal'd been. He'd stayed at Soyer's Symposium with a friend who'd spotted him as we were on our way out. Suited me. I'd had enough of hearing that machines were going to do away with manual labour.

But when we got back inside the Crystal Palace, it was all more of the same, wasn't it? Improvements, inventions. Modern this, extraordinary that, revolutionary the other.

Still, Lleu was only a boy, and he'd been thoroughly excited by the whole thing. And not just the machines. He'd especially loved the elephant in the Indian section. It was a huge stuffed specimen, wrapped in so much gold cloth you could hardly see it, and saddled with a canopied pavilion for people to ride in.

The boy'd also stood for a long time looking up at a huge eagle, wings outstretched, holding the flag of the United States. I'd wondered if he was imagining himself going to America, finding his fortune. I'd considered it for myself, to tell the truth. Still did, every now and then.

But the thing that'd impressed Lleu the most had been the Crystal Palace itself. We'd gone right to the topmost gallery, and as we were looking down on the people far below, he suddenly spoke up. 'I've decided,' he said. 'I'm going to be an engineer.'

'What'll Miss Gwatkyn have to say about that?' Lleu was about to go off to school at Phoebe Gwatkyn's expense.

'She'll be pleased. She's always telling me to be ambitious. Saying I don't need to think about where I've come from, just where I'm going.' He looked round at me then, and I had the peculiar impression that I wasn't just seeing the boy he was but the man he was going to be as well. Eagerness and determination in the same face.

'The other day,' he said, 'she was telling me about a man called John Lloyd Davies – he's the High Sheriff of Cardiganshire, and Miss Gwatkyn says he's going to be an MP as well. But he started off as a pot boy in a hotel.'

He didn't need to say any more. Pot boy. Hall boy. If this John Lloyd Davies could do it, so could Daniel 'Lleu' Williams.

The thought brought our own hall boy at Glanteifi, Wil-Sam, to my mind. I wished it hadn't. Wil-Sam's father was one of the tenants in arrears. One of those Mr Ormiston wanted to get rid of. How would I ever be able to look the boy in the eye again, let him clean my boots and run errands for me, if I stood by and allowed his family to be thrown off their farm? More than likely they'd end up in the workhouse.

I didn't honestly know which was more terrifying, the thought of letting that happen and having to tell Wil-Sam, or standing up to Mr Ormiston and trying to prevent it.

—

I mentioned Lleu and his engineering ambitions to Gus's father that evening at dinner.

'If he's got ideas of being an engineer, he should study technical drawing,' Mr Gelyot senior said. 'That's the coming thing. I know my father would've insisted on it if there'd been such a notion when I was a youth.'

I didn't know where Miss Gwatkyn was sending Lleu to school, but I was pretty sure he wouldn't be able to study this new technical drawing there. Latin and Greek and mathematics, yes. But nothing that would fit him to design buildings or machines. 'Do the National Schools teach technical drawing?' I asked.

Mr Gelyot put his wine glass down. 'I doubt it very much. Your boy might have to come to London.'

More talk of leaving Cardiganshire. And if he left, would he go back, Miss Gwatkyn's little Lleu? Perhaps he would if there were enough people like Jem Harborne wanting to build weaving mills there.

'Such a shame you're not able to stay longer, Mr Davies,' Mrs Gelyot said, waving a footman over to fill my glass up for me again.

'I'm afraid I'm needed back at Glanteifi, Mrs Gelyot,' I said. 'The Michaelmas quarter-day will be here before long and I have a lot to do before then. As well as assisting Harry when he's acting as coroner, of course.' I looked up and offered a smile to the wine-pouring footman. He ignored me.

'Knowing Harry,' Gus said, 'he's probably been out to half a dozen suspicious deaths while you've been away.'

I glanced across at him. As usual, he was exaggerating for effect, but everybody in the Teifi Valley knew that Harry wanted to be informed about any unexpected death, so he might well have been called out.

I didn't want to think about that. If Harry went out to view a body while I was away, he'd have to take Lydia Howell with him to act as his assistant. And she'd be very competent. More than competent. She'd barely been in Cardiganshire for five minutes when she'd joined us on the coroner's hustings in April and found herself in the middle of an inquest. Without any fuss, she'd taken charge of two witnesses who would've run rings around Harry and me without her. She was quick, Lydia, and she could read people as easily as reading a book.

In her previous life, she'd had years of being trusted to lead people, make decisions on their behalf. If she got the chance to show what she could do as coroner's assistant instead of just his private secretary, Harry might decide that I was too busy as under-steward and he'd do better with Lydia at his side.

'Has he had to deal with many poisonings?' Mr Gelyot wanted to know. 'Not a week goes by here but the papers are full of some-body going on trial for poisoning their master or their husband.'

I glanced at Mrs Gelyot, but she seemed to be taking talk of murder in her stride.

'No. To be honest, we haven't seen any,' I said.

'The Welsh, Papa, are an unusually law-abiding people.' Gus grinned at me. 'Apart from their drunkenness, obviously.'

I didn't rise to the bait.

'Is that true, do you think, Mr Davies? Are your people unusually law-abiding?'

I smiled, trying to make it look as if I didn't mind Gus needling at me. 'As it happens, Mrs Gelyot, I think we just have less detectable ways of killing each other if we feel the need.' To be honest, I didn't think we *were* as inclined to murder each other as the English, but 'unusually law-abiding' sounded more like an insult than a compliment. Made us sound as docile as cattle.

'I do find Harry's enthusiasm for the post of coroner somewhat surprising,' Mrs Gelyot said. 'He was always such a dedicated social reformer that I was certain he'd end up in Parliament. Of course, I suppose he still could.'

The notion that a blind man might become an MP one day didn't seem as foolish this evening as it would've done yesterday. On one of the display stands in the American section of the Exhibition I'd seen a specimen of something called 'tactile ink', designed to let the blind read. That was the kind of invention that might change everything for Harry.

Gus opened his mouth to say something, but I got there before him. 'He could indeed, Mrs Gelyot. Like Thomas Wakley. An MP *and* coroner for Middlesex.'

'Ah yes, Mr Wakley. Such an interesting, energetic man.'

Of course. Thomas Wakley had eaten dinner with the Gelyots. Anybody who was anybody in London had eaten dinner with the Gelyots. Reading Gus's letters to Harry was like reading about the doings of high society in *The Times*.

'Yes, but then he'd be MP for *Cardiganshire*, Mama,' Gus said, waving the footman over for more wine. 'And nothing ever *happens* in Cardiganshire so what would be the *point*?'

I couldn't tell whether he meant it or was just trying to provoke me for his own amusement, but I'd had a few more glasses of wine than I should have. The footman kept refilling my glass, and I didn't want to make a fuss by saying no, so my tongue was looser than usual.

'I think you might be surprised, Mr Gelyot,' I said, feeling the heat creep up my neck and onto my face. 'I met a man today at the Exhibition – a man from near where we live in Cardiganshire – and he'd laugh if you told him nothing happens there.' Unwisely, I tried to cool myself down by drinking more wine.

'Oh, and what does he do? Is he a farmer, or a preacher?'

'Neither. He's a textiles producer.' I put my empty wine glass down. 'As it happens, he's building the first wool factory in the Teifi Valley.'

'Is he, by God?' Mr Gelyot senior joined the conversation.

'Yes. He thinks West Wales can steal the American market from Manchester and the other northern towns.'

Mr Gelyot leaned his elbows on the table and looked intently at me. It was an invitation to say more, so I did. 'He's got ambitious plans for a Cardiganshire woollen industry and he's in London to look for investors. He's got wind of various plans for new railway and sea links to and from West Wales. And those plans mean that the sooner he can get his factory built and running, the better placed he'll be to capitalise on transport to his markets – including America.' Considering how much I'd had to drink, I was pretty pleased at how sober I sounded. Lucid, even. Articulate.

'And what's his name,' Mr Gelyot asked, 'this Welsh wool wizard?'

'Jeremiah Harborne,' I said. And then I did something I regretted as soon as I was sober. I took my card case out of my pocket and put Jem Harborne's calling card into Mr Gelyot's outstretched hand.

Harry

Before I could begin speaking to the family, Mrs Rees was obliged to deal with neighbours who had come to offer their condolences on Lizzie's death. Custom dictated that they be welcomed in and offered hospitality while the solemn circumstances of the death were shared, but of course that was out of the question while Reckitt and I were in the house.

We listened to Esther Rees gravely accepting words of comfort then saying firmly, 'Dr Reckitt's here to see Lizzie, and Mr Probert-Lloyd with him, so I can't have you in, but thank you for coming. If you see anybody else on the way over, can you tell them tomorrow would be better?'

She latched the door behind her visitors and immediately began marshalling her daughters to pour the tea, insisting that Reckitt and I take the only two decent chairs in the place. It was hard to reconcile her demeanour with that of a mother who not five minutes before had overseen the examination of her deceased daughter's body.

As she stood in front of the dresser, arms folded, Esther Rees was a commanding presence, but it was essential that I take control of the situation now. In putting off her neighbours, she had made it common knowledge that the coroner was on the premises; a considered judgement must be made public as soon as possible. However, unaccustomed to dealing with coroner's business without John at my side, I felt disconcertingly exposed.

'If I may, I would like to speak to you individually, please, starting with you, Mr Rees. Nobody here is under suspicion,' I clarified when neither Mic Rees nor any of his family moved.

'But I do need to speak to you all if I'm going to decide whether to ask Dr Reckitt to look more closely at Elizabeth's body.'

For a few moments there was total stillness in the room. Then, without warning, Esther Rees clapped her hands. 'Girls! Come on – out! Leave Mr Probert-Lloyd and your father to talk.'

'Would you like me to leave as well, Probert-Lloyd?'

'Actually, Reckitt, would you mind taking notes?'

I took my seat in a heavy chair made of dark wood, whose silken patina beneath my fingertips suggested great age. 'So, Mr Rees, tell me about this man your wife mentioned – the one who brought the wool. Who is he?'

Mic Rees, squatting opposite me on a stool, sighed audibly. 'He's just a servant on one of the farms nearby.'

'And why did the notion that he'd been here agitate your wife so much? Was he paying court to your daughter – sweet on her?'

'There were several young men who were sweet on Lizzie.'

I noted this evidence of the dead girl's popularity and, presumably, prettiness. 'But Mrs Rees didn't favour him?'

'No. She didn't.' Rees shifted his slight frame on the stool as if he was uncomfortable, and thrust his legs out in front of him. 'She has strong opinions about people, Mr Probert-Lloyd. Like Dr Reckitt, here – she sets great store by him. Heard a lot about what he's done at the workhouse, hasn't she?'

Since taking up the post of physician to the Cardigan Workhouse Union, Reckitt had been responsible for improvements in diet and hygiene at the workhouse, changes that had significantly improved the health of the inmates.

'Do you think you'll be able to tell us why Lizzie died, Doctor?' Rees asked.

'That depends on what examinations I am permitted to carry out.'

As Reckitt spoke, I ran my fingertips back and forth along the smooth underside of the chair's arm, thinking. Rees had adroitly deflected my attention from his daughter's would-be suitor, and in good time I would find out why. But first there were procedural matters that needed to be settled.

'Mr Rees, your wife told Dr Reckitt that a doctor had certified your daughter's death as being from natural causes. Who was that?'

'Dr Gwynne, the local—'

'*Doctor* Gwynne?' Reckitt was suddenly galvanised. 'Cadwgan Gwynne is no *doctor*. He's a hedge witch, a charmer—'

'He's in the medical directory!' Rees protested.

'That means nothing. Half the quacks in the country are listed—'

'That may or may not be so,' I interrupted, aware that this was a subject on which Reckitt could hold forth indefinitely, 'but Dr Gwynne is entitled to be consulted and to certify a death. Had he attended your daughter before, Mr Rees?'

'Not recently. Only for the usual childish things, years ago. His remedies for the chickenpox were very good, I remember. Stopped them scratching straight away.'

'So he hadn't seen her recently for any reason?'

'No.'

'Was Lizzie still feeling under the weather yesterday evening?'

'A bit.' Did Rees sound a little defensive?

'I only ask because when Dr Reckitt examined her body, he didn't find any of the reddening or chapping that you'd expect from a cold.'

'Well… it wasn't a bad one. Just one of those summer things, you know.'

'But bad enough to keep her here rather than go to Ffynone with her mother and sisters?'

'She was tired, like I said to you earlier. After walking home.'

Reckitt was right, there was something here. But if Mic Rees was going to insist on this cold, I might do better to leave it and see whether Lizzie's sisters had any light to shed on the matter.

'When he came, did Dr Gwynne offer any opinion about *when* your daughter might have died?' It seemed a gentler formulation than 'how long she had been dead'.

'No.'

'And what sort of examination did he perform?' I asked before Reckitt could.

'He looked in her mouth… as best he could.' Rees swallowed audibly. 'He opened her eyes. He looked at her hands and then at her throat and chest. And he felt all over her head.'

Whatever Reckitt thought of his medical qualifications, Dr Gwynne had obviously had the wit to look for the most obvious signs of trauma.

'Did he remove any of her clothes?' As was his custom, Reckitt had not touched the body before asking that Lizzie Rees's garments be removed.

'No. Well, not exactly. He lifted her petticoat.'

'Did he examine her private parts?' Reckitt asked.

'I don't know,' Mic Rees muttered. 'I couldn't look at her like that.'

'The young man who brought the wool,' I said. 'Why had your wife taken against him?'

Rees sighed. 'In my wife's eyes, nobody will ever be good enough for any of our girls. Not unless they've got a hundred acres, money in the bank, and no brothers and sisters to keep.'

'And your daughter? Was she as interested in this young man as he was in her?'

Rees hesitated, and again I missed John fiercely. He would have guided me, indicated whether I should push on this.

'Mr Rees?'

'It doesn't matter whether she was or not. Like I said, Esther wouldn't have it.'

'And you, Mr Rees, what did you think?'

'Not married, are you, Mr Probert-Lloyd?'

'I'm not, no.'

'No. Well you'll find, if you don't mind me saying, that it's best not to oppose a wife in matters relating to marriage.'

I allowed a small silence to develop while I constructed my next question. Let him think he had offended me; if it put him on edge, that might work to my advantage. 'Just so I'm clear about who was here the day your daughter died, did this young man in fact bring wool for her to spin?'

'He did, yes. But that wool didn't cause her death, did it? Dr Gwynne said she just died in her sleep. That's all.'

Though Rees's tone fell short of belligerence, he seemed to be losing patience. Perhaps it was easier to do so with me than with his wife.

'Your wife thinks you're hiding something, Mr Rees. Why might that be?'

In my peripheral vision, Mic Rees's head drooped. 'She wants somebody to take the blame. Somebody she can shout at.' He raised his head once more. 'As far as she's concerned, it's my fault. I was here and I let Lizzie die.'

I had heard similar sentiments before. Human beings do not readily accept randomness, and the notion that there must be something that might have been done was common after an unexplained death – a greater vigilance that might have been observed, some extra precaution that had been overlooked.

'And you, Mr Rees – do you blame yourself?'

Rees drew in a long, shuddering breath. 'What man wouldn't? There I lay, in my bed, while my girl breathed her last. The thought of it will haunt me every time I close my eyes to sleep.'

John

It was a long two days' journey home. Train from London to Bristol then coaches from Bristol by stages all the way back to Newcastle Emlyn, with a night's stop on the way.

But if I didn't enjoy the journey, I was enjoying the thought of being home even less. As soon as I was back, I had to try and change the way Mr Ormiston was running the estate. I was dreading it. He hadn't exactly been impressed when I'd tried to make him see things from the tenants' point of view, and what I was planning now was a lot worse. I was going to go directly against his wishes.

The novelty of railway travel had worn off pretty quickly for me, and now I just felt the discomfort of it. Which included the endless prattling of the Alltybela servants. Thank God for Lleu – I made him sit with me and practise his English so he'd be ready to go off to his new school.

He got very excited when I told him what Mr Gelyot senior had said about learning technical drawing. 'D'you think I could do that instead of going to Miss Gwatkyn's school?'

I shrugged.

'Or perhaps I should go for an apprenticeship instead – with an engineer?'

'Do you know any?'

'I know Mr Harborne.'

The boy was going to go far if he counted a casual meeting like that as knowing somebody.

'I could go and live in Llandyfriog and be Mr Harborne's apprentice at his new factory.'

When Jem Harborne had told us where he was building his wool factory, I'd been shocked. Llandyfriog was barely three miles from Glanteifi, and I couldn't understand how we hadn't heard of his plans. But then it was possible that Harry knew all about Harborne. I hadn't had much time recently for anything except the estate and preparing for the solicitor's exam in November. That'd been a good excuse to keep my distance after Harry refused to listen to what I had to say about the estate, and most evenings I left Lydia Howell reading to him in the drawing room while I studied in the library.

'Building work on the mill started in June,' Harborne'd told us. 'This time next year we'll be in production.'

As Lleu sat there thinking about his future as an engineer, I stared out of the carriage window at the stubbled end-of-summer English farmland and tried to forget that I might've put Mr Gelyot on the path to investing in Harborne's factory.

I shouldn't've let Gus annoy me with his digs about Cardiganshire being backward, should've kept my big mouth shut instead of boasting about Harborne's mill as if it was already producing thousands of yards of flannel a year. If I'd kept quiet, his factory plans might have never got off the ground. I knew he was looking for more investment, because he'd told me and Lleu, as plain as you like, that he'd come to the Great Exhibition to find 'forward-thinking men' – by which he meant ones with deep pockets who could fund his factories full of machines.

I knew exactly what effect those machines would have. They'd be as bad for local people as a threshing machine arriving on the estate would. Half the women in the area made extra money by carding or spinning for the local weavers. What were they going to do when Harborne's machines spun all the yarn he needed?

My mother'd been a spinner. Her strong, evenly drawn yarn had been in demand, and we'd never have paid the rent without the money she brought in. One winter, when things'd been really bad and there wasn't enough extra labouring work for my father away from our little farm, my parents'd come to an agreement. My mother would work full time at her spinning and my father'd do the rest of her work. They never told anybody – my father was afraid of the other men laughing at him – but they'd had no choice. Mind, it wouldn't've surprised me if that kind of thing went on quite a lot. It was easier for women to make extra money in the winter than men.

As I sat there staring at big open fields where hay could easily be cut with one of those new mowing machines, I thought of all the cottagers' wives around Newcastle Emlyn who kept the family going with their carding or spinning, and a cold shadow walked through me at the thought of what Jem Harborne's mill would do to them if it was a success.

-

I parted company with the Alltybela lot in Newcastle Emlyn. They were changing coach one last time and I was going to walk back to Glanteifi. As we parted, Lleu took me by the arm. 'When you see Mr Harborne, will you ask him about me being his apprentice?'

'I don't know that I *will* see him.'

'He said he'd see you soon.'

'That's just what people say, isn't it?'

'And Llandyfriog's not far from where you live, he said.'

'Yes, but—'

'So when you see him, will you ask him? Please?'

I stared at him. He was a boy with a passion now. The Great Exhibition had fired him up and he had a purpose. 'All right. When I see him.'

-

I left the Emlyn Arms coachyard and headed down to the bridge, walking quickly, eyes on the road. I didn't want to have to stop and answer questions about the Great Exhibition. With Harborne's factory already being built in Llandyfriog, it felt like the world of the Exhibition had followed me home.

But crossing the bridge over the Teifi, I couldn't stop people wishing me good day and welcoming me home. I think I did a fair job of pretending everything was all right; I even managed a few smiles But inside I felt like a cat whose fur's been stroked the wrong way. Because everything might *look* the same now I was back, but it wasn't, was it?

The river might run bright and clear under the bridge the same way it always had, the Carmarthen coach might've pulled in to the Emlyn Arms just like it had all my life – but for how long? According to Jem Harborne, the railway'd be here in about five minutes, so there'd be no more coaches and the Emlyn Arms'd lose a lot of its business. And the Teifi – how long before there were woollen mills all along its banks, and the water was filthy with the stuff they used for fulling? How long before the river meadows were full of machines instead of people?

As I walked out of town up Adpar hill, I glanced across the road at Mr Schofield's office. Five years I'd worked there as his solicitor's clerk, and with every year that'd passed, I'd wished more and more that something would happen to change my life. Anything.

Now I could see that what I'd really been wishing for had been a fairy story where my fortunes changed but everything else stayed the same. And when Harry made me under-steward, I'd thought that was what I'd got. But everything was different from how I'd expected it to be. It wasn't just me and Harry at the dinner table, or in the library afterwards; Lydia was there. And after old Mr Probert-Lloyd's death, instead of carrying on his improvement works on the estate, Mr Ormiston'd stopped spending money and was coming down hard on the tenants. And Harry expected me to help him do it.

As soon as I'd exchanged greetings with the tollgate keeper and turned off the hill onto the road back to Glanteifi, I stopped and took my watch and its little key out of my pocket. Sunrise and sunset were about fifteen minutes later here than in London, and I'd changed the time on our journey up there so that we wouldn't get in a muddle with trains and coaches, which followed what they called 'railway time'. I hadn't been going to bother changing my watch back to normal till I wound it last thing, but suddenly I needed to do it now. This very second.

I put my carpet bag down and opened the back of my watch to put the little key into the mechanism. Moving the hands back to the right time made me feel a bit better, and as a pair of buzzards started mewing overhead, I suddenly realised how quiet the air around me was. My ears'd been full of noise for a week – the noise of London and travel and people. Hundreds and thousands of people. Chattering, shouting, laughing, drunk, excited, bragging, begging. The sound of wheels and hooves and whistles and whipcracks and orders. A world of noise like a waterfall battering down onto rocks, each voice and sound being pulled into the general din.

But as I picked up my bag again and walked along the road – past fields and cottages that looked unbelievably clean and bright after London's grey sootiness – each sound I heard was completely distinct. It was like individual drops landing in a quiet pool. A girl singing as she gathered in dry washing. A man whistling on his way home from a day's work. Birds twittering as they fed the last of their fledglings.

I breathed in, deep down into me, and tried to still my thoughts, stop them racing on London lines.

But I couldn't get Harborne and his factory out of my mind. Nor Mr Ormiston and his plans for the estate. Everything I'd seen and heard in the last few days'd made it more important for me to try and protect Glanteifi people from losing their farms.

But to be honest, without Harry on my side, I wasn't sure I was going to be able to do anything.

Harry

I decided to speak to Esther Rees last of all, once I had heard what her younger daughters had to tell me. I asked the sisters to come in together; given their youth, I was afraid they would be intimidated if interviewed alone. Besides, experience had taught me that rivalry often induced siblings to say more if they were questioned together.

However, the ploy produced no revelations. On the contrary, Gwen and Ann were somewhat unforthcoming on the subject of their big sister, and I could not help wondering whether John, being closer in age to them, might have induced them to be more open.

The unsatisfactory interview concluded, and wanting relief from sitting, I accompanied the girls outside, leaving Reckitt to finish his notes. Though afternoon was now becoming evening, the sun was still bright above the western horizon.

The girls scampered off in search of their mother and I leaned my back against the house's sun-warmed gable end, mulling over what I had learned. It was precious little, and so far I could see no reason to doubt that this was a natural death. Only Reckitt's observation that the body showed no signs of the head cold that Lizzie had supposedly been suffering from gave me any pause for thought at all.

But perhaps he was making too much of this in an attempt to persuade me to allow a post-mortem examination; might not a mild cold – one of those summer things, as Mic Rees had called it – simply be invisible after a day or two of sleeping in her own bed again?

A thought occurred to me and I went back into the house. 'Reckitt, have you examined the girl's bed yet?'

'Not yet.'

'Would you mind doing so now, while we wait for Mrs Rees?'

Reckitt pocketed his notebook and pencil and rose with a grunt of discomfort while I went back out into the sunshine. Watching Reckitt about his task would be pointless, as I would gain only the most general idea of what he was doing; besides, he would give me as full an analysis of his findings as I would permit, in due course.

'Here I am, Mr Probert-Lloyd.'

I jumped, startled once more by Mrs Rees's silent, barefoot approach.

'I've left the girls in the orchard – I hope that's all right? They said you'd finished talking to them.'

'Yes. Of course.'

She did not ask whether her daughters had been helpful, which I found interesting; most parents were keen to know that their offspring had not shown them up in any way. Perhaps she was so sure of her authority over her children that she regarded such a question as unnecessary. In which case, I wondered whether she had had similar confidence in her authority over Lizzie, and whether such confidence might have been misplaced.

As I stood aside to allow her into the house, Reckitt emerged.

Before even allowing Mrs Rees over the threshold, he asked, 'The petticoat I asked you to take off your daughter before I examined her – was it the one she was wearing when she died?'

'Yes.'

'You're sure your husband didn't put a fresh one on her?'

'Quite sure. He said she was clean. I thought, because she was young...'

Like most women of her age and station, Esther Rees would be no stranger to laying out the dead. However, it seemed that her experience had been confined to the bodies of the elderly, as she clearly believed that only those whom age had weakened were apt to void bowels and bladder post-mortem.

'I see,' Reckitt said. 'And has the bedlinen been stripped and replaced?'

'No, I didn't want...' Those few strained words contained more emotion than anything I had so far heard from Esther Rees.

It was a common belief amongst uneducated people that the soul stayed in the house for several days after death, taking its leave of all that it had known and loved before departing. Even in the absence of such a superstition, my father's death had taught me that for the first few days, the dead seemed not yet fully gone; so to look at Lizzie's bed, at the indentation her body had made in the mattress, and instruct Ann and Gwen to take the sheets and wash them while she went to consult Dr Reckitt would – even for a woman as stoical and determined as Esther Rees – surely have felt like erasing her daughter's last precious hours of life.

Reckitt stood aside to allow us into the kitchen and asked no more. But he would not have raised the question of Lizzie's clothes and bedlinen had it not been relevant.

'Mrs Rees,' I began, once we had assumed our places, 'why did you ask Dr Reckitt and me to come here today?'

'Begging your pardon, Mr Probert-Lloyd, but I didn't ask for you. Dr Reckitt insisted.'

It was as I had suspected: Reckitt had hoped to persuade me to call an inquest and allow him to perform a forensic dissection. Sometimes his determination to unravel the mystery of death got the better of him. 'Very well,' I amended. 'Why did you ask for Dr Reckitt's opinion?'

'People don't just *die*! Not when they're young and healthy.'

Despite her vehemence, Mrs Rees volunteered nothing more. 'You told Dr Reckitt that you thought your husband was hiding something.'

There was a pause. Given that voicing her suspicions to Reckitt had resulted in his involving me, perhaps Esther Rees regretted her candour. 'Not *hiding* exactly,' she said. 'But I thought there was something he wasn't willing to tell me.'

'Such as?'

'I don't know.' Sensing her discomfort, I waited. 'I thought it might be something Dr Gwynne had said,' she admitted eventually. 'Something my husband didn't want to tell me.'

I did not think she was lying, but neither was I confident that this was the whole truth. Keen not to misdirect her – nor to give her a way out – I said nothing.

'The point is,' her tone was suddenly more decisive, 'everybody knows Dr Reckitt's the one who can tell you why somebody's died. He knows what to look for.'

I wondered whether she understood just how deeply Reckitt looked. But if she knew of his reputation, she must surely be aware of his almost invariable resort to dissection.

'So far, Dr Reckitt has been unable to find any clue as to why Lizzie died,' I said. 'Would you be prepared to allow him to open her body?'

Welsh lacked a commonly used word for 'dissection', which made the question so much starker than it would have been in English, but if Esther Rees flinched, I did not see it. She remained stiffly upright on the stool before me. 'Yes. I want to know why my daughter died.'

'It's an expensive business,' I said. 'The fee for such a post-mortem examination is two guineas.' Did her eyes widen, even fractionally, at such a sum? John would have noticed and told me later; I could not rely on Reckitt doing the same. 'Normally the fee is paid as part of the inquest costs,' I told her, 'but as things stand, I'm not sure I can justify calling an inquest. There's nothing to suggest that your daughter died anything but a natural death.' I heard Reckitt take a breath to disagree and held up a quelling finger in his direction. 'The county magistrates already complain that I hold too many inquests and ask ratepayers to pay for too many post-mortem examinations.'

'Are you saying that Dr Reckitt can't look inside my Lizzie's body to see why she died unless you hold an inquest?'

'Unless you have two guineas.' Again, though less ostentatiously this time, I signalled that Reckitt should stay silent. I knew perfectly well that he would carry out an examination of Lizzie Rees's viscera gratis, simply to further his own knowledge, but I wanted to see if Mrs Rees knew, or even suspected, more than she was currently telling us.

When she did not respond, I asked gently, 'Do you have any information that might justify holding an inquest, Mrs Rees?'

A silence gathered, then lengthened. Had John been there, he would have been able to signal to me, simply by leaning backwards or forward in his chair, whether I should be patient or press on with further questions. Reckitt might have inferred the mechanics of our wordless system during the many inquests he had attended with us, but if so, he was too caught up in his own feelings to make use of it now. So as best I could, I studied Esther Rees in my peripheral vision. But her posture was unmoving, and I learned nothing from it.

'Your husband told us that there was a young man who was sweet on Lizzie,' I suggested.

Mrs Rees made a dismissive sound. 'Foolishness.'

'You didn't favour this man?'

'I didn't favour any of the young fools!'

'But this one in particular, the one who brought the wool – what is his name?'

'He may be unsuitable, but I'll not bring trouble down on his head, not without reason.'

'But we may wish to speak to him.'

'If there's evidence that he did something, I'll tell you.' It was clear that I would wait in vain for her to relent. 'We don't have the money for a post-mortem examination.' She pronounced the Latin words carefully, as if she was drawing them syllable by syllable from her memory. 'So if it's evidence you want, Mr Probert-Lloyd, I'll just have to trust you to do what's right.'

John

Walking up the drive to Glanteifi, I knew I wasn't in a fit state yet to talk to Harry and Lydia Howell about the exhibition – or anything else – so I decided to go to my room and change for dinner first.

Wil-Sam rushed up to me as I came through the door, all smiles and greetings. I was glad I didn't have to deal with the starchy English butler, Mr Moyle, any more. He and Harry'd never got on, so he'd left soon after old Mr Probert-Lloyd had died, and Harry hadn't replaced him.

'What was it like?' Wil-Sam wanted to know. 'Did you see anybody important?'

I'd seen Jem Harborne. Who knew how important he was going to turn out to be?

'No, *'machgen i*, I didn't. I'll tell you all about the Exhibition later, all right? I need to go and get changed now.' And I needed not to have his trusting little face in front of me. I didn't want to think about what might happen to his family's farm if I couldn't persuade Mr Ormiston to change his mind.

But before I could go anywhere, Lydia appeared. 'Wil-Sam, go and ask Mrs Griffiths to send some tea for Mr Davies, will you. And cake.'

The boy scampered off and the two of us were left alone in the hall. 'Can you get somebody to bring the tea up to my room?' I asked her. 'I need a wash and change before I sit down with you and Harry. I'll join you both for dinner.'

'Harry's in Eglwyswrw. He's dealing with a sudden death with Dr Reckitt.'

Harry going out to see a body without me was just what I'd been afraid of, and my mouth started speaking before I could think. 'Just him and Reckitt? Why didn't he take you with him?' As soon as the question was out, I wanted to take it back. I looked away, but I could feel her eyes on me.

'I'm sure Dr Reckitt will be ample assistance,' she said steadily. 'Why don't you come and sit down in the library to have your tea – you can change later.'

If I insisted on going up to change, she'd think I was embarrassed about what I'd just said. And then dinner'd be awkward when I came down. Best to drink tea with her now, try and smooth things over.

In the library, I almost went straight to the chair I usually sat in, by the fire, but it didn't feel right, sitting down with just me and Lydia there. So I went to the long windows at the far end of the room. It was a nice evening – standing there looking out onto the terrace wouldn't seem odd. The windows were still open and the wallflowers in the beds outside smelled so sweet it was like breathing in sugar.

'What did you think of the Great Exhibition?'

I shrugged without turning around. 'Lleu was very taken with it.'

'Lleu's a child; of course he was impressed.'

Meaning that she thought I should be a bit more selective. That she expected me to make some intelligent comments on what I'd seen.

Instead, I just stared out of the window. The mansion stood on a hill, and below us the Teifi wound around in a wide, slow-moving loop. The new grass in the hayfields on the far bank was bright green and gold in the sunset, and I could see the swans that'd built their nest on the little island in the middle of the river settling for the night. It was as different from London, with its dusty worn-bare grass and litter in Hyde Park, and its clamouring noisy streets, as night was from day. Like a different world.

'If you want to know the truth,' I said, still keeping my back to Lydia, 'I thought it was loud and crowded and expensive and incredibly boastful.' With those last two words, my throat closed up and I felt tears sting my eyes. I'd been trying to keep my worries about everything on a tight rein, but admitting what I really felt about the Exhibition had loosened something. Thank God Lydia couldn't see my face.

'Look on my works, ye mighty, and despair.'

I swallowed, hard, and cleared my throat to make sure my voice wasn't going to crack. 'What book of the Bible is that from?'

'It's not from the Bible. It's from a poem. About a vast ruined statue from a vanished empire. The poet sees it lying in pieces in the desert sand. Nobody remembers the ruler it commemorates, but there's an inscription on it: "I am Ozymandias, king of kings / Look on my works, ye mighty, and despair!"'

I turned to face her. 'Is that what you think'll happen to our Empire?' The word brought a memory to mind – the Indian elephant Lleu had admired so much, standing there stuffed and draped in gold.

'Of course. It's what happens to all empires. They rise, they grow, they overreach themselves and they crumble.'

I stared at her. This was the kind of conversation she usually had with Harry, not with me.

I felt stranded. I knew what I should do – just march over to the hearth, take the chair opposite her and join in, like Harry would have. But I wasn't him.

Lydia was looking at me, as if she was trying to draw me over there by sheer force of will. As soon as I could bring myself to meet her eye, she spoke. 'I didn't come here to try and steal your place, John.'

It was such an unexpected thing for her to say that it felt as if she'd kicked my legs from under me. I felt the guilty blood rushing to my face. 'I didn't think you had.'

'But you've been worried that perhaps that's what Harry wants, haven't you?'

I didn't move. I couldn't think what to say. What gave her the right to sit there calmly telling me what was in my head?

'Come and sit down,' she said.

I didn't move.

'John—'

'I should change for dinner.'

'There's only me here, and I'm happy for you to eat dinner as you are. Please.'

My legs seemed to move of their own accord, but I only let them take me as far as the big table in the middle of the room. The one Harry and I had played shuffleboard on in the evenings before Lydia'd come to Glanteifi. Like everything else in the library – the carpets, the dusty books, the long curtains – it seemed old and faded after the Gelyots' house.

The way she was looking at me made me very uncomfortable. I put a hand out, as if touching the table would give me more reason to stand there.

'John, I don't want to be coroner's assistant.'

I shrugged. It wasn't what she wanted that mattered, was it? My fingers found an old dint in the table that somebody'd tried hard to smooth away, and I worried at it. I could feel Lydia willing me to look at her.

In the end, she won, and I looked up. The way the light was falling into shadows showed me the lines that were gathering at the corners of her eyes.

'Thing is,' I said, wanting to show her I was being reasonable, that I wasn't a child worrying over nothing, 'you'd be good at it. We all know that.'

She leaned back in her chair, her hands clasped in her lap, and looked at me. 'Are you determined not to be reassured?'

I turned my eyes away.

After a long silence, she stood up. 'Well, I can't *make* you believe me.'

Just then the door opened and Elsie, one of our maids, came in with the tea. Thank God.

Once Elsie'd gone back to the kitchen, Lydia passed me a slice of cake.

'Harry received a letter this morning. From the county magistrates.'

'About?'

'When we've finished our tea, I'll fetch it and you can see for yourself.'

—

Whatever Lydia'd said about not bothering to change, I felt dirty after all the travelling I'd done, so I went upstairs. The magistrates' letter could wait a few minutes. I wanted to sit down to dinner in clothes that didn't smell as if they'd been screwed up and sat on by every passenger on the Carmarthen coach.

When I walked into the dining room five minutes later, washed and changed, Lydia was already sitting at the table. 'Refreshed?' she asked.

I nodded. One of the things I'd got used to since coming to live at the mansion was having water brought to my room whenever I wanted it. *Warm* water, too. Not that I'd bothered anybody to bring me warm water just now. Not with dinner waiting. Wouldn't want to annoy our cook, Mrs Elias, by keeping dinner waiting.

'I hope you don't mind,' Lydia said, 'but I told Elsie not to bother lighting the fire. By the time the room warmed up, we'd be leaving it again.'

She and Harry had got into the habit of going back to the library after dinner to drink tea or brandy, or to finish the decanter of wine we'd started at the table. I joined them if I wasn't busy, but until I'd taken the solicitor's examination that Harry and I had agreed I should do before I took over from Mr Ormiston, I had other things to be getting on with. I wondered if Lydia was expecting me to join her when we'd eaten our dinner.

'No point wasting coal,' I said as I sat in my usual place. I wondered whether the chandelier'd been left unlit to save money as well. It was one of the first things Harry'd ordered after his father died – a huge twenty-four-candle specimen that hung low over the table. What sight he had left was as good as useless in poor light, and he said he was fed up with not being able to see his food.

'Why don't you sit there instead?' Lydia asked, nodding at Harry's place at the head of the table. 'It might be easier if we're not staring across at each other.'

I didn't really want to take Harry's seat. But she was right about us staring at each other, so I moved, and before I could tell him I'd do it, Ianto the footman came and shifted my plate and cutlery. I watched him place things just so. Was he mocking me? In my mind's eye I could see his expression when he went back to the kitchen. *Guess who sat in the master's place?*

'I thought we'd manage with a more moderate quantity of candles,' Lydia said. 'Since it's just you and me.'

I nodded, but still, I was glad Ianto hadn't pulled the curtains. The pinkish gold of sunset brought some light into the room and made it look warm instead of just gloomy. Bit different from the Gelyots' dining room, mind. While I was there, I'd got used to eating by the incredible brightness of gas light, and to be honest, the light in Glanteifi's dark-panelled dining room was worse than at the cheap hotel we'd stayed in on our journey home.

Lydia waited until our food was in front of us, then said, 'Do you want to read the magistrates' letter now, or would you rather enjoy your food and read it later?'

I glanced at Ianto. He was standing in the corner, looking at the wall opposite as if he'd turned to stone. It was all very well asking whether I'd rather read the letter now or later; the truth was I'd much rather she hadn't asked at all. If she'd just put the damned thing in front of me, that would've been fine. But now, if I said I'd rather wait, Ianto'd think I didn't want him to know anything about it.

'Let's have it now.'

She took it out of a pocket and opened it before passing it to me.

It could've been a letter I'd written – neat and carefully legible. No room for error. It was addressed to Harry, but from the way it

58

was worded, I was willing to bet that identical copies'd gone out to any number of people – inspectors of police, registrars, local justices of the peace.

The letter begged to inform 'all interested parties' of a decision taken at a recent meeting of the county magistrates.

> *The Cardiganshire County Constabulary now having complete oversight of all areas however remote, it said, the magistrates judge it inappropriate, henceforward, to remunerate any parish officer for duties which belong more properly to the uniformed constabulary.*
>
> *These duties include, but are not limited to, dealing with vagrants, taking action against drunkenness, bringing malefactors before the petty sessions and – I looked up at Lydia, who could see that I'd reached the meat of the thing – informing coroners of sudden suspicious deaths, empanelling inquest juries and bringing forward witnesses for inquest proceedings.*
>
> *If individual parishes saw fit to continue to employ a local constable, that must be their own affair, the letter advised, but no county finances will be disbursed to defray expenses for any of the above activities. Likewise, local registrars will no longer be remunerated for bringing news of suspicious deaths to the attention of the coroner but must take any relevant information to the nearest police station.*

I looked up. 'They're basically putting him under the thumb of the police. He'll only be able to act on their instructions.'

Lydia nodded. 'More or less. Obviously this doesn't actually *prohibit* anybody else from informing him of a suspicious death…'

'No, but if the parish constables don't get paid, they're not likely to bring deaths to Harry's notice. Same with the registrars.'

Registrars were busy men, and registering deaths – and births, if they could persuade people to remember – was a sideline for them. They weren't going to spend time coming to see Harry about a death that might or might not be suspicious if they weren't getting paid for it.

Still, most of the sudden deaths we went out to came to Harry from family members, so perhaps there wasn't too much to worry about. It wasn't supposed to happen, strictly speaking – they were supposed to go through somebody official – but people'd soon realised that the only reliable way to make sure that Harry knew about a sudden death was to tell him about it themselves.

I glanced at Ianto in the corner. Still pretending to take no notice. Back in the kitchen, he'd be giving them chapter and verse.

I read the letter again, turning it to the nearest candle and wishing we had the Gelyots' gas light. I remembered what Jem Harborne'd said about Soyer's Symposium at night – that all the lights were reflected again and again around the room by silvered glass. Maybe we should get some here and put them amongst the candles in the chandelier. Anything to make the dining room a bit cheerier and brighter.

The letter was going to cause trouble. It might be addressed to 'all interested parties', but Harry'd see it as the bench of magistrates calling him to heel, and he'd fight it, I knew he would. And the last thing I wanted was another fight. The one I was going to get into with Mr Ormiston was all I could manage at the moment.

'I assume Harry took this pretty personally?' I asked.

'He did. The question is, was he right to?'

'Well, the number of inquests has gone up almost threefold since Mr Bowen's time, and Harry can't say that's *all* because Mr Bowen was ill for so long – he definitely investigates more deaths than most coroners, so he costs more money than the magistrates think he should. But they haven't come up with this just to annoy Harry, have they?' I folded the letter up and passed it back to her. 'Other counties are bringing in similar rules. The county magistrates in Dorset,' – or was it Devon? – 'did something similar a while ago.'

Harry was a member of the Society of Coroners, which kept us up to date with goings-on like this. Since I'd been working with him, it'd been my job to read him anything that came from the Society.

My dinner was going cold in front of me, so I picked up my cutlery and made a start. A fish knife still felt odd in my hand. A tricky implement.

'You know as well as I do,' Lydia said, 'that he won't comply with anything that puts the coroner in a subservient role to the police.'

I swallowed a mouthful of salmon. It might as well have been sawdust. I didn't want to be having this conversation. I might be at odds with Harry, but it still didn't feel right talking about him behind his back.

Lydia picked up her knife and separated skin from flesh along the whole length of her fish in one deft movement. 'But whatever he decides, you and I know that it'll be up to us to make sure he doesn't do anything too unwise.' She looked up from her plate. 'Because if he alienates the whole of the county magistracy at this stage, I don't think his tenure as coroner will be very long-lived, do you?'

Harry

As we left the family at Rhosdywarch, Reckitt suggested that we might break our journey back to Cilgerran at the Sergeant's Inn in Eglwyswrw, and as the tea we had been given by Esther Rees had served only to make me realise how thirsty I was, I agreed readily.

Though I had not visited the inn for years, I was familiar with it from my younger days. In the autumn before an 'inappropriate association' had seen me banished to Oxford, I had stayed there when I went to Eglwyswrw for Ffair Feigan, the Meigan Fair, with my boyhood friend Davy Thomas.

The fair had made Eglwyswrw as busy as a Soho street, crowded with hundreds of people in whatever finery they could muster, and the main road had been dangerously narrowed by stalls offering revellers everything from ribbons to rice pudding.

Davy and I had been there, like every other unmarried person, to attract the attention of the opposite sex. Groups of young men and women paraded up and down, calling out to each other; ambassadors flitted from lads' gangs to girls' in order to press the suit of one of their number; girls gathered fairings from as many admirers as they could and spent the rest of the time comparing trophies and giggling behind their hands.

I remembered the deftness with which Davy had attached the two of us to a group of lads from Cilgerran. Somehow, though we were from the other side of the river, he had known one of them, and that had been sufficient introduction to see us accepted; especially as he had omitted to mention my surname.

Davy had been as ardent a suitor of pretty girls as anybody, and with his muscular frame and dark good looks – so different from my own pale slightness – he had not waited long for his attentions to be reciprocated.

For myself, I had enjoyed the carnival atmosphere at first and had smiled at my own fair share of young women. But as the day had worn on and more than a few individuals of both sexes found themselves the worse for drink, good-natured flirting had turned into something more sinister and threatening. Young men who had spent all their money on fairings prowled the stalls looking for a carnal return on their investment, and some girls were sufficiently drunk to find themselves obliging.

There had, I remembered, been a good deal of manhandling of young women who had become separated from their friends, sometimes in fun but often with lustful intent. Once or twice I had seen men I took to be parish constables intervening, but more frequently, it was a girl's friends who had swarmed up to defend her honour with hat pins and knitting needles.

Now, as our horses ambled up the almost deserted street to the Sergeant's Inn, my thoughts turned from those young women to the one whose death had brought us here. Elizabeth Rees had been nineteen years old – she must have attended her fair share of Meigan Fairs. Had the farm servant who had been sweet on her bought her favours and sought to catch her eye last November? Perhaps he had succeeded and things had gone too far. Something, after all, had made Esther Rees wary of her daughter's suitors. But I should not be looking for suspects – Reckitt had seen nothing to suggest that Lizzie's death had not been a natural one.

Like any coaching inn, the Sergeant's was prominently positioned on the main road, standing opposite Eglwyswrw's church. As we pulled up before the facade, I looked past the grey whirlpool at the centre of my vision and along the road as it sloped down to a little bridge. Here and there I could just make out the occasional figure wending its way home or to one of the alehouses at the end of a long working day.

Roused by the sound of our horses' hooves, a boy rushed out of the stables opposite the inn and laid hold of each bridle as we dismounted. 'Staying, sirs, or just stopping?'

'Stopping.' I reached into my pocket for a penny and tossed it to him. 'We'll be on our way again in an hour.'

The inn was a sturdy two-storey establishment, stone-built and white-rendered beneath a slate roof. Inside, it had a well-kept, prosperous air, with a malty smell of ale in the first stages of preparation somewhere on the premises.

Though the ceiling was low, betraying the inn's age, the ground floor was spacious and the flagstones beneath my feet, far from being sawdust-covered like those of an alehouse, were swept clean and had the slightly slick surface that I associated with the kitchen at Glanteifi. I wondered if the servants here used buttermilk to scrub the floors as ours did.

'Good evening, gentlemen! Dr Reckitt, isn't it? And would this be Mr Probert-Lloyd, the coroner?'

The ability of innkeepers both to remember faces and to keep abreast of local goings-on never ceased to impress me. But of course, news of Lizzie Rees's death was already common knowledge; the fellow who had given us directions earlier had shown us that.

Our host ushered us to the settles on either side of the fire in the main room, then, having brought us a jug of ale, at Reckitt's request he agreed to provide us with some dinner.

'Are you in funds, Reckitt?' I asked, once we were alone. He was not in the habit of treating me to dinner.

He stretched his legs towards the fire. 'I hope to be, directly. To the tune of two guineas.'

'I think planning a post-mortem might be a little premature,' I said, keeping my voice down lest we attract the attention of the two other men sitting within earshot. 'We've seen nothing to suggest foul play.'

'Nothing except a perfectly healthy young woman dying for no apparent reason and her father lying about it.'

'I beg your pardon?'

'Rees lied. He told us his daughter died in bed. But I think it *extremely* unlikely.'

'Reckitt, please, moderate your tone,' I hissed, inclining my head towards the drinkers at the other end of the room.

He reached to the floor for his mug. Was he embarrassed at my pointing out his inappropriate loudness, or irritated? I had only his silence to go on, and that was insufficient.

'Your evidence for that statement?' I asked, barely above a mutter.

He leaned towards me and lowered his voice a fraction. 'When people die in their sleep – unless they've been unconscious for some time and unable to take in fluids – there is almost invariably urine leakage, because the bladder fills up through the night. Unless death occurs very soon after retiring, when the sphincter is released, urine is expelled.'

Physiology lesson over, he retrieved his mug and drank.

'You're telling me there was no evidence of urine in Lizzie Rees's bed?'

'I am. It was completely dry.'

'What's to say that she didn't die soon after she went to bed? There would have been no time for her bladder to fill up then.'

'It's possible. But unlikely. You recall Rees telling us that the quack doctor had looked in the girl's mouth *as best he could*?'

I ignored his denigration of Dr Gwynne. 'Yes, of course.'

'If she had died early in the night, and the doctor didn't see her until the morning, her jaw would have stiffened, making it impossible for him to look into her mouth. Rees's testimony suggested that it had merely been *difficult*. Similarly, to have examined her intimate female area, it would have been necessary for him to be able to move her lower limbs.'

'Except that her father couldn't say whether he'd done so.'

'Why else lift her petticoat?'

'To look for bruising on the torso?'

'Nevertheless, if it's true that he was able to conduct at least some kind of examination of her mouth, it's unlikely that rigor mortis was much advanced. When I examined her, at five o'clock however, rigor was pretty well established.'

'Which means?'

'That she had probably been dead at least twelve hours, and therefore died before five in the morning. So if the quack managed to open her jaw, he must have seen her before eight, which seems unlikely. My conclusion, therefore, is that Rees exaggerated and that the quack merely parted her lips.' Reckitt's voice had resumed its normal lecturing tone, so despite the fact that it meant I could no longer see him, I leaned closer to encourage a reduction in volume.

'Let me understand you. You think that Dr Gwynne's physical examination was not as thorough as we've been led to believe, and that there might be something in her mouth that could indicate how she died?'

'Very possibly.'

'You also believe that it was impossible for her bladder not to have been at least partially full. Therefore, her father must have removed soiled clothes and put clean ones on her?'

'Ah, as to their cleanliness, there's something interesting there. I'm not persuaded that the garment she was wearing was completely clean – by which I mean freshly laundered. It wasn't soiled, but from its smell, it had been worn.'

Putting aside the mental picture of Reckitt breathing in the scent of the dead girl's underlinen, I asked, 'Does the petticoat's having been worn not argue against you?'

'If you consider my earlier reasoning, you will see that it cannot.' He paused. 'Furthermore, her body had been washed. You will have noticed that it did not smell of urine.'

When Mic Rees had drawn back from the sight of his daughter's body being undressed, had he been driven by guilt rather than decency? 'Do you have any theories as to why her father might have lied about where she died, and when?' I asked.

'I do not. However, I can tell you that as far as I have been able to ascertain from a surface examination, she was not the victim of violence. Not physical violence, anyway. As yet, rigor has prevented me from determining whether she had been forced against her will.' He took another swallow of his ale. 'I'll need to examine the body again when rigor mortis has receded, but now that I've apprised you of the suspicious circumstances, I hope you'll agree that a full post-mortem examination is indicated.'

I sighed. 'Reckitt, I'm coming under a great deal of pressure from the county magistrates to reduce the number of inquests.'

'Which county?'

'What...' I had been going to ask what relevance that could possibly have, but half a second's thought gave me the answer. 'Cardiganshire,' I admitted, 'for the most part, but—'

'She died in *Pembrokeshire*.'

'Yes. I know. But each of—'

'You can't allow the magistrates to dictate!' Reckitt's volume rose once more. 'They are medical ignoramuses!'

'But look at it from their point of view. If there's no actual evidence of—'

'*No evidence* was the response of the imbecilic officers in Norfolk when faced with the Balls family! You do *remember* the Balls case?'

Reckitt might be vague about the names of his patients, and scarcely ever exerted himself to remember the names of people to whom he was introduced socially, but he never forgot a name if it was concerned with medical research or jurisprudence. And well he might remember this particular one, for the case argued strongly for the routine examination of corpses by dissection.

Jonathan Balls had killed at least eight members of his family, and possibly many more, before he and his baby granddaughter died on the same day. When repeated appeals from his neighbours finally forced the authorities' hand and the two bodies were exhumed, it was discovered that he had poisoned himself and the infant. Subsequently, the bodies of ten of his other relatives were exhumed and seven were discovered to have been poisoned.

My fellow feeling for the Norfolk coroner in the case had risen considerably in the last twenty-four hours, as prior to the two final deaths, he had been unaware of the unusually high rate of sudden death in the Balls family; Norfolk's magistrates had ruled that before a parish constable could take news of a death to the coroner, he must obtain written permission from a minister of religion, parish overseer or church warden.

The relevant men in authority not wishing to seem profligate with ratepayers' money, evidently no such permission had been granted. Children suddenly taking sick and dying, they might have argued, was commonplace. And Balls's wife had been over eighty at the time of her death, hardly an obvious murder victim.

The same could not be said of Lizzie Rees, a vigorous, healthy young woman who had, it seemed, simply died. But not, apparently, in her bed and not in the garments in which her corpse had been presented to us.

Still, I was loath to allow Reckitt to think he could manoeuvre me into ordering a post-mortem simply by mentioning Jonathan Balls.

'What exactly would you be looking for if you dissected the body?'

'I'd be looking for poison in the first instance. After that, a haemorrhage on the brain, a ruptured aneurysm, pulmonary embolism or *asphyxia idiopathica*.'

A haemorrhage on the brain. Reckitt was proposing not only to cut into Lizzie Rees's torso and examine her viscera but to take his saw and shear off the top of her skull in order to remove her brain. But that would go beyond the remit of an inquest post-mortem. For that, he needed only to rule out foul play, and apart from poison, none of the causes of death he had mentioned qualified.

Before I committed myself, there were more questions to be answered. If we were to determine time of death with more accuracy, I needed to know at what time Mic Rees had summoned Dr Cadwgan Gwynne to certify his daughter's death. I also wished to speak to whoever had taken the awful news to Esther Rees at Ffynone. Why had Mic Rees sent somebody else to speak to his wife rather than going to fetch her himself? Might the reason have any bearing on the timing of Lizzie's death? The answers to those questions might help me understand why Rees had lied to us about where his daughter had died.

'I shall speak to Rees again tomorrow,' I told Reckitt, 'and make some other enquiries.'

'Excellent.'

'And depending on the answers I receive, and your own findings as to whether Lizzie Rees had been sexually molested, I will *then* decide on the advisability or otherwise of a post-mortem.'

I ignored his harrumphing and called a servant to take a message to the stables that we would be staying after all. It crossed my mind to send another to Glanteifi with a message for John, who was due home today. However, given that I would not now be returning home tonight, I felt l could confidently leave it to John to infer that there was an investigation in hand.

He would know that he was needed.

John

I'd expected to sleep well after all the travelling I'd done, but with Harry still over on the other side of the river, I lay awake half the night arguing with myself about what to do in the morning.

It looked as if this death in Brynberian or Eglwyswrw or wherever it was had turned out to be suspicious. Harry'd be investigating and he'd expect me to go over there first thing with my assistant coroner's hat on.

But why should I? He'd run off to the other side of the river when by rights he should've told Reckitt to go and look at the body by himself and only come to him if there were suspicious circumstances. Those'd been the rules even before the magistrates' letter.

And anyway, I had enough on my plate. I had to decide how I was going to broach things with Mr Ormiston on Monday, as well as sort out all the work he'd left for me to do.

On the other hand, if I didn't go over to Eglwyswrw to find Harry, goodness only knew what foolishness Reckitt would lead him into.

By the time the dawn light started poking its way into my bedroom around the curtains, I'd batted the arguments backwards and forwards for hours until I'd finally made a decision. Harry had to start playing by the rules, and it wouldn't help if I encouraged him to think that he could go rushing about doing as he pleased and I'd follow like a lap dog. I was staying here.

-

I hadn't expected Mrs Griffiths, the housekeeper, to be up and about at dawn with the other servants, but she came into the kitchen as I was finishing off some of yesterday's bread with butter and honey.

'I see you're not in riding clothes, Mr Davies. Does that mean you're not going over to Pembrokeshire to meet Mr Probert-Lloyd?'

I swallowed a mouthful and shook my head at the same time, which almost made me choke. 'No,' I croaked. 'Estate work to do.'

She gazed at me, her expression hard to read. I thought she liked me well enough, but I knew she was devoted to Harry, and perhaps she thought I was being disloyal to him.

'Did you enjoy the Great Exhibition?' she asked.

Chewing again, I nodded. 'Strangest thing happened up there, mind. Me and Daniel Williams – Miss Gwatkyn's hall boy – were standing looking at mowing machines when somebody came up behind us and started speaking to us in Welsh!'

I told her the whole story, and when I mentioned Jem Harborne's name, she surprised me.

'That's the young man who's putting up some big construction in Llandyfriog.'

'Yes,' I said. 'A wool factory.'

'He'll be lucky to see it built, the way he's going.' Ianto's tongue was a lot looser in the kitchen than it was in the dining room.

'What d'you mean?' I asked.

'People are against it. This factory.'

The other footman, Fred, dumped a bucket of anthracite in front of the range. 'So they should be. That wool man took a smallholding that'd been promised to somebody else.'

'How?' I asked. A promise to sub-let was generally as good as a written contract.

Fred shrugged. 'New squire over at Plas Blaengwyn wanted the factory on his land. Tenant didn't have a choice, did he?'

71

'So who's going to do the land work?' I asked. I couldn't see Jem Harborne turning out whenever the farmer who'd sub-let the land to him needed an extra pair of hands, which was the usual agreement with sub-tenants.

Ianto shrugged. 'Pay some poor bugger of a labourer, won't he?'

'Ianto Jones!' Mrs Griffiths said sharply. 'Language.' With no butler, she was having to keep a firm hand on the footmen.

It was time I left. Ianto'd hold it against me for ever if I stood there watching him getting a telling-off, and I didn't want to give him a reason to 'accidentally' pour soup in my lap.

Harry

The following morning, before I sat down to breakfast, I asked the Sergeant's landlord if he could find somebody to take a message over to Glanteifi for me.

'Present my compliments to my under-steward, Mr John Davies,' I told the young man who eventually produced himself, 'and ask if he'd be so good as to meet me here at his convenience. Take a horse from the stables and charge it to my account.' At this rate, I was going to be significantly out of pocket if I decided not to call an inquest. Still, the quicker John got here, the more efficient my investigation would be.

Half an hour or so later, I went over to the stables to find Sara tacked up and waiting for me. Standing next to her was the skewbald animal Reckitt had been riding, also ready to go.

'The doctor not going with you, sir?'

I turned to the grey-haired, slightly stooped little man who had spoken. 'No, not this morning.' All I required from Reckitt was that he re-examine Lizzie Rees's body once rigor mortis had released her from its grip, a process that would not yet be far enough advanced. 'You can stall his horse for a while yet.'

The man whistled and issued instructions to somebody I could not see.

'And your mare, sir – will you be needing a stall for her later?'

'I'm not sure. Possibly.' I took the reins from him. 'I've just sent a messenger over to Glanteifi—'

'Yes, sir, young Dai Davies. First-class rider – he'll be there in no time.'

'If I'm not back before my assistant, Mr John Davies, arrives, direct him to the smallholding of Rhosdywarch, will you?'

I started to give him directions, but he forestalled me. 'I know the Reeses' place.'

'Did you know the young woman who's died?' I asked. 'Lizzie Rees?' Being of a different generation, it was possible that he had not been acquainted with the girl.

'Only to pass the time of day with if I saw her in the street, sir. She only came to the village for church as a rule, and I'm chapel.'

'Have you heard anything about her death? Have people been talking?'

'Gossip, you mean?'

I smiled, pointing my gaze in his direction. I had been practising with John and Lydia and had learned to look pretty well infallibly at a speaker's face, but looking them squarely in the eye would, I feared, always be beyond me. 'I find there's often a seed of something even in the worst kind of tittle-tattle, don't you?'

He took a confiding half-step towards me and lowered his voice slightly. 'I heard Dr Gwynne'd given it as natural death, but Esther Rees wouldn't have it – went straight off to Cilgerran for Dr Reckitt. Why would she do that?'

I hesitated, but sometimes it was necessary to give a little in order to get what one wanted. 'That's what I'm trying to find out. So, *have* you heard anything?'

He looked over his shoulder as Reckitt's horse, now unsaddled once more, was led away by a small boy. 'There *was* something. But it was just lads talking in their cups really...'

'And what did they say, these lads?' I asked when I realised that the old man would say no more unless prompted. It was a common trick amongst people who wanted to tell me what they knew but were afraid of being accused of passing on information that others might not want shared: if the coroner asked a direct question, there was no choice but to answer him, was there? It was the law.

'They were going on about this one lad,' he said, keeping his voice down lest the boy hear. 'The Englishman, they call him.'

'And what did they say about him?'

The old man sucked his teeth. 'Only gossip it was, sir...'

'Even so, it would be useful to know what people are saying.'

'They said Lizzie Rees's death wasn't right. That it must be something to do with the Englishman. That's all I know.'

And try as I might, I could get nothing more out of him.

–

The ride to Rhosdywarch was pleasant and my new familiarity with the route meant that I seemed to reach the smallholding much more quickly than we had the previous day.

As I forded the stream below the Reeses' home, I slowed Sara to a walk, then pulled her up and closed my eyes for a moment. I was not used to conducting interviews without John, still less alone, and I needed to collect my thoughts. As soon as my eyelids closed on the whirlpool and the effort of trying to see the world around it, I became aware of birdsong all about me: in the trees along the water's edge, in the sky above, in the hummocky, gorse-strewn fields ahead. I tilted my head the better to distinguish individual calls and songs, and felt the early sun on my cheek, smelled the sweetness of earth and plants warming from a chilly night.

It is a cliché to say that a blind man's other senses become more acute in order to compensate for the one he has lost, and I do not believe it to be the case; it is simply a matter of paying attention to senses that are often ignored because of the overwhelming primacy of vision. In the year or so since my sight had failed me, I had forced myself to learn everything I could from my other senses and had been astonished at the amount of information human beings routinely disregard. As a boy, I had often heard farmers say that they could smell rain and had dismissed the notion as metaphorical, but now I knew it to be true. Similarly, music now seemed sweeter than any I had heard before, and I had been forced to wonder how often in my previous life I had failed to properly appreciate a performance because I had been distracted by the beauty of the singer or the bored twitchings of my fellow listeners.

Vision, I had come to understand, masks and weakens our other senses. Why else would a young woman close her eyes as she breathes in the scent of a rose she has just been given?

The thought, and with it the accompanying memory of a once-beloved face, sent over me a wave of acute melancholy. If I were to fall in love again, to marry, I would never know the face of my beloved in any but the most tantalising way: *visible* but never to be gazed at, drunk in, fixed upon.

Nudging Sara into a walk once more, I turned my ears to the birds again, catching the high, sweet twittering of a lark and seeing the fluttering littleness of it, high above, in my mind's eye.

–

Rhosdywarch was quiet when I arrived, and I was afraid that despite my early start, the family might already have left for chapel. However, my shouts soon roused an answering greeting from the field on the other side of the little orchard, and one of the girls came running.

'Is it my mam or my dada you'd like to speak to, sir?' she panted as she pulled up in front of me.

'Your father if he's not too busy,' I said, dismounting.

'I'll see if he's out yet,' she answered, already taking to her heels with my message.

Damn. I had been too slow on the uptake and now Mic Rees and I would both be embarrassed when he cut short his private business in the privy and presented himself.

John would have been quicker, would have called the girl back and asked her to fetch her mother. But then I knew perfectly well that John would have argued strongly against being here in the first place.

Dr Gwynne saw nothing suspicious, he would have said, *and neither did Reckitt. You're making too much of her father's white lie.*

76

He just didn't want to let Cadwgan Gwynne see her wet and stinking of piss.

'Mr Probert-Lloyd!' It was not Mic Rees's voice that pulled me from my thoughts, but his wife's. 'I'm sorry, I know you wanted to see my husband, but he's...' She faltered to a halt.

'Don't trouble yourself. I know you'll all want to be getting off to chapel. Besides, you will be able to answer at least one of my questions.'

And indeed, it suddenly seemed serendipitous that I found myself speaking to Esther instead of to her husband. I might do well to defer my discussion with Mic Rees about the circumstances in which he had found his daughter's body until I had more information about his own movements the previous morning.

'I'll help if I can.'

'I've asked Dr Reckitt to come over later today to finish his examination,' I began, hoping that this would predispose her to cooperate with me. 'Once he has done so, he may find that he does not need to conduct a post-mortem.'

She did not reply, simply waited to hear what I wanted from her.

'Meanwhile, I would like to speak to the man who came to bring you the dreadful news of Lizzie's death. Can you tell me his name and where I can find him?'

There was something about the ensuing silence that told me that though Esther Rees might want to know how her daughter had died, she did not want me riding around the parish asking questions.

'He didn't see Lizzie. Just came to Ffynone to tell me.'

'It's just that there are protocols – ways of doing things – to be followed,' I said, hoping that the use of such an officious, English term would deter her from asking more questions. 'You yourself believe your husband may be hiding something,' I reminded her, blinking as the sun came out from behind a cloud.

I waited, but she made no reply.

77

'I'll also be going to see Dr Gwynne,' I said.

'Why? Dr Reckitt's seen her now.'

'But it was Dr Gwynne your husband consulted.' I gathered Sara's reins. 'Therefore I need to speak to him to see if he observed anything of note.' I was particularly interested in Gwynne's observations on her husband's state of mind when he had appeared at the doctor's door.

'He didn't see anything!' Esther Rees's vehemence spun me around to face her. The tension in her posture was visible even to me, her arms rigid at her sides, fists clenched. 'That's why I wanted Dr Reckitt! I want him to look inside her – to find out *why she died*!'

Before I could stop myself, I had taken a step toward her. 'Mrs Rees, don't upset yourself.'

'If you're not going to have an inquest, I'll pay Dr Reckitt to do his examination. I can't pay two guineas, but I've got the money Lizzie brought back from the south. It's no good to her now.'

I could not allow her to take control of the situation in this way. 'Mrs Rees, please be so good as to do nothing until I have consulted with Dr Reckitt myself. He will be here later, and if he arrives before I get back, I would be obliged if you would not make any such request.'

Esther Rees clutched at her apron with both hands as if she wanted to tear it to shreds. 'But he said the longer it is, the more difficult it'll be!'

Damn Reckitt and his impatience. 'Poisons persist for a long time. Another few hours won't make any—'

'*Poisons!* You think somebody killed my Lizzie with poison?'

I was taken aback; was that not what *she* thought?

'I don't think anything,' I said, striving for a calming tone. 'But poison is one of the things Dr Reckitt would look for, certainly.' As well as haemorrhaging and whatever *asphyxia idiopathica* was. My Latin was rusty, but it sounded suspiciously like a doctor's obfuscating way of saying 'died due to unexplained lack of breath'.

'Now, if you'll just tell me where I might find the man who fetched you from Ffynone, I'll be on my way.'

John

As I left the kitchen and made my way to the estate office at the front of the house, I was still thinking about Jem Harborne and his wool factory. I wasn't surprised about what Ianto'd said – there would be bad feeling, wouldn't there? It was only to be expected. And not just from the family that was supposed to have been sub-letting the land Harborne was building on, either. Even if his factory was mostly producing cloth for South Wales or America, I could see that it'd affect local weavers in the end.

Of course there was bad feeling towards him.

I thought about the farmer who'd been forced to go back on his previous agreement to sub-let the smallholding. Harborne must've gone over his head, straight to the new squire at Plas Blaengwyn, and offered a lot more money. Half for the tenant and half for the squire, most likely.

Mr Ormiston would approve. As far as he was concerned, the only thing that had to be considered when renting out land was bringing in as much money as possible for the estate. I'd lost count of how many times a tenant'd complained to me that this wasn't how old Mr Probert-Lloyd had done things.

Ever since Harry'd given Mr Ormiston a free hand to manage the estate, everything had changed. Trouble was, with the same steward in charge, as far as the tenants were concerned it must be the new squire's fault that they were suddenly being dealt with differently. So it was Harry people blamed when a farm up for re-letting went to the highest bidder instead of the next family member in line; or when a new tenancy agreement made the tenant, not the estate, liable for maintaining the property; or when the rent went up because the tenant'd made improvements in recent years and raised the farm's value.

I'd tried to tell Mr Ormiston that he was causing trouble for Harry, but he wasn't having it. 'The tenants have had it too easy for too long,' he'd said. 'Mr Probert-Lloyd senior was far too understanding. The tenants took advantage. The balance needs to be redressed.'

But whatever he said, I knew things couldn't go on like this.

When I opened the study door, the place smelled unused. Cold soot, ink, and a lingering smell of vinegar. The maids must've come in to clean the windows while I'd been away. Did that mean Mr Ormiston hadn't been here for the last few days?

There was a pile of documents on my desk, along with a note in Mr Ormiston's jerky, upright hand telling me that the contracts and agreements he'd left for me were needed tomorrow – two copies of each as usual. He wouldn't be in the office until midday, the note said, so I should have plenty of time to finish the work. The thought popped into my head that if I didn't have to get everything done today, I'd have enough time to go over to Eglwyswrw, but I ignored it. I had more work to do than just the drafting that Mr Ormiston'd left me.

My desk was in the little annexe that had been Mr Ormiston's office when Harry's father'd been alive and this had been his study. But I wasn't going to sit at my desk today. Today I was going to take steps for the good of the estate, so I was going to sit at the big desk, the one that had been Mr Probert-Lloyd's.

As I arranged my papers and unstoppered the ink bottle, I wondered what Harry would've said if Jem Harborne had come to him and asked to sub-let some Glanteifi land for his wool factory instead of the land in Llandyfriog.

Thank God that hadn't happened. It was bad enough having the tenants complaining about the way the estate was going – we didn't need all the local weavers up in arms against us too.

But I'd done something just as bad, hadn't I? If Mr Gelyot put money into Harborne's factory, I'd be responsible for weavers losing their jobs.

I just had to hope and pray that nobody ever found out it was me who'd given him Harborne's name.

Harry

It was not far from Rhosdywarch to the farm where Mic Rees had gone in search of a messenger, but the short ride gave me ample time to berate myself for my own incompetence. I should not have allowed myself to be caught up in what amounted to a confrontation with Esther Rees.

If John had been here, it would not have happened. His presence at my side gave my position a certain weight, and without him I felt insubstantial, lacking in significance.

Esther Rees's directions had told me to look out for a farm lane immediately after crossing a small stream, and I soon found myself riding up to the farm she had referred to as Dolbannon.

I followed the sound of voices past a substantial farmhouse and into a courtyard surrounded on three sides by stone buildings. Most were thatched, though the largest – and presumably newest – boasted a slate roof; evidently whoever owned the land hereabouts was still in the process of improving his farms. I wondered sourly whether he, like my father, had decided to fund his renovations by mortgaging the estate.

The yard was busy with young men and women and I realised that I had arrived to find everybody ready for chapel. The farm's harvest had just been brought in, and there was something of a holiday atmosphere in the air, with girls teasing the lads about the soaking they'd given yesterday to the *caseg pen fedi* – the harvest mare – which was the name given to the last sheaf of corn to be tied. By tradition, the young men's task was to bring it to the farmyard unmolested, while the young women's was to soak it. This year, the girls had won.

My unexpected arrival caused a silence to fall, and I looked around the dusty uncobbled yard before dismounting as if I was nothing more than a neighbour.

'Good morning! I'm Harry Probert-Lloyd, the coroner.'

They returned my greeting with restraint, uncomfortable at being addressed in Welsh. John was forever insisting that as an officer of the Crown, I should speak in English, but I could not bring myself to do it. Welsh was my native language as much as it was theirs, and I would not pretend otherwise. Eventually everybody would get used to it.

'I'm looking for whoever took the message about Lizzie Rees's death over to her mother at Ffynone yesterday,' I said, trying to disregard the skin-crawling discomfort caused by the concerted gaze of eyes I could not see. For a moment or two there was no response, then one of the young men took half a step forward.

'I-it was me, M-Mr Coroner,' he stuttered.

I nodded. 'I'd better just have a word with your master, then. Ask his permission to detain to you for a while.'

He led me out of the yard and over to the farmhouse.

'C-coroner's h-here for Master,' he said when a small female figure answered his knock at the door.

Master. Though I had used the word myself, many older farmers still preferred 'Uncle', so I assumed that Dolbannon's tenant was one of the younger generation. And so it proved. The man who came to the door had the bearing and dark hair of a man not much older than me.

'Mr Probert-Lloyd, is it?' he asked in fluent but heavily accented English, not waiting for an answer before introducing himself. 'David Jones. Dai Dolbannon.' Modern he might be, but he did not attempt to shake my hand, bowing instead as his father and grandfather would have done. But I had become inured to handshakes on the hustings that had elected me, so I thrust my hand out and found it being gripped enthusiastically.

'I heard you were at the Sergeant's last night, so I was half expecting you to come and talk to Barti here. A young woman,

84

dying suddenly like that – I thought you'd be bound to want to have a look.' Courteously he refrained from commenting, even obliquely, on my visiting on such an errand on a Sunday.

I took his lead and chose to offer no excuse for my Sabbath-breaking. Perhaps he already knew that I was a persistent offender. 'Do you know the family at Rhosdywarch, Mr Jones?'

'I see Mic Rees at the market, and the farmer he rents his holding from is one of those that makes hay with us. Most years he pays Mic to be an extra scythe. And my wife buys flannel from him.' He paused, slightly. 'He's a good weaver, I'll grant him that.'

'And are there respects in which he isn't so good?' I asked, in Welsh.

Jones gave a bark of laughter, though whether it was caused by my sudden linguistic switch or by my directness, I could not tell. 'He's from away, isn't he?' he said, folding his arms. 'Nobody knows who or what he was before he came here.'

I ignored a stirring from Barti at my side. If David Jones had an opinion about the Rees family, it would be as well to hear it from him now. Barti could wait. 'I heard he was a drover.'

'Yes. And we all know about the kind of things *they* get up to.'

Drovers were a law unto themselves, and some, at least, had no respect for any other kind.

'But he hasn't driven cattle for years,' Jones continued. 'So why didn't he go back where he came from to settle down? Makes you wonder.'

I recalled Mic Rees saying that he had not seen his family home since he was sixteen. Perhaps, like John, he was an orphan and had been obliged to make his own way in the world wherever he could.

'And his wife?' I asked, suddenly curious. 'Is Esther Rees from away, too?'

'No. She's from around here.'

I detected something in his tone and trained my gaze where I hoped his face was. 'But?'

Jones shrugged. I wondered whether he cast a glance at the slight, dark figure of Barti, still and silent in my peripheral vision, to see what he was making of this conversation. 'She didn't stay where she was put, either. Went away when she was young. She was one of the *merched y gerddi*.'

I had never heard the term. 'Garden girls?'

'Went up to London, didn't they? To work in the market gardens. Earned a fortune.'

I waited to see if he would offer more, and he obliged.

'I remember my father saying that when she came home, Esther Rees thought she was too good for the boys here. Airs and graces she had. Speaking English. Too proud to even wear a *betgwn*! Came back in English clothes.'

'Was she a farmer's daughter?' I wondered whether some of the pride had been there already.

'No! Not her. Her dada was a labourer.'

'So,' I said, 'when she got back, she was too grand to marry a man like her father, but none of the farmers' sons would have her?'

'You know how it is, Mr Probert-Lloyd. Farmers' sons marry farmers' daughters. Labourers' sons marry labourers' daughters.'

And those caught uneasily in the middle – smallholders like Mic Rees – might marry up or down depending on their fortunes and prospects. Rees had told me that his wife was determined not to have her daughters courting anybody but a farmer's son. What was it he had said? *Not unless they've got a hundred acres, money in the bank, and no brothers and sisters to keep.*

But Esther Rees's maternal ambition was unlikely ever to have been realised. Farmers were not apt to consider brides for their sons who would not bring animals or capital to the match, however pretty they were.

David Jones cleared his throat. Had I been so obviously distracted? Or was he reminding me that time was going on and he, like his servants, wanted to be off to chapel?

'Did you know her?' I asked. 'Lizzie Rees?'

'I'm a married man, Mr Probert-Lloyd. The likes of Lizzie Rees are of no interest to me.'

My gaze still on Jones, I saw something move in the gloom behind him. Peripheral vision may lack precision, but it is sensitive to movement, and I suspected that the maid who had summoned her master had hung back to listen to our conversation. Did she just want to take some juicy gossip back to the kitchen, or had she known Lizzie?

Jones must have seen something in my gaze, because he spun around. 'Don't stand there, girl, get back to your work!'

'Actually, if that's your maid, can I just have a quick word with her, please?'

'I thought you were here to see Barti?'

'Even so.'

Jones jerked his head. 'Barti, go back to the others while Mr Probert-Lloyd talks to Elen. We'll come and find you when it's your turn.'

At my side, Barti hesitated. 'Look, *ngwas i*,' Jones reassured him, 'if you're worried about being late for church, you can come with me and Mrs Jones in the trap. You'll be there in plenty of time.'

As Jones disappeared into the house in search of the little maid who had, evidently, fled back to her work as instructed, I wondered why he had sent Barti away; it seemed unnecessary. But before I could come to any kind of conclusion, he returned in the company of the same diminutive figure who had answered the door to us.

'Elen, this is Mr Probert-Lloyd,' he said in Welsh. 'He's the coroner. Do you know what that means?' Evidently something indicated to her master that Elen was either ignorant or unwilling to answer. 'It means that when people die, if nobody knows what they died of, he has to find out.'

'I only want to talk to you for a minute, Elen,' I said, gently.

'I don't know anything! I don't know who killed her!'

It was not a surprise that my visit to Rhosdywarch had led people to believe that Lizzie Rees's death was suspicious, but I wished that my involvement was not inevitably seen as evidence of foul play; people's perceptions are influenced by the notion of murder, even if they are unaware of the fact.

I tried for a soothing tone. 'We don't know that *anybody* killed her. I just wanted to find out a bit about her. Did you know her?'

'Go on, girl, answer Mr Probert-Lloyd!'

Had Elen looked to Jones for help, or had he just become impatient when she did not answer me immediately?

'I didn't know her to talk to,' she said, so softly it was only just more than a whisper.

'She was a lot older than you, I expect?' Elen sounded like a child rather than a young woman.

'Yes.'

It suddenly struck me how intimidating it must be for her to be standing there between her master and a strange gentleman, looking up at one then the other. I was of no great height – not as tall as Jones – but I doubted that Elen measured more than four and a half feet. 'Shall we sit down?' I suggested. 'Perhaps there's somewhere in the yard?'

Jones sighed gustily but led us to the side of a byre, where he indicated a horse trough. 'Will that be all right?'

'Of course.' I put my hand on the edge of the trough to gauge its height, then lowered myself gingerly, feeling the sun-warmed topstones through my britches.

Though Jones did not sit down with Elen and me, he showed no inclination to leave. Was his instinct to protect his servants or to know their business?

I turned to the girl. 'Elen, did you know Lizzie Rees by sight – enough to say good day to if you met her?'

Sitting at my side rather than having to face me, Elen seemed more at ease. 'No. I go to chapel, and Lizzie Rees was church.'

'So you only know her name from things you've heard?'

I caught her nod. Ordinarily, I would have explained that I could not see well and that she would need to speak rather than just nod or shake her head, but I feared that she would take any such comment as a criticism and become even more reticent. Still, I could stare fixedly ahead and apparently avoid looking at her while actually keeping her in my peripheral vision; perhaps if she did not feel that she was being scrutinised, the nervousness that was making her screw up her apron in her little fists might relent a little.

'Did you hear about her from the other maids?'

Another minimal nod.

'Were any of them friends with her?'

I saw a shrug, then Elen turned to look at me. 'They said she went away.'

'That's true. But not for long. Only a month or so.'

'They said she'd gone to catch a better husband.'

'A better husband? Did she have an understanding with somebody, then?'

'I don't know!' That wail again. 'That's just what they said.'

'Who said it – the other female servants here?'

'Yes.'

'Did they say anything else about her?'

The child's fingers worried at her apron; I did not want to make her cry.

'Elen – did any of the other girls here say anything when they heard that Lizzie Rees had died?' I asked gently.

'Elen.' Jones's voice held a note of warning in it. She was to answer my question or face the consequences.

'They said… serve her right.'

Serve her right?

'Did they say *why* it served her right – what she was supposed to have done?'

Elen's head could not have dipped further towards her chest unless she had dislocated her neck, and I barely heard her response. 'They said she thought she was better than everybody else.'

'Better how?'

'I don't know! Mistir, can I go back to my work, now? Mrs Jones'll be waiting for me to go to chapel. I don't want to get into trouble.'

As it seemed unlikely that I would get any more useful information from her, I nodded in Jones's direction, and a second later, Elen almost flew off her perch.

'Right then,' her master said as she fled. 'Is it all right if you talk to Barti now, so that we can get off?'

'Of course. I'm sorry.'

'No, no. No need to apologise. I just don't want to feel the edge of the vicar's tongue if we're late. He'll have enough to say about all the gossip that's going round about Lizzie Rees. I don't want to give him anything more to put in his sermon.'

John

The hall clock hadn't even struck nine and I was already sick of drafting and copying. And if I'm honest, a little bit sick from nerves at the thought of going against Mr Ormiston's instructions with the new contracts when I'd finished this lot. When the messenger from Eglwyswrw arrived a few minutes later with Harry's note, half of me was delighted – I could get out of the cold office into the sunshine and leave my plans for rebellion until later – but the other half was furious. What gave Harry the right to think he could just call and I'd come like a sheepdog to its master's whistle? We had an agreement: I wouldn't go out with him as assistant coroner if I had estate work pressing. And however scared I was of what I was planning, it *was* pressing. It had to be done.

I ignored the treacherous little voice in the back of my mind that said Harry didn't know that.

'Shall I tell him to wait for you?' Wil-Sam asked, meaning the messenger, who he'd left on the front steps.

No, tell him to go back to Eglwyswrw and tell Harry Probert-Lloyd I'm not coming because I'm busy running his estate!

'No. Ask him to wait for me to get changed, and I'll ride back with him.'

As I ran upstairs, I told myself I could always use the journey to think again about how I was going to word the contracts that I'd decided needed changing.

–

But of course I didn't do that. Instead, like a good little assistant coroner, I spent the ride over to Eglwyswrw digging for information.

The man who'd been sent to fetch me introduced himself as David Davies. 'But they call me Llwyo,' he said. Davies was the most common surname in the area, so anybody with a name like his and no farm to identify him would need a nickname.

I looked over at him, sitting easily on his grey mare. He was a stringy kind of individual with a long face and a beak of a nose. 'Llwyo? Why?'

'Because "Dai Llwyau" isn't so handy.'

Dai Spoons. 'You make spoons, then?'

'Yes. But not for eating. Course, I can do those as well, but—'

'Oh! Love spoons, is it?'

He looked at me sidelong, to check whether I was mocking him. 'I make a good bit out of it. Everybody wants one of my spoons.'

I gathered both the reins in one hand and leaned forward to put the other on the mare's warm neck. My fingers were still stiff with cold from the study. 'I've never really understood why you'd buy a love spoon to give a girl. Isn't the point supposed to be that you show her how much you love her by how much time you've spent carving the thing?'

'Yes, but some people can't carve to save their life. They could spend months on it and still end up with something that looks as if a blind man made it left-handed.'

I glanced at him. I could see that as soon as he'd said it he'd remembered who my boss was.

'Sorry. I didn't mean…'

'Don't worry about it.'

He was blushing. Still managing to ride like a gentleman, mind. He'd obviously been taught properly, with a saddle, rather than learning to ride bareback on a farm horse like most of us.

'But thing is, right,' he said, falling over himself to make me forget his poor-taste joke, 'what's going to impress a girl more –

a clumsy spoon somebody's made himself but that she can't show off to her friends, or one he's bought that'll make the other girls envious enough to curdle milk?'

'Fair point.' I turned to look at him properly. 'You're that good, are you?'

'So they say.'

'Anybody come to you for a spoon to give this girl that's died?'

He shrugged, but in a way that made me think he knew something. 'They did, then?'

He looked me in the eye. 'What's it worth?'

'You want paying for *gossip*?' If I sounded scornful enough, maybe he'd tell me for nothing.

He cocked his head at me. 'Not gossip. Information.'

I tried to think how much money I had on me. I didn't tend to carry much when I was with Harry, because his word was always enough to get us credit, but I had a few shillings in my pocket.

'Half a crown,' I said. Would that be enough? It should be – it was probably a day's wages for him.

'Five shillings.'

'*What?* Get off! D'you think I'm made of money?'

'No. I think you work for the coroner. He'll be on expenses, won't he?' He rubbed a thumb and forefinger together. 'County money, isn't it?'

Dear God. If only he knew how difficult it was to part the county magistrates from a single penny. But he worked at the Sergeant's, where the petty assizes were held. He'd see all sorts going on expenses for that and assume it was just the same when it came to inquests.

'I'm not giving you five shillings. I'm not giving you anything until I know a bit more about this so-called information.'

He reined his mare back to a walk as we started up the hill that'd take us along the top of Cenarth gorge. I shivered a bit. The road was overshadowed here by the stunted oak trees that were all that would grow on the steep slope. 'All right then,' he said. 'I can give you the names of three lads who paid me for spoons to give to Lizzie Rees.'

'That's the dead girl?'

'Obviously.'

'And would one of your spoons have done the trick?'

'Who knows? Not easily pleased, Lizzie Rees, by all accounts.'

'So just making her friends jealous with a spoon wouldn't've been enough for her to start walking out with somebody?'

Llwyo sucked his teeth. 'Far as I could see, she didn't *have* many friends. Only one girl she went about with. Not that I knew her, not really. Just saw her about.'

'Got sisters, has she?' I'd noticed that girls with a lot of sisters tended not to be so bothered about having a pack of friends. All their need for gossip and foolishness was already seen to.

'Two. But they're younger. It wasn't that.'

'What, then?'

Llwyo looked at me sideways. Probably thinking of asking for money for this information as well. 'Family's a bit odd,' he said, in the end. 'Keep to themselves, mostly. The father's from away. Her mother met him on the road.'

I was obviously supposed to ask, so I did. 'On the road – like vagrants?'

He grinned. 'No. Esther Rees'd been working in London and she was on the way home. He was a drover. Or working with a drover. One or the other.'

'And he came back with her?'

Llwyo made a face that told me he was running out of facts he knew for certain and beginning to rely on things he'd heard older relatives saying when he was little. 'No. I think he turned up later. When he'd saved enough.'

'For the land, you mean?' No man'd ask a woman to marry him unless he could provide a home for her.

'Yes.'

'And is that the place where they live now, or have they moved up in the world?'

'No. Always lived at Rhosdywarch. He's got a weaving shed there and they've got an orchard as well as the land. Sell some cider.'

Lydia Howell had told me that according to Reckitt, the dead girl's mother'd been working away from home when the news came that her daughter had died. So if the family was scraping a living together with weaving and selling cider and taking work where they could to pay the rent, where did Miss Haughty's attitude come from?

We were out in full sun again now, heading down the steep slope to the river and the Llechryd road. I hated riding down that sort of hill, so I slid off my little mare, Seren's back and walked at her side.

'So why am I going to pay you five shillings for the names of three lads who were sweet on Lizzie Rees?' I asked, craning my neck to look up at Llwyo, who seemed perfectly happy in the saddle. 'From what I've heard already, there were no suspicious circumstances about the death.' Best to make it clear to him that I already had some useful information; that I wasn't going to roll over and give him money for just any old gossip.

'If there aren't suspicious circumstances, what's your boss doing riding about asking questions?'

Oh God. Harry'd started without me. 'He'll be wanting to make sure. If somebody calls him to a body, Mr Probert-Lloyd'll give full consideration to all the circumstances of the death. He's not one to just say "looks like natural causes" and go home.' Especially not since an innocent man'd been transported to New South Wales on account of him not investigating hard enough during the coroner's election campaign back in April. 'If he was really suspicious, he'd've asked Dr Reckitt to do a post-mortem examination. To cut the body open, I mean.' I turned to him. 'He hasn't, has he?'

'Dunno. Might've by now. Heard they were arguing about it in the Sergeant's last night. Dr Reckitt says they can't know for sure that it wasn't poison unless he opens her up.'

'Who'd want to poison her?'

Llwyo shrugged.

'You're never accusing one of the lads who bought spoons off you?'

95

Another shrug. He wasn't going to go as far as accusing them, but he wasn't going to jeopardise his five shillings by defending them, either.

I reached into my pocket and pulled out a handful of coins. 'Three shillings,' I said.

'Four.'

'Three and six.'

'Done.'

I handed the money over and put the remainder back in my pocket. 'Come on then – names.'

Harry

'Before you call for Barti,' I said as David Jones made to follow his little maid, 'why did you send him away while I questioned Elen?'

'He frightens her.' Jones drew a deep breath, as if he was fortifying himself before saying something difficult. 'She's got no reason to be afraid, because he wouldn't hurt a fly, but... well, you won't have been able to see, but he looks a bit... unusual. His eyes don't work together – one of them wanders. He used to wear an eyepatch – that's where he got his nickname from, Barti Ddu. Like the pirate,' he added, in case I'd never heard of Bartholomew Roberts, also known as Black Bart – Barti Ddu.

'Why doesn't he wear the patch any more?'

Jones put his hands in his pockets. 'There was a bit of horseplay when he first came here to work.'

'The others took it off him?'

'They didn't mean anything by it. It's just not something you see every day, is it – a young lad with an eyepatch.'

'But he won't be able to see properly without it.' I felt outraged at this young man's treatment at the other servants' hands.

'He keeps the wandering one closed, mostly.'

'I don't suppose that improves his looks either! No wonder Elen's frightened of him.'

'It's not just that.' I was not sure whether Jones was defending himself or his servant. 'He's a bit odd. Walks around a lot at night. Doesn't sleep with the rest in the loft.'

'I'm not surprised, if they treat him like that.'

'As it happens, he asked if he could have a place by himself when I first hired him. Says he can't sleep when he can hear other people breathing and snoring.'

'So where does he sleep?'

'In the brewhouse. Not that he does sleep much. When he's not walking around the fields at all hours, he's drawing things. Spends any money he's got on paper and pencils and lamp oil.'

Perhaps it was not simply his squint that made the other lads pick on Barti. Somebody who behaved differently, who refused to conform, would always be treated with suspicion; I knew that to my cost. 'So why did you choose him to deliver the message about Lizzie Rees's death?'

'Because we were harvesting and he's the least handy with a sickle. With it being Sunday today, I wanted the corn in yesterday, while the weather held. If it'd been any other news, I'd have told Mic Rees to look elsewhere for a messenger, but in the circumstances... Besides, whoever went needed to take a spare horse for the girls, and I knew he'd be the best to ride and lead at the same time. He's good with horses, Barti is. I'll miss him for that, when he's gone.'

'What do you mean, when he's gone?'

'It's his last day with us today. He's got another job to go to.'

As Jones walked off across the yard to fetch the young man, I hoped that Barti would find better treatment at the next farm he worked on, though it seemed unlikely if he was as different from his peers as it seemed.

Had Lizzie Rees also been different? It seemed so, if what Elen had said was true. *They said she thought she was better than everybody else.* Different, perhaps, but not in the way that Barti was.

Perhaps I had been wrong to assume that Lizzie did not share her mother's ambitions for her. But if that was the case, did it have any relevance to her apparently natural death? Before I could give the matter any more thought, Jones was back with Barti.

'Thank you, Mr Jones,' I said as they approached. 'I'll come and speak to you again, if I may, when Barti and I are finished.'

A perceptible hesitation hinted that Jones did not appreciate being dismissed in his own yard, but his tone was civil enough. 'Very well. I'll be in the house. I was writing a letter to George the auctioneer when you arrived.'

And with his status thus reaffirmed, he left us.

'Barti,' I said, fixing the whirlpool just to the young man's left so as to see as much of him as I could in my peripheral vision, 'I gather that you were the one Mr Jones trusted to go over to Ffynone to tell Esther Rees that her daughter had died?'

'Y-yes.'

'Can you tell me exactly what message Mic Rees gave you to take to his wife?' I asked. I did not know whether Rees had actually told her that their daughter was dead or had simply asked her to come home.

'Th-th-that Lizzie had d-died in her sleep,' he said. 'M-Mr Rees said he'd w-woken up in the morning and f-found her dead and D-Dr Gwynne had been and c-c-certified her death.' He gasped in a breath. 'N-natural c-causes. He said to t-tell Mrs Rees to p-please come home straight away.'

So distracting were the painful blockages of his stutter and the subsequent barely intelligible rush of words that I almost failed to catch the significance of what he had said. 'Wait a moment. Did you say that Dr Gwynne had been to Rhosdywarch *before* Mic Rees came here?'

There was a brief silence.

'Th-th-that's right.'

Odd. In my experience, most people delayed calling in the doctor to certify death as long as they could, as if some part of them clung to the belief that their loved one might yet revive. Certification made death a reality. Final.

So why had Mic Rees felt the need to ask Cadwgan Gwynne to see Lizzie's body before he had even sent word to his wife and daughters?

'What time was it when Mic came to Dolbannon yesterday?' I asked. Rees had told me that the house cow had woken him up well after sunrise. If he had gone to fetch Gwynne first – having already washed and re-dressed his daughter, if Reckitt's theory was correct – he could not plausibly have reached Dolbannon before half past eight at the very earliest.

'I-I don't know, M–Mr Probert-Lloyd. Th–there's nobody here has a pocket watch and M–Master's clock is in the house.'

'I don't need to know the exact minute. Was it before or after you'd all been in for breakfast?' Farm servants ate breakfast only after all the early work was done, which at this time of the year would be between half past seven and eight o'clock.

'B–before breakfast,' he answered. 'B–but not long before.'

Almost an hour too early to fit the chronology of Mic Rees's account.

'What time did you get back from Ffynone?' I asked, in an attempt to establish the exact sequence of events. 'Before midday, would you say?'

I could not tell whether his hesitation was a result of uncertainty or a different manifestation of his stutter. 'D–definitely.'

'How much before, would you say?'

He did not respond, and as I waited for him to speak, I realised my mistake. Lacking a watch, he had no reference points for fractions of an hour. 'How far could you have walked, do you think, in the time before midday?'

A considered pause. 'To Eglwyswrw.'

Somewhere between half an hour and three quarters of an hour, then, depending on how fast a walker he was. So he had returned by half past eleven or thereabouts.

'You were able to leave Ffynone pretty swiftly, then?'

'M–Mrs Rees went to tell her niece what had happened and the girls went to fetch their things. Th–then we came back.'

I wondered what kind of grief-stricken truth lay behind those few words. Surely Esther Rees had not remained so stoical in the face of such an enormous blow, still less her young daughters? I pictured Ffynone's female servants gathering around, Lizzie's sisters crying and comfort being offered. Work would have been set aside for a few minutes in the face of such a tragedy, but once Esther had chivvied her girls onto the horses, whoever was in charge of the laundry work must have breathed a sigh of relief. I did not know the Colbys of Ffynone personally, but they were successful businessmen. They would be unlikely to tolerate delays out of sympathy for their servants' relations.

I had assumed that Barti had simply come back here after his trip to Ffynone, and I had asked about timings accordingly. But perhaps I had underestimated Mr Jones's generosity with his servant's time. 'Did you take Mrs Rees and her girls all the way back to Rhosdywarch,' I asked, 'or did you just bring them back here and let them walk home?'

'M-Mr Jones said t-to take them home first, th-then come back.'

'And it was still well before midday when you got back here, to Dolbannon?'

'Y-yes.'

I believed him. People who measure their waking hours by daylight do not need to consult the height of the sun in the sky at any given moment; it is as much part of their awareness of their surroundings as the ground beneath their feet or the smell on the air they breathe.

All of which made it very clear that one way or another, Mic Rees had not told me the truth. Either he had discovered his daughter's death far earlier than he had been prepared to admit, or he had not fetched Dr Gwynne to certify her death before coming to Dolbannon for a messenger. Indeed, if he had already fetched the doctor, why would he need to send a messenger to Ffynone? Surely he could have begged the loan of two horses and gone himself?

Lizzie Rees's father was hiding something.

John

Harry wasn't at the Sergeant's when I arrived in Eglwyswrw, but an old ostler told me that he'd left a message for me to meet him at the Rees family's place, Rhosdywarch, and told me how to get there.

As Seren trotted along, I wondered if there was any value at all in the gossip I'd paid Llwyo three and six for. Three names. Three lads who'd bought spoons to give to Lizzie Rees. Or at least, so he suspected. None of them had said who they were for, but according to him 'everybody' knew that the three of them were fighting over her.

'Mind, they were only the ones with the money for spoons,' he'd said. 'I'm not saying there weren't others sniffing after her. I'll give you one name for free. Nattie Stockton.'

I turned to eyeball him. 'Go on.'

'From down south. Heard it was serious between them. Stupid, mind, if it was. People wouldn't stand for it, would they?'

People being the local lads. They'd see any man from away as poaching on their patch if he tried to court a local girl. And poachers don't get treated well as a rule.

I took the next road on the right and found myself going down and down towards the stream Llwyo'd said I'd cross at a ford. On either side of me, the hedge-topped banks sprouted hogweed that narrowed the road by half its width and left its pollen on Seren's chest and my boots. The piggish smell of it got up my nose as Seren trotted through it, and as my head went back for a sneeze, I caught a glimpse over the hedge of the stubbly bank field beyond. It'd not long had some late hay taken off it, and I wondered if it belonged to Mic Rees. It wasn't bad land. South-west-facing so it'd get a lot of sun, which brought the grass on no end.

But of course, once Seren'd splashed through the almost dry ford, I realised that the Rees's land would be on *this* side. North-east-facing wasn't such good news. Less sun, so less profitable.

A little way up the hill, I saw the apple trees I'd been told to look out for and pulled up. Rhosdywarch wasn't a bad-looking place. The land was well kept and the house was better than I'd been expecting. Not a full two storeys, but a window'd been knocked into the roofline at one side, so Mic Rees had made the loft a decent space for sleeping in, not just a dark attic under the thatch. To one side of the house was a low-roofed lean-to. Probably the weaving shed Llwyo'd mentioned. The thought of weaving made my stomach lurch, and I pictured Mr Gelyot senior listening to Jem Harborne's big plans for wool factories in the Teifi Valley, then shaking hands on a deal. My fault. And all because Gus had poked fun at us.

I stared at the Reeses' place and tried to forget about Jem Harborne.

I'd heard that in some parts of Pembrokeshire the houses were pink from adding pigs' blood to the limewash, but the Rhosdy-warch cottage was white like those on our side of the river. Perhaps the pink ones were only in the south, where they spoke English and gave themselves airs.

There was no sign of Harry's little mare, Sara, so either she was on the other side of the house or Harry wasn't here. To be honest, a bit of me was relieved at the thought of putting our first meeting off for a bit longer. Harry and I had barely been speaking to each other before I went up to London.

Still, we'd have to talk now, wouldn't we? We were on coroner's business. And anyway, who knew, perhaps me disappearing off up to London to see the Exhibition'd given Harry time to think, take stock a bit.

I looked up and down the road as far as I could see which was about twenty yards in either direction. Nobody. I was going to have to face Lizzie Rees's bereaved parents and ask them if they knew where Harry was.

It was generally Harry who dealt with grieving relatives. He was good at it, didn't just stick to the usual phrases everybody trots out when there's been a death; he sounded as if he meant it. Seemed as if he could sense what people needed to hear. Don't know how he did it without being able to see, but it was a valuable talent for a coroner to have.

I carried on sitting there for another minute, nerving myself to go up to the house. But then I remembered what day it was. I took my watch out. Nearly eleven o'clock. They'd almost certainly be at chapel, so I could wait here for Harry without worrying.

I nudged Seren with my heels and up we went to the cottage. The door stayed shut, but I slid down out of the saddle and knocked just in case. Didn't want to be caught sneaking about the place.

When there was no answer, I moved to one side and looked through the window. Another point in Mic Rees's favour. The window had glass in it, not just a shutter. Inside, I could see a fair-sized room with a dresser pretending to be a wall. The fire was banked up, so they must still be out. I moved to the other side of the door and peered in through the second window. Box bed. Rag rug. Chest of drawers. Stool. Was the corpse in the bed?

Another couple of paces and I was standing at the lean-to window. It was covered with a sheet, so now I knew where the body was.

Suddenly I heard some scuffling coming from the far end of the house and turned to see two faces peering round the gable end at me. They pulled back as soon as they saw me looking at them, so I dropped Seren's reins, tiptoed up to the end of the house and peered around. They were hiding there – two little girls. They squealed and grabbed at each other and started laughing in that high-pitched, half-excited, half-terrified way girls have. I could tell they were about to run away, so I spoke to stop them.

'Good morning, ladies! My name's John Davies and I'm the coroner's assistant. Is Mr Probert-Lloyd here?'

They shook their heads and stared at me, eyes wide.

'Don't be scared,' I said. 'Mr Probert-Lloyd left me a message to meet him here. Did he say when he'd be back?'

More shaking of heads, mouths tight closed.

'Not at chapel today?' They weren't in Sunday best.

No answer to that either.

'Is your mam or dada here?'

They stared at me like two baby birds in a nest looking at a boy who's climbed the tree to steal eggs. The one who looked to be the younger of them – maybe nine or ten years old – shook her sister. 'You say.' But the older girl kept her mouth clamped shut.

I waited. I'd learned that from Harry. Don't ask too many questions.

'Dada's gone to talk to the carpenter about a coffin for Lizzie,' the younger one blurted. 'And Mam's gone to church to see about her burial money.'

Sounded as if Lizzie Rees's mother was part of one of these friendly societies where women saved money for a rainy day.

'Has Mr Probert-Lloyd been here today?' I asked.

Both heads nodded. 'And yesterday,' the younger one said.

'D'you know where he was going when he left here today?'

Just then, Seren clopped up behind me, hooves muffled on the dusty path, and butted my back. She didn't like me dropping her reins and leaving her. I took hold of them again and stroked her neck.

The girls laughed, but thanks to the mare, they sounded less shrill now, more normal.

'So do you?' I asked again. 'Know where he was going?'

'To Dolbannon,' the older one said.

'To see Barti Ddu,' said her sister.

Barti Ddu. Must be quite a character to deserve a pirate's nickname.

'And what did Mr Probert-Lloyd want to see this Barti Ddu for?'

The younger one jutted her chin and opened her mouth, but before she could say anything, her sister said, all in a rush, 'It was him brought the news to us about Lizzie being dead. To Ffynone.'

Their faces crumpled then. Just for a few moments, me arriving – and Seren's antics – had made them forget that their big sister'd died. I felt sorry for them, the way their faces suddenly ran with tears.

But they didn't stop at tears. They started clutching at each other and sobbing fit to break their hearts. I didn't know what to do.

In the end, I couldn't bear it any more and I cleared my throat before asking, 'Has Dr Reckitt been here today?'

The question seemed to remind them that I was there. They hiccuped and wiped their eyes with their fingers, and before long the crying'd stopped.

'No,' the older one said. 'Only the coroner.'

'Can you come a bit closer?' I asked. They were cowering at the far end of the gable wall and I was afraid they'd suddenly disappear around the back of the house.

They looked at each other and the older one nodded. She wasn't much taller than her sister, but she was less of a little girl – maybe twelve or thirteen years old. The pair of them had the same thick golden-blonde hair, and even if they were a bit on the underfed side, their eyes were clear and they had some pink in their cheeks. I felt sorry for the older one because you could see that her little sister was going to be a beauty. Like Lizzie, by all accounts.

I fixed my eyes on her. 'Like I said, my name's John Davies. What do they call you two?'

'I'm Ann and she's—'

Her sister slapped her, wanting to speak for herself. 'I'm Gwen.'

Looking at the two of them, I reckoned I was still just about of an age where I could ask them the kind of questions Harry'd never get away with, especially as they'd landed in my lap while their parents were away and there was nobody to shush them.

I took my specs off and pulled out a shirt tail to polish them. There was a neatly pressed handkerchief in my pocket, but using that would've made me look like a gentleman. 'So, Dr Reckitt – what did you think of him? Bit like a bear in clothes, isn't he?'

The girls giggled but didn't say anything.

'It's a long way for your mam to go and fetch him, from Cilgerran.'

Still nothing.

'Why d'you think she wanted to speak to him? The local doctor'd already said it was natural causes Lizzie died from, hadn't he?'

Ann stared at me. Her eyes were brown, I noticed. Unusual combination, golden hair and brown eyes. She didn't say anything, just stared as if she was trying to send her thoughts straight into my head, like those mesmerists were supposed to be able to do.

Then Gwen's chin went up again. 'It was because Lizzie stayed—'

'Gwen, *husht*!'

'Stayed where?' I asked. Gwen's eyes weren't like her sister's; they were blue – the colour of Willow pattern china.

She shook Ann off and took half a step towards me. 'Here.'

'While you two and your mother were away working?'

Ann stepped forward too. 'Yes, Mam said she should come with us but Dada let her stay.'

'Because she *said* she had a cold but sh—'

Ann's hand went over her sister's mouth, shutting off whatever she'd been about to say, but it was too late. Gwen thought her sister'd been shamming this cold.

I was about to ask why she'd do that, but before I could open my mouth, I heard a horse trotting up to the house and a man's voice calling out, 'Mr Rees, Mrs Rees?'

The girls turned and fled.

Benton Reckitt's timing couldn't have been worse.

Harry

Having left Barti to go off to church with his master, I rode over to Eglwyswrw, only to find that John had already left for Rhosdywarch.

As Sara and I trotted back towards the Reeses' smallholding, I wondered how frosty a reception I should expect from John. I knew that he would resent being summoned for what I still had no reason to suspect was anything other than a natural death, and I could only hope that Reckitt's further examination of Lizzie's body this afternoon might shed sufficient light on her father's lies and evasions to justify my involvement.

However, whether that justification would make John any less taciturn than he had been of late remained to be seen.

Ever since he had begun working under Micah Ormiston, he had never seemed entirely at ease. Initially I had assumed that this was a young man's impatience to be given more responsibility, but having seen him ride out on estate business unaccompanied by Ormiston, I had been forced to revise my opinion. Something else was clearly at the root of his discontent.

As my father's man, I recognised that Ormiston might be a little old-fashioned in his approach, and in truth, John had suggested that I become more actively involved in Glanteifi's affairs, but I was reluctant to be seen to interfere in estate business when I had no experience to back up any opinions I might have.

Ormiston had worked for my father, man and boy, and shared his encyclopaedic knowledge of tenants, land and future plans. Since my father's death, whenever I might have interested myself in the estate's management, I had found myself paralysed by an unwillingness to admit that my own knowledge was less thorough; that during the months before the series of apoplectic strokes that had killed my father, I had neither sought his advice nor allowed him to discuss estate business with me. My bitterness at being forced home from London had coloured all aspects of life at Glanteifi with a bilious resentment, and I had seized on the excuse offered by my alternative occupation as coroner to effectively dissociate myself from my inheritance.

And now I was suffering the consequences. I knew John was right, that I should discuss matters with Ormiston, but I simply could not bring myself to allow my steward to see just how ignorant I was when it came to knowledge of my father's methods and plans. Bad enough that I knew myself to have been a poor excuse for a son; I could not face the prospect of Ormiston knowing it too. Instead, I persuaded myself that it would be best simply to allow him to get on with the job he was uniquely qualified to do, while I tried to do the same. So, having asked him to run the estate in the most profitable way he could, I made it my job to seek out investment opportunities.

To that end, I had begun to reintroduce myself to Teifiside society. After spending almost a decade away from Cardiganshire, first at Oxford, then in London, I was scarcely on nodding acquaintance with those who should have been my friends and allies, and Lydia had been quick to point out that I must rectify this if I wished to make a success of my new life. Joining forces with my housekeeper, Mrs Griffiths, who had firm opinions about the social duties of the gentry, she had issued invitations on my behalf with a liberal hand, and with an alacrity due as much to curiosity about me and my novel household as to good manners, those invitations had been accepted. Subsequently, my person and my manners having obviously passed muster, reciprocal invitations began to arrive, and I found myself re-embraced by my Teifiside peers.

Much to my relief, conversations at several mansions had revealed that I need not look far for a business venture worthy of my capital. Virtually every local gentleman with thruppence in the pound to spare had declared his intention of investing in the South Wales Railway's proposed extension between Carmarthen and Cardigan, and again and again I had been encouraged to lay my hands on as much ready cash as I could in order to be ready to buy shares when they were issued. If Micah Ormiston succeeded in the task I had set him, returns on such an investment might yet save Glanteifi.

—

There were two horses standing in front of the Reeses' cottage, and with them, two men. I knew John by his voice before I could get close enough to see his familiar figure, and the voice that answered him was equally recognisable. Reckitt.

'Well met, gentlemen!' I called, feeling a flutter of discomfort as I wondered what they had been discussing.

John came towards me as I dismounted.

'Thank you for coming straight away,' I said, my voice pitched so only he would hear. 'Don't worry, I'll smooth things over with Mr Ormiston.'

'It's not him I'm worried about. It's all the work that won't get done while I'm here. He left quite a bit for me to do.'

'Did you enjoy the Crystal Palace?'

John sighed. 'It was... I don't know. There was a lot to take in. Shall we talk about it later, when there isn't a body to inspect?'

'Reckitt's already done his preliminary examination,' I said. 'There's no need for you to see her.'

Though he had become accustomed to the more grisly aspects of our work, I knew that John did not relish the viewing of the body, something he was obliged to do in my stead.

'Why are you standing out here?' I asked, including Reckitt in the question. 'Family not back from chapel yet?'

'Girls are here, parents aren't,' John summarised. 'Mr Rees is arranging a coffin and I think Mrs Rees must've been putting money by for a rainy day with a local friendly society. She's gone to get it to pay for the funeral.'

'Or possibly to pay me,' Reckitt said. 'Are you going to allow—'

'Where are the girls?' I interrupted him.

'Ran off when they heard the doctor arrive,' John replied.

'Did they say when their parents were likely to be back?'

'No. But it could be a while. If their dada's gone to speak to the carpenter, the business'll probably get done in the pub after chapel.'

'Right. Let's not waste time here, then. You and I'll go and see Dr Gwynne.'

'I'll come with—'

'No, Reckitt. You wait here. When Mic and Esther Rees return, you can do whatever bits of your examination you weren't able to do yesterday.'

'And if Mrs Rees wants a full post-mortem?'

I sighed. 'That, I suppose, becomes a private matter between you and her if there is no reason to call an inquest.' Keen to end the subject, I turned to John. 'Do you know where Dr Gwynne lives?'

'More or less, but can you give me a few minutes first?' John asked. 'I'd like to speak to the girls again. Dr Reckitt arrived just when they were about to tell me something.'

I failed to see the urgency. 'They'll still be here when we get back.'

'Yes, but their mother might be here by then and she'll tell them not to gossip.'

'Not if it's official coroner's business. I had no interference when I spoke to them yesterday.'

'And did you get anything useful from them?'

I had to admit that I had not. But still, that was no reason to delay. Given the discrepancies in timing between Mic Rees's original statement and the information Barti had given me, I wanted to see whose testimony Dr Gwynne's account tallied with. It was possible, of course, that Rees, distraught at the discovery of his daughter's body, had become confused about the course of events, but still, it would be useful to have two independent witnesses to events when we confronted him.

'We can speak to the girls when we get back,' I said. 'We need to see Gwynne now.'

John

I could see Harry wasn't going to change his mind, so I backed down. I'd have to find a way of talking to Ann and Gwen by myself when we got back. I knew they'd tell me more than they'd told Harry. He was a squire and they'd be afraid of him.

Dr Cadwgan Gwynne was famous enough for me to know he lived next to the old college in Felindre Farchog, so we pointed our mares' noses in that direction and on the way Harry told me what he'd discovered so far.

'Right, let me see if I've got it all,' I said when he'd finished. 'This Mic Rees says his daughter died in her bed, but she didn't. He told his wife he didn't change the girl's clothes, but he did. Then he went over to – what was the name of the farm where the pirate works?' If there was an inquest, I'd be writing all this up and I needed the details clear in my head.

'Dolbannon.'

'Right. Yes. And this Barti Ddu works for David Jones. All right then. Mic Rees rides over to Dolbannon after he's had the doctor to his dead daughter and asks for a messenger to take the news to his wife at Ffynone.'

'Yes.'

'Why? Why didn't he want to go and tell his wife himself?'

Harry knew what I was getting at. 'Presumably because he still had things to do at home before his wife got back.'

'Exactly. And what things might those have been?' Most likely he'd been catching up with little jobs that'd been left undone while his wife was away, but there was always the possibility that he'd had things to cover up.

As we trotted along, we passed people dawdling home from chapel in the sunshine and a coach thundered past us on its way to Cardigan, forcing us almost into the ditch. It didn't seem possible that I'd been on a coach myself yesterday. And the day before that, I'd been in London. Since I'd been back, it'd all started to seem like something from another time. The Crystal Palace. Soyer's Symposium. Even Jem Harborne.

My stomach knotted up at the thought of the wool man. He'd told me and Lleu that he'd be back in Llandyfriog this week. Maybe he was there already.

'Harry, d'you know a man called Jem Harborne?'

'No, I don't think so. Who is he?'

'I met him at the Exhibition. Says he's building a wool factory in Llandyfriog.'

'A *wool* factory?'

'A weaving mill to begin with. Then the rest. Carding, spinning, fulling. The lot.'

Harry turned to look at me, even though it meant he'd lose me behind the blind patch in front of his eyes. He couldn't help himself – when he was really surprised, I think he forgot he was blind. 'What, all under one roof?'

'All on the same site, certainly.' I was pretty sure that was what Harborne had said.

Harry frowned. 'And he's starting with a power loom?'

'Yes. Just like the ones in Yorkshire, according to him.'

'Steam-powered?'

'No. Water, like normal mills.'

'Where's he from? Not here, I assume?'

Was he going by Harborne's name, or the fact that nobody'd ever talked about mechanising weaving in the Teifi Valley? 'He is, as it happens. From Llandysul, but he went to Newtown in Montgomeryshire to be apprenticed. Then Leeds. Bigger, better machines according to him.'

'And now he wants to bring those machines here.'

'Yes, to make pots of money shipping cloth down to the new towns in the coalfields. Reckons he can steal the market because of being on the doorstep. But never mind him for now.' I slowed Seren to a walk. Felindre Farchog's odd little college building was in sight ahead of us, so Gwynne's house would be close by. 'Stop a minute, Harry.'

'What's the matter?'

'Nothing. Just hold on.' I pulled Seren up and Sara stopped alongside. 'What do you know about Cadwgan Gwynne?' I asked.

'Nothing. Hadn't heard his name till yesterday.'

I'd thought as much. Harry might like to present himself as the local boy – he'd certainly played that card every chance he'd got during the election for the coronership back in April – but he'd been back in Cardiganshire less than a year. Before that, he'd spent the whole of his adult life somewhere else.

'Dr Gwynne's a wizard,' I said. I could tell I'd shocked him, but he was trying not to show it. 'He'd probably call himself something else – *dyn hysbys* or something.' Good job we were speaking in Welsh because I wasn't sure what the English for *dyn hysbys* would be. It meant something like 'knowing man'. Not quite 'wise man', but somebody who knew things other people didn't.

'I heard that his name was in the medical register,' Harry said. 'For what that's worth.'

'I'm not saying he's not medically qualified. Everybody knows his father sent him to London, to the university. But he came back to take over the practice when the old man died.'

'His father was also a *dyn hysbys*, I take it?'

'Oh yes. Llywelyn Gwynne. They used to say he could raise the dead and change the weather. Or cure you of piles or tell you who you were going to marry. He was also supposed to be able to see what was wrong with people just from looking at them.'

Could he? It was on the tip of Harry's tongue to ask; it was written all over his face. 'And his son, Cadwgan – is he similarly gifted?'

'So they say.'

Dr Gwynne's house sat back from the road a good way, tucked into the hill behind it, and looked as if it'd been there a while. The windows were small and the house'd seen so many years of limewash – a century at least from the look of it – that you couldn't see the shape of the stones underneath, only smoothed-over bumps in the walls.

There was nobody handy to take charge of the horses, so we stood there, reins in hand, while I grabbed the rope hanging from the lintel and rang the bell.

Mrs Gwynne came to the door herself. She had to be the doctor's wife – no servant would've been that haughty-looking.

'Good day to you, I'm John Davies, coroner's assistant, and this is Mr Harry Probert-Lloyd, coroner for the Teifi Valley.' She looked like the kind of woman who'd be impressed by titles. 'Do we have the pleasure of addressing Mrs Gwynne?'

'You do.'

I glanced across at Harry. He couldn't see her expression, but he'd've worked out that she wasn't exactly welcoming from the way I'd spoken to her.

'Good day to you, Mrs Gwynne,' he said, giving her a little bow. 'Might it be possible to have a few words with your husband?'

'I'll see if it's a convenient moment,' she said eventually. 'I know he went back to his charts after a busy morning.'

Charts? Of course – astrology. Gwynne's father'd been famous for saying, 'Tell me the moment of your birth and I'll tell you the moment of your death.' Cadwgan must've carried on the star-consulting tradition. Mind, why anybody would want to know exactly when they were going to die was beyond me.

We waited on the doorstep while Mrs Gwynne disappeared inside. Not very genteel, leaving us standing here; she could've invited us in. Then again, we still had hold of the horses, so perhaps not.

She was back in less than a minute. 'Dr Gwynne will see you now.' She turned and jerked her head at somebody standing in the hall. A boy slipped past and took the mares' reins without looking at us or uttering a word. Son or servant? Difficult to tell. Either way, he was firmly pressed down under Mrs Gwynne's thumb.

We followed her through the hall and into a passage that separated the rooms facing the road from those that looked up the hill. I don't know what I'd been expecting from a wizard's house, but you'd've seen the dark paintings and red-tiled floor in any number of well-off people's homes. Then again, there was mistletoe over the door Mrs Gwynne opened for us.

The consulting room – if that was what this was – was surprisingly light. Granted, it was south-facing, but the windows were small. Then I saw them. Mirrors. They were on every wall, cleverly angled to catch and reflect the light. And the room needed a lot of light, because it was full of plants. Pots and pots of them on long, deep shelves that ran around the room. The air was filled with the summer tang of them, as if somebody'd walked past and put a hand out to disturb the leaves of each one before we'd walked in.

Dr Gwynne was standing in front of a small desk to one side of the fireplace. The fire wasn't lit, but I noticed that the fat-bellied coal scuttle was full of decent chunks of anthracite, not cheap dusty coal or culm. The doctor must be doing all right for himself.

'Gentlemen. It's a pleasure to welcome you to my home. I assume you're here to ask me about the death of poor Elizabeth Rees.'

Didn't take a fortune-teller to know that, did it – why else would we be here?

'We are,' Harry said. 'I hope you don't mind our coming unannounced.'

Harry was matching his Welsh to the doctor's – the kind of elevated, educated language you'd expect of a professional man. He could go up and down the scale with the best of them, and hearing him talk to a stable boy in exactly the kind of language the boy'd use himself was a sight to behold, I can tell you. Or rather, the stable boy's reaction was.

I wondered if Gwynne did the same, or if he always spoke like this, to show his patients what a learned man he was.

'Please, do sit down.'

There was only one place for us to sit – a small chaise longue upholstered in dark-red velvet. It was an unsettling colour. Like dried blood.

Gwynne turned his chair towards us and sat waiting. He was as thin as a pole and very tall – sitting down, his arms and legs seemed to extend further than they should from his body – and his chestnut-coloured hair fell in long ringlets over his collar. Mind, he was soberly dressed. Grey wool and white linen that wouldn't've shamed a preacher.

Harry pointed his eyes in Gwynne's direction. 'To begin at the beginning, Dr Gwynne, what time did Mic Rees arrive at your house yesterday?'

The doctor leaned forward and clasped his hands together on his knees. 'Just after I'd broken my fast. It's my habit to rise with the sun, walk for an hour and then come home to eat. Then I am fortified for the day ahead.'

I looked about. There was no clock in the room, but Gwynne had a watch chain. 'Do you know *exactly* what time it was, Doctor?' I asked.

'Yes, it was just after half past seven. I always make a note of the time at which my patients choose to consult me.'

'Why?' I asked, when Harry didn't.

'Sometimes it proves significant. Not often, but I keep it as a rule, nonetheless.'

'And how would you describe Mr Rees's demeanour when he came to your door?' Harry asked.

While Dr Gwynne collected his thoughts, I glanced around the room. It was completely different from the chaos at Reckitt's place, but then Reckitt didn't generally see patients at his house.

Those who could pay summoned him, and he saw the rest at the workhouse.

If everything I'd heard about Dr Gwynne was true, people came as often to ask him to tell their fortune as they did to consult him about his specialisms – skin disease and madness. He wasn't a bone-setter and I'd never heard of him stitching a wound. No, what Gwynne was famous for was curing the disfigured and the mad. As well as knowing things other people didn't. And I'm not talking about the kind of things Benton Reckitt knew.

Still, I'd expected shelves with jars and bottles, like a chemist's or druggist's, but all there was here were cupboards and drawers. Some of the drawers were so small you'd barely have got a shilling's worth of pennies in there. Obviously hiding rare and valuable stuff.

'I would say that Mr Rees seemed as you might expect,' Gwynne said in the end. 'He'd found his daughter dead in her bed. He was confused, upset, not entirely articulate.'

'And what did he tell you about the circumstances in which he'd found her?'

Gwynne's eyes went up towards the ceiling, as if what he wanted might be written there for him to read. People often did that, in my experience, which was odd, really. You'd've thought it would be more helpful to shut your eyes, wouldn't you? Memories are inside your head, when all's said and done, not in the air in front of you.

After a few seconds, he shook his head. 'I can't remember precisely. Let me find my notes.'

He unfolded himself from the chair, squatted down to open one of the three drawers in his drop-leaf desk and took a book out. When he stood up again, he did it in one effortless movement, without putting a hand to the floor, as if his joints were oiled. Back in his chair, he started flipping through the pages. He settled on one and scanned it quickly.

'Mr Rees told me that he'd been woken sometime around sunrise by a sound. He didn't know what it was, only that it had woken him and he was *filled with dread*.' He was obviously quoting Mic Rees's own words. '*I couldn't shake off the feeling that something terrible had happened,*' he read, '*so I went to rouse Lizzie. It was nearly time to milk the cow, but really, I just wanted to know that she was all right.*' He looked up. 'Mr Rees told me his daughter had had a cold, though I could see no sign of that when I examined her.' He scanned the book again, then closed it, leaving a thumb in to keep his place. 'When he went up to the loft to rouse her, he found Lizzie "with no breath in her body", as he put it.'

'Mr Rees told me that he was woken by the cow lowing,' Harry said. 'He didn't mention that to you?'

Cadwgan Gwynne checked his notes, but you could tell that he already knew.

'No. Just that he felt something was wrong.'

So Mic Rees'd felt the need to come up with something better than 'a sound woke me' and 'I felt something terrible had happened' by the time he spoke to Harry. Because he was lying? Or because he'd been afraid the truth sounded weak?

'Mr Rees's first thought was to come to you,' Harry said. 'Not to go and fetch his wife. Why do you think that was?'

Dr Gwynne gave a thin smile. 'You think Mr Rees might have come to ask me to raise his daughter from the dead, is that it?'

I knew that wasn't what Harry'd been thinking at all, but fair play to him, he didn't turn a hair. 'You do have a certain reputation, Doctor.'

'A reputation that is out of all proportion to my abilities, I assure you. I have never done anything half as dramatic.'

'But your father was supposed to have worked a miracle,' I said. 'So perhaps people think you could too, if you wanted to.'

There wasn't even the pretence of a smile now. 'My father never claimed to have raised anybody from the dead, Mr Davies. What he in fact accomplished, on one occasion and one only, was to revive somebody from a state of utter unresponsiveness that had persisted for three days, during which the afflicted man neither ate nor drank, did not speak nor respond in any way, even when pins were stuck into him. He had suffered no seizure, no fit, no fever nor other sickness. He had simply lain down and ceased to behave like the living. He was not dead – he still breathed and his heart beat, if slowly – but in all other respects he might as well have been.'

That was a story he'd told before. Irritated or not, he was word perfect.

'As a matter of interest, Doctor,' Harry asked, 'how *did* he revive the patient?'

Patient. Clever. Giving the old man credit as a proper medical man.

'By throwing him into the river.'

'That's not very medical!'

Cadwgan Gwynne turned to me. 'You're assuming that all cures must be based in science, Mr Davies. In anatomy and physiology or the administration of drugs. But as Shakespeare knew more than two centuries ago, there are more things in heaven and earth than are dreamt of in anybody's philosophy. He knew that the greatest mysteries lie in the human heart and mind. We may bring about our own cures if we understand that, without medicines. Jesus Christ also knew that. Otherwise why would he tell the woman with the persistent haemorrhage that it was her faith that had made her well?'

So he didn't just dress like a preacher, he spoke like one as well. That was unexpected.

'But if not for a miracle, why would Mic come here first?' Harry persisted. 'I'm at a loss to know why he wouldn't have gone to convey the sad news to his wife and asked you to come and certify the death afterwards.'

Gwynne nodded. He could see the sense in the question. 'Mr Rees wanted to be able to tell his wife – and to be certain himself – that nobody else was responsible for his daughter's death.'

Harry looked as confused as I felt. 'But there was no evidence of any injury on her body. Why did he think…?'

'He wasn't looking for evidence of physical foul play, Mr Probert-Lloyd. He wanted me to tell him whether Lizzie'd been cursed.'

Harry

'You should not scoff at things you do not understand, Mr Probert-Lloyd,' Gwynne said. Evidently my incredulity had been clear. 'For people who believe in such things, the power of a curse is strong. It works on the mind and may indeed provoke illness or even death.'

'But did Mr Rees have any reason to believe that somebody had cursed his daughter?'

The doctor did not respond immediately. At my side, John remained still, silently counselling patience.

'Mr Rees gave me to understand that his daughter was a headstrong girl, apt not to take too much notice of what other people thought of her,' I prompted, then waited once more as Gwynne drummed his fingers softly on the arm of his chair.

'She was courting a young man,' he said. 'Not a local boy. Some of the other young people in Eglwyswrw felt that she shouldn't be encouraging him.'

'Not local? Was it, perhaps, a young man I've heard called the Englishman?' I asked, remembering what the old groom at the Sergeant's stables had said.

'Possibly.'

'Or Nattie Stockton?' John asked. Where had he heard that name?

'Ah, Nattie – do they call him the Englishman? Perhaps. I know he doesn't speak Welsh. You've heard the rumours, then?' Cadwgan Gwynne seemed relieved, as if this removed a burden of discretion from him.

'I was given his name as somebody who might have been sweet on Lizzie,' John said.

Gwynne sighed. 'There was a certain amount of bad feeling about her favouring him over the local lads, I believe. It even turned the other young women against her, according to Mr Rees.'

She thought she was better than everybody else. Had a belief in her own superiority made Lizzie Rees cast her eye beyond the usual pool of suitors?

'And were you able to sense anything when you looked at her body?' John asked. 'Anything that told you she might've been cursed?'

This time Gwynne's response came immediately. 'No. Nothing at all.'

I found it interesting that the doctor took seriously not only the existence and efficacy of curses but his own ability to discern such a thing post-mortem.

Inquests, however, could only deal in facts, so I steered away from superstition onto the path of solid evidence and asked Gwynne where Lizzie's body had been lying when he had examined her and what condition her petticoat had been in. As expected, he told us that he had examined her in her bed in the loft and that her petticoat had been quite dry. 'Though I did not lift the body to see the condition of it underneath.'

'Did you not find such dryness odd?'

'Each death is different, Mr Probert-Lloyd. And each body likewise. We cannot expect one to react in the same way as another.'

I knew that Reckitt, fond of what he called *fundamental physiological facts*, would disagree.

–

Once we were back on the road and I was able to voice my scepticism as to Gwynne's claims, I was taken aback by John's response.

'I don't know. Perhaps he's right. From what you've told me, Reckitt's basing all his suspicions on a dry petticoat. And even he says it wasn't a clean one. Where would Mic Rees have got one she'd already worn if the one she was wearing was the one that got wet?'

'Point taken. But what about this curse business?'

'I don't believe in curses. Not if you mean someone using bad magic on you. But I think Dr Gwynne's right – if you know you've been cursed, it might work on the mind, as he said. Make you worried, afraid even.'

'But you can't worry yourself to death!'

'I don't know. You do hear of people dying of fright.'

'Only in sensationalist fiction.'

John sighed in a way that told me he didn't entirely agree but knew logic was on my side.

I urged Sara into a trot. Wherever the boy had taken the mares while we had been speaking to Gwynne, they had obviously been in full sun. My saddle had been uncomfortably warm as I mounted up and it had not cooled down with me on it. Rising to the trot was a relief.

'You know what we should've asked him?' John said, drawing alongside again.

'What?'

'Whether Lizzie'd ever consulted him.'

'I asked her parents that. They said he'd treated all the girls when they had chickenpox, but that was the only time.'

'I'm not talking about seeing him for that sort of thing. She might've gone to speak to him about this supposed curse. He's well known to cast horoscopes, and I know for a fact that people go to him to ask who they're going to marry.'

'You're joking.'

'No.' John's face turned towards me. 'If you think about it, seeing your future in the stars isn't that different from what people get told at chapel. Well, some chapels anyway – the Calvinists. You know, everything's predestined, whether you're going to heaven or hell, everything you're ever going to do. Even if he's not that way inclined, your minister'll still tell you God knows everything about you – now and for ever. Except God keeps it all to himself, doesn't he? But if all that knowledge is there somewhere, why shouldn't it be readable in the stars or planets? That's what people think, anyway,' he added.

'All right, yes, I can understand that, even if it is nonsense. But tell me why you think it'd make any difference if Lizzie Rees *had* consulted him.'

'She might've mentioned names,' he said. 'I know there were some lads sweet on her. I got their names from Llwyo – Dai Davies, the messenger who came to fetch me. Twm y Gof, Dai Blaengwndwn and Wil Llain. And the one English-sounding one I mentioned to Gwynne – Nattie Stockton. But maybe it's girls we should be looking for. Jealous girls.'

'But what would those girls have done? You can't honestly think they scared her to death? We'd have a hard time proving that.'

However, poison was a great deal easier to prove, and Reckitt had yet to rule that out.

–

Back at Rhosdywarch, we found Reckitt in the middle of an argument with Mic Rees; an argument that became audible as we rode up to the house, even though it was taking place somewhere out of sight.

John and I dismounted and walked around the end of the house to the patch of ground where the family's garden was laid out. I could not make out what vegetables occupied the tidy rows, but it was clear from the weed-free earth between them that the garden was meticulously kept.

Reckitt and Mic Rees stood between house and garden, Lizzie's body on a table in front of them. Even I could see that the body was naked and the abdomen open.

'There's no need to cut her any more!' Mic Rees protested, his voice loud with anguish. 'You said you wanted to look in her stomach for poison, and you've done that. You don't need to look inside any more of her.'

'Mr Rees, as I explained to your wife—'

'My wife's not in charge here, I am!'

'Nevertheless, if you'd let me—'

'*We're* paying for this so we decide how it's done.'

'I beg your pardon! Nobody's paying anything. Did your wife not tell you that I'd agreed to do this without payment? I just wish to fully investigate—'

'No! Just take whatever you got from her stomach and look at it to see if there's poison there. That's all we want you to do.'

Reckitt raised his voice further. 'Mr Rees do you or do you not want to know what killed your daughter? Because the most likely thing, in my estimation, is—'

'Gentlemen!' I called, as much to stop the argument as to alert them to our presence.

'Probert-Lloyd!' Reckitt strode towards us. 'Have you come to a conclusion yet? Will you be holding an inquest?'

'That rather depends on the talk I need to have with Mr Rees. Meanwhile,' I lowered my voice slightly, feeling the delicacy of the question, 'can you analyse the stomach contents here?'

'No. I'll have to take them back to Cilgerran.'

Damn it. I had hoped to have a definitive answer as to foul play before leaving Rhosdywarch. Still, it couldn't be helped.

I moved in Mic Rees's direction. 'Mr Rees, what is your wife's opinion? Does she too merely wish to know whether or not foul play has taken place?'

'Meaning no disrespect to you, Mr Probert-Lloyd, but I'm the head of this family, not my wife. It's me that'll decide how far this cutting of my daughter's body goes.'

I found his insistence perplexing; why, when he had he felt unable to stand up to his wife in the matter of who might marry their daughter, did he feel able to oppose her on this?

'I'd like to speak to you in private, Mr Rees, if I may?' I turned to walk towards the house, only for John to put a hand on my arm and draw me aside.

'Listen,' his voice was pitched for my ears only, 'I should speak to Ann and Gwen now.'

'Very well. We'll see the girls first, then—'

'Not *we*. Me. I'm sure they were going to tell me something before. Then Reckitt arrived and scared them off.'

He might be right, but I needed him with me when I questioned Rees; the man had lied to me once and I had to be sure he did not get away with it a second time.

'It needs to be me by myself, Harry,' he said, seeing my hesitation. 'They're little girls, and you're the coroner. I'm more like the lads they know.'

I breathed in deeply, the pungent smell of sun-baked straw and cow dung from the byre midden filling my lungs. 'Then I'll wait, talk to Rees when you've finished.'

John's stance shifted, and in the restless movement I read his impatience. 'No. If you're standing about waiting for me while I take them off, it'll look like I think they've got something really important to say. They'll be scared.'

A bead of sweat ran down between my shoulder blades, but it was frustration, not heat that was making my skin prickle. This refusal to acquiesce to my wishes was new.

'Take Reckitt with you,' John said. 'He knows Mic Rees lied to you now. He'll be wary this time.'

His reasoning was sound; I only wished I shared his confidence in Reckitt.

'Meanwhile, I'll find the girls and get them to show me where the mares can have a drink. Then I can talk to them without them thinking anything of it.'

My mouth was barely open to agree when, without a word, he turned away abruptly. Belatedly I realised that he was trying to give the impression that he had lost the argument we had supposedly been having, just in case the girls were watching. Joining the charade, I fixed a grim look on my face. 'Dr Reckitt, will you and Mr Rees come into the house with me, please? There are things we need to discuss.'

The kitchen was dim after the bright sunlight outside, and I knew I would see next to nothing until my eyes adjusted. The feeling of physical inadequacy made my skin crawl as if I was louse-ridden, compounding my fear that Mic Rees would once more persuade me with plausible lies.

I had half expected to find Esther Rees back and presiding over her kitchen, but the place was empty.

'Will you take a drink, gentlemen?' Mic Rees asked. 'Some cider?'

We had drunk tea the last time we visited. Perhaps Rees was in need of Dutch courage.

'Yes, thank you.' I had had nothing to drink since my breakfast at the Sergeant's that morning.

Rees took a jug to the barrel in the corner of the room and opened the tap. At the edge of my vision a tabby cat, disturbed from its lazing in a patch of sun, bent a leg around its head and began washing itself.

'Mr Rees,' I said, seizing a moment while he was off guard, 'why did you lie to us about where your daughter died?'

The jug clattered against the side of the barrel as Rees's grip on it faltered, and I heard a splash of cider on the kitchen floor.

'Dammit,' he said, thrusting the jug back under the stream.

The cat, roused from its ablutions, sprang up and trotted over to the spill.

'I didn't lie to you, Mr Probert-Lloyd. I don't know why you'd think I did.'

'You told us she died in her bed.'

'It's the truth. She died in her sleep.'

'You also lied about not having put her in clean clothes, didn't you?'

He turned around, and this time he must have closed the tap, for there was no splash. 'What? You never asked me about her clothes.'

'No, but I asked your wife. And she told me you claimed you hadn't changed her. But that's not true, is it?'

'Yes!' He stood with both hands wrapped around the cider jug in front of him, as if it might ward off my accusation.

Moving to the chair I had occupied on my previous visit, I signalled to Reckitt to sit. Rees would be at a disadvantage, stranded in the other half of the kitchen while I sat in his place at his fireside. 'Mr Rees, if you persist in lying to me, I must assume that you're concealing the true circumstances of your daughter's death. That being the case, I would have no choice but to hold an inquest and ask you these questions, on oath, before a jury of your peers.'

My hope was that the thought of giving testimony at an inquest, his neighbours watching while I asked incriminating questions, would persuade Mic Rees to tell me the truth. Because whatever answers he gave in public, it was the questions that would stick in people's minds.

You claim to have found your daughter dead in her bed. You further claim that you did not remove her clothes before the doctor saw her to confirm death. But – on your oath – neither of those things is true, is it?

Hearing those words, an image would appear in the mind of every person present: Mic Rees standing over his dead daughter, looking around furtively while he removed her petticoat. He could lie all he liked, but it would do him no good: that picture would be fixed, and he would never shake it off.

I waited while he found three wooden mugs and poured cider into them, lip knocking against rim as his hands shook.

Reckitt and I accepted the mugs without a word, and Rees lowered himself heavily onto the stool.

'She did die in bed,' he said. 'But not in *her* bed.'

John

If the pile on the grass behind them was anything to go by, Ann and Gwen were supposed to be collecting rushes. What they were actually doing was plaiting crowns and bracelets. I hoped they were keeping a good eye out for their mother – Esther Rees didn't sound like a woman to tolerate time-wasting.

'My little sister used to love a rush bracelet,' I said, walking up to them.

'Doesn't she still?' Gwen asked, looking up at me with those china-blue eyes.

'No. She died when she was only nine.' It wouldn't do any harm for them to know I'd lost a sister too.

Gwen's eyes went wide. 'How old were you when she died?'

Compared to how the pair of them'd behaved when I first laid eyes on them, Gwen was very chatty now. Maybe it was because I'd already spoken to them once, so they knew me. Or maybe it was because I had both the mares with me, so I looked more like a servant than a gentleman, riding clothes or no riding clothes.

'I was twelve.'

Ann left off plaiting and looked up at me too. 'And how old are you now?'

'How old do you think I am?' I didn't want them to think I was too grown-up to talk to.

Gwen tilted her head on one side, and I wondered if she'd got that from her big sister, Lizzie. 'I think you're—'

'Eighteen,' Ann said, getting in first.

'Close enough,' I said. And if that made them think I might only be seventeen, so much the better. At twenty, I was very nearly of age. Seventeen would demand a lot less respect.

I unfastened the mares' reins from one side of their bridles so they were long enough for me to hold on to them while the animals grazed a few feet away, then sat down on the grass next to the sisters.

'How long's your mam been saving with the friendly society?' I asked. Best to start off with questions they'd have no reason not to answer.

Gwen looked at her sister. As the older one, she'd be more likely to know. Ann shrugged. 'Don't know. A long time.'

I picked a rush off their pile and began stripping it till the pith was only supported by one long strip of green, ready to be dipped in bacon fat and dried for a rushlight. They were watching me carefully. A gentleman wouldn't know how to make rushlights. 'Where's she gone for the money?' I asked, eyes on what I was doing.

'Mrs James y Gof's house in Eglwyswrw. That's where they meet. The society.'

'They knit,' Gwen butted in.

'What, they meet to do knitting together?'

'Yes,' Ann said. 'They were knitting together before they started saving.'

'The knitting came first.' Gwen wasn't going to be left out.

That made sense. If a group of women'd been meeting for knitting nights for a while, it would be natural for them to start doing other things together. My mother'd been a great one for a knitting night. Or any gathering, really. Singing, knitting, studying the Bible. Interesting that the society met at y Gof, the Smithy. Twm y Gof, the blacksmith's boy, had been one of the lads who'd bought a love spoon from Llwyo. Perhaps he'd had some encouragement from Esther Rees about courting Lizzie.

'I'd've thought your mam'd go to Brynberian for her knitting and saving, not Eglwyswrw.' Brynberian was much closer.

I caught the look Ann gave her sister, but Gwen turned her pretty little face up to me anyway. She wasn't going to let Ann take Lizzie's place as the sister who bossed her about. 'The women in Brynberian don't have knitting nights.'

That didn't seem very likely. Esther Rees probably just wasn't invited.

'They're not very friendly,' Gwen said, as if she'd heard my thought. She tied a knot in the end of her rush plait and slipped it over her hand, turning it this way and that to admire her handiwork.

'Not very friendly to everybody, or just to your mam?'

Again that look from Ann, and this time Gwen stayed quiet. Which was an answer in itself.

The afternoon sun was hot. I held the reins out to Ann to hold, shrugged my way out of my jacket and sat there in my shirtsleeves, necktie undone. Now I'd look even more like the boys they knew. Mind, I was careful not to roll my sleeves up. My arms were pale from indoor work, and that'd ruin the notion that I was one of them.

'Go on then,' I said, taking the reins from Ann and lying back on one elbow. 'What about people who were friendly with Lizzie? I know there were young men sweet on her – Twm y Gof, Wil Llain, Dai Blaengwndwn and Nattie Stockton – but which one did she like best?'

I watched them from under my eyebrows while I picked seeds off a stalk of grass. Ann started biting the skin around her thumb-nail, but Gwen gave a sly little smile. 'Guess!'

I grinned. 'All right then. But tell me first, who's got the biggest farm?'

'Hah!' Gwen said. 'That shows how much you know. Nothing!'

'Well, Twm y Gof probably isn't a farm boy,' I said, 'unless he's the blacksmith's apprentice, not his son.'

'No. He's the son.' Ann got there before her sister could.

'But you two obviously know more about the others than I do. I suppose they're labourers, are they?'

'No!' Gwen was enjoying herself. 'Wil works at the quarry in Cilgerran.'

'Not all the time,' Ann said. 'Not when the rent work has to be done.'

Rent work. Hay and harvest work that smallholders did for the tenant farmer they rented their land from. So Wil Llain was a smallholder's boy who had no choice but to work off the farm. Definitely not a candidate for Lizzie's hand in Esther Rees's mind.

'So Dai's the one with the money, then.' I made it sound as if I thought I was clever to work it out.

'He's the eldest Blaengwndwn boy,' Ann said. 'But their farm's not much. Thirty-five acres, maybe.'

'So who was it, then? Strong-arm Twm, Dai with thirty-five acres coming to him,' I counted them on my fingers, 'quarryman Wil, or maybe the one from away – Nattie Stockton?' Dr Gwynne had said it was Stockton she favoured, but it'd be interesting to see if Ann and Gwen thought the same. She'd been their sister and they'd be more likely to know than the doctor.

'Guess!' Gwen said again, and tossed the daisy chain she'd been making at me, trying to get it to sit like a crown on my head. Instead, it slid down and hung from one ear.

They laughed like the children they were, then Ann reached out to straighten the crown and went bright pink as she touched my hair.

'I think it's Dai Blaengwndwn,' I said.

'Wrong!' Gwen jutted her little chin at me. She was going to be a handful in a few years' time.

'Gwen. *Husht!*'

'Why? Makes no difference now, does it? And anyway, Mam's not here.'

Gwen wanted to tell me, I could see that, so I let them fight it out with their eyes while I looked over at the south-facing slope on the other side of the little valley. There were a dozen or so cows standing under a tree, nose to tail so they could keep the flies off each other's faces. August was a terrible month for flies.

'No!' I heard Ann hiss at her sister.

I looked around at them. 'Go on, you can tell me – who was it?' I tried to sound like one of the older boys they'd know at chapel, teasing after a secret only they knew about their big sister.

134

Hopefully, with me lying here in the grass with them and the mares grazing a yard away, they'd forgotten who – or rather *what* – I was. 'I won't tell your mam,' I whispered. 'Promise.'

'Cross your heart and hope to die?'

I looked into Gwen's eyes and raised the elbow I was leaning on just slightly so I could draw an X on my chest somewhere over my breastbone. The movement felt awkward, but I didn't want to sit up properly in case it brought the girls to their senses. Mind, my elbow was sore from the little stones that were digging into it, and the maids at Glanteifi weren't going to be happy about the dirt I was getting on my shirt. Still, all in a good cause.

'Nathaniel Stockton,' she said.

I raised my eyebrows. So Dr Gwynne had been right. *Had* Lizzie been to see the doctor, confided in him?

'They call him the Englishman—' Ann tried to take over.

'Or Nattie Gilfachwen, 'cos that's where he works,' her sister interrupted. 'But he's really called Nathaniel. And he's not from here. He's from down south. A place called St Florence—'

'And he came here because of Lizzie,' Ann finished. 'He fell in love with her when she was working down south last year and he came up in the autumn and got himself hired by Mr Preece at Gilfachwen.'

'So did she fall in love with him as well?' I asked.

'I don't—' Ann began.

'Yes! She did. And everybody knew because she gave him the *coron fedw*,' Gwen finished triumphantly.

'Did she indeed?' The giving of the *coron fedw* – the birch crown – was as good as saying that you had an understanding; that you'd get married as soon as you could afford it.

A shadow went over the sun and the warmth on my skin cooled. I looked up. Clouds coming in from the west. Rain tomorrow, most likely. I sat up.

'So. Were they going to get married?' I asked. From what Harry'd told me, they'd have had to step over Esther Rees's dead body first.

Ann and Gwen exchanged a look. 'What?' I said, as if I didn't understand what was going on. 'Weren't your mam and dada willing?'

More looks. More silence.

After the conversation we'd had with Cadwgan Gwynne, and the questions we'd failed to ask, I decided to take a risk and lead them a bit. 'If I'd been Lizzie,' I said, watching the mares grazing nose to nose, as if I was more interested in them than in what I was saying, 'I think I might've gone to see Dewin Gwynne' – I gave him the title local people used, Wizard – 'to see if he could tell me what my future was. Because if he said I was going to marry somebody, then it wouldn't matter what anybody else thought, would it? That'd be my future.'

Looked like I'd hit the nail on the head. The girls fidgeted, and Ann shifted her position so that instead of sitting with her legs crossed under her apron, she was sitting up, legs beneath her. She looked more alert, more wary, and she kept darting glances at her little sister, who was making another daisy chain, weaving buttercups into it after every third daisy.

'Is that why she didn't go with you to Ffynone?' I asked. 'Because she wanted to go over to Felindre Farchog to see Dewin Gwynne but she knew she'd never be able to get away from your mother?'

Even Gwen looked troubled now, and her sister's mouth might as well have been sewn shut for all the sound she was making. But if I could guess what had happened, I was pretty sure they wouldn't deny it if it meant lying to me.

'I know your mam doesn't think much of Dr Gwynne,' I said. That must be true, because she'd gone straight for Reckitt, no matter that Gwynne had already been here and given his opinion. 'But your father trusts him, doesn't he? Did Lizzie persuade your father to let her stay home so she could go and see him?'

But that wasn't it, I could tell. Ann looked ready to bolt now, and even though Gwen was still working at her daisy chain, she was crying quietly.

Her sister put a hand on her shoulder. 'Don't cry, Gwen *fach*…'

But her gentle words made things worse. Gwen looked up, tears streaming down her face. 'If she'd come with us, she'd still be here.'

'We don't know that.'

'Yes we *do*!' Gwen wailed, spit or tears coming out of her mouth. 'Sally Sips must've told everybody what Lizzie was going to do, so they came here that night. They must have! You saw her things…'

'Gwen, *husht*!' Ann put her arm around her little sister, but I could see her trying to watch me out of the corner of her eye.

A sudden breeze had come with the clouds, and it was swirling about in the little valley where we were sitting, turning the leaves of the trees upside down to show their pale undersides. I shifted, trying to move into a more comfortable position without tearing a hole in my britches – there was a nasty sharp stone making itself felt under me. Seren didn't appreciate me accidentally pulling on her, and threw her head up, almost yanking both reins out of my hand.

'Gwen,' I said gently, 'do you think somebody came to the house on the night your sister died?'

'She doesn't know anything,' Ann said, pulling her sister closer. 'She's just being silly. You know you are, Gwen.'

'No I'm *not*!' Gwen wailed, looking more and more like the little girl she was with every new tear that ran down her blotchy cheeks. 'I'm *not* being silly. They hated Lizzie! And Sally Sips must've told them what she was going to do and they came to frighten her. They *killed* her! They killed our Lizzie!'

I looked at Ann. She wasn't telling Gwen off any more. There was something going on here, something more than a little girl getting upset about people's spitefulness to her big sister.

'I think you'd better tell me what Lizzie had in mind that night,' I said. 'Don't you?'

Harry

'I let her sleep in the box bed,' Mic Rees said. 'Like I told you, she hadn't been well, and I wanted her to have a good night's rest. The box bed keeps the draughts out – and the early morning light – so she could sleep in a bit. There was only the two of us here…'

The implication was clear: his wife would never have agreed to such a thing.

'Why didn't you tell us this straight away?' I asked.

'My wife…' He pulled himself up, then regrouped. 'She'd've said that if I'd made Lizzie go with her, she wouldn't've died,' he said. 'And perhaps she's right.'

'Nonsense,' Reckitt said. 'I suspect it was a brain aneurysm that killed your daughter. If I'm right, it would've been far more dangerous for her to be doing hard work like washing sheets and tablecloths.'

Rees's head came up. 'Is that true? Do lots of people have them, then, these…?'

'Aneurysms. Yes, I'd say they're one of the most common causes of sudden death in the young. They're badly formed vessels that burst.' There was a brief pause while, apparently, Reckitt took in the fact that Mic Rees was very little the wiser. 'It's like when you blow up a pig's bladder for football,' he went on. 'Sometimes there's a weakness and the wall of the bladder bulges out in a bump instead of being nice and round, and it might burst. An aneurysm is like that. A weakness in the wall of an artery.' He used the English words for *aneurysm* and *artery*. I wondered whether Cadwgan Gwynne would know their Welsh equivalents.

'The arteries are the pipes, if you like, that carry blood from the heart around the body,' Reckitt's explanation went on. 'Sometimes the pressure of the blood is too much and the stretched-out bulge bursts. That's one of the things I wanted to look for in your daughter's brain and heart vessels.'

'But what could've made it burst when she was in bed?' Rees's voice was barely above a whisper, his desperation suggesting that if he could only understand what had killed his daughter, somehow he might contrive to turn back time and change the circumstances that had led to her death. It was, I had discovered, a common reaction to the death of a child.

Reckitt, oblivious to the man's anguish, simply answered the question. 'In somebody with a cold, a sudden attack of coughing or sneezing is most likely.'

'A *sneeze* could have killed her?'

'If an aneurysm's wall had been weakened enough, yes.'

As Rees sat there, his mug cradled in his hands, I realised that I had drunk none of my own cider. I lifted it to my mouth, and immediately the warm, dry sensation of cider-cured wood on my lips and the apple-laden aroma transported me to another time: to those days in my childhood and young manhood when I had roamed the farms of the estate. I had been oblivious to my status as Glanteifi's heir then, accepting the hospitality shown to me as nothing more than that due to another pair of hands at hay or harvest, not understanding that I was welcomed by virtue of my position rather than my usefulness.

'Mr Rees,' Reckitt said, 'Cadwgan Gwynne told us that he had examined your daughter in her own bed, in the loft.'

Mic Rees hesitated. 'Yes.'

'Was it difficult – moving her?'

I shifted uncomfortably. 'Reckitt...'

'I'm not asking whether moving your daughter's body was upsetting,' Reckitt clarified. 'I'm asking whether it was physically difficult.'

Rees did not reply straight away. Was he looking to me for help? 'She's not a very big girl,' he began. 'Not very heavy.'

'But carrying her up a ladder must have been unwieldy?'

Rees swallowed audibly. 'I put her round my shoulders. Like carrying a ewe.'

'Then death stiffness hadn't set in?' Reckitt used a colloquial Welsh term rather than the Latin one Rees was unlikely to understand.

'No.' Mic Rees let the word out gradually, as if he might want to pull it back at any moment.

Reckitt turned to me. 'QED, Probert-Lloyd,' he said. Then he switched back to Welsh. 'If she was not yet at all stiffened, then your daughter had only recently died, and so late in the night her bladder would've been quite full. Therefore, when you found her, her petticoat must have been very wet. You changed her underclothes before anybody saw her. Why?'

Reckitt's certainty seemed to breach Rees's defences. I heard him take a long breath, and when he spoke, his voice was unsteady with emotion.

'I couldn't stand the thought of Dr Gwynne seeing her soaked in her own piss.' Again he sucked in air, as if he needed more breath than usual to get the words out. 'It was the last service I could do her. To let her have that dignity.'

I conjured up the likely sequence of events in my mind's eye. 'The mattress in the box bed must have been wet where Lizzie lay,' I said. 'How did you prevent your wife noticing that?'

Rees ran a hand under his nose before replying. 'Before I went for Dr Gwynne, I dragged the mattress into the yard. Rinsed the worst of it out. Then I hung it from a beam in the byre – for the water to drip out. After the doctor'd left, I laid it in the sun to dry while I went to Dolbannon.'

'And her wet petticoat?'

'Washed. Three times I had to soap and rinse to get the stink out.'

I waited to see if Reckitt would ask anything further, but it seemed he was content with having been proved right.

Mic Rees sat between us, head bowed, cider apparently forgotten. I found that I had lost the appetite for mine, too, and set it on the floor under my chair. My fingertips brushed the ground, and feeling the kitchen floor's cold smoothness, I wondered whether its dark colour came from pigs' blood. I had heard that combining it with mud and lime produced a durable surface, and Esther Rees was the kind of woman who would use what she had to hand in the most resourceful way.

'Reckitt,' I said softly, 'would you go and see if you can find any evidence of dampness on the feather mattress in the box bed?' It was as well to be sure; Mic Rees had lied to us before.

As Reckitt rose from his creaking chair, Rees roused himself. 'You'll need to feel underneath the mattress, Doctor. I turned it over in case it was still damp when we went to bed.'

I tried to imagine what it must have been like for Rees, lying down to sleep in the place where the previous night his firstborn child had breathed her last. Though I had not been excessively attached to my father, still for weeks after his illness and death I had barely been able to enter the room where he had died.

'Please, Mr Probert-Lloyd, don't tell my wife.'

Rees's plea, along with the sound of the box bed's door being slid open, pulled me back from stark recollections of my father's deathbed. 'As long as there's no need for an inquest,' I said, 'your wife does not need to know.'

'But there *won't* be an inquest now, will there?' His voice rose half an octave. Had he hoped that telling us the truth would ensure that no further action would be taken?

'There's something else you haven't been honest with us about,' I said.

'What?' Did I imagine the edge of desperation in his voice?

'The time. If you didn't discover Lizzie until the cow started complaining, by my reckoning there wasn't time for you to wash her and put her in her own bed, then go for Dr Gwynne and still be over at Dolbannon by the time I'm told you arrived.'

'I…' He faltered. 'Lizzie was always up at first light to milk.'

'Even so…'

'And it didn't take me long to get to Dewin Gwynne's – I ran along the river.'

It might be true. There was nothing of Mic Rees; he was as thin as a whippet. But I did not think Cadwgan Gwynne would have run back here with him. And had Rees, subsequently, run all the way to Dolbannon too? Yet I could see no good reason for him to be lying. I did not ask him about the other discrepancy – the cow's lowing he had told us about but omitted when he spoke to Gwynne – for it seemed petty in the light of the anguish that had driven him to hide the truth about where his daughter died. No doubt by the time Reckitt and I had arrived, he'd had sufficient time to reflect on the sound that had woken him and conclude that it must have been the cow.

Reckitt rejoined us. 'Some residual dampness confirms it,' he murmured to me before resuming his seat. 'Mr Rees, will you allow me to examine Lizzie to see if I can find a burst aneurysm? If that's what killed her, you and your wife will have peace of mind that no matter where she'd spent those final hours, your daughter would still have died.'

'But what if you *don't* find one? What then?' The man's distress was clear, but Reckitt was not fond of hypothetical questions. 'No,' Rees said when he received no reply. 'I don't want you cutting my Lizzie up any more.'

'I'm offering you—'

'Reckitt, Mr Rees has made his feelings clear,' I said. 'We have what we need to determine whether an inquest is required. At this point, anything further is vexatious.'

I stood, hoping to avoid further argument, and as I did so, the door opened. I turned my head to see the tall figure of Esther Rees.

'Doctor! I'm so glad to find you here. And you, Mr Probert-Lloyd—'

Her husband interrupted. 'Did you get the money for the funeral?'

She spun around. 'Funeral? Is that all you can think about – getting her safely into the ground?' She stepped towards Rees, who had risen to his feet as she entered. They were a similar height, and when she stood toe to toe with him, it was he who seemed the smaller, as if he shrank before her. 'Do you think burying her is going to stop the gossip? Because if you do, Michael Rees, you are as wrong as wrong can be. Do you know what I heard everywhere I went? *His* name. That damned foreigner's name!'

John

By the time I walked into the Rhosdywarch kitchen, the battle about Reckitt taking his scalpel to the rest of Lizzie's body was almost over. Mic Rees was still fighting, but you could tell from the beaten look of him that he knew he wasn't going to win.

And looking at Esther Rees, I doubted that he won very often. Nothing her husband said seemed to have any effect on her – it was like watching a man try to drill a hole with a mallet.

I didn't want to stand there with them arguing, so I backed out.

Harry followed me.

'Looks like you've got what you wanted from Mic,' I said quietly, so that Gwen wouldn't hear. She was at the weaving-shed end of the house, holding Seren for me.

'Yes, he lied about not changing Lizzie's petticoat.' Harry kept his voice down too. 'He just didn't want Gwynne to see her like that.'

'Right then. I'll get back to Glanteifi.' I was already walking towards Seren, keen to be gone now we knew there was nothing more to Mic's lies than embarrassment. But Harry followed me.

'At least stay until Reckitt's completed the examination,' he said. 'Then we can ride as far as Eglwyswrw together and I'll go on to Cilgerran with Reckitt. I want to be on hand while he analyses the stomach contents, then there'll be no delay if I have to call an inquest.'

'You stay if you like,' I said, 'but I've got work I need to do before tomorrow. By rights, I shouldn't have come at all.'

'Surely Ormiston—'

'No. There are things only I can do at the moment. And they need to be done today.'

He wasn't happy, but in the end he had to let me go.

–

I trotted Seren away from Rhosdywarch, furious that Harry put nursemaiding him above my estate work. And that he thought I should just let Mr Ormiston get on with it. Fair enough if he'd been a competent steward; maybe I could've picked and chosen what work I did when. But he *wasn't* competent. At least not now, when the estate's future was hanging by a thread.

Micah Ormiston thought the solution to the estate's financial difficulties was simple. Just replace tenants who were stuck in the past with more ambitious men who'd pay higher rents and who'd be more forward-thinking about crops and stock. But it wasn't that simple. Farmers didn't work on their own, not like weavers or carpenters or blacksmiths. They had to cooperate or nobody'd survive.

The tenants Mr Ormiston wanted to get rid of all had something that couldn't be easily replaced. Sam Dangraig had a boar that was always in demand for on-heat sows because it sired big litters and was docile to walk between farms. Tomos Iscoed, father to our hall boy, Wil-Sam, had inherited his position as leader of the local haymaking group from his father; without him, haymaking on the ten farms that worked together would be a shambles, because there was another farmer who thought he should be in charge and only Tomos could handle him. Dan Penralldywyll had a plough pair that went out to every neighbouring farmer, and if he sold them – which was Mr Ormiston's 'simple solution' – it wasn't only him who'd have no means of ploughing his land.

And it wasn't just the men, either. The farmers' wives were in charge of gleaning, and they were often better shearers than their husbands. Mari Cwmderi was known as the midwife who'd take over from Ann Davies when she retired, and Sally Treloyw had a reputation as a marriage healer. If their families were turned off the land, their skills would be lost.

Then there was Deio'r Gwahoddwr – the bidder-to-come – who carefully crafted wedding invitation verses and sang them to every farm in the district. He could no more be replaced by whoever took over his holding than could the distinctive staff he carried. It'd been carved for his grandfather when he'd served twelve years as the Gwahoddwr, and old Wil y Gwahoddwr hadn't given it up until his grandson'd proved a worthy successor.

If all those people ended up in the workhouse, or on a farm miles away doing drudge work for a charitable relative, all their skills would be lost and Glanteifi'd be the poorer for it. In both senses.

But, after Harry'd told him that he should do whatever was most profitable for the estate, all Mr Ormiston cared about was retiring next April with as much money in the Glanteifi bank account as possible. Or at least with our debts not increased. Then he'd go off and live with his daughter, and I'd be left with the impossible task of knitting the community he'd unravelled back together.

I tried to put it out of my head and think of something else, but then my mind filled with the bizarre story I'd got from Ann and Gwen.

I was glad Harry hadn't had time to ask me whether I'd got any sense out of the pair of them. The story they'd told me was completely fanciful and I didn't want him to think I believed in such nonsense. And if there was still a chance that Reckitt might find a brain aneurysm or poison when he did the rest of his examination, there'd be no need to repeat any of the girls' fancifulness.

Of course, if Reckitt found nothing when he opened her up, it'd be a different story. I'd have to tell Harry then.

But as I rode on, I was already arguing with myself. What was the point of telling him such an unlikely tale at all? Some people just died for no apparent reason. Why did Lizzie Rees's death have to be somebody's fault?

146

Trouble was, what Ann and Gwen'd told me fitted in with what Llwyo had said about Lizzie not getting on with the other girls.

I saw Gwen's tear-stained little face in my mind's eye, her words tumbling over each other as her fears poured out, little drops of spit catching the sunlight as she wailed at her sister.

Sally Sips must've told everybody what Lizzie was going to do, so they came here that night. They must have! You saw her things…

Ann hadn't wanted to tell me what Gwen meant. She'd tried to shut her sister up and say it was nothing. But in the end, I'd got the whole story.

'There was a girl,' Ann'd said, sitting up primly on the grass with her legs folded under her, 'up Lampeter way. It was in the papers. She died of fright after her friends tricked her when she washed the midnight shirt.'

She looked at me as if she expected me to know what that meant. I made a face that told her I didn't.

'It's to find out who you're going to marry. Before you go to bed, you wash something you wear next to your skin and put it by the fire to dry. Then, at midnight, you watch to see what happens. If you're going to die a spinster, a coffin goes through the house. But if you're going to marry, the spirit of your husband-to-be comes to turn the shirt for you.'

I knew girls giggled over divination games but surely nobody took them seriously?

'Does it work?' I asked. But of course that was a stupid question. A girl would never admit that she hadn't seen her future husband, any more than a lad would admit he'd been refused when he asked a girl to walk out with him.

'The girl in Lampeter – she was at a boarding-out school,' Ann went on, 'and she did the midnight shirt with the other girls in the house. One of them knew that there was a man who was in love with her but who the girl hated. So to pay her back over an argument, she dressed up like that man – made herself red whiskers and everything – and when the girl peeped round the door at midnight and saw him turning her shirt, she was so shocked that she fell down in a dead faint! They had the doctor to her and everything, but it was no good. She died.'

Lampeter was on Harry's patch. If this'd really happened, we'd have heard about it for sure. 'When was this?' I asked. 'Recently?'

Ann gave a little shrug. 'I don't know exactly, but everybody knows about it. It was in the papers.'

She'd already said that, but it didn't make it true.

'And you think this Sally Sips played the same trick on Lizzie?'

'Not Sally. I don't think it was her. I think she's a real friend to Lizzie. Was, I mean. But she was the only one. The others were always spreading lies about Lizzie on the sly. And they could've easily made Sally tell them what the Dewin'd said. She's got a kind heart, Sally, but she can't keep a secret to save her life.'

I shifted my weight under me. As well as the sun going in, insects were starting to crawl into my clothes, and I was keen to finish this story. 'But I don't understand why Lizzie would've done this midnight shirt thing if she'd already given Nattie Stockton the *coron fedw*?'

Ann bit her lip. 'Mam told Lizzie she'd never let her marry Nattie. But Lizzie loved him.' She didn't say anything else, just looked at me with a worried little face.

'You think she went to see Dewin Gwynne to ask him whether she *was* going to marry Nattie, is that it?' I asked slowly. 'You don't think *he* told her to wash the midnight shirt?'

Gwen could see I didn't believe it. 'She *did* do it!' she said, sitting up suddenly as if somebody'd slapped the back of her head. 'Her nightgown was still drying on the back of the chair by the fire when we got back from Ffynone!'

Something in my riding boot bit me and I twitched. But I wasn't going to take it off, not in front of these two. 'Nightgown?'

'The one she'd embroidered for her bottom drawer,' Ann said.

'She never wore it,' Gwen butted in. 'It was for when she was married.'

'But she might've thought that if she washed something important like that, then the spell would be especially powerful.' Ann's face said she didn't know what to believe.

'Did your mam see the nightgown?' Esther Rees struck me as a woman who was about as likely to believe in divination as she was to believe in marrying for love.

Ann nodded.

'And did she ask your father what it was doing on the back of the chair?'

'He said Lizzie'd had it out to put more embroidery on it and the cat had jumped on it with dirty paws and she'd had to wash it.'

'Did she believe him?'

Ann shook her head miserably. 'I don't think so. Will you tell Mr Probert-Lloyd?'

I don't know whether she was afraid that I would or that I wouldn't.

Harry

Lizzie Rees had not died of an aneurysm. Reckitt's saw and scalpel revealed nothing out of the ordinary, neither in the dead girl's viscera nor in her brain.

Her stomach's noisome contents, carried back to his house from Rhosdywarch for analysis, proved equally innocent. He had ruled out laudanum or prussic on first dissecting the body by the simple expedient of sniffing the stomach contents for their characteristic odours, but he had wished to test for arsenic as it was the most freely available of all poisons.

'I can't rule out strychnine because I can't test for it,' he told me the following morning, after he had woken me to deliver his news, 'but I doubt it's involved here. It causes seizures, and the body showed no indication of the girl having suffered any.' He poured the coffee his maid-of-all-work had brought in and handed me a cup. 'I'm no expert on plant poisons,' he said, 'but she didn't appear to have ingested anything unusual. Her last meal was no longer evident, so she didn't die very soon after eating it.'

Placing my cup and saucer on the floor, I divested myself of the blanket Reckitt had provided me with and retrieved my jacket and necktie from the back of the ancient, battered couch on which I had spent the night. 'She really did die of natural causes, then?' I asked, looping my tie around my collar.

'It would appear so.' Another man might have been pleased at the result of his forensic investigations, but not Reckitt.

'In that case, the certified cause of death stands. No need for an inquest.' That would please John.

Reckitt gave a weighty sigh. 'No, I suppose not.'

'Not happy with your own findings?'

He sat heavily on one of the mismatched chairs that occupied his untidy parlour-cum-dining-room. 'People don't just *die*, Probert-Lloyd. There may have been no foul play involved, but *something* killed Lizzie Rees. Medical science simply lacks the knowledge, as yet, to say what that something might be.'

I drank my coffee and waited for the rest.

'Her brain showed no clots, no haemorrhaging, no tumours. All her organs were in perfect health, including her heart. And yet it simply stopped beating.

'This is why properly trained medical men must be allowed to dissect every corpse before burial,' Reckitt said, as if this was a novel opinion and not one he aired every time we had this conversation. 'Instead of just being satisfied with discovering *gross* changes in the viscera, if we were mandated to examine *every* body after death we would learn to look for much more subtle signs, even those only visible under a microscope.'

'But how would you know that such small changes were actually responsible for a person's death?'

'That's exactly the point! You wouldn't know if they were very rarely seen. But if many case histories were to correspond both in the circumstances of death and the histology—'

'Histology?'

'Bodily tissues under a microscope. The point is, Probert-Lloyd, if there were small – apparently insignificant – changes in people who lived in the same circumstances or worked in the same occupation or had ingested the same substance, one might reasonably draw the inference that that common factor had contributed somehow to their death.'

Shivering, I finished fastening my waistcoat buttons and searched the floor for my coffee cup. 'But what then, Reckitt? Would you go about like some harbinger of doom telling people to move from where they live or to cease plying the family trade? Lizzie Rees worked as a farm servant – what could she possibly be counselled to avoid?'

'You may mock, but there are cases in which going against the accepted orthodoxy has had remarkable results. There's a Swiss doctor who has dramatically reduced maternal mortality in his obstetric hospital by simply insisting that all doctors wash their hands in chlorinated lime before conducting their examinations. He'd noticed that the women who'd been treated by a doctor were three times more likely to die than those who had been treated by a midwife. *In the same hospital.*'

'Why?'

'The doctors were coming straight to the ward from conducting dissections. Something was obviously being transmitted on their hands.' He fell silent, and I had the familiar and perpetually uncomfortable sensation of being stared at. 'We don't have to understand exactly what's causing illness and death to stop it. We may simply change habits. We know that moving people out of the stench of London to the countryside materially improves their health – and that's just one example.'

I sipped my coffee. It was burned, as usual; Reckitt's maid never drank the stuff and consequently had no idea how her carelessness affected the taste. Nevertheless, I was glad of its warming effect. The fire was not lit and the room, with its small window, was cold, a fact to which Reckitt seemed oblivious.

I added the two chunks of sugar in my saucer to the coffee and stirred it, wondering what Cadwgan Gwynne would say to the idea of universal autopsy. Few medical men saw it as practicable, even if it might ultimately prove informative. For if every single death in the country were to result in a post-mortem examination, doctors' time would be monopolised by the dead to the detriment of the living.

My stockinged feet tingling with the cold, I finished my coffee and pulled on my boots. 'Will you go to Lizzie Rees's funeral tomorrow?' It was Reckitt's usual habit to attend the interments of those he had dissected, as a mark of respect.

'I see no reason why not.'

I rose to my feet. 'Keep an eye out for me, would you?'

'What for?'

'Malicious gossip,' I said. 'It would be helpful if you could quash any rumours you hear of foul play. The family's not altogether trusted locally – Mic Rees is an incomer, and you know how people can be.'

I had seen often enough where a parish full of rumour and mistrust led, and I did not relish the thought that my becoming involved might have given rise to suspicions that would not now be allayed by an inquest.

John

I woke up on Monday morning with a sense of dread. That afternoon, if Mr Ormiston had his way, we'd be going out to tell six families that they were going to be turned off their land. Six families who'd probably spent yesterday on their knees praying that instead of giving them notice we'd take whatever small amount they could pay for last quarter's arrears and give them another quarter's grace. And I was going to try and persuade Mr Ormiston that we should do exactly that. In fact, I'd spent hours writing carefully worded contracts to that effect.

The previous evening, I'd been in the office slogging through those – and the paperwork I'd abandoned to go rushing off after Harry and his ridiculous suspicions of Mic Rees, a man who was guilty of nothing except doting on his daughter – when Clara, one of the maids, bobbed in to tell me dinner'd be ready in five minutes.

I saw her looking at my boots. That meant that Mrs Griffiths, who missed nothing, knew that I was still in my riding clothes after going straight to the office when I got back from the other side of the river. She'd want to give me time to get changed like a gentleman before sitting down to dinner with Lydia Howell.

I hadn't seen Lydia since I got back, so when I took my place at the dining table, a bit breathless and damp from a quick wash and change, I should've been prepared for her first question.

'How did the pair of you get on in Brynberian?'

The pair of you. She was yoking me and Harry together like mischievous boys or a pair of dumb oxen. It got under my skin like a tick. Set me right on edge. What did she think – that I'd been *happy* to go haring off when Harry crooked his finger? How dare she think she knew me, knew what was most important to me?

I took my time laying my napkin in my lap, watching her out of the corner of my eye. She looked the same as she always did, clean and neat and governess-like in her plain high-collared dress. Calm and steady. Respectable, even. But she hadn't always been this person, had she? She'd been fiery, once. A rabble-rouser. She of all people should know better than to judge.

'Bit of a wild goose chase, as it happens,' I said. Good. I sounded calm.

But fake calm couldn't stop an image of Ann and Gwen sliding into my mind. Lizzie Rees's sisters didn't think it was a wild goose chase. They were convinced Lizzie'd been killed by the Eglwyswrw girls' spitefulness.

I pushed the thought out of my mind.

'Didn't deserve a minute of Harry's time as far as I could see.' I felt my heart pushing against my ribs. Dismissing Lizzie Rees's death like that felt wrong, but I wanted Lydia to know that I wasn't always delighted to go chasing around three counties on a whim of Harry's. 'To be honest, my time would've been better spent here. And his, come to that. There are far more serious things happening on the estate than he realises.'

She looked at me. 'Go on.'

I glanced over at Ianto, standing there like a statue, and Lydia caught my eye. 'Ianto, we'll manage by ourselves,' she said. 'You can go back to the kitchen with the others. We'll call you when we're ready.'

He left, but not without a quick glance at me. Lydia might've spoken, but he knew whose fault it was he was being sent packing.

My hands were trembling. Now I'd started, I wanted to tell Lydia everything, but hours writing my replacement contracts had chipped away at my own faith in what I'd decided to do. When I'd tried to talk to Mr Ormiston, weeks ago, about how we could help the tenants in arrears, he'd accused me of thinking too much like a farm boy and not enough like a steward. At the time, I'd told myself that that just showed he didn't really understand how things worked – but what if he was right?

I picked up my knife and fork, looked at my dinner and put them down again. Lydia started eating, eyes on her plate, which I was grateful for. 'When I first met Harry,' I said, 'he told me that he didn't want to be squire. He didn't want to own the farms that people work on. He thought everybody should own their own land. Everybody should be equal.' I picked up my wine glass and took a drink. It jerked against my lips, my hands were shaking so much. 'He was probably talking similar nonsense when you first met him,' I said. 'Not in Ipswich, I mean. When you were here before.'

As I put my glass down again, I risked a glance to see how she'd taken that. She was looking at me with that steady, self-composed look of hers. I didn't have a clue what she was thinking, and my heart sped up. Maybe I shouldn't've mentioned her previous life, but I was sick to the back teeth of all the things she and Harry never spoke about. And if I'm honest, I wanted her to tell me that Harry hadn't really changed from when he'd been a lad riding out with her Rebeccas to break tollgates. That deep down he still believed in equality between people. That he wasn't going to be just another don't-know-don't-care squire.

Because if he was, I'd made a hell of a mistake taking the under-steward's job.

I watched her cutting up her chop with dainty movements that reminded me a bit too much of Reckitt's precise scalpel work. 'I know he's given Micah Ormiston free rein to run the estate as he sees fit,' she said finally. 'Are you saying he's favouring the estate over the tenants?'

I swallowed the mouthful of mutton that I seemed to have been chewing for the last ten minutes and forced it down with a swig of wine. 'If you don't mind me saying, seeing the estate and the tenants as two different things is exactly the problem. The tenants *are* the estate!' I drank some more wine.

Lydia nodded and put her knife and fork down. 'Like a chapel,' she said, looking me in the eye. 'Without the people – without the *minister* – it's just a building. Is that what you mean?'

The *minister*. Laying emphasis on it like that, she was meeting me on the dangerous ground I'd stepped onto when I'd mentioned her previous life. She knew I'd be picturing who she'd once been. Or pretended to be. Did a day go by without her thinking about it?

'Yes. Exactly like a chapel. An estate's just land until it's got people on it. It's the people who matter and I thought Harry knew that. But he's let Mr Ormiston loose, and as far as *he's* concerned, as long as every farm's got a tenant, everything'll be fine.'

'But it won't.'

'Of course not! Think about what you just said – a congregation's not just any old collection of a hundred people just to make up numbers, is it? It's people who know each other, who depend on each other. They know who's good at things – who can preach and who can sing, who can read and write, who's always got a newspaper, who'll lend you money and who won't. Who'll pay you back and who won't. Who's a true Christian and who's a hypocrite!' I picked up my wine glass once more, and drained it.

Her face didn't change, but her chin jutted out just a little bit when I said the word *hypocrite*. Had I meant it for her? If the cap fitted…

As she moved her head, the pins in her hair caught the light, and just for a second I found myself wondering what she'd look like with her hair down. It wasn't an interesting colour – kind of mouse-brown – but it was thick and vigorous and always seemed to be trying to escape. She pulled it tight to govern it, but having it scraped back so severely didn't suit her face. How had she worn it when she was living under her brother's name, wearing his clothes, doing the job that would've been his if he hadn't died? Minister to Treforgan chapel.

How had she got away with it? She didn't look like a man. I mean, she was plain, but she was obviously a woman. But then, as she'd said herself when we'd met in her employer's house in Ipswich, put a person in a man's clothes and give them a man's job and that's what people see. A man.

If I dressed in a *betgwn* and apron and scrubbed floors or milked cows, would people see a woman?

My hands were still shaking as I poured myself some more wine.

'Anyway,' I said, scrambling to pick up where I'd left off, 'what I'm saying is that the estate's not just separate farms with tenants keeping to their own land. You can't throw a family off their farm without altering the balance of things.' I could hear myself getting louder, so I stopped, took a deep breath and picked up my knife and fork. There was cold gravy on the handle of my knife. I wiped if off with my napkin.

Lydia's eyes were fixed on me, waiting. But I couldn't look at her. It wasn't just that I'd talked about her previous life. I felt as if I'd crossed a line, stood with her instead of with Harry. But Harry didn't want to listen, did he?

'It might be all right if you just give one or two tenants notice,' I said. I couldn't have her thinking I was a child who wanted everything to stay the same for ever. 'But it all depends on who takes over their land. Mr Ormiston thinks it's better to let well-off farmers take a second tenancy to run alongside their original one, but that'll throw things out of balance. Especially if that new tenant makes even more money and takes a third farm. Then suddenly you've got too many cottagers and smallholders and not enough farmers. A lot of poor people and only one who's doing all right. Maybe more than all right. And that causes jealousies, resentment. Blame.'

'And that's not good for the estate.' She said it like a statement, but it was a question.

I shook my head. 'It's not good for *anybody*.'

And now – this afternoon – I had to see if I could stop that happening.

Harry

After leaving Reckitt's house and retrieving Sara from the livery stable tucked away behind Cilgerran's main street, I spent most of the journey down to Llechryd bridge and the Cardiganshire side of the river trying to persuade myself that Lizzie Rees's death was no longer any concern of mine. But try as I might, there was something about the case that would give me no peace. Of course, Mic Rees's admission that he had allowed Lizzie to sleep in his own bed and that he had stripped, washed and re-dressed her went some way to explaining why he had felt the need to lie to us, but I couldn't shake the feeling that we had failed to get to the bottom of his daughter's death.

My thoughts were interrupted by the sound of a horse cantering up behind me, and I steered Sara to the side of the road lest we get in the newcomer's way. But instead of passing us with a wave, the rider pulled up alongside me. 'Mr Probert-Lloyd, I'm glad I've caught you!'

My impression was of a youngish man, dressed in brown homespun. 'It's all right,' I said, in Welsh, 'you don't need to speak English with me.'

'Thank you, but do you mind if I do? I need to practise.'

I was surprised at the request, but perhaps my speaking Welsh to him had encouraged him to be bold. 'Very well.'

'I'm the constable for Cilgerran parish. Caleb Richards. A body's been found in the river and I'm asking you to come and see it. In your position as coroner.'

I am ashamed to admit that I was pleased to have a legitimate reason not to return to Glanteifi; neither John nor any county magistrate could disapprove of my being officially summoned.

As we rode back towards the town, Richards told me that Cilgerran coracle fishermen had caught the body in their net early that morning.

'Drowned, I assume?'

Richards hesitated. 'Possibly, but it's an odd one if he did.'

'As you can see, I'm lacking my assistant today,' I said. 'If it's a suspicious death, I'll need someone to view the body with me.'

'I've already asked for Dr Reckitt's help,' Caleb Richards said. 'All being well, he'll meet us there.'

'There?'

'I told them to take the body to the Pendre Inn to wait for you.'

'Was it you who decided I needed to be called?' If he had made the decision without reference to any higher authority, he should make the most of the privilege while he could. No doubt Pembrokeshire's magistrates would soon follow Cardiganshire's lead and make him seek permission.

'I'm the *plwyfwas*, so yes, it was me who decided.'

I smiled. I might well have an ally in Caleb Richards.

Soon we were riding back up the shallow slope into Cilgerran, passing two girls with bundles on their heads and a boy driving a pig along the road with liberal use of a switch.

'Has the dead man been identified?' I asked.

'No. Nobody knows him.'

'Is that because of the state the body's in after coming out of the water?' As yet, I'd not been called to a drowning recovered from the Teifi, but having been dragged to dissections by my medical friend, Henry Grey, while I was a pupil barrister, I knew that unless a drowned corpse was recovered quickly, it rapidly became grotesque. Fish fed on the soft parts and the river's currents would dash it against the bank and floating objects; add to that damage the slippage of saturated skin and it took a strong stomach to view a victim of the water.

'No. From the look of him, I don't think he was in the river long at all.' Richards pulled up. 'Here we are.'

From what I could see, the Pendre Inn was a decent-enough place. It had obviously been there since my grandfather's time and seemed to have been much added to and changed over the years. The roofline had sprouted irregular dormer windows, and the roof itself, once probably thatched, was now covered in slate tiles – more than likely from the quarries downriver.

Richards put his head around the door and gave a whistle that brought a lad out to take our horses, leaving us free to enter the gloom of the inn and to make the acquaintance of the corpse that lay within.

John

The office was quiet, and as I listened for sounds of Harry coming home, the only thing I could hear was my own pen scratching out the contracts Mr Ormiston'd left notes for. I'd finished the ones he hadn't asked for – the ones he wasn't going to like – before going to bed.

There was a part of me that wanted to know what Dr Reckitt had found when he opened up Lizzie Rees's body – of course there was. But I still hoped Harry wouldn't get back before Mr Ormiston came in. I needed to get these papers finished.

Time ticked by. Had there been poison in Lizzie Rees's stomach? Had Reckitt and Harry gone back to Rhosdywarch?

Concentrate, John! But my ears stayed pricked for any sounds outside the office door. At one point I heard Lydia Howell and Mrs Griffiths going past talking about where the 'shower bath' should go.

That shower contraption'd caused a bit of a stir when Gus Gelyot had sent it as a birthday present for Harry a few weeks ago. Mind you, with the newspapers full of all the modern inventions at the Great Exhibition, nobody at Glanteifi had been quite as surprised when it arrived as they would've been before.

My dear P-L, Gus's birthday note'd said, *I hope this will afford a little luxury in the taking of ablutions until such time as you are able to join the modern world and install actual plumbing.*

To be honest, the shower bath might be an engineering miracle in brass and copper, but it didn't look all that robust, and I wasn't going to volunteer to be the first one to use it. A hip bath or a quick wash all over was fine for me. Having hot water carried about the house whenever I wanted it was enough of a luxury, I didn't need it to come down on me like rain.

The shower bath was designed to be movable, but Harry had decided that it would be better to give it a room of its own, so as not to damage it with constant shifting about. Trouble was, building walls and putting in doors was expensive, so for now, the shower was still standing in the corner of his bedroom, unused.

Hearing Lydia Howell's voice made me sweat at the thought of all the things I'd said to her last night. I'd had too much to drink, hadn't I? And now I'd changed things between us. She knew my worries about the estate. And she knew I wasn't going to pretend she'd never lived as a man.

To be truthful, half of me was glad my tongue had run away with me – it'd all needed saying. But now I didn't know where I stood with her. I'd avoided her so far this morning by getting up early and having breakfast in the kitchen before I started work.

But I'd have to face her eventually.

–

Mr Ormiston came into the office on the stroke of twelve. Had he been waiting in the hall till the clock chimed?

I looked up as he opened the door into my little inner room. I'd moved back to my own desk this morning in case he came in earlier than he'd said.

He took one of the contracts I'd written and scanned it. 'What's this nonsense you've written for Jones at Ffynnonwen?' He glared at me.

'A compromise.'

'It says we'll pay him money.'

'Only if he's forced to leave the farm after making improvements. And only for the next five years.'

'*Only* for the next five years? Where do you imagine we'd find the money to *compensate* him,' he waved the contract at me, 'for making improvements to his *own buildings*?'

I took a deep breath. Here we go… 'But they're *not* his own buildings, are they? *He'll* build them, but they'll belong to the estate.'

'Be that as it may, as you know very well, the estate can't afford to finance the improvements.'

'No, but don't you see how unfair that looks to John Jones?'

'Unfair?'

I barged ahead before he could tell me that running an estate wasn't about fairness. 'Yes, because half the farms on the estate had new buildings put up for nothing when Mr Probert-Lloyd senior was alive, but now we're expecting the rest to do it for themselves, with no reduction in the rent and no guarantee that they won't lose out if things go wrong!'

'So you want us to guarantee compensation we can't afford?'

'I don't think we'll have to pay any compensation, because it'll make Ffynnonwen profitable and then we won't have to give John Jones notice in a year or two's time.' While he was taking that in, I rushed on with the rest of the argument I'd practised. 'If we can show him that he's not risking anything by building another byre, he'll do it. And then he'll have room for four more milking cows. That's a lot of butter to sell. And calves.'

'But if he's got enough money to build another byre and buy four cows—'

'He won't need money – he'll quarry the stone on the farm and fell the wood for the roof. His servants'll do the labouring. And he'll only bring in one new cow at a time, and not for cash; there'll be—'

'Another one of your local *arrangements*?'

That was something else Mr Ormiston couldn't seem to understand – that most farmers didn't use cash for anything except their rent. Everything else was done by fair exchange. That was why you had to know your neighbours. You had to know who you could trust – who was good to deal with and who wasn't.

'It's the way things are done,' I said, afraid that I'd annoyed him and still lost the argument.

He dropped the contract back on the pile. 'I'll overlook the fact that you've gone against my instructions. All things being equal, a steward does well to think of the future, and I can see that's what you're trying to do. But I can't just do as I please. Mr Probert-Lloyd has asked me to lay my hands on as much money as possible this quarter—'

'To invest, I know. But he's not going to need money for the railway shares for at least a year.'

'There are other, more immediate investment opportunities. Glanteifi could take a quarry over at Cilgerran, for instance – the demand for slate is going up all the time with the building that's going on in the coalfields.'

Slate? Surely Harry wasn't going to put his money into that? There was a lot of bad feeling about the Cilgerran works – the quarries were blocking the river with waste, and there was talk of a court case. And, anyway, it could only be a matter of time before the coalfields found slate somewhere nearer than Cilgerran. Then where would we be?

'Can we have look at some of the other suggestions I've made?' I asked, putting my hand on the pile of contracts and agreements.

Ormiston hesitated, so I pushed on. 'If we end up giving notice to everybody on the list, we'll end up with six farms needing new tenants.' I looked him in the eye. 'But I'm worried we may find we've given ourselves more problems than solutions.'

'By which you mean?'

'Stepping in to bid for a tenancy where the farmer's going unwillingly can cause a lot of bad feeling. Feuds, even. We don't want that at Glanteifi.'

I watched him wavering. His eyes moved from my contracts to the window and back to me.

'Why don't I go and ask Mrs Griffiths for some coffee and we can have a look at what I'm proposing? Then you can decide what's best.'

Harry

Like similar hostelries everywhere, the Pendre Inn smelled of beer, pipe smoke, tobacco spit and stale sawdust. It was not a combination I was fond of, but I had become used to it. Inns were a coroner's natural home, with inquests commonly carried out in their large public rooms and unclaimed bodies routinely laid in the outhouses where barrels were stored.

The taproom was low-ceilinged, and north-facing windows let in little light, which meant that I had to feel my way as I followed Richards through to a back room. There I found Reckitt's unmistakable figure bent over what I presumed was the corpse. The doctor had a lamp in his hand, which he raised towards me as I walked in. 'Ah, you're here. Can you ask them to move our friend here outside, where I can see him better? They wouldn't do anything until you got here.'

I nodded to Caleb Richards, who ducked back into the taproom.

'They'll need to move the table as well,' Reckitt called after him, as if the constable might think he wanted the corpse deposited on the ground, then strode through the back room's open door into the yard beyond.

I followed him, squinting. Though the sky was overcast, the light was uncomfortably bright after the gloom within.

'The *plwyfwas* seemed to think he hadn't drowned,' I said. 'Why's that?'

'Because it'd be damned odd if he'd drowned sitting down,' Reckitt said.

I waited, knowing an explanation was on its way.

'He's in an almost foetal position. Thighs tight to chest, though his arms are loose at his sides. *Were*, I should say. He's in full rigor, so there's nothing loose about any of his limbs at present.'

'And it's impossible that he could for some reason have adopted that position in the water?'

Reckitt drew in a long breath, considering the question. 'Highly unlikely – can you think of a possible mechanism?'

'Could he have been bound?'

'There's no sign of that, but I'll know more when I can get his clothes off. And lividity'll give us more information, of course.'

Lividity – the pooling of blood in corpses under the effects of gravity – was a sure sign of the body's position in the hours after death. In those who had gone into the water soon before or after death and had been buoyed up and moved about, it was usually almost entirely absent.

'You say he's in full rigor – so he's been dead, what, at least twelve hours? Always assuming,' I added, before Reckitt could give me a lecture, 'that he wasn't somewhere very cold or unusually warm.'

'Correct. Somewhere between twelve and twenty-four hours, I'd say. Though it might be much longer, depending on how long he was in the water. Having said that, from the condition of his skin, he seems unlikely to have been submerged for long.'

Reckitt's confirmation of Caleb Richards' opinion raised my estimation of the young constable's judgement.

Muttered sounds from within the outhouse were followed by a scuffling and shuffling, which preceded the emergence of two men carrying the trestle board bearing the crouched corpse. Richards carried the trestles, which he stretched out, and once the table was reassembled, its porters left.

'Do you mind if I stay?' Richards asked. 'It might help me find out who he is.'

'Of course,' I said, pleased at his volunteering to help. Parish constables generally melted away once I arrived, lest I find them things to do.

'If you're staying,' Reckitt said, 'be a good fellow and see if you can find some shears. It's going to be next to impossible to get the clothes off him in any normal way.'

'Do you think we should…?' Richards didn't finish the question, but I knew he would want to hand the dead man's clothes over to the bereaved family intact if he could.

'I don't think Mr Probert-Lloyd's going to want to twiddle his thumbs for twelve hours until the corpse is in a fit state for me to undress it.'

I knew perfectly well that Reckitt's impatience had nothing to do with my convenience and everything to do with his own eagerness to begin, but nevertheless, the examination was better done swiftly. An inquest was inevitable, and the more quickly I could begin my investigations, the better for all concerned, so I indicated that Richards should do as Reckitt asked.

Somewhat surprisingly, he was back within a minute.

'These are tailor's scissors,' Reckitt said as he took the proffered item.

'My mother's a seamstress. She lives next door,' Richards said. I could not fathom his wish to practise speaking English; he was fluent, confident. Perhaps he had ambitions to become a uniformed police officer; if so, he would have to cross the river. As far as I knew, there were no imminent plans for a county constabulary in Pembrokeshire.

Reckitt moved to the other side of the table and began his removal of the corpse's clothing. I shuffled closer. The dead man was lying on his side, his chin on his knees, his arms half flexed at the elbows. As far as I could tell, he was fully clothed.

'What are his clothes like, Reckitt?'

'Decent-quality Sunday best. He wasn't down on his luck, but he wasn't a gentleman either, I'd say.' Reckitt put the shears down and crouched over the corpse. 'He doesn't have a gentleman's hands, either.'

'Any signs of violence – broken skin on the knuckles?'

'All in good time, Probert-Lloyd, all in good time.'

Reckitt had his method and he did not like to be diverted from it. I turned to Caleb Richards. 'What time did the coracle men find him?'

'A bit before sunrise.'

'And they caught him in their net?'

'Yes. Whoever threw him in probably thought the tide'd take him all the way to the estuary – out to sea if they were lucky. It was bad luck for them that the nets caught him instead.'

–

A little while later, after much snipping and tearing and teasing and pulling on the part of Reckitt and Richards, the curled corpse lay naked on the table.

'There, just as I thought,' Reckitt said. 'The lividity pattern tells the story. Blood in buttocks and feet, in his hands and the lower part of his face. And here,' he tapped at the man's buttocks, 'you can see contact blanching. I'd say he'd been sitting on a rough, stony surface for some time. The lividity's fixed, which means he didn't change position for a period of several hours while the blood was settling.'

'And you're sure he wasn't on the stony bed of the river – at low tide, for instance?'

'Quite sure. The body was forced into this position either before or soon after death. There's no indication that he'd been bound, and I can think of nothing on the bed of a river that might restrict him in that way. He was put into the water in this state.'

Reckitt continued his examination, and I heard a grunt that indicated the discovery of something significant. 'What?'

'There are no injuries to his hands, but there are marks – contusions – on his left wrist.' He bent to the pile of now-tattered clothing that lay beneath the table and withdrew what looked like a shirt sleeve. Gathering it up in his hands, he leaned over the corpse again and touched the shirt to the left wrist.

'Buttons,' he said, straightening up. 'At some point not long before he died, the little buttons on the cuff of his sleeve dug into the flesh on his wrist hard enough to leave marks.'

'Any other signs of violence?' I asked.

'Difficult to tell until he uncurls, though...' Reckitt bent down and stared at the man's side, 'there may be the beginnings of a bruise here, on his ribs. And...' he moved again, craning his neck to try and see the man's face, which seemed to have adhered to his kneecaps, 'there might be some damage here, too. I'll know better when I've been able to look at him properly. But you'll have to call an inquest, Probert-Lloyd. It's most definitely a suspicious death. And given that somebody threw him into the Teifi when he was good and stiff, I'd be amazed if he wasn't murdered.'

John

Mr Ormiston and I parted company after we'd visited the last defaulter's farm. He said he had business in Newcastle Emlyn, but I knew he just didn't want to ride back to Glanteifi with me. Not after what we'd just done.

I don't remember the ride home. Seren got no instructions from me. I couldn't think, couldn't see what was around me. I was weighed down, weary with sadness and guilt. My head and my heart were full of it. I couldn't stop hearing the voices of families pleading not to be put off their farms, promising to find more money, to do better, begging not to be thrown into the workhouse. They'd kept looking at me, speaking to me in Welsh so that Mr Ormiston wouldn't understand, accusing me, shouting that I knew what would happen to them now. They couldn't understand why I was letting this happen; how Harry could do this to them.

'His father would never have seen us treated like this,' one farmer wept, tears running off his grey-stubbled chin. 'Never. He was a good man, old Mr Probert-Lloyd. He looked after his tenants.' He glared at me, his eyes running with tears. 'Is this what it's going to be like on Glanteifi land now? Pay up every penny every quarter or go? Never mind that our families have lived here for a hundred years?'

A hundred years in which their lives would've been inseparable from the lives of the masters of Glanteifi. They'd have celebrated heirs' coming-of-age up at the big house, they'd have raised hound pups for the hunting squires, they'd have turned out to make hay and shear sheep and harvest corn for their masters before cash rents came in. And now they were being cast aside. All for the sake of ready money.

It was every bit as bad as I'd known it would be, but even though they ranted at me and Mr Ormiston, the families didn't really blame us. Because they knew where the real blame lay. With young Mr Probert-Lloyd.

And the truth was, Harry *was* to blame, wasn't he? He'd told Micah Ormiston to get him as much money this quarter as he could, without putting so much as a single caveat in place.

I'd looked around the kitchen at one of the tenancies we were ending, tears clutching at my throat and stinging my eyes. Everything the family had to sell had been sold, you could tell. No china on the dresser, only a few wooden plates and mugs. No chairs, just a rough bench knocked together for them all to sit at. It looked as if their table'd been sold too, because now there was just an old byre door on trestles, the bottom edge rat-gnawed, the grain stained with the red paint that'd been mostly scrubbed off, except for the stubborn edges of planks and the dents from feet and tools and horns.

When I was a boy, our dresser at home'd had a pot on it. An old Toby jug. And that pot'd been the difference between solvency and debt. Every coin my mam earned with her spinning and knitting and butter-making had gone into that jug and it hadn't come out for anything – not salt, not shoes, not bread, not school – until the rent'd been paid.

You could tell this'd been a prosperous home once. Decent floor, not just beaten earth. A second storey to the house. Glass in the windows even, though the curtains were gone. I wondered what there was upstairs, whether they'd sold the beds, the good sheets.

I looked at the weeping farmer. Did he drink? Was that where the money'd gone? Or had his wife insisted, once upon a time, on having things they couldn't afford? Neither, probably, but Mr Ormiston'd still say it was their own fault. Because their land was worked out. Like most farmers in the area, they'd just carried on working the land in the same way their fathers'd done – cropped and cropped on the same acres year after year with no enrichment for the soil and only the odd fallow year here and there. And like everybody else, they'd sold their best animals because they needed the rent money, and left themselves with the weakest and smallest and most evil-tempered to breed from. So the sheep were small and scrawny, and every year, the lambs they produced got smaller and scrawnier. Same with the cows. Every year, unless there was a new bull, the cows gave less milk and were more trouble about it.

With less butter to sell, stuff from the house'd begin to go, and then the family was on the slippery slope to ruin unless they got help from somewhere.

Old Mr Probert-Lloyd had bled the estate's bank account dry trying to prop up farmers who Mr Ormiston described as backward and inadequate, and if I'm honest, the old squire hadn't had a lot of help from the tenants. Land'll only be productive for so long unless you feed it – that's one thing Mr Ormiston'd learned from Mr Probert-Lloyd senior and I'd learned from him. Harry's father had tried to persuade tenants to rotate what they planted and include green crops, like clover. But the tenants hadn't been keen. It was a new idea, and new ideas don't take root very easily in traditional soil.

And this was the result. A cashless family who couldn't pay the rent.

As I'd stumbled out of that house trying to keep my dignity and not be seen with tears running down my face, the wife had caught my arm. 'Can't you do something? Speak for us?'

'I've tried, Aunty.' I'd wiped my tears with the back of my hand and tried not to sniff like a child. 'I promise you, I've tried.'

It wasn't a word of a lie. I *had* tried. Hard. I'd plied Mr Ormiston with coffee and Mrs Elias's fruit cake and tried to make him see what the consequences of his actions would be for the estate. And in the end, after pleading and reasoning and raising my voice and apologising for raising my voice and proposing new strategies and saying *shouldn't we talk to Mr Probert-Lloyd before making so many people homeless*, I'd managed to save half of them. Three families who'd stay on the farms their grandparents had been born on – for now, at least – and who'd try every way they could to find a way to pay the rent next quarter.

And perhaps it'd been my lucky day or perhaps I was just – finally – learning how to persuade Mr Ormiston, because I'd also convinced him to issue the contracts I'd written promising that the estate'd pay compensation in the event of eviction to the two farmers most likely to ensure that the improvements they made would turn a profit.

But now, as I rode back up the drive to the mansion at the end of the longest day I could remember, I knew it wasn't enough. Of course it wasn't. But at least it was something. I'd managed to do *something*.

Still, my heart was heavy with the knowledge that this time tomorrow, there wouldn't be a single person on the whole estate who hadn't heard about the heartlessness of young Mr Probert-Lloyd. Harry's reputation with the tenants was going to take a battering.

But there was something else that was making me feel low. Something that had nothing to do with Harry's poor judgement and everything to do with mine. Because what'd happened today would happen again and again if Jem Harborne's mill was a success. No extra money coming in to pay the rent. More families destitute. The guts ripped out of a community.

In my mind's eye I saw Mr Gelyot senior's face as I told him about Harborne's plans that night in London, and I wished like I'd never wished before that I'd had the sense to shrug off Gus's mockery and keep Harborne's calling card in my pocket.

Harry

I rode back to Glanteifi after instructing Caleb Richards to gather a jury to view the body the following morning and to bring in the publicans of Cilgerran to see if they recognised the dead man. He might be a stranger to the village, but it was possible that he had stopped to drink in one of the public houses.

John was out on estate business with Ormiston when I got back to the house, but Lydia proved a ready audience, interested not only in the coracle men's grisly catch but in what Reckitt and I had learned the previous day. And as I told her everything we had discovered, my concerns that Mic Rees had not been entirely honest with us resurfaced.

'Does it matter?' Lydia asked. 'Perhaps he does have something to hide, but if Reckitt says his daughter's death wasn't suspicious, then it's not your responsibility to find out, is it?'

I pushed aside the plate that had held a late lunch of bread, cheese and pickled onion and carefully accepted a cup of tea.

'John thinks it might have something to do with what Cadwgan Gwynne told us,' I said. 'He thinks that if Lizzie knew she'd been cursed, it might have affected her mind, her health even.'

'You should take more notice of John's opinion,' Lydia said. 'He's very astute.'

I fixed the whirlpool over the crockery between us so that she appeared in my peripheral vision. 'That was a little pointed. Are we still talking about his opinion on curses?' Though I smiled as I asked the question, I felt a sudden apprehension.

Lydia stood and walked over to the French windows, where her sturdy, habitually upright frame was silhouetted against the light.

'John surprised me yesterday evening.' Despite the fact that her face was turned to the window, her voice carried to me clearly, and I had a sudden disconcerting memory of hearing that same slightly husky contralto directing a torchlit crowd of men, holding the reins of their compliance as confidently as a postilion on an old and favoured horse. 'He confided in me. He hasn't done that before.'

John's confidences must concern me; she would not have raised the subject otherwise. 'Are you going to tell me what he said?'

Lydia turned, and her skirts swirled visibly around her legs with the sudden motion. 'No. But I'll tell you what I've observed. He's struggling to understand your attitude to the management of the estate.'

'I leave that to Ormiston.'

'Precisely.' I could feel her gaze fixed on me. 'What would the Harry Probert-Lloyd I first met – the young firebrand who wanted to ride with my Rebeccas – say to you now? What would he think of you letting your steward run the estate in whatever way he sees fit, without even bothering to ask whether the tenants are treated well or badly?'

I was stung. 'Ormiston's been managing the estate since before I was born! It's not for me to interfere while he's still steward.'

'So you're content to let him do as he likes and shelve any notion of a more enlightened management of the estate until John takes over in April?'

She had teased me often enough that I had abandoned my principles, and even in jest, it rankled. This time, she was serious, and her words struck me dumb. Had she really no idea how difficult it was to embody Radical philosophy as a Cardiganshire squire when notions like equitable land tenure baffled the very people they were designed to benefit?

Since coming back to Glanteifi, I had been forced to understand that as a barrister in London, surrounded by like-minded company, it had been easy for me to maintain the self-delusion that when I inherited the estate I would do something extraordinary with it. That I might sell it piecemeal, at a knock-down price, to my tenants; or form a model estate in which all the workers had an interest. That I might sell it to a rich industrialist looking to acquire the social standing of the landed classes and use the proceeds to set up some charitable foundation.

Once blindness had left me unable to support myself and forced me back to my father's house however, the realities of life in the Teifi Valley had soon become abundantly clear. Not one tenant in a score would contemplate taking the risk of becoming an owner-occupier, and there were no surplus funds with which to establish any kind of model venture. But even worse had been the unpalatable realisation of how completely dependent I was on the estate. Unable to work for my living, I would be reliant for the rest of my life on the rental income from Glanteifi's tenants; an income that was currently proving insufficient to pay the bills.

In the silence, Lydia strode back to the table and, palms planted, leaned towards me in a forceful, unladylike posture. I had to resist the urge to leap up and respond to the challenge.

'Harry, I think you overestimate Micah Ormiston's competence. And his role under your father. I've had sight of all the estate documents, don't forget, and there's not a single plan, not even so much as a note, written by Mr Ormiston. The only things in his handwriting are contracts and receipts.' She paused while I took this in. 'It was your father and his principles that ran the estate. I suspect Mr Ormiston was little more than a glorified rent-collector.'

Feeling horribly at a disadvantage under her gaze, I pushed my chair back and moved away from the table. I wanted to tell her she was wrong, that she did not know what she was talking about, but the fact that she had read the estate papers, that she had first-hand evidence for her words, prevented me. I had no facts of my own with which to launch a counter-attack, and that was nobody's fault but my own.

Throughout my years in Oxford and London, my father had written weekly letters that had laid out not only his plans for Glanteifi but also a meticulous account of the execution of those plans. Bloodlines improved on the home farm and his attempts to encourage his tenants to do likewise. Farmhouses, barns and byres rebuilt, extended, renovated. Drainage projects undertaken. Cropping rotations established. Trees planted. Rents lowered. Rents remitted. His pleasure at seeing one generation of an estate family hand on the reins to another.

Since his death, I had been filled with self-contempt at my failure to respond as I should have to the steadfastness of purpose with which he had tried to teach me what he himself had taken such great pains to learn; and I had squirmed as I recalled the solipsism with which I had persuaded myself that his punctiliously regular letters were nothing but hectoring rebukes to my own dilatory correspondence. If I had kept those letters, I would now have what amounted to a comprehensive manual on how to run Glanteifi. Instead, I had used them to light the fire in my lodgings.

Allowing Ormiston to continue to run the estate in the way he had under my father had felt like some kind of penance.

I cleared my throat, trying to dislodge the lump that appeared whenever I was forced to confront the myriad ways in which I had been a negligent son and an undeserving heir. 'You think I shouldn't have stood for election as coroner?'

'I don't think that at all, though I'm interested that you should ask the question.' Again she paused. 'You're a thorough and conscientious coroner. But that shouldn't prevent you being equally conscientious in the running of the estate.'

'But if what you say about Ormiston is true…' I held up a hand as she drew breath to respond. 'I don't dispute it but if all Ormiston ever did was to carry out my father's instructions, then all he has to do is continue in that vein. My father spent years planning the improvement of the estate. I don't see how I can be expected to do better in less than six months.'

'But Mr Ormiston *isn't* following your father's instructions, Harry. He's following yours. Because the one instruction you *have* given him countermands everything your father ever said. You've told him to raise as much money as possible this quarter so that you can invest it. Do you honestly think you can save the estate with clever investment?'

'If it's the right investment, yes! How do you think the likes of the Colbys at Ffynone came by their wealth? Not by cropping rotations and better cattle! No, by investing in industry. Iron. Coal.'

She did not reply. What was she thinking? I could feel her gazing at me. When she finally broke her silence, her voice was low, sombre.

'Do you know that they've gone out today – Mr Ormiston and John – to throw half a dozen families off their farms? John's distraught.'

Before I could respond, there was a soft click as the library door opened, and I heard Elsie's voice. 'Is it all right to take the tray away now?'

The question had obviously been directed at Lydia, who ushered the girl in with a gesture and began helping her to stack the crockery on the tray while I tried to take in what she had just said. Six families to be thrown off their farms? I did not think my father had evicted six tenants in half a century. Ormiston would not take such drastic action, surely? He must understand that I had never intended that my request for money to invest should come before the welfare of Glanteifi's people?

In the corner of my eye, I watched Lydia hold the door open for the departing girl then close it before sitting down at the fireside.

'I think you sometimes forget who John is, Harry. Where he's come from.'

I sank onto the chair opposite her, keeping my eyes on the faded colours of the carpet beneath our feet. I would let her say her piece without trying to catch fleeting, invisible expressions;

the effort rarely did anything but remind me how little I could see that was of any real use.

'Before he met you, John had very little prospect of ever being anything but a solicitor's clerk, however bright and promising he might be. You've raised him up in a way he could never have imagined, and you treat him like an equal, *but*,' she had obviously seen me look up, ready to defend myself, 'has it ever occurred to you that he can't afford to see himself in the same way? You may consider yourself his friend, but you're also his employer. And in making him under-steward, you put Ormiston between you. You've made it clear to him that Ormiston's word is law on the estate, so because he knows Ormiston is making mistakes, instead of coming to you he's trying to battle it out with him face to face.'

In my mortification, I could not look at her. 'What should I do?'

'*Involve* yourself, Harry! Talk to John, then sit down with him and Ormiston.'

'But how can I suddenly insert myself into estate affairs without giving Ormiston the impression that John's come tittle-tattling to me?'

'I don't think the news that six families have been given notice would be seen as tattle. Now's the time to be squire, Harry. Glanteifi needs you.'

John

'Beg pardon for asking, but are you all right, Mr Davies?'

I turned to look at the groom who'd spoken. Twm. I'd asked him a hundred times to call me John, and today of all days, I wished he had. I didn't want to be a gentleman today. Not when gentlemen could throw people off their land.

'Tired,' I said. 'Up late working.'

'Suppose you had a lot to catch up with, after you'd been to London then over the river to Mr Probert-Lloyd yesterday.'

'Is he back?'

'He is, sir.'

I nodded. 'What's your surname, Twm?'

'Same as you, as it happens. Davies.'

'Right, well from now on I'm going to call you Mr Davies, unless you call me John.'

He stared at me. *This isn't right.* I could see him thinking it. But what did right have to do with it – it was all luck, wasn't it? It'd looked like terrible luck when my parents'd died, but if they hadn't, I'd never have gone to Mr Davies's school as an orphan scholar, never ended up clerking for Charles Schofield, never had a chance to work with Harry or live in the mansion.

'I can't,' Twm said. 'What would Sarge say?' Sarge was the head groom. As far as I knew, he'd never been a soldier; somebody must've just given him the nickname because he was such a stickler for people following his orders.

'Tell him I told you to.'

'He still won't like it. He'll say you don't know your place. That you shouldn't be encouraging me to behave as if I don't know mine.'

'All right then. We'll both be Mr Davies.'

I left him standing there wondering whether he'd won or lost, and went into the house. The front of the mansion faced east, and with no sun on it since midday, the hall was on the cold side of cool. I shivered as I took my coat off, and was just going into the cloakroom to hang it up when Wil-Sam appeared at my side. He had keen ears and he could hear the front door opening from anywhere on the ground floor.

'I can hang up my own coat, Wil-Sam,' I said, though I knew that wasn't why he'd come so quickly.

'I know, Mr Davies.' His voice shook. He was terrified that his family'd lost their farm.

'Everything's all right, Wil-Sam,' I said, putting a hand on his shoulder. 'Your father's got another quarter to find the rent.' If I hadn't been able to persuade Mr Ormiston to give Wil-Sam's family another quarter's grace, I wasn't sure I'd have been able to stay as under-steward.

Wil-Sam was eleven years old, and his top teeth still looked too big for his mouth when he beamed. He liked to swagger about in the decent clothes he'd been given when he came to the big house, pretending he was a young man, but just at that moment he looked like the child he was.

'Your father's agreed to sign a new contract,' I told him.

'What for?' Wil-Sam knew what a contract was. He'd put his mark on one when he came to work at the mansion, and he'd be able to write his name when he signed the next one. Mrs Griffiths'd seen to it that he went to school.

'To say what crops he'll grow and how often he'll change them round.'

'But it's his land! You can't tell him what to grow!'

I sighed. 'It's Mr Probert-Lloyd's land, Wil-Sam. And your dada could take a lesson from you and learn some new ways of doing things.'

I pulled my riding boots off and handed them to him. 'There you are. I might hang my own coat up, but I'll let you clean my boots.' Then, before he could dart off, I added, 'Could you ask Ianto and Fred to bring some hot water up, please? I need a bath.'

–

The bath didn't exactly wash my sins away, but I felt better after dipping the jug into the water again and again and pouring it over my head. There was something about sitting there with the warm water running down my face. Soothing.

When I finally got dressed and went downstairs, Harry and Lydia were in the library. That morning, I'd been all in a knot about how to face Lydia after the things I'd said last night, but after today, those worries seemed stupid, childish.

They both looked at me as if I might break, so I knew Lydia must have spoken to Harry about what I'd told her. If I'm honest, I'd half hoped she would. But I didn't want to talk about any of that now. I couldn't face it.

I went and stood in front of the fire, hands out to the glow of the culm. I'd thought about staying in my room till dinner, but that would've brought on all sorts of questions.

As it was, neither of them said anything, which was worse. In the end, I had to turn round.

'You look tired, John,' Lydia said gently.

'Up till all hours,' I mumbled. I was glad she hadn't asked what had happened with the tenants. Just the thought of the tears running down old Matthew Thomas's face as he asked me why we were doing this to him was enough to stick a lump like a crab apple in my throat.

Harry made a small movement, and something in his face told me that he was about to say something important. And I didn't want him to.

'You were late back from Cilgerran,' I said, trying to sound normal. 'Did Dr Reckitt find out what killed Lizzie Rees?'

That brought Harry up short, like a man greeted with a handshake instead of a slap. 'Uh… no. There was nothing suspicious. But that's not what—'

'Not even poison?'

He tried a smile, but it was strained. 'You know Reckitt. Won't say *absolutely* not. But no, no poison.'

I turned back to the fire. My hands were damp with sweat. How could they be cold and sweaty at the same time?

'Anyway,' Harry said, 'as there's no inquest required, I don't think there's anything more to say about the death of Lizzie Rees.'

If I turned round, he'd ask me about our visits to the defaulters, I knew he would. 'There might be *one* more thing to say about Lizzie Rees,' I said, still looking at the fire.

'Oh?' Harry sounded surprised.

'Something I got from the Rhosdywarch girls, Ann and Gwen.' An image of the two of them sitting on the grass flashed into my mind, Gwen making her daisy crown, Ann trying to stop her telling me what their big sister had done. 'I know why Lizzie didn't go with her mother and sisters to Ffynone,' I said.

Then I turned to face them. 'Do you know what washing the midnight shirt is?'

Harry

I stayed in the library long after Lydia and John had retired and I had sent the last maid up to bed. I kept telling the servants they did not need to stay awake in case I wanted anything, that I was perfectly capable of fending for myself. But habits are hard to break, I suppose, and my father would not have dreamed of making tea for himself or fetching more fuel to keep a fire burning into the small hours.

Over dinner, John had finally been persuaded to provide us with the bare bones of the visits to last quarter's defaulters. Thanks to his efforts, only three families had been given notice rather than six, but nevertheless, I had heard tears in his voice. For his sake, I hoped they had remained unshed – he would not wish to appear unmanly in front of Lydia.

The hall clock started to chime midnight and an old reflex in me waited for the rest to join in. As a young man, my father had been a horological enthusiast, and there was a long-case clock in virtually every major room downstairs. It had been his lifelong ambition to persuade them all to chime simultaneously, but however hard he tried, and whatever minute adjustments he made, there had always been a cacophonous half a minute or so while the various clocks went about their ill-synchronised business. Since his death, I had seen to it that only the clocks in the hall and the study were wound. It made for a quieter house.

Midnight or not, I was wakeful, my mind darting restlessly from one thing to another. The estate and my failures in its stewardship. The odd questions still clinging to Lizzie Rees's death. The viewing of the body that John and I would oversee in

Cilgerran the following day. Life seemed determined to set my responsibilities to the estate at odds with my duty to the dead.

I stood at the library window as Lydia had done earlier, the darkness of the whirlpool merging into the darkness beyond, rendering me totally blind. I could not see the weak light of the candles on the mantelpiece reflected in the glass.

A wave of smothering claustrophobia threatened to engulf me, and I turned around, took a pace or two into the darkness of the library; I needed to feel movement, action, to throw off the black deadness. One of the great losses that blindness had brought in its wake was an inability to move swiftly and surely. All movement now had to be careful, considered, lest I run into things, knock them over, fall headlong. Blindness had prematurely aged the way in which I navigated the world, and I bitterly resented the caution that had been forced upon me.

However, in recent weeks, Lydia had provided me with a partial remedy. In preparation for a season of balls, she had decided that I must learn to dance. Or rather, relearn. For I had been a proficient and enthusiastic dancer before losing my sight.

Despite the fact that she was not here, I found my feet moving now of their own accord; shuffling at first as I moved sideways up the library towards the table, then more fluidly back towards the window. Becoming bolder in the open space, I tried to skip and turn, but blindness is not conducive to good balance and I found myself staggering and almost falling.

Righting myself, I took a deep breath. No. I would not be thwarted. I would try a polka, even if I ended up flat on my back. I was twenty-seven years old and needed to feel the blood singing in my veins.

New to me on moving to London, the polka had quickly become my favourite dance. Now, cautiously, at half-speed, I tried skipping and dipping with an imaginary partner. And even slowed as they were, the familiar movements brought with them joyous memories of the open-air dancing platform in Cremorne Gardens, where Gus and I had danced away many a carefree day;

young gents and slightly less respectable young women whirled up into a dancing frenzy by the music of strings and woodwind, the pleasure gardens green and lush around us, studded with the jewel colours of flowers whose shapes had blurred as my vision declined.

The waltz had its enthusiasts, but I had always been a polka man.

Suddenly, the music in my head stopped, brought to a halt by a different sound, the clicking of the library door catch. I swayed to a standstill.

There was a candle. Dim, almost imperceptible above the whirlpool, but I saw it because I was looking for it. And faint, almost silent footsteps that suggested slippers or bare feet.

The blur of light moved closer and closer until I could see the faint paleness of a face behind it.

'Harry?'

Lydia.

I do not know what possessed me; I held out a hand. 'Come and dance with me.'

'*Dance?*'

'Yes. It's no fun on my own.' As I waited for her response, I could feel my heart beating. Had I been exerting myself so much?

Eventually she stepped forward.

'Do you know the polka?' I asked.

'No.'

'It's not difficult. Even a guardsman can do it.'

She laughed softly, understanding that my weak joke required some response in lieu of a smile, and after turning aside to put her candle on the table, came and gave me her hand.

Was it the darkness that made the placing of my arm around her back, my hand on her waist so very intimate, or the simple fact that it was many, many months since I had held a woman in my arms? I tried to fix my mind anywhere but on the sensation of Lydia's warmth, the closeness of her body. I did not want my inconvenient arousal to alarm her.

'I know several waltz tunes,' she said, 'but I don't believe I've ever heard a polka. Can you hum a tune?'

Even as I began to hum the first polka that came to me, memories flooded back. The thrill of moving as one with another person, their feet following yours, their body responding to every move of your own. The in and out and round and round of dancing so as not to collide with other couples, holding your partner's gaze with the laughter and recklessness of it all, catching the eyes of other young men, exchanging triumphant or envious looks depending on the attractiveness of respective partners.

But Lydia's unfamiliarity with the steps, coupled with the darkness and my disinclination to hold her too close lest my body betray me, made for a stumbling, clumsy attempt. I stopped, released her hand.

'I'm sorry,' she said. 'If it wasn't dark, it might be easier.'

Suddenly consumed by a painful, physical longing for the blithe days in Cremorne's sunshine, I moved away from her. 'Why did you come down?'

'I didn't hear you come upstairs. After our conversation earlier, and John's distress, I thought you might be in need of company.'

I stared into the darkness where she stood. 'I don't know what to do, Lydia. Should I visit those farms myself tomorrow, tell them I've changed my mind? Or would that make me look weak?'

'Oh, you men!' I saw a swift movement as she picked up her candle once more. 'Why must it be weak to change your mind and show compassion?'

'Changing your mind and showing compassion are two different things.'

'Don't you *dare* split hairs!'

'I'm not.'

'Yes. You are. Like every other man in the world, you think there's a time to be compassionate and a time to be businesslike. As if compassion has no place in business. But that's not the Radical line, is it? That's pure Tory.'

I felt as if she had slapped me.

Held in place by the darkness around me, I watched her candle move towards the fire and come to rest as she put it on the table next to one of the wingback chairs. I heard the hinge squeak as she raised the glass on the mantelpiece lamp and lit the wick, its light combining with that of the candles to restore a measure of sight to me.

As she sat down, I moved cautiously over to the hearth, one hand tracing the outline of the wingback chair, the other searching the air around the fire for the poker. I thrust it into the banked-up fire, revealing a sullen red glow and allowing air in under the blanket of coal dust that Lydia herself had thrown on before retiring so as to keep the embers alive until morning.

I poked and prodded at the fire until I felt calm enough to speak.

'Precisely what would you have me do, Lydia?' I asked. 'How can I be compassionate but not let the estate go bankrupt?'

'By doing what I advised earlier – talk to John.'

'Just to him? Are you saying I should exclude Ormiston?'

'Mr Ormiston will be gone in a matter of months. He only promised a year to train John, didn't he? Agreeing new policies with John now will make things easier when Ormiston leaves.'

I sighed, but she had not finished.

'But working with John on estate business means that sometimes you may have to restrain yourself from rushing off the minute you hear of a sudden death.'

The implication – that I was like a bored schoolboy abandoning resented lessons when something more appealing offered itself – infuriated me, a reaction that must have been visible to Lydia.

'I'm sorry,' she said, retreating into formality, 'that was poorly put. I didn't mean to offend you.'

'I wish you wouldn't do that, Lydia.'

'Apologise?'

'Retreat behind your good-servant facade.'

'Have you forgotten that you *employ* me, Harry?'

'Technically, yes.'

'No, not technically. *Actually*. On what basis would I live here if not as your private secretary?'

I stared blindly at her, unable to answer. The truth was, I did not think of her solely – if at all – as my secretary. I thought of her as my friend, an irreplaceable part of my household family.

'Harry,' she began again, her tone softer now, 'I understand that you don't want to be the sort of squire your father was. But I don't think you know what kind of squire you might be instead.'

Her words went to the miserable heart of the matter. She was right. I did not know how to *be* here. I had failed to apply myself adequately to the task of being squire of Glanteifi because what I really wanted was my old life, the life that had been mine in London before my sight put a stop to it. A life of satisfactory employment as a barrister engaged by charities to represent impoverished defendants. Of attending lectures by Radicals and free thinkers. Eating raucous dinners with other barristers. Dancing with Gus. The life that I had chosen and clung to in desperation – even as my blindness tore me away from it – now felt as if it had belonged to another man. A happier, more carefree man.

I wanted to be him again, but I did not know how to find him here.

Somehow Lydia understood my distress. She left her chair and came to kneel in front of me, taking my hands in hers. At her touch I felt an almost overwhelming desire to fall on her breast and weep all the stifled tears that were stiff in my throat.

'Harry...' she said. Was she waiting for me to look up, meet her eye? If so, that was a fool's errand. 'If anybody can be a Radical and a squire, it's you. You manage it in the coroner's chair, after all.' I heard the smile in her voice. 'But you must stop looking back to your old life and put your hand to the plough of this one. It's the only way.'

John

When we set out for Cilgerran the next morning, I felt as if I hadn't properly woken up. After everything that'd happened yesterday, I'd slept like the dead – overslept, in fact. Ianto'd had to come and wake me up, else we'd've been late for the jury's viewing of the body.

I don't know how Harry'd slept, but he didn't have much to say either. He told me what Reckitt'd said about the sitting corpse the previous day, and then we rode in silence. I still couldn't stop thinking about old Matthew Thomas at Nantyddwrgi – how he'd cried when we told him he was going to have to leave his home. *Is this what it's going to be like on Glanteifi land now?*

Well, if that *was* the future at Glanteifi, I didn't want to be part of it. And I'd decided something. When we got back later, I'd go over to Nantyddwrgi and make sure Matthew and his wife had somewhere to go. If their son couldn't take them in, I'd try and find them a cottage somewhere on the estate. I should've thought of it yesterday, but I hadn't been in a fit state, if I'm honest.

When we got to the junction with the Cenarth road at the bottom of Rhiw Siôn, I looked over to the west. You could see the course of the Teifi marked out by the early-morning mist down in the bottom of the valley. That happens in summer – the mist hangs low over the river like a long cloud until it gets burned off by the sun in the heat of the day.

Seren trotted down the steep little slope and I sat down deep in the saddle and breathed in the early morning air. It left a chill in my nostrils that wouldn't've been there a month ago, and the scents of sun-drying hay and wild flowers that'd sweetened the warm air of high summer were gone. The grass and flowers growing up the hedge banks on either side of me had nearly all gone to seed now, and their stems were dry and dead. Autumn was coming, you could feel it. Some of the smaller trees were already turning, their leaf edges brown and dry, and the dog roses in the hedge were bright with hips, not flowers. Everything was running out of life.

We couldn't get to Cilgerran fast enough for my liking. Harry and I'd never had so little to say to each other, and by the time we reached the Pendre, the silence was like a third person riding between us.

At the inn, Dr Reckitt already had the body out of the back room. He was bending over it when we arrived.

'Good morning, gentlemen!' He had that glint in his eye that you only ever saw when he had a dead body in front of him. Like a pig in muck, he was.

'What have you found?' Harry said. 'You've managed to straighten him out, I see.'

'Yes, by seven this morning he was amenable to the anatomical position.' Reckitt waved his hand over the corpse. 'The young constable was here soon after, and he's already paraded the publicans of the town past to see if they know him.'

'And do they?' I asked. Dr Reckitt sometimes left out the bit of information you really needed, as if he thought it was obvious.

'No. Not one of them. Claim never to have seen him, even. Shall we go through what I've discovered?'

Harry nodded. He knew I preferred to get as much noted down as I could before the jury came, then I wasn't rushing to take names at the same time as I was writing a description of the corpse and its wounds.

I took my notebook and pencil out. 'Off you go, Doctor.'

'Before us is a man in his early to middle twenties. Of average height, and slim though muscular build. No abnormalities of the facial features or indications of any kind of malformation. No obviously broken bones.'

'In other words, a perfectly healthy individual apart from his being dead?' Harry said, straight-faced.

'That I could not say without performing a dissection.'

I wrote the man's probable age down as twenty-one to twenty-five years, his height at five feet seven, my own height – I was getting good at estimating that by now, and I hardly ever needed to use the measure I carried – his hair colour as dark brown and its length as longer than average. 'Eye colour?' I asked. The corpse's eyes were closed.

Reckitt glanced up. 'Brown.'

'Right,' I said. 'Wounds. Looks like somebody gave him a bit of a kicking.' The ribs and abdomen were an angry mass of red and purple.

'Not if you mean that literally, Mr Davies. The bruising is exclusively from his being punched. In one or two places you can see the knuckle marks quite clearly. Furthermore, kicks usually result in broken ribs, whereas this man's ribs are intact.'

I wrote that down. 'Anything on his back?'

'Some light grazing across the shoulder blades. But come and see for yourself.'

I helped him turn the body over. I was still feeling slow and useless, and we almost had the board off the trestles at one point, but Reckitt managed to jam his thigh up against it just in time. Gave me a look, mind. He wasn't used to me being cack-handed.

Once the dead man was safely on his front, I stared down at the pale skin, the knobs of his backbone and the bony bands of his ribs. My clumsiness'd left one of his arms trapped under him and his shoulder blade was sticking out. I felt sick – the dead skin was stretched so tight over the bone I was afraid it might split. Maybe Dr Reckitt was worried as well, because he freed the arm and laid it down at the corpse's side.

I quickly looked at the grazing he'd mentioned, which turned out to be quite hefty scratches slanted just off the horizontal across his back. Some were broad and red, some thin and faint as if somebody'd drawn them in diluted ink with a fine-nibbed pen. None of them seemed to have broken the skin much – you could see that just the very surface layer'd been torn and was ridged up on the edges of the most noticeable marks.

'What do you think caused them?' I asked.

'We'll come to that in a minute.' He did like to give information in a logical manner, Reckitt. Wasn't keen on telling you things in any old order. 'While he's prone, observe the lividity, if you please. It is significant.'

I did as he asked, writing down the pattern Harry'd already described to me – settled blood in the buttocks, feet, hands and face. 'Seen anything to change your mind since straightening him out?' I asked. 'Or do you still think he was kept in a sitting position after he died?'

'I stand by my earlier conclusions. And he wasn't simply kept seated – it seems likely that he was wedged into a small space, face on his knees, which is why you see the settling of livor mortis there too. The pattern tells a story.'

'And that story is?' asked Harry from behind me.

'Patience, Probert-Lloyd! Let us first consider the manner of his death.' Reckitt leaned towards us over the table. I braced myself for one of his lectures, but that wasn't what we got. What we got was a surprise.

'Yesterday, gentlemen, I told you that this man had not drowned in the river. I was wrong.'

I think my mouth might actually have fallen open. I'd never heard Benton Reckitt say those words before.

'He did drown,' he went on, 'but not in the Teifi.'

Harry stared hard in his direction. 'How on earth can you know that?'

'Because there's no pond weed in the river – it's far too fast-flowing.'

'Pond weed?'

'When I compressed his chest to confirm my assumption that he had not drowned, I was surprised to see the characteristic pinkish froth of death by drowning. It brought with it a small quantity of mud and a green substance that I subsequently identified—'

'As pond weed,' I finished.

'Indeed. I believe he inhaled it when his head was being held under the water.'

'How do you know he was being held?'

'Didn't Harry tell you about the small contusions I found on his left wrist? Here, look.'

Harry hadn't mentioned any injuries to the corpse's wrist. Had he forgotten, or did he think the doctor had been making something out of nothing? I shot him a look as I moved towards the body, but of course it was wasted. Dr Reckitt raised the man's arm and twisted it so I could see the inside of his wrist. There were three small red marks. 'What are they?'

'Bruises, essentially. The little mother-of-pearl buttons on his shirt sleeve dug into his flesh while somebody was gripping his wrist. You can see there's some reddening of the arm – light bruising.'

I thought about it. 'So somebody pulled him out of wherever he drowned?'

'That might be a plausible explanation if not for his face.' Reckitt put the corpse's arm down gently and moved to his head. I followed. 'Do you see these small wounds?'

I peered at the dead face. The day before yesterday, this man had been as full of life as I was now. Now he was just a collection of skin, muscles, bones and organs. Whatever had made him human was gone.

Against the background of his blood-saturated face, I could just make out small cuts and gouges to his chin, nose and forehead. My stomach did a quick lurch as I put all Reckitt's clues together and worked out what must have happened. 'You think somebody pushed his arm behind his back and forced him face down into the water?'

'Yes. Shallow water with small stones at the bottom. The stones cut his face as he tried to move his head to breathe or escape his captor.'

I stared at the corpse. Somebody had deliberately held this man's face under the water while he drowned.

Harry

The jury arrived, as instructed, at ten o'clock and were guided through their viewing of the body by Dr Reckitt. John read his notes to them – omitting our conclusions – and asked them to confirm that there were no other wounds visible nor anything else of note.

Then, despite the fact that the answer was already evident from their scattered comments, I asked them whether they knew the man's identity.

'Not a Cilgerran lad,' one of them observed. 'Nor from the farms about.'

His fellow jurors mumbled and grunted their agreement.

'And none of you had seen him before?' It seemed unlikely. Caleb Richards had asked the town's publicans to come and view the body, and none of them had reported having seen him.

Heads were shaken. 'Maybe he went into the river from the other side?' an older man suggested. 'A Cardi?'

A Cardi. A Cardiganshire boy, like John and me.

'Thank you, gentlemen,' I said. 'Mr Richards will let you know once I've set a date for the inquest.'

The jury dismissed and the corpse restored to the dark little back room, Reckitt announced his intention to ride over to Eglwyswrw for Lizzie Rees's funeral.

'Eglwyswrw?' John said. 'Don't you mean Brynberian?'

'I do not. Miss Rees is to be interred at the parish church in Eglwyswrw. Apparently that's the church she attended with her mother.'

'What about the rest of the family?' While Reckitt always had to be dissuaded from detailing every single fact he had gleaned about the bodies of the sick or the dead, he displayed very little interest in the daily lives of healthy people.

'I gather Mr Rees attends Brynberian chapel with his younger daughters.'

'Well that explains why it was mostly Eglwyswrw boys who were chasing Lizzie,' John said. 'If she went to church there she'd be one of them, even if the family lived closer to Brynberian.'

While John was speaking, Reckitt, clearly seeing no further role for himself in the conversation, left without another word.

'Bye, Doctor,' John said wryly.

'Never mind him,' I said, 'nor poor Lizzie Rees, come to that. Our pressing task is to identify our dead man.'

'Can I make a suggestion?' Caleb Richards asked.

'Of course.'

'I could speak to the foremen at the quarries and see if any of them are missing a quarryman.'

I was about to tell Richards that according to a recent decision by the magistrates he would not be paid for his services when I realised that I was not in Cardiganshire now.

'If Mr Richards does that, we can go back to Glanteifi,' John said when I did not respond immediately. 'There's no point us riding about the place asking questions as well.'

He was right. I should simply let Richards go about his business. We had already shown the jury all the evidence they would need to come to a verdict of unlawful killing, and strictly speaking, the only other duty that fell to me was the identification of the deceased. Once we knew who he was, we could convene an inquest. But I had never yet held an inquest into what was clearly an unlawful killing without at least some idea of who might have been responsible.

Still, it would do no harm to let Richards go and talk to the quarrymasters. 'Thank you, Mr Richards. If you'd be so good, I'd appreciate that. And if you do happen to discover who he is, see if you can find out who his friends and associates were, will you? We'll need to speak to them, call them as witnesses.'

Once Richards had left us, I turned to John. 'Why are you so keen to get back? I thought you and Ormiston had visited all the tenants in arrears yesterday. Surely things are quieter now until we actually get to Michaelmas?'

Michaelmas was the next quarter day on which rents would be due. The tenants Ormiston and John had visited the day before had failed to pay the Midsummer rent, and like as not the Lady Day rent too.

'I want to see what we can do for the tenants who're losing their land.' His voice was tight. What emotion was boiling away in him. Anger? Shame?

Keen to be gone, he set off around the side of the inn.

'John!'

He stopped but did not look round.

'I'm sorry about the tenants who've been given notice. You should have come to me.'

In an instant he had turned and was striding back to where I stood. 'No, Harry. *You* should've come to *me*. Or to Mr Ormiston. You should have given him proper instructions that would've looked after the tenants instead of telling him to squeeze as much money out of them as possible so you can invest it!' He stood there panting slightly, waiting for me to defend myself. But I had no idea how to tell him how ashamed I was of my inaction.

'Right. Well. If you want to stay here, fine. Do as you like. I'm going home to try and look after Glanteifi's people.'

–

I let him go. I did not have it in me to follow him and endure his silent fury all the way home; it had been bad enough on the ride over. Besides, it seemed prudent to stay in Cilgerran until I knew the results of Caleb Richards' visit to the quarries.

I walked back into the odorous gloom of the Pendre's interior and asked the landlord to let Richards know when he returned that he could find me at Reckitt's house. The inn had now become my de facto base in Cilgerran, and the landlord no doubt took it for granted that I would hold the inquest here.

'Would you happen to have some bread and cheese?' I asked. I had deprived John and myself of anything but a slice of bread and honey in my haste to leave Glanteifi that morning. John, I knew, had assumed that I wanted to get here in time to talk to Reckitt before we met with the jury, but in truth, my primary reason for leaving in such haste had been to avoid having to face Lydia over breakfast. The intimacy of our midnight encounter in the library would, I feared, make our next meeting uncomfortable for both of us.

Still, discomfort notwithstanding, I could not stay in Cilgerran indefinitely. I had accepted an invitation to lunch tomorrow at Plas Blaengwyn, one of the bigger local mansions. Its new residents, Mr and Mrs Anthony Saunders-James, had only recently returned from an extended honeymoon tour of the Continent, during which the house had been much renovated and modernised, and immediately on their return they had begun issuing invitations in order to show off their refurbished home.

Lydia had been invited to accompany me to Plas Blaengwyn, a fact that was not as notable as it might have been three months ago. Much to my surprise, I had discovered that the social world of the Teifi Valley readily encompassed invitations for private secretaries, though I doubted whether the same would have been true had the secretary been male, and therefore of less interest.

The new Mrs Saunders-James – previously Eleanor James, heiress to the Blaengwyn estate – had, prior to her engagement, been in danger of being written off as an old maid, having reached the advanced age of twenty-nine unwed. Lydia, I knew, must be at least three years her senior, if not more, yet she had not felt like an old maid when I took her in my arms. Not at all.

Had she felt the same stirring when we danced, or had she simply been humouring me – her employer?

'When will you hold the inquest?'

Having not seen the landlord return with the requested food, his sudden question startled me. 'I'm not sure,' I said, putting down the beer mug whose contents had sloshed over my hand when I jumped, and shaking the beer from my fingers.

'Just wondering how long he'll be out there in the back room. It's still warmish, and he'll start to stink soon.'

I knew he was right. In the ordinary run of things, now that the jury had seen the body it would have been claimed by the family and buried. But as yet no family had been identified. 'If it gets too bad, we'll have to think of somewhere else to put him,' I said. 'Meanwhile, let's hope Caleb Richards can find out who he is.'

As the landlord seemed inclined to linger at my side, I asked, 'Been *plwyfwas* long, has he, Richards?'

''Bout five years, far as I can remember.'

'Well liked?'

'Does his job. Conscientious. Can't be bribed or threatened.'

Which put him in a minority in my experience.

'Then I have hopes that he'll come back with a name for our corpse,' I said.

'Let's hope so,' came the morose reply.

In the event, however, it was Reckitt who brought news that identified our dead man.

But another death was to intervene before that.

John

When I got back to Glanteifi, I didn't manage the quiet word I was hoping for with Mr Ormiston about what we could do for Matthew and Mair Thomas. As soon as I closed the door behind me, Wil-Sam came dashing over the black-and-white tiles of the hall towards me. 'Mr Davies!' He sounded agitated. 'Is Mr Probert-Lloyd with you?'

I hung my coat up and looked around. No sign of Lydia. 'No, he won't be back till later – tomorrow, perhaps.' Harry hadn't been able to get down to Cilgerran fast enough this morning, so I didn't suppose he'd be in a hurry to come back.

'There's somebody here to see him.' Wil-Sam's eyes were troubled, and he was shuffling from foot to foot as if he needed a piss.

'Who?'

'Owen Thomas. Matthew and Mair Nantyddwrgi's son.'

My stomach gave a lurch. What was he doing here? Whatever it was, he was likely to be angry about his parents being turned out of house and home.

'Have you told Mr Ormiston he's here?'

'He said to leave it to Mr Probert-Lloyd. Then he went home.'

Oh did he indeed? Harry didn't want to be here, Ormiston didn't want to take responsibility, which left me. I didn't want to face Owen Thomas either, but I couldn't have Wil-Sam thinking I'd dodge this the way Micah Ormiston had. 'Come on, then. Let's see if he'll talk to me.'

Wil-Sam walked ahead of me from the hall to the passageway that led to the back of the house. The kitchen was warm with steam and the smell of baking, but nobody seemed to be working.

Isabel Griffiths came to my side. 'Where's Harry?'

She must be worried. Mrs Griffiths never usually called him Harry in front of me or the servants.

'Still in Cilgerran,' I said. 'Trying to find out who the dead man is.' Why was I making excuses for him? He should be here. Should've let Caleb Richards do the leg work; the man was willing enough. 'Do we know what Owen Thomas wants?' I asked.

She shook her head. 'All he'll say is he wants to see the squire.'

I walked towards the back door, which was standing open. My riding boots sounded loud on the flagstones and every eye in the kitchen was watching me.

Outside, there was a man sitting on the steps to the washhouse. He stood up but didn't come over. 'Where's Mr Probert-Lloyd?' he called.

I was getting sick of hearing the same question. 'Not here. Not likely to be here till tomorrow. You'll have to deal with me.'

'And you are?'

'Under-steward.'

He glared at me. 'Your master refused to see me.'

I wasn't going to get into an argument about who was and wasn't my master, so I just eyeballed him back. He didn't seem sure what he should do now he knew Harry wasn't coming, so I nudged him along. 'You're Owen Thomas, I'm told. Matthew and Mair's son.'

'Yes.'

'What did you want to see Mr Probert-Lloyd about?'

That seemed to decide him, and he marched over. 'I wanted to tell him, face to face. Tell him what he'd done.'

I waited. There was no point asking what he meant. He was blaming Harry for his parents losing their farm.

'Yesterday Mr Ormiston gave my father and mother till the end of the month to leave their home. Harry Probert-Lloyd didn't have the decency to tell them himself, like his father would have. Except his father would never've thrown them out, he'd've found a way to help them, because he *cared* about his tenants. Harry Probert-Lloyd doesn't give a wet fart, does he? He's too busy running around being coroner. Instead of talking to tenants man to man, he sends his steward to do his dirty work for him.'

It felt as if his words were sticking into me, tearing me like thorns. 'Mr Thomas, Owen—'

'My father was *born* on that farm! And so was his father and his grandfather. *I* was born there, too.' He took a step towards me, within spitting distance. Punching distance. 'And today, my father *died* there. He got up at dawn, he milked the cows, then he hanged himself in the cowshed. My mother found him when she went out to see what was keeping him.'

Owen Thomas stood there panting. I could hear the kitchen filling up with shock behind me.

'That's what I came to tell the *squire*,' he spat. 'But I've got a message for the *coroner* as well. He doesn't need to bother himself to come to the farm, you can tell him – the police have been and they could see what'd happened clear enough.' He took a final step forward. 'But seeing as how he loves his inquests so much, *I* want an inquest. I want *everyone* to know who's responsible for my father's death. I want it to be clear as day that he died because Harry Probert-Lloyd was too busy being coroner to take any interest in the people who've made his family's fortune.'

Fred and Ianto had come to stand on either side of me, but they didn't need to lift a finger to Owen Thomas. He'd said his piece. Without another word, he walked away.

I watched him go, my heart pounding.

Too late. I'd left it too late to show proper concern for Mair and Matthew Thomas. I should've gone back over there yesterday and sorted something out for them, told them we'd find them somewhere. No. I should have done it before I left. Because I'd known what losing the farm would mean for them. I couldn't blame Mr Ormiston; he was from another class. He'd never known the fear of the workhouse. But I had.

I stood there. Two minutes ago, the idea of moving Matthew and Mair into a cottage somewhere had seemed like the right thing to do. Now it felt like a cosy children's story.

Isabel Griffiths took my arm and steered me to a tall stool by the table. I'd seen our cook, Mrs Elias, perching on it when she was working there sometimes. 'Sit down.'

I did as I was told and she put a cup of tea in front of me, along with a good chunk of sugar. I put it in the cup and stirred till I couldn't hear it clunking any more. Around me, nobody was saying anything. They were all waiting for me to speak. But what was there to say?

The sweetness of the tea made my teeth sing, but it seemed to help. At least my heart wasn't trying to batter its way out of my chest any more.

We'd've had to hold an inquest even if Owen Thomas hadn't come to demand one. By rights, the constable who'd gone out to Nantyddwrgi should have given formal notice of Matthew Thomas's death by now, and I was surprised that the constabulary'd let a chance to humiliate Harry slip past them. This inquest couldn't help but shine a bad light on things at Glanteifi, could it? Then another thought came to me – what if they were going to ask another coroner to hold the inquest? Owen Thomas wouldn't have held back from putting the blame on Harry, I was sure of that.

No. They wouldn't do that. It was clear that Harry wasn't directly involved. The constable was probably just following procedure, going back to check with his sergeant. The police had never asked us to hold an inquest, not once since Harry'd been elected in April, so I didn't know how quickly they'd get round to it.

Is this what it's going to be like now? Matthew Thomas had been talking about how the estate was run, but the words applied just as well to how things would be for me and Harry now that we'd have to wait for the police to inform us about sudden deaths.

I swallowed some more tea. No, I shouldn't be thinking about deaths that hadn't even happened yet. Matthew Thomas's death was the only one I should be thinking about.

The old man's face, yesterday in his kitchen, was clear in my mind. Tears running down his lined cheeks, his eyes staring at me and at a future where he could see no place for himself. Had he thought it'd be easier for his son to make room in his house for Mair if there was only her to take in?

I finished my tea down to the leaves and stood up. 'I'd better go and see to getting a jury called.' I was going to make sure this inquest was organised before Harry got back. Present him with it. Organised. Done.

'Perhaps you should wait until Miss Howell's back. Talk to her first,' Mrs Griffiths said.

'Why, where's she gone?'

'When Owen Thomas wouldn't tell us why he wanted to speak to Mr Probert-Lloyd, she was worried, so she got Twm to drive her over in the trap.'

'When you say over…?'

'To Nantyddwrgi.'

—

While I waited for Lydia, I wrote the standard 'the coroner requires your attendance at an inquest' letters. What a waste of time it was writing those notes every time. I wondered how much it would cost to have them printed pro forma. Still, it gave me something to do.

I'd nearly finished when I heard the front door open and Wil-Sam scurry into the hall. I'd left the office door open, and as she came past, Lydia looked in. 'Thank goodness you're back.'

'Just me. No Harry.'

'No. Sarge said you'd come back by yourself.' She looked at me steadily. 'Owen Thomas has told you about his father, then?'

'I'm writing jury calls now.' I hesitated. 'How's Mair?'

She looked me in the eye. 'If she survives the shock, it'll be a miracle. She collapsed when she found him. I think she might have had an apoplexy. She can't speak properly.' Lydia drew a deep breath. 'Are you going to ride back over and fetch Harry?'

'I should get these out. I'll ask Twm to go.'

'I could deliver them. They'll be less likely to want chapter and verse on the doorstep from me.'

And you're in no fit state. I could see her thinking it.

'He should've *been* here, Lydia.' It shouldn't've been me that had to hear the news.

Lydia came towards me. 'Let me finish those notices and take them out. Just give me the list of addresses.'

I knew I should let her – it was the sensible thing to do. But the truth was I couldn't face going to fetch Harry. I wasn't sure I'd be able to bite my tongue and not accuse him of causing Matthew Nantyddwrgi's death. 'No. I'll go to the jurors and send Twm over there.'

She sighed. 'If you're not going, I'll take the trap and fetch him.'

Did she think I'd argue, change my mind? If she did, she was disappointed.

'Tell him I've scheduled the inquest for eleven tomorrow, jurors to gather at Nantyddwrgi to see the body at half past nine. We know all the witnesses we need. Me. Mr Ormiston. Mair Thomas and her son. I'll go to the police station and make sure the constable Owen called out comes to give evidence.'

I knew she was staring at me. I didn't look up.

'We're supposed to be at Plas Blaengwyn tomorrow,' she said, 'eating lunch with the new Mr and Mrs Saunders-James.'

'I know. But Harry puts inquests ahead of Glanteifi. He can put this one ahead of hobnobbing with the *crachach*.'

Harry

A suicide on a Glanteifi farm; I could not recall such a thing ever happening before, and the knowledge that I had been responsible made me feel physically sick.

I sat down at Reckitt's cluttered table and swallowed hard. 'Are they sure?'

Lydia's silence was response enough.

'Yes,' I mumbled, 'of course they are. I'm sorry.'

What, after all, was the alternative? That somebody had strung the old farmer up not twenty-four hours after he had received news that had effectively ended the life he had always known? That he had somehow lynched himself by accident? In truth, the latter was scarcely less improbable than the former.

–

'I'm sorry that John had to bear the brunt of Owen Thomas's anger,' I said as we walked to the Pendre Inn, where Lydia had left the trap. 'It isn't his responsibility.'

At my side, Lydia's stride did not falter. 'You've made it his responsibility, Harry. That's what I was trying to tell you yesterday. John knew that ending those tenancies was wrong. He came home today to try and rescue the situation, to find somewhere for Matthew and his wife to live—'

'And I stayed here. You don't have to say it.'

'Harry, you *must* find a better way to carry out your duties as coroner without neglecting the estate.'

'Believe me, Lydia, John made that point very forcefully this morning, even before he'd heard about...' I did not know how to refer to Matthew Thomas's suicide, so I simply plunged onwards. 'There's one obvious solution. When John is occupied on estate business, you might assist me—'

'No. Absolutely not.'

Shocked by her vehemence, I turned to face her without thinking, and immediately she disappeared into the whirlpool. I looked away again. 'You're very certain, considering that you don't know what I was going to suggest.'

'Of course I know what you were going to suggest – that I act as coroner's assistant. But *think*, Harry! Think for half a second about how John would see that!'

Her presuming to know John's mind irked me. 'John's a reasonable man. He'd obviously see the need—'

'I'm not disputing his *reasonableness*.' Lydia did not raise her voice – she would not wish to attract attention – yet she left me in no doubt of the strength of her feeling on this matter. 'But you're at loggerheads at the moment, and any suggestion of my stepping into his shoes – whatever the reason – will make him feel he's being punished because he dared to challenge you.'

'That's nonsense! John would never think that; he knows how essential he is to me – how irreplaceable!'

'And yet still you took me on as your private secretary.' Plain words, spoken without heat, but freighted with feeling. 'I'm hardly overworked, Harry. If it wasn't for the time John spends studying for his exams, he and Isabel Griffiths could easily manage everything I've done since I've been here – you must know that. John certainly does. And he must be asking himself why, then, you employ me. Sometimes I find myself asking the same question.'

Her words recalled what she had said in the half-lit library. *On what basis would I live here if not as your private secretary?*

Was she thinking of leaving? Had her expectations of life at Glanteifi not been fulfilled?

What, I asked myself belatedly, had her expectations *been*?

That was the question I should have asked when she had arrived unannounced seven months before to enquire whether I would consider employing her. But starved of congenial company since my return from London, and delighted at the prospect of continuing our epistolary discussions in person, I had agreed immediately, never asking myself what the future might hold for Lydia were she to take such a step. With the mansion a mere five minutes' walk from the chapel where she had previously held the pulpit, there was a significant possibility that at some point her previous identity might be suspected, but I had not allowed myself to contemplate the almighty scandal that would erupt were that to happen.

In my desperation for companionship, I had been too selfish to give any thought to what Lydia's future might hold and wilfully blind to the effects the discovery of her previous identity might have on my local standing.

Unable to face riding home with her in the trap and continuing our acutely uncomfortable discussion, I took Sara and headed for Newcastle Emlyn.

I had to speak to Micah Ormiston.

John

When I'd finished delivering the jury notes, I went to talk to the police constable who'd been out to Nantyddwrgi to see Matthew Thomas's body. I'd get his testimony at the inquest, but I needed to make sure that he knew when to turn up.

'He's in the back,' the sergeant told me, 'writing his report.'

He didn't offer to fetch the constable, so I just walked past him into Newcastle Emlyn police station's tiny back room. Even though I was pretty sure he'd have heard me talking to the sergeant, I introduced myself and told him why I was there. 'Mind if I sit down?' I asked. If Harry and I were going to have to work with the police in future, it did no harm to be friendly.

He nodded and waved a hand at the only other chair. Fair play, he'd stood up when I came in, too. He wasn't any older than me from the look of him – younger, even. His face still had spots and I don't suppose he shaved every day any more than I did.

'You know the worst thing?' he said, after he'd told me how Owen Thomas'd turned up in a rage making accusations and demands. 'The rope. The one he hanged himself with.'

'What d'you mean?'

'It was all cobbled together. That's how bad things'd got out there. The poor dab didn't even have a length of rope long enough to hang himself properly.'

He had more to say, I could tell.

'He'd cut the handles off the milking buckets – three of them – and knotted them together with another old bit of rope from somewhere. Even then, it was only just long enough to go round the beam and his neck. He'd rubbed the top of his head raw on the beam where he...'

He stopped, didn't know how to say what he meant. But I knew. I'd never seen a man hanged – people were hardly ever hanged at Cardigan gaol and I wouldn't've gone anyway – but I knew what happened. The hanged man couldn't stop himself struggling, could he? If Matthew Thomas's head'd been close enough to the beam to rub on it, then the rope he'd knotted together for himself must've been pitifully short.

'He'd left the buckets outside the cowshed. Tidy, in a row, with a sack over the top of them to keep the birds and the cats off. And every one of them was without a handle because he'd cut them off to hang himself with.'

I swallowed. Matthew Thomas'd obviously been very determined to kill himself. If he hadn't had enough buckets, he'd probably have taken his trousers off and hanged himself with those. I was glad he hadn't. The picture of him hanging there in his flannel underwear would have stuck in people's minds. And he didn't deserve that.

But then he didn't deserve to die at all, did he? He might not've been a profitable farmer, or one who was keen to try new things, but he didn't deserve to have his farm taken away either. And I knew it wasn't only me that thought that. The news'd gone around the parish the way gorse goes up in a fire – all of a red-hot rush – and I'd got some disapproving looks from people as I went about delivering jury notes. One woman stood on her doorstep, her husband's jury call in her hand, and stared me in the face. 'Is there such a verdict as "died of a broken heart"? Because whatever was round his neck, that's what killed Matthew Nantyddwrgi.'

I don't think I'd ever been as worried about an inquest.

Harry

Yesterday's still air and river mists had blown away overnight, and the morning of Matthew Thomas's inquest greeted me with a blustery wind that swirled around the stableyard, sending the cats skittering away to wherever they waited out ill-tempered weather.

John was not at my side as I waited for my horse to be saddled up. He had left the breakfast table early to ride into town, ostensibly to oversee all the necessary arrangements, but he had never felt the need to form a vanguard before.

I knew he blamed me for Matthew Thomas's death. But I did not know how to penetrate the cold reserve his feelings wrapped around him and would have paid good money to have him shout at me instead. At least then I might have understood how he thought I should atone for my blind pursuit of solvency for Glanteifi. As it was, my current plan – to pay Ormiston off early and promote John to the rank of agent now, rather than in April as we had planned – might only make him despise me more if he, like Lydia, saw it as an attempt to foist my responsibilities onto him. Yet I was well aware that something must be done to reassure Glanteifi's tenants that things would be different from now on, and I had tried to speak to Ormiston on my return from Cilgerran yesterday.

I recalled now the hesitancy of the maid who had come to the door.

'Mr Ormiston's not at home, sir.'

So frustrated had I been at not being able to resolve matters there and then that I had almost challenged her, demanded to know whether her master was genuinely absent or simply not at home to me, but fortunately I had stopped myself in time. It was not fair to drag innocent servants into the mess I had made.

The chilly tension between John and myself on my return home had clearly been visible to Lydia, and after dinner she had done her best to relieve it, suggesting that she might read something amusing to cheer us up. But I had declined the Pickwick Club's papers in favour of making preparations for today's inquest.

–

I had not been foolish enough to expect a quiet inquest; I was only too well aware that news of Matthew Thomas's death would have spread in that almost preternatural way that bad news does. However, as John and I returned, with the jury, from the viewing of the body at Nantyddwrgi, we discovered that the taproom of the Lamb Inn was already crowded beyond any reasonable capacity.

'We're going to have to move proceedings outside,' I said, leaning towards John to make myself heard. 'Can you see about setting things up in the marketplace?'

John stepped up onto a chair. 'All right!' he shouted. 'We can't conduct an orderly inquest in here. We'll set up outside. Everybody who's here for the hearing, out, please.'

The crowd grumbled and grunted its way outside, pint mugs in hand, while Mrs James, the landlady, reminded everybody to come back when it was over. 'It's thirsty work watching an inquest, gentlemen!'

As John made arrangements for the jury's seating and coroner's table to be taken out into the square, I retreated from the crowds and found a quiet corner in which to wait until eleven, when I would begin the inquest.

I was not left alone, however. Several local gentlemen were kind enough to seek me out and offer their sympathies at my predicament; one even offered to deputise in order to spare me the need to preside at an inquest that could only hear testimony to my disadvantage. But though I was more grateful for his kindness than I could adequately express, I declined the offer. Given that I had no choice but to subject John and Ormiston to the ordeal of giving evidence, I felt that the least I could do was not to flinch from hearing it.

Finally John strode back in. 'It's time,' he announced, and we walked side by side in a parody of unity into the marketplace.

The fully sighted might imagine that in this particular case, my inability to see the inquest crowd was a blessing, but nothing could be further from the truth; the crowd that parted to allow us free passage to the coroner's table could not feasibly have been as judgemental of me as the mob of my imagination. And whatever blame or reproach those gathered in the market square might wish to fling at me, nothing could have tormented me more than my own conscience.

Mair Thomas being too unwell to appear, the farm labourer who had found her insensible on the ground in front of her husband's suspended body gave evidence as to the circumstances of his master's death; followed by the police constable, who testified as to the obvious cause, and the absence of any indication that Matthew Thomas had not been responsible for his own destruction.

Then I called Ormiston to come forward. Throughout a wretchedly wakeful night, I had been unable to prevent myself obsessively rehearsing the questions I would ask, and to begin with, his answers were almost exactly as my conscience-stricken mind had foreseen.

'Is it usual for tenants to be turned off their land for arrears, Mr Ormiston?'

'It would depend on the circumstances and the landowner concerned—'

'But at Glanteifi,' I interrupted. 'Is it usual at Glanteifi?'

He hesitated. 'No, sir.'

'So Mr and Mrs Thomas wouldn't have been expecting this blow?'

'They had been late in paying for two quarters and in arrears for another two.'

'But still, they probably wouldn't have anticipated losing their home?'

Again, he wavered before replying. 'I don't believe so, no.'

'Can you tell the jury why, in that case, they were given notice to quit their tenancy?'

Though Ormiston prevaricated – perhaps to defend his own reputation, perhaps to defend mine – he eventually admitted that he had been acting under instructions to maximise rental income this quarter and next.

Then, having done my best to lift the responsibility from his shoulders and lay it on my own, I called John to give evidence.

Unlike Ormiston, he made no attempt to obfuscate.

'Mr Davies, did you consider the notice to quit that was issued to Matthew Thomas to be justified?'

'No, I didn't.'

'And did you try to persuade Mr Ormiston against such a course of action?'

'Yes. Not just in this case, but in others. And we agreed on three quit notices instead of six.'

I did not ask him why Matthew Thomas was one of the three who had been evicted. 'There was no prospect of him paying' was not a judgement I wanted the spectators to associate with John, preferring to leave them with the knowledge that he did not consider the eviction justified. It would be to his advantage when he took over from Ormiston if Glanteifi's tenants saw him as their advocate rather than their enemy.

'And, given that an eviction notice *was* delivered, what do you feel should have been done to prevent such a tragedy?'

'Mr and Mrs Thomas had been tenants for many years. Mr Thomas had taken over the tenancy from his father. They were getting on in years and didn't have much prospect of finding work. So, in my opinion, they should have been found alternative accommodation on the estate.'

'Why was that not done?' I asked.

'I had intended to do so yesterday but coroner's business detained me elsewhere,' John said, his tone flat. 'But the time I got home, it was too late.'

There was no justification for a verdict other than suicide, but I took what steps I could to comfort the family and ensure that Matthew Thomas would receive a proper funeral. Criminal suicides might no longer be buried beneath crossroads with a stake through their heart, but a burial at night, without rites, would only stoke resentment and anger against the estate.

In the library after dinner the previous evening, I had asked John to fetch Sewell's *Treatise on the Law of Coroner*, and to read out the section on types of insanity.

'*Nostalgia*,' he had read when I told him what I wanted, '*is a form of melancholy originating in despair, from being separated from one's native country.*'

Welsh has its own word for the phenomenon: *hiraeth*. But *hiraeth* is not simply caused by being exiled from a *nation*, rather by a sundering of a more intimate kind from the terrain, customs and people of one's birth. Given that my instructions to Ormiston had effectively enforced such a separation in the case of Matthew Thomas, it seemed only right to inform the jury of this particular form of insanity before they withdrew to deliberate. They had received the information gratefully, and their subsequent verdict, swiftly arrived at, was that Matthew Thomas had taken his own life *while not of sound mind, memory or understanding as a result of the acute nostalgia occasioned by his eviction from the only home he had ever known.*

Having confirmed the jury's verdict in writing, instead of dismissing the now voluble spectators I rose from my seat, quit the security of the coroner's table and stood in front of the crowd.

The hubbub that had broken out at the apparent end of proceedings died away, and those who had been in the process of gathering themselves and their families to depart fell still. The buffeting wind stirred the air, laden with dust from streets long deprived of rain.

I swept what remained of my gaze from one side of the crowd to the other, a blur of unidentifiable faces slipping past my peripheral vision.

A hush fell, every eye fixed on me, waiting.

My mouth was as dry as chalk. 'You've heard the verdict of the jury,' I said, my voice as confident as I could make it. 'When he was not in his right mind, Matthew Thomas hanged himself. But though he took his own life, it is I who am responsible for his death.'

If they had been quiet before, they were pin-drop silent now, and the air seemed suddenly thick in my throat, as if the words I had to speak would choke me.

'If his death had happened on another estate, I would have taken the squire who gave Matthew Thomas notice to task for not having sufficient care of his tenants. For not having provided for Matthew and Mair's welfare when they had been deprived of their home. And I can promise you, I condemn myself every bit as much as I would have condemned another man. *Every bit.*'

My voice broke on those last words and a small ripple of something I could not name went through the crowd.

I dry-swallowed and forced myself to make the promise I had determined on sometime during the darkest hours of the night. 'I should have had more care of Glanteifi's people. And in future, I will.'

Then, my piece said and my humiliation complete, I turned away and retreated behind the table.

But if I had hoped that the spectators would be content to discuss my self-abasement amongst themselves and leave me to lick my wounds in peace, I was to be disappointed.

'Ah, the gentlemen of the press,' John said, alerting me to the identity of the approaching figures. 'Good afternoon, Mr Pritchard, Mr Foster.'

Journalists attended almost every inquest I conducted, and these two were familiar to me. The taller and slimmer of the two was Foster, from the *Carmarthen Journal*; his shorter, portlier companion wrote for *The Welshman*. Unlike the *Journal*, which was a stridently Tory organ, Pritchard's newspaper represented the Radical view and could generally be relied upon to support my stance as coroner. However, I dreaded his commentary on this particular inquest.

'Can you confirm the rumour that you'll be paying for Matthew Thomas's funeral?' Foster asked.

I stood up straight and pointed my blind gaze in the direction of his face. 'I can.'

'And do you think that's sufficient reparation?' Pritchard asked.

'No. You heard me say how I will make reparation. By ensuring that I do better by Glanteifi's tenants in future.'

'Words, words, words,' Pritchard scoffed. 'Will you make good on them, that's the question.'

His tone was goading, and everything in me wanted to pivot on my heel and punch him on the nose, not because he was questioning my integrity, but because his words were a horrible echo of my own fears.

John packed up the writing box and put it in the saddlebag on the table in front of him. 'Right, we'd better be off,' he said affably. 'What's next for you gentlemen? Lunch in the Emlyn Arms?'

'No such luck,' Foster said. 'We're off to Llandyfriog now. Got a tip-off this morning that there's been some damage to this factory that's being built there.'

'Jem Harborne's wool mill?' There was an odd eagerness in John's tone that caught my ear.

'That's it,' Pritchard said. 'D'you know him?'

'We're acquainted. I met him in London. At the Great Exhibition.'

'You should come with us then. He'd probably appreciate a friendly face.'

'I don't think so. Not today.'

Not in the aftermath of this humiliating inquest was what he meant. But perhaps he could persuade them to be less condemnatory of me if he went with them, smoothed their path with this

219

Harborne. 'No – you go, John. It would do you good to be away from Glanteifi for an hour or so. Take your mind off things.'

Riding home alone, I could at least endure my wretchedness in peace.

John

If I'm honest, one of the reasons I'd called the inquest at such short notice was to get it done before the press could hear about it. It was my bad luck that Foster and Pritchard'd happened to be in the area the day before and heard what had happened at Nantyddwrgi.

Their newspapers were on opposite sides politically speaking, but they weren't any keener to waste money than the rest of us, so the pair of them'd come to Newcastle Emlyn together. They offered me a ride out to the factory in their carriage, but I wasn't in the mood for conversation after the inquest, so I said I'd catch them up and went to find the boy who was looking after Seren.

He was letting her graze on the grass behind the church, and as well as her reins, he handed me a letter. 'The Glanteifi steward gave me this for you.'

I took the folded page. On one side it was addressed to H. Probert-Lloyd Esq., and on the other there was an instruction for me.

> John, please be so good as to read this to Mr Probert-Lloyd for me.

I gave the boy his penny and watched him skip away before I unfolded the letter.

> Dear Mr Probert-Lloyd,
> It is with great sorrow that I must inform you that I no longer feel able to act as steward to the Glanteifi estate. Recent sad events have persuaded me that I must acquiesce

to my daughter's long-held desire that I go and live with her
and her family in Aberaeron. Mr Davies has an acute mind
and a knowledge of your tenants' ways that will stand him
in excellent stead as my successor.

With every good wish for the future, I remain,
Your humble servant,
Micah Ormiston

My thoughts were all over the place on the way to Llandyfriog. The Teifi flowed very close to the road along one stretch, and usually, if you listened hard enough over the sound of your horse's hoofbeats, you could hear it rippling and swirling around rocks and tree roots in the bank. That day, I didn't hear a thing. All I could think about was Mr Ormiston's letter.

I didn't know whether I was thrilled to bits or scared stiff. A year ago, I hadn't even met Harry, and now here I was about to be steward to the Glanteifi estate and, as long as I passed the exam, a qualified solicitor.

Unbelievable. Literally unbelievable. If you'd told me the previous September that in ten months' time I'd be living in the mansion, calling the squire Harry and working with him, I'd have laughed in your face.

And now I was going to be in charge of the whole estate. The old-fashioned title could retire with Mr Ormiston. I'd be Glanteifi's agent.

For months, I'd been looking forward to next April, when I'd been supposed to take over, but now that the moment had come early, I was terrified. Because it'd be up to me now, wouldn't it? Everything. Making sure the estate didn't go bankrupt. Keeping the tenants happy. Making sure they could pay their rents. Stopping a tragedy like Matthew Thomas happening again.

Could I do it?

I honestly didn't know.

Since leaving town, I'd been trotting along not really taking any notice of where we were going, but then, up ahead, I saw the pressmen's carriage turn off the turnpike and up a little road on the side of the hill. I kicked Seren into a canter to follow them.

The road zigzagged up the hillside. Ahead of me the springs of the pressmen's open-topped carriage were working hard over the ruts and potholes. I could hear the sound of rushing water away to my right, and through the trees I got glimpses of a fast-flowing little stream. I peered down at it through the greenery. Barely more than a running jump wide. Was that big enough to power a mill?

'Is Mr Harborne expecting you?' I called to the newspapermen.

Pritchard, who was sitting facing me, grinned. 'Not unless he's clairvoyant. Bound to be there, though, isn't he – surveying the damage?'

The word *clairvoyant* called Cadwgan Gwynne to my mind, but I wasn't going to start thinking about him, nor Lizzie Rees, thank you very much. Harry rushing off to investigate her death when he shouldn't've done had caused enough trouble without me wasting time thinking about it.

Just then, I caught sight of something through the trees on the other side of the little stream. I couldn't see it very clearly, but there was definitely building work in progress.

Another hundred yards further on, the road levelled out and there was a newly built bridge over the stream into the fields on the other bank. The timber of the uprights hadn't weathered yet, but you could see there'd been a lot of toing and froing over the bridge, because the planks of the bed were filthy from hooves and feet and wheels.

The carriage driver pulled his horses up and sat there frowning, as if he had doubts about the bridge. It was quite long, because it didn't just go across the stream – it carried on over the slope of the bank on the other side to where the field levelled out.

I looked around at what I suppose Harborne'd call the factory site. To my right, back down below us, the building work I'd seen turned out to be a tall timber-framed building. There were cart tracks all the way down to it and piles of timber dotted around the place. Twenty yards or so to my left, there was an earth bank, and beyond that, a pond.

At least, there should've been a pond. You could see that water'd gathered in the basin behind the bank because it was a mess of mud and puddles, and the yellowish grass around the edges looked as if it'd been combed flat. The water must've rushed out at a hell of a rate to make the grass like that – the way the water drains into a mill race when you open the sluice gate.

And that was exactly what'd happened. Only instead of just opening the sluice gate, somebody'd smashed the earth bank where it'd been built across the stream.

It didn't seem much in the way of damage to me. The main structure of the dam was still intact, and the section directly over the stream would be easy to rebuild – that and the gate. Two men could've easily done it in a morning.

'You haven't come all the way just to see this, have you?' I asked.

The journalists looked around at me, but it was the carriage driver who answered. 'Main damage is down the way.' He waved in the direction of the building.

Pritchard and Foster climbed down and the three of us went over the bridge, me leading Seren. The carriage driver didn't have much choice but to follow us – he was blocking the road and there was nowhere else to turn around.

Once we were on the other side, I got a good look at Harborne's factory. I was surprised that he wasn't building in stone. But then, when I thought about it, I realised that it was quicker to build in timber, and you could have much bigger windows in a wooden building than in a stone-built one. Because Harborne was going to need daylight for his looms, wasn't he? There was no gas light here like there was in Newtown and Leeds.

Mind, quick to build they might be, but it stood to reason that wooden-framed buildings'd be quick to knock down as well. And somebody'd put a good bit of effort into knocking this one down. There were planks and poles scattered all around the site, and window frames hung half in, half out of the walls, smashed out of place by a well-aimed sledgehammer. When we got right up to the building, I could see that a lot of what was scattered about on the ground wasn't building material at all. It was bamboo scaffolding poles, some of them roped together to make walkways.

At first I thought there was nobody about; then a stocky older man appeared from behind a pile of timber. The look on his face said, *Who the hell are you and what's your business here?* But we were too well dressed for that kind of greeting.

'Good day to you.' When he opened his lips, I could see that somebody'd knocked out one of his front teeth for him.

We introduced ourselves and Pritchard said they were hoping to speak to Mr Harborne.

'Gone for the police,' the man said. His voice lisped a bit through the gap in his teeth, which made him sound a lot less intimidating than he looked.

'Any idea when he'll be back?' Foster asked. He must've been glad the man spoke English. Foster couldn't speak Welsh, and it drove him mad that Harry always held his inquests in Welsh and he had to find a translator.

'He's been gone a while. Be back soon, prob'ly.'

If he'd gone into town for a constable, I wondered if he had got caught up in the crowds at the marketplace. Had he stopped to watch the inquest? I hadn't seen him, but then I'd tried to keep my eyes away from the spectators.

Pritchard kicked a pole to one side and stepped over a long timber with notches cut into it. It looked as if whoever'd wrecked the building had smashed as much as they could reach from the walkways, then pulled the whole scaffolding structure down. I could see that it was going to set work back a bit and send costs up, but I didn't think it'd stop a man like Jem Harborne.

The foreman – if that was what he was – followed us as we stepped up into the two-storey skeleton of the building. The clean smell of freshly cut timber was strong, and I breathed it in as

I looked around. From inside, you could see that somebody'd intended to do a lot more damage. Every supporting timber had a bundle of pitch-soaked rags nailed to it at about head height. Whoever'd been here had intended to burn the place down.

I thought of the family who'd been promised this parcel of land. Was it them who'd been responsible? If it was, I couldn't honestly say I blamed them.

'Looks like they were interrupted,' Foster said, flicking a finger at a clump of black-clotted rags.

'Yes, me and the boys put a stop to it,' the foreman said.

'The boys?' I asked.

'The carpenters and labourers. We're on site all the time.' He jerked his head towards a wooden building further down the slope that I could see through the gaps in the walls. 'Came up as soon as we heard the banging, but they had a couple of dogs, so there was only so much we could do. Saw them off in the end, mind.'

'How many were there?' I asked.

'Four or five,' he said.

'Do you know who they were?'

He spat on the ground and wiped his mouth with the back of his hand. 'Didn't say a word, so I don't know. And I didn't know 'em 'cos I'm not from here, see?'

That explained why he didn't look familiar to me.

'Mr Harborne brought me and the boys in from home. We've been making the frame up for months – only waiting to know where to bring it, we were.'

'Where's home?' I asked.

'Llandysul I'm from. Mr Harborne wanted the job done quick, so I had to find men from where I could. Mostly from Llandysul, but a couple are from Llanybydder and Pencader.'

I nodded. Not local, but not from far away. Even Llanybydder wasn't more than half a day's walk. Well worth it if there was decent work to be had, especially if you were given lodgings on site.

The foreman stood in the empty doorway, watching me and the newspapermen walk around his sledgehammered building. I stepped over a plank, minding my footing so I didn't step on a nail or a peg, and noticed something on the wooden floorboards – a brownish stain about six inches in diameter.

Dried blood.

The foreman saw me looking at it.

'That's where one of my lads fell. Jaco,' he told me, speaking in Welsh as the newspapermen were at the other end of the building scribbling notes.

'What did they hit him with?' I asked.

'Plank. Went down like a sack off a wagon. Nasty cut right here.' He pointed to his own head, just behind his right eyebrow. 'Thought he was dead at first because we couldn't rouse him. That was when they ran off. Hadn't come to do murder, had they?'

'How is he now?'

The foreman shook his head. 'Still not come round. We had the doctor out to him and he said there was nothing he could do. We'll just have to wait and see if he wakes up. One of the boys has gone up to Llandysul to tell his family. They'll probably bring a cart to fetch him home. Live or die, he'll be with his own.'

Just then, I heard horses coming up the road on the other side of the stream. In less than a minute, Jem Harborne was walking down the slope towards us with a police constable.

The wool man looked different from how I remembered him. His hair was untidy from his ride to town and there was no silky angola suit for him today – he looked much more like a practical man in brown wool.

He sent the police constable off to talk to the foreman, then turned to me and the newspapermen. 'Jeremiah Harborne at your service.' He looked at me and I could see he recognised me but couldn't think where from.

'The Great Exhibition,' I said. 'We went to Soyer's Symposium together.'

He snapped his fingers and pointed at me. 'John Davies! How the devil are you, sir?' He thrust his hand out to me as if we were old friends.

'This'll put your schedule back,' I said, shaking his hand and nodding at the mill.

He waved the hand I'd just let go as if he was flicking off a fly. 'Minor setback. Just need to make sure it doesn't happen again. But I'm pretty sure I know who's behind it. A spell of hard labour should sort him out.'

I realised that Harborne didn't care what people thought of his factory. People could hate him for what he was doing here, but as long as he was making money, it made no difference to him.

After what'd happened to Matthew Thomas, I had a feeling that was what people might think Harry was like too. He was going to have to work damned hard to prove them wrong. Or rather, now that Mr Ormiston'd gone, *I* was going to have to work damned hard.

'You don't feel any sympathy for him – the man who'd been promised the land?' I asked. I knew it was Matthew Thomas's inquest that was making me angry, as much as Harborne's attitude, but I couldn't help it.

The newspapermen's pencils started working and Jem Harborne frowned. 'You think this is justified?'

'Not justified, no. But understandable. You've got to admit, he's got good reason to feel hard done by.'

Harborne shook his head, eyes still on me. 'I don't agree. But anyway, as it happens, I don't think he's the man responsible. A windbag weaver's been making a lot of noise. Goes round saying that factories have no place in the Teifi Valley and that folk here want honest cloth made by people they know.'

People like Mic Rees in his one-man weaving shed. There'd be no weavers like him soon if Harborne had his way. I felt sick at the thought. By giving Harborne's card to Mr Gelyot, I'd put myself on the side of machines instead of men, and that thought churned away in my gut along with guilt over Matthew Thomas's death.

Harborne was watching me. I don't know what he saw, but he changed the subject pretty sharpish. 'You had a young lad with you in London,' he said. 'Struck me as a proper bright spark.'

I swallowed. *Lleu*. This was my chance to speak up for him and his dreams. 'Daniel Williams. Yes, you made an impression on him too. Matter of fact, he wanted me to ask you if you'd take him on as your apprentice.'

'*My* apprentice? What as?'

'An engineer.'

'I'm not an engineer. I'm a weaver – or was. And not a very good one, as it happens. Now, I'm a businessman. Still, my engineer'll be here by the end of the week – he might take the boy on.'

He took out his pocket watch and flipped it open. 'Right, if I go now, I might just be in time to join the tail end of the Saunders-Jameses' luncheon.'

We fell into step as we walked back up to the bridge. 'D'you know Mr Saunders-James well?' I asked.

'Only since I've been looking for land. Lucky to find him. He's very interested in the factory. I'd never have got so far so quickly without him.'

'Invested, has he?'

'A little. But the main thing is, he's offered to stand surety for me in some loans. Most of the landowners I approached laughed at the idea of a factory here. But Anthony's not like other squires.'

'No. Made his money from guano, I heard.'

'Yes. Started off importing it, now he's digging the stuff up in East Anglia.' He looked sidelong at me. 'I know your Harry Probert-Lloyd's home-grown, so to speak, but I wonder whether he might be cut from the same cloth. Forward-thinking, you know. I'd very much like to meet him.'

Shame for him that Harry'd had to send his apologies for the Saunders-Jameses' luncheon party.

'I'm sure you will eventually,' I said.

'Oh, I'll make sure of it,' Jem Harborne said. 'Don't you worry.'

Harry

After John had left in pursuit of the journalists, I went to the Emlyn Arms hotel to pick up anything that had come for us on the mail coach.

'Only a hand-delivered letter for you today, Mr Probert-Lloyd,' the servant in charge said. 'No big parcels this time.'

I don't know if he made the same remark to Twm, who normally came for the mail, or whether he simply could not think of anything else to say to me, but he had repeated the same weak quip every time I had fetched the mail since Gus Gelyot's damned shower bath had arrived a few weeks ago. The carrier had stopped in Newcastle Emlyn to ask directions to Glanteifi and seemed to have informed the town's entire population about the wonder he was carrying to us.

I smiled, thanked the post clerk, and stowed the letter in my pocket as if it was of little consequence, but in truth, as I rode over the bridge and up Adpar hill, I could think of nothing else. Had I still had my sight, I would have unfolded it as soon as I had left the hotel and read it immediately. As it was, I had not the slightest indication even of who it might be from, though the good-quality paper suggested that it was from somebody of significance. I profoundly hoped it was not another billet-doux from the county magistrates.

Of all the trials and inconveniences my blindness caused, not being able to read was, I think, the most frustrating. There was simply no circumventing it.

John had been excited by the so-called 'tactile ink' that had been exhibited at the Crystal Palace, but I doubted my ability to make much sense of fractionally raised writing. At the very least, it would be painfully slow, as reading by magnifying glass had become during the last stages of my sight's deterioration. Struggling to read one word at a time, finally reduced to guessing at each by its blurred shape, I had usually forgotten how a sentence had begun by the time I reached its end. The notion of something even more painstaking was unappealing, however much John and Lydia thought it might revolutionise my life.

But even my frustrated curiosity as to the provenance of this letter could not long blot out the vivid, painful moments from the inquest that kept obtruding themselves upon my thoughts, however much I might try to turn them aside. Particularly difficult to displace was the comment Owen Thomas had made after describing how he had found his father hanging from the beam of one of the cowsheds, the milking stool he had stepped off kicked aside. 'His toes were only six inches off the floor,' he had said. 'It didn't seem far enough to have killed him.'

–

In the stableyard at Glanteifi, I slid off Sara's back, handed the reins to Twm and went inside without a word. God alone knows what he and the other grooms made of such incivility, but I did not feel equal to conversation.

As I stepped into the hall, I was greeted by Isabel Griffiths. Had somebody nipped through from the stableyard to the kitchen to tell her I was back?

'Dr Reckitt's here,' she said. 'Miss Howell's entertaining him in the library.'

The letter in my pocket – was it from Reckitt? Was he here to talk about something he already expected me to be aware of? I passed the folded sheet to Mrs Griffiths. 'Would you see who this is from, please?'

She took her pince-nez from an invisible pocket and unfolded the letter. 'It's from Mr Anthony Saunders-James. Regretting that you can't attend his lunch today and asking if you and Miss Howell would join him on Saturday instead, as there's somebody he would like you to meet.'

It was gratifying that Saunders-James was so keen to meet me but my response would have to wait; I could not think of luncheons at the moment, not while I had yet to set a date for an inquest on the unidentified man in Cilgerran. I thanked Mrs Griffiths and made my way to the library.

'Ah, finally!' Reckitt rose to his feet as I walked in. 'I have news.'

'Good day, Reckitt. I trust you're well?' I took my seat and handed Saunders-James's letter to Lydia.

He brushed my pleasantry aside. 'Yes, very well, thank you. As I say, I have news. I would have delivered it yesterday, but on my way home from the funeral in Eglwyswrw, I was asked to oversee a difficult birth. I was there all night. But I believe I may have identified our corpse.'

'Really? Who is he?'

'I said "may", Probert-Lloyd.' Reckitt sat down again. 'At Lizzie Rees's funeral, I seemed to hear nothing but muttering about somebody who had failed to attend. People were considerably more interested in discussing why he wasn't there than they were in speaking well of the deceased.'

'And the "he" they were referring to?' I asked.

'A Nathaniel Stockton – a farm worker from somewhere near Felindre Farchog.'

Nathaniel Stockton. The incomer who had been sweet on Lizzie Rees. Her sisters had told John that he had found a job in the area so as to be near Lizzie after they had met while she was working in south Pembrokeshire. 'Did you get a description of him?' I asked.

'I did. And it fits him in every particular.'

'Had he been missed before the funeral?'

'That wasn't clear. Nobody else from the farm he worked on was there – they weren't neighbours or fellow parishioners. But I'm told that this young man walked over to Eglwyswrw every

Sunday to attend church so that he could see Lizzie Rees. And that he was there last Sunday, presumably not having heard that she was dead.'

'What's the name of the farm where he works? Or worked.'

'Gilfachwen. And I have directions.'

John

On Thursday morning, we were back in Cilgerran bright and early to meet Caleb Richards and a farm servant from Gilfachwen who was going to tell us whether the body in the Pendre's back room was Nathaniel Stockton.

In theory, that was all we needed to hold an inquest. A name and the body to put before a jury. But that'd never been enough for Harry before, and it wasn't going to be enough this time.

When we got to the Pendre, it seemed a lot longer than a couple of days since we'd been there. What with Matthew Thomas's death and inquest and now Mr Ormiston going, I felt as if I'd aged a year in less than half a week.

Harry and I hadn't talked much about the resignation letter. I'd read it to him and Lydia when I got back to Glanteifi from the wool factory, but we'd agreed to talk about it all when we'd finished with this inquest. 'But you need to know,' Harry'd told me, 'that I'd very much *like* you to take over from Mr Ormiston. We just need to decide how exactly things are going to be run from now on.'

I knew how I wanted things to be run, but I wasn't sure Harry would agree. Still, best not to think about that for now.

When we walked into the Pendre's taproom, I had a surprise. Caleb Richards and our witness weren't there yet, but Benton Reckitt was. I'd never seen him up before nine o'clock in the morning before, unless there was a dead body to be looked at.

We sat down at the table with him. 'If this does prove to be Nathaniel Stockton,' Harry said, 'I assume we all agree that his death must be related to Lizzie Rees's? It surely can't be a coincidence that a young man who was by all accounts courting her turns up murdered two days after her death?'

'Circumstantial,' Reckitt said, 'but definitely worth bearing in mind. Incidentally, if this is the young man we suspect it is, the gossip at Lizzie Rees's funeral suggests he wasn't well liked.'

'Not surprising,' I said. 'A foreigner courting a local girl's never going to win friends, is he?'

'There seemed to be more to it than petty jealousy.'

I stared at him. *Petty* jealousy? Hadn't he stitched up enough men after fights over women to know there was nothing petty about it? Jealousy in one form or another caused more violence than anything else, in my experience.

'What kind of comments did you hear, Reckitt?' Harry asked.

'People seemed to feel he thought a lot of himself. That he considered himself better than the locals.'

'He thought himself better than them?' Harry asked.

'That sort of thing, yes.'

'But that actual phrase?'

Reckitt blinked. I could almost see the effort as he tried to remember.

'The thing is,' Harry said, 'I heard something similar said about Lizzie Rees. The little maid at Dolbannon told me that's what the older servants said about her.'

It didn't seem like much to me, but Harry wanted the two deaths to be related, didn't he? Because then he could go back and question Mic Rees again.

He hated being lied to, Harry, and he knew Mic'd lied to him.

–

Before long, Caleb Richards arrived with our witness, who he introduced as Evan Evans.

'But they call me Cadi,' Evans said. I could see why. It'd be short for *cadno* – fox. He had that colour hair.

'Been working at Gilfachwen long?' I asked as we trooped through to the back room.

'Longer'n anybody else on the place. Must be nearly ten years now. Since I was a *gwas bach*.'

If he'd been there since he was a boy, I could see why he'd been the one to come and talk to us. Over the years, he'd have seen enough servants come and go to know a bit about the men who hired themselves out at the fairs. He'd be able to tell us the kind of man Nattie Stockton'd been.

Caleb Richards uncovered the body and Cadi leaned forward to peer at the battered, blood-filled face before stepping back as quickly as he could from the body's putrefying stench. 'Yes, that's Nattie, poor dab. Caleb says he was pulled out of the river?'

Harry nodded. 'Do you have any idea why he might have been in Cilgerran? Did he know anybody here?'

'If he did, he never said. Far as I remember, he never mentioned Cilgerran at all.'

We went back into the taproom and Cadi answered Harry's questions while we drank the beer the landlord'd brought for us.

'Nattie was only here because of Lizzie Rees,' he told us. 'He didn't need to look for work. His family's got their own farm – and not a tenancy, either – down in the south. Place called St Florence. Never heard of it before Nattie came. Don't have much to do with people down there, do we?'

We all agreed. The Teifi Valley might only be thirty miles or so from the south coast of Pembrokeshire, but that was a two-day walk, and unless there was a good reason to go there – like Lizzie Rees going for harvest work – it might as well be on the other side of England.

'He was a good boy, though,' Cadi went on, picking at some dried wax on the table. 'Never a shirker, never tried to come the boss, if you know what I mean. He taught us to swear in English and we taught him some Welsh. One or two of the boys don't speak much English – only "good day" and "if you please", you know.'

I did know – those were the bits of English you needed to know if you didn't want to get into trouble for being disrespectful.

236

'And how did his courting Lizzie go down with the other servants at Gilfachwen?' Harry asked.

Cadi shrugged. 'Didn't matter to us. Not one of our girls, was she? Out of our parish, Eglwyswrw. But the boys over there didn't like it at all.'

'Oh?' Harry raised an eyebrow and looked somewhere past Cadi's left ear. I could understand him wanting to try and look people in the eye, but when he missed, it made him look more blind than if he hadn't bothered.

'Tried to warn him off, didn't they?' Cadi said. 'One Sunday, after the end of hay, some lads grabbed him on his way home from church and gave him a proper hiding. Told him he'd better stop chasing Lizzie or there'd be worse to follow, type of thing.'

'Was that before or after she gave him the *coron fedw*?' Harry asked.

Cadi looked up from his pint. 'You know about that, do you?' He shook his head, eyes focused on the past. 'Came back from a church outing one Sunday with a grin all over his face and the crown on his head.' He grunted at the memory. 'The beating came after that. *Because* of it, I suppose. Boys in Eglwyswrw getting worried things were serious between them.'

'Do you know the names of any of the men who attacked him?' Harry asked.

Cadi wiped his mouth with his knuckles. 'Nattie only knew Eglwyswrw people by name if they went to the church. Knew them by sight, mind. Said he'd seen them about when he walked home from church.'

'Did it work – the beating?' I asked. 'Did Nattie stop seeing Lizzie?'

'Didn't have to. She went away just after that, down south for the harvest.'

'When did you hear that Lizzie Rees had died?' Harry asked.

Cadi started picking at the wax again. 'On Sunday at chapel. We thought that was why Nattie hadn't come back from church – that he'd gone down to Rhosdywarch to see her family.'

'And when he didn't come back by evening?'

Cadi shrugged. 'Thought he might've just gone back to St Florence.'

'What,' I said, 'and left all his things behind?'

'Didn't have much. Only his working clothes and boots. Oh, and a writing box. But Mistir kept that in the parlour for him. Used to go in the house once a week and write home, he did. Regular as clockwork.'

'You didn't think he'd come back for that?'

Another shrug. 'Didn't really think about it at all till now.'

'Did you think he might've run away because he'd had something to do with Lizzie's death?'

Cadi looked me in the eye and shook his head, definite. 'He couldn't have. He hadn't seen her for weeks.'

Hold on, hadn't Mic Rees said he'd been there the day she died?

I turned to Harry. 'Didn't you tell me Mic Rees said that Nattie'd dropped some wool off for Lizzie to spin on Saturday?' I asked. 'A few hours before she died?'

He frowned. 'That's what I remember, yes. Though I wasn't taking notes, obviously.'

Cadi shook his head. 'No. Whoever took wool to Rhosdywarch, it wasn't Nattie – wasn't any of us, come to that. Gilfachwen's got people closer to home to do our spinning. And Nattie never left the farm last Saturday. I was with him every minute until he went off to church on Sunday.'

'You slept in the same loft?' I asked.

'Yes. The two of us and another outdoor servant. If Nattie'd gone anywhere, we'd've known about it.'

Harry looked as if he was staring at the battered, beer-stained table, which meant he was really looking at Cadi over the top of his blind patch. 'Well somebody brought wool,' he said, 'because Mic Rees said Lizzie'd been spinning on the evening before she died, and according to Esther Rees, there'd been no wool to spin when she left for Ffynone. It had to've come from somewhere.'

'So Mic Rees lied about who brought it,' I said.

He was looking troubled. 'Or maybe I've misremembered.' That meant he thought he had. 'I don't have quite your recall for conversations, John, but I'm not absolutely sure Mic ever mentioned Nathaniel's name.

Damn. This wouldn't've happened if I'd been there. It was my job to nail details right down, because I was the one who had to write the inquest report, so I kept asking questions until I knew exactly what a witness was saying and what they weren't. But Harry wasn't so meticulous – he was prone to going off down other rabbit holes if they appeared, then forgetting to go back to where he'd been.

And things got missed like that.

'So was there anybody else trying to court Lizzie?' I asked.

Cadi made a face that stood in for a shrug. 'From what Nattie said, half the boys in Eglwyswrw were after her. But I don't know if any of them went any further than looking. Don't go to church over there, do I, so I don't know what was going on.'

Church and chapel. The two main places for young people to meet. What with Sunday school and Bible studies and hymn-singing practice and a second service in the evening, you could spend most of your Sunday with the same people if you wanted to. And you'd definitely want to if you were courting a girl – it'd be the only chance you had to see her.

If there'd been another man trying to court Lizzie, he had to be our main suspect, didn't he? We were going to have to go and speak to Mic Rees again.

Harry turned to Caleb Richards. 'Did you ask the farmer at Gilfachwen where I might contact Stockton's family?'

The *plwyfwas* reeled off an address, and I remembered my father giving Mr Price the name of our holding when I was hired out, aged eleven. *In case of anything*, as Price had said.

'Thank you. I'll write to his parents today. That'll give them time to get here if I hold the inquest on Monday. Meanwhile, I think we'll go and pay Dr Cadwgan Gwynne another visit.'

Harry

As we dismounted outside Gwynne's house, before I could ask John to ring the bell, the doctor appeared around the side of the house. With his long limbs and flowing hair, he was a sufficiently unusual-looking man that even I could recognise him.

'Mr Probert-Lloyd, Mr Davies! Is all well?'

'As far as John and I are concerned, perfectly, thank you. Might we come in for a few moments?'

Once the horses had been led off and the maid instructed as to refreshments, we found ourselves invited once more into Gwynne's house. But not this time to his consulting room.

'We might be more comfortable in the drawing room,' he said, opening the door to a room at the front of the house. As we walked in, I had the impression not of a conventional drawing room but of an orangery. There were plants everywhere: on tiered stands and windowsills, in huge pots on the floor and on tiny tables set here and there about the room. Some were in flower, some had huge striped leaves, others – as far as I could tell – were feathery and fern-like. I had assumed that the plants in Gwynne's consulting room were evidence that he made up his own salves and tinctures, but it seemed that plants were not simply of professional interest to him; if this room was any guide, they were his passion.

The room had been adapted in order to admit sufficient light for vegetation to flourish; as well as a large east-facing window at the house's gable end, French windows had been installed on the south side. And just as in the consulting room, what I had initially taken to be paintings on every wall proved, as I moved past them, to be mirrors endlessly reflecting greenery back and forth.

Gwynne clearly saw my surprise. 'Being surrounded by plants is good for the soul.'

The soul? I was unaccustomed to that kind of comment from a medical man.

At Gwynne's invitation, I sat on a small sofa while John took the high-backed chair that stood at right angles to it.

'This chair is far more comfortable, Mr Davies,' Gwynne said, inviting him to sit opposite me. But I knew John would decline; he had seated himself where he would be most visible to me.

Instead, Gwynne himself sat in the wingback chair. 'How may I help you, gentlemen?'

'The body of a young man called Nathaniel Stockton has been recovered from the river in Cilgerran,' I told him.

'Oh no! The poor boy!'

'You knew him?'

Gwynne cleared his throat. 'I believe we discussed Elizabeth Rees's preference for Nathaniel the last time you were here Mr Probert-Lloyd?'

'We did,' I confirmed.

'He was brought to me for treatment a few weeks ago after a severe beating.' Gwynne paused. 'The man who brought him here – a servant on the same farm – told me that his attackers had intended to warn him off Lizzie Rees.'

'Did he give you any names?' I asked. Cadi Evans had told us that Nattie had known his attackers by sight but not by name. However, it did no harm to ask.

'No. Neither would he go to the magistrates about the matter. With no witnesses, he said it was his word against theirs. But whoever they were, they'd underestimated his determination. Or perhaps the nature of his attachment to Elizabeth.'

'He didn't take the warning to heart?'

'If you mean did he forsake Elizabeth, then no, I do not believe he did. In point of fact, he told me that he was going to ask her to marry him.'

Something in Gwynne's voice told me there was more to be learned here if I only cared to dig for it. I fixed his face in my peripheral vision, the whirlpool over his chest. 'Dr Gwynne, did you encourage Nathaniel Stockton to ask for her hand?'

'It's not for me to encourage or discourage such intentions.'

'What if somebody's asked you to cast their horoscope,' John cut in, 'and a certain person seems to be identified as a future husband or wife? Or if they wash the midnight shirt and see a vision?'

If Gwynne gave credence to horoscopes, did it follow that he believed in the powers of divination?

'Horoscopes are never so specific as to provide names, Mr Davies.'

'But did you have any reason to believe, one way or the other,' I asked, 'that Lizzie would say yes if he asked her to marry him?'

Abruptly Gwynne rose to his feet and went to the door. 'Where is the girl with that tea?'

As he left the room, I turned to John. 'There's clearly something he doesn't want to tell us.'

'Agreed. Still,' his voice brightened, 'a cup of tea would be nice.'

I grinned, my mood lightened by his sudden levity. Perhaps now that Matthew Thomas's inquest was over and Ormiston was gone, we could put past trials behind us.

After a minute or so, Gwynne returned carrying a tea tray. 'Apologies for the delay, gentlemen.'

John and I watched in silence as the doctor poured milk and tea, and proffered sugar. When he had seated himself opposite me once more, I put my teacup next to a plant on the table beside me.

'Dr Gwynne, we've been told that Lizzie Rees came to see you before she travelled south to go harvesting. Is that true?'

Gwynne hesitated. 'It is.'

So Lizzie's sisters had been right about that, at least. 'What was the nature of the consultation?'

Gwynne shook his head. 'I can't tell you that. It was between me and Elizabeth.'

Should I press him, or try a more subtle tack? John leant forward decisively. *Press on, hard.*

'Dr Gwynne, whatever you disclose to us now cannot hurt Lizzie Rees. But we believe that her death and Nathaniel Stockton's are related, and without wishing to prejudge the jury's verdict, Mr Stockton was clearly murdered. He intended to marry Lizzie Rees and she came to consult you. If you know anything pertinent, I would urge you, in the interests of justice, to tell me.'

Gwynne hung his head as if the condition of the polished floorboards was suddenly of enormous interest to him. I waited while he wrestled with his conscience.

'Lizzie's sisters are convinced she asked you to tell her who she was going to marry,' John said.

The doctor's head remained lowered.

'Dr Gwynne?' I pressed.

I heard him draw in a deep breath. 'No,' he said, 'she didn't ask me that.'

'But she did ask you something, in your capacity as...' I hesitated, unable to bring myself to use the word *wizard*, 'as somebody who she believed had an insight into the future?'

'Not even that.' He took another deep breath and sat up straight. 'On your last visit, we discussed Mic Rees's belief that his daughter might have been cursed. Lizzie had a similar fear.'

I waited.

'Elizabeth had given the *coron fedw* to Nathaniel Stockton—'

'Yes, we know,' I interrupted before he could begin an unnecessary explanation.

'What she wanted me to tell her was whether her marriage would be cursed if she married somebody else.'

John

It was threatening to rain as we left Dr Gwynne's house, so we put our coats on before we got into the saddle. Easier not to have to ferret around in the saddlebags once it'd started.

'According to what I got from her sisters and Llwyo,' I told Harry as we trotted away from Felindre Farchog, 'Lizzie Rees only really had one friend. Girl by the name of Sally Sips. If anybody knows who this other man is, it'll be her.'

So off we went to Eglwyswrw.

I don't know what Harry was thinking – probably wondering how a doctor trained in London could still believe in curses – but I was trying to get everything straight in my head. I was going to need to write all this up at some point, and if I thought it through now, it'd be easier; half the work would be done.

And to be honest, thinking about Nattie Stockton's murder kept my thoughts away from Matthew Thomas's suicide. We were going to have to go to his funeral tomorrow and I was dreading it. Half the people there would've been at the inquest and they'd want to know what Harry was going to do – how he was going to make sure nobody else was thrown off their land. And at the moment, I didn't have a clue.

But we did know quite a lot about what'd happened to Nattie Stockton, and I stopped my thoughts wandering by making a mental list.

Fact: his body had been pulled out of the river at Cilgerran.

Fact (as good as, seeing as it came from Reckitt): he had drowned somewhere else, in water where pond weed grew.

Fact: the body had been put (hidden?) somewhere after Stockton'd died and before he was thrown into the Teifi. A place where for some reason he'd been propped up in a sitting position. Probably somewhere stony, given the wounds on his back.

Fact: he'd been in that position for up to twelve hours, according to the lividity and rigor.

Unsubstantiated fact (but probably reliable, coming from Reckitt): somebody had held one of his arms (twisted behind his back?) and forced his head down into stones at the bottom of – let's say – a pond. (Because of pond weed.)

Fact: as yet we had no evidence as to who'd drowned him or why, but it seemed likely to be related to the death of the girl he'd been courting, Lizzie Rees.

Fact: Lizzie Rees had been sweet enough on Stockton to give him the *coron fedw*.

Fact (I couldn't see any reason to disbelieve Dr Gwynne): Lizzie had had second thoughts about Nattie Stockton and was considering marrying somebody else.

Unsubstantiated fact: Lizzie wanted to stay home to wash the midnight shirt so she could find out who – or rather, which one of two men – she was going to marry.

When Ann and Gwen had told me their story, I'd thought it was romantic nonsense that they'd come up with because of a nightgown drying. But what if it was true? Maybe, if there were two men in the running, Lizzie might've thought she needed a bit of a supernatural nudge in the right direction.

Harry'd asked Dr Gwynne if he knew who the other man was, but according to him, Lizzie hadn't said and he hadn't asked. Harry'd also wanted to know what answer Gwynne had given when Lizzie'd asked him whether her marriage would be cursed if she married somebody else after she'd given Nattie Stockton the *coron fedw*.

'I told her that her marriage would certainly be cursed – in the metaphorical but no less effective sense – unless she was quite certain who she wished to marry. If she wasn't, she faced a lifetime of wondering whether she might have been happier if she'd made a different decision.'

'And did you give her any indication of how she might be so certain?'

'I told her to pay specific attention to her dreams and to how she felt on waking from any dream about either young man. Sometimes our dreams tell us things our waking minds shy away from.'

And maybe Lizzie'd taken that to mean that she should wash the midnight shirt. Because when you thought about it, unless a girl pinched herself to stay awake into the small hours after putting out her intimate garment to dry, the so-called 'visions' of a coffin or a husband were likely to be dreams, weren't they?

So perhaps Ann and Gwen's story wasn't so far-fetched after all. Except for the bit about girls who hated Lizzie coming and pretending to be another man to frighten her. That was obviously nonsense. You might get away with that sort of thing in a boarding school full of impressionable girls, but not at Rhosdywarch.

Back to facts.

Fact: Nattie Stockton'd been killed sometime on Sunday, after he'd left Gilfachwen for church. Which raised two questions in my mind. First, had he got as far as Eglwyswrw church? And second, was it possible that whoever'd killed him hadn't known that Lizzie Rees had died?

When Cadwgan Gwynne'd told us there'd been a second man in the running, the thought that'd leapt into my head was that Nattie must've been killed to avenge Lizzie. That for some reason the other man believed that Nattie'd killed Lizzie, and thought he'd get away with it because of Gwynne's 'natural death' verdict. Everybody in the parish would've known by Sunday morning that that was what Gwynne had said.

But what if Lizzie's other man wasn't from the parish and – just like Cadi Evans – hadn't heard about her death by Sunday morning? What if he'd just chosen a really bad time to go looking for Nattie Stockton to get rid of the competition?

As we trotted into Eglwyswrw, I told Harry what I'd been thinking and he nodded, with that look on his face that told me

I'd had an idea he hadn't. 'Excellent reasoning. Which means that one of the things we need to ask Sally Sips is whether Nattie Stockton ever got to church that morning.'

–

Before we could talk to Sally Sips, we had to find out where she lived. Llwyo, the groom who'd fetched me from Glanteifi, seemed like somebody who might know, so we stopped at the Sergeant's Inn stables and Harry stayed outside with the horses.

'Sally Sips?' Llwyo said when I asked if he knew her. 'Who'd you hear calling her that?'

'Ann and Gwen – Lizzie Rees's little sisters. Why? Isn't that what people call her?'

'No, no, it is – well, Eglwyswrw people anyway. It's just odd hearing a stranger call her that. Not very complimentary, is it – Sally Sipsi?'

Ah, so Sips was short for Sipsi. Gypsy.

I watched Llwyo, waiting for him to tell me more. He was rubbing a horse down, keeping the animal between me and him.

'So if you know her, I expect you know where she lives?'

He dipped down to brush under the horse's belly. 'Course I do, *'machgen i*!'

But he didn't tell me. Did he think that because I'd paid him for the names he'd given me before, I'd pay for the address now?

'Well then?' Harry said from behind me. 'Where can we find her?' He must've found a boy to hold the horses.

Llwyo straightened up and I saw him dry-swallowing. His Adam's apple went up and down like a chicken trying to peck its way out of a sack. 'Her father keeps the grocer's shop at the other end of the village,' he said, all helpful now. 'That's where she'll be. Mind,' he said, looking away from Harry to me, 'I haven't seen her out and about since Lizzie's funeral. Hit her hard, it has.'

Harry came to stand at my side and Llwyo ducked down out of his way to brush the horse's legs. He could be very commanding when he chose to, Harry.

'We've been given information that Lizzie Rees was courting somebody else, at the same time as Nattie Stockton,' he said. 'Happen to know if that's true, would you?'

Llwyo stayed down. Preferred having his face within kicking distance of an iron-shod hoof to facing Harry. 'No, sir, I wouldn't. Like I told Mr Davies, half the lads in Eglwyswrw would've liked to be courting her, but it was only the Englishman had the ball— the guts to actually do it. Mind, he should've seen sense and left off, instead of...'

'Instead of what?' I asked.

'Nothing.'

'No, come on. If he didn't see sense after the beating he got, what was he doing?'

Llwyo straightened up, started pulling the horse's mane tidy. 'Who told you about the beating?'

'Dr Gwynne.'

He sucked his teeth. 'Proper mess he was, from what I heard. Couldn't hardly see, his eyes were so swollen.'

Poor dab – somebody'd given him quite a hiding. 'So what was he doing when he should've been seeing sense?' I wasn't going to let it go.

'Nothing.'

'It's not nothing, though, is it?'

'Just gossip, that's all.'

'Tell us anyway and we'll be the judges,' Harry said.

Llwyo gave him a look that said he'd rather punch him than answer him, but Harry was the coroner and Llwyo knew he could make him give evidence at the inquest. And that'd be worse than telling him what he wanted to know now. At the inquest, everybody'd *see* him passing on gossip. 'Somebody saw him – Stockton – coming away from Rhosdywarch,' he said. 'Before sunrise on the morning Lizzie died.'

'Somebody – who?' I asked.

'Dunno. Told you. It's just gossip.'

'And what does the gossip say he was doing there at that time?'

Llwyo stared at Harry. Probably wondering how much he could see, like everybody did when they first met him. 'If he wasn't up to no good, there's only one thing he'd be doing coming from there at that time, isn't there?' His eyes switched back to me, dared me to say it.

I nodded. Of course! Looked at in that light, it all made sense. Made sense of Mic Rees lying to us. Made sense of Lizzie being in the box bed.

'*Caru yn y gwely*,' I said. Courting in bed.

Harry

Courting in bed. I remembered how much of a Welsh bumpkin I had felt when I first realised that this was not something people did in other parts of the country. In England, young couples did not meet at night, bundled up in clothes and blankets in a bed or on the floor, bolsters often thrust between them by wary parents. Elsewhere, it seemed, courting was carried out in the light of day. But here, in a farming community whose every daylight hour was spent working to keep bread on the table, time had to be found after dark for a couple to decide whether they suited each other. And such a decision was vital, for unlike people of my station, who might easily choose to avoid their spouse by occupying separate parts of a large house, a husband and wife in a Teifi Valley cottage or farmhouse lived and worked cheek by jowl, all day, every day. If there were not, at the very least, a bond of friendship or mutual respect, the union would be miserable for both them and their children.

I had done my share of courting in bed in the dark of a night-time hayloft, but I did not wish to dwell on the memories of those dark hours of whispered lovemaking. They had, ultimately, resulted in her betrayal and murder.

'So,' I said, as John and I walked down the high street to the grocer's shop, leaving our mares in the stables, 'as Cadi told us quite categorically that Nattie hadn't seen Lizzie since she'd been back from harvesting, and that he was in the loft with the other servants on the night she died, if there *was* a man with her in the box bed, it was this other suitor – agreed?'

'Yes.'

'Having said that, we need to avoid jumping to conclusions. We both know how rumours start after a sudden death. This one might have no truth in it at all.'

'Yes, but it fits what we know, doesn't it? Her being in the box bed instead of her own bed. Her lying about having a cold. And I'll tell you something else that fits now, too – Mic Rees stripping her petticoat off.'

John obviously saw a significance there that I didn't. I stopped in my tracks; sometimes the effort necessary to make out where I was putting my feet made thinking while walking nigh on impossible.

Mic Rees had told me that he had not been able to bear the indignity Lizzie's memory would suffer if Dr Gwynne had seen her in her urine-soaked petticoat – that putting her in fresh linen was the last thing he had been able to do for her. Clearly, John now thought otherwise.

'How does that fit?' I asked.

'Some people have courting sacks,' he said. 'They cover the girl all over so only her arms and her head are free. But if you haven't got one, if you want to be sure nothing goes on, you can sew up the middle of a petticoat. Or nightgown. We know Lizzie'd had her wedding-night nightgown out because Ann and Gwen saw it drying on the back of the chair. That's where they got all their nonsense about washing the midnight shirt from.'

'And if Dr Gwynne'd seen her in that, with a line of additional stitches to ensure chastity, he would've known what'd been going on and might've asked awkward questions.'

'Exactly. So Mic took it off her and put the petticoat she'd been wearing earlier back on.'

Which meant that Reckitt had been right about her petticoat having previously been worn. I imagined Mic Rees – and possibly this mystery lover – unpicking Lizzie's careful stitches from her sodden nightgown by the light of a rushlight or candle. If we asked to see that garment, examined it, would we see stains where the flame had dripped tallow onto the fabric?

This new evidence raised as many questions as it answered. Chief among them the question of whether Mic Rees had hidden his daughter's courting in bed in order to avoid having to answer to his wife, or to protect the man concerned. But if it was the latter, why would he do such a thing? Surely any man who had been with Lizzie on the night of her death must be complicit in it, Reckitt's failure to find any evidence of foul play notwithstanding?

As soon as we'd finished with Miss Sips – whose surname, we had been told by Llwyo, was Jones – we would need to speak to Mic Rees again.

-

The grocer's shop was much smaller than the one in Newcastle Emlyn and, lacking a large front window, was not well lit. Immediately feeling at a disadvantage in the poor light, I let John introduce us and ask whether we might speak to Sally.

As her father went to fetch her, I sniffed the air, trying to identify the scents that lay just out of reach of anything but a concerted effort. I caught the rich, deep notes of molasses, and something that might have been tea. But the dominant note was the beeswax and turpentine of wood polish. Evidently Mr Jones kept his counter clean and buffed.

'Miss Jones,' I greeted the dark-haired young woman who followed the grocer back into the shop, 'would you be so kind as to come for a short walk with me and Mr Davies so that we can talk to you about Lizzie Rees?'

Her father started to object, trying to insist that he be present, but Sally put a hand on his arm and spoke quietly. 'It's all right, Dada, it'll be nice to have some fresh air. I'll just get my shawl, if I may, Mr Probert-Lloyd.'

When she had gone, her father spoke up again. 'She's been very upset by what happened to Lizzie, our Sally has. I don't know why you have to speak to her. Dr Gwynne said it was a natural death.'

'There's been another death, Mr Jones. A young man who was courting Lizzie. We'd like to talk to Sally about him.'

'What – the Englishman? He's never killed himself over her, has he?'

'No,' I said. 'He hasn't.'

Outside, we walked back along the road. 'Shall we step into the churchyard?' I suggested. It would get us off the public thoroughfare and provide a modicum of privacy. I must confess that I also hoped it would induce Sally to be more truthful with us than she might otherwise be; if she and Lizzie had been close friends, it seemed likely that Sally had also attended this church rather than the chapel in the village.

We skirted the side of the Sergeant's Inn stables and walked through a gate into the churchyard, where the church sat on an area of gently raised ground. Under the lee of the west end, partly hidden from the main road by a tree, I turned to Sally.

'It must have been a shock losing your best friend so suddenly like that,' I said, offering her the chance both to express her sorrow and to deny any such closeness with Lizzie if she wished. We had, after all, only Ann and Gwen's word for it that the two had been confidantes.

'It was,' she said, her voice low and subdued. 'I've never had such a shock in my life. Not even when my *mamgu* died. But it's different when it's an old person, isn't it? There isn't all the sadness about things they'll miss.'

Sally had been presented to John as something of a frivolous personality – his exact phrase had been 'Ann made her sound like the sort of girl who'll tell secrets to anybody' – so it came as a surprise to hear such a philosophical outlook from her. I scrutinised her as best I could, wondering whether it was just her dark hair that had earned her the nickname, or whether there was more to it.

'Sally, have you heard that the body of a young man was pulled out of the Teifi in Cilgerran on Monday morning?'

'Yes.' The distraction in her voice told me that her mind was still on her friend.

'Yesterday, that young man was identified as Nathaniel Stockton.'

'*Nattie?* Had he... I mean, did he...'

She had jumped to the same conclusion as her father. 'No,' I said. 'Mr Stockton was murdered.'

'But *why*?' Her question was anguished. 'He hadn't even *seen* Lizzie after getting warned off.'

It was interesting that she had assumed that whoever had been responsible for the beating Nattie had received was also guilty of his murder. Had there, I wondered, been other threats made against him?

'You're sure Lizzie hadn't seen Nathaniel Stockton since getting back from harvesting in the south?' I asked.

'No... Well, that's to say, I hadn't seen her. So I suppose... I don't know. Perhaps she had? All I know is, I went to church on Sunday looking forward to seeing her, and her mother told me she'd died.' Her voice broke and she turned her head away from me.

'I'm sorry, Miss Jones.'

Before I could ask anything else, a shout from the Cenarth road on the south side of the churchyard made me jump. 'Sally! You all right, are you?'

The road was much lower than the church and the distance involved meant that I could not see who had called out.

'Yes thanks!' Sally called back, her voice still catching. 'Just having a word with Mr Probert-Lloyd. The coroner.'

Evidently her would-be saviour moved away on hearing this as there was no more from him. 'Somebody's keeping an eye on you,' John remarked.

'It's just Twm y Gof – his father's forge is only just over the road. He must've seen us walk by.'

'Sweet on you, is he?' I asked.

'Not me, no.'

'No, he was after Lizzie, wasn't he?' John said. Twm y Gof must be one of the names Llwyo had given him.

254

'Not just him. Plenty of boys fancied Lizzie.'

I expected John to drop the subject, but he did not. 'What's he like, Twm?'

'All right. Bit under his father's thumb, but then everybody is. Only one blacksmith in the parish, isn't there? It's him or walk a long way.'

'Did you ever see Twm arguing with Nattie Stockton?' John asked.

Sally did not reply straight away. Was she trying to recall or wondering how truthful to be? Twm had implicitly offered to rescue her from us a minute ago, and looking after one's own must cut both ways if it is to work. 'Once,' she said, eventually.

'Go on,' John encouraged her.

'Me and Lizzie were standing over there,' she indicated the corner of the churchyard with a raised hand, 'one Sunday after church, with Nattie and another young man, and Twm came over from the forge. Told Lizzie she shouldn't be hanging around with foreigners.'

She seemed disinclined to say any more, busying herself with resettling and fastening her shawl. 'Did Nattie say anything in return?' I asked.

'He did.' She stopped her pulling and twitching. 'I think he was trying to impress Lizzie. He said it was no wonder she preferred his company when the only bachelors on offer here were... I don't remember the word he said, but Lizzie told me it meant somebody who can't read.'

Insulting Twm by using unfamiliar English words was hardly the wisest course of action, but it did explain Stockton's reputation for behaving as if he was superior to everybody in Eglwyswrw.

'Dr Gwynne told us that Lizzie Rees went to see him a few weeks ago,' I said, changing the subject. 'Did you go with her?'

I heard Sally draw in a long breath, as if she was fighting back tears at the memory of the last visit she had made with her friend. 'Yes, I did.'

'Did you go into Dr Gwynne's consulting room with her?'

'No. Dr Gwynne doesn't allow that. It's always private with him.'

'So you don't know what they discussed?'

'Oh no, I do, yes. She wanted to ask him if she had to marry Nattie because she'd given him the *coron fedw*.'

'Had she changed her mind about him?'

Sally did not reply.

'We heard that there was another man she was interested in,' John said.

'There were lots of other men interested in *her*.'

'Do you know which of those men warned Nathaniel Stockton off – beat him?' I asked.

Sally shook her head.

'Twm y Gof?' I suggested.

'I don't know. You'd have to ask him.'

Unless she had seen Nathaniel Stockton being attacked, Sally was unlikely to name anybody, even under oath. We would soon be gone, but she would have to live cheek by jowl with the resentment of young men who would feel betrayed by her if she spoke up.

'So Lizzie never said anything to you about another man she might've fallen for?' John asked.

'No. I mean, I knew there was *somebody*. Asked her straight, I did, when she told me why she wanted to go and see the *dew*— Dr Gwynne. But she wouldn't tell me. "Not yet," she said to me. "I'll tell you when I'm sure. *If* I'm sure."'

'What do you think she meant?'

John let Sally take her time. 'Sometimes,' she said warily, 'when you know a man likes you, it makes you more warm towards him, if you know what I mean. But you can't get carried away with that. You have to wait awhile. Test it out.'

'Test how?' John asked. 'By courting in bed?'

'*No!* If things'd gone that far, she'd have told me. She *would*!' she insisted when John did not reply immediately. But evidently Sally Jones had not been trusted as implicitly as she had believed.

I changed tack, dropping my voice so as not to be heard by the driver of the cart that was trundling by on the road below us. 'Do you know why Lizzie stayed at home when her mother and sisters went to Ffynone?'

'No, like I said before, I hadn't seen her since she'd come back from down south. At the funeral, her father said she hadn't been well – she had a cold.' She stopped, but John obviously saw something that made him think she had more to say.

'Go on,' he prompted.

'Her sister – Gwen, I mean, the little one – she told me that Lizzie didn't have a cold, that she'd just said that so that…' Sally hesitated again, 'so that she could stay at home to wash the midnight shirt.' She waited for a reaction, but when neither of us showed any scepticism, she went on more steadily. 'Gwen thought I knew all about it, but I didn't. I hadn't seen Lizzie.' She began to fiddle with the edge of her shawl once more, and I could feel her looking at me.

'You don't think…' She checked herself, then surged on again. 'Her mother said her heart'd just stopped. You don't think she died of a broken heart because of who she saw in her vision, do you?'

I shook my head. 'No.'

'One more thing,' John said. 'Did Lizzie know anybody in Cilgerran?'

She appeared to give this a few seconds' thought. 'No, I don't think so. Why?'

'You're sure?' John pressed. 'No old family friends, no third cousins, nothing like that?'

'No.'

'And you'd definitely have known, would you?'

'I would, yes.'

'All right then, what about Nattie Stockton – did you see him at church last week?'

'Yes.' I heard a bleak note in Sally's voice as she answered him. 'It was me told him about Lizzie. When he couldn't see her, he

257

came straight to me. He could see I was crying, knew something was wrong.' She lifted the edge of her shawl and dabbed her eyes. It must be cotton, I thought, rather than wool; probably her Sunday best. Perhaps, if her father was doing well, it might even have some silk in it.

'Did he stay for the service?' John asked. An excellent question.

'No. He tried to talk to Esther – Lizzie's mother – but all she'd say to him was that the workhouse doctor'd been to Rhosdywarch and seen Lizzie. Esther wanted him back to cut Lizzie open to see if he could find out why she'd died. I don't think Nattie liked that idea. He just walked out of church then, and I didn't see him after. He must've gone home.'

–

Once we had seen Sally back to the grocer's shop and were out of earshot, I turned to John. 'You think Nattie might've gone to Cilgerran looking for this other man; that's why you asked whether Lizzie knew anybody there?'

'He had to be there for some reason, didn't he? Reckitt hadn't done his post-mortem then, don't forget, so Nattie might've jumped to conclusions about what'd happened.'

'What if he went to see Reckitt? Everybody knew that Reckitt and I'd been to Rhosdywarch. Stockton might've wanted to ask him what he'd seen when he examined Lizzie.'

John drew in a considering breath. 'Possible, I suppose. But don't you think it's more likely that if Nattie'd got wind that Lizzie was seeing somebody else – if she'd told him, even – he'd've blamed this other man for what happened to her? Or he might've heard the rumour about somebody coming away from Rhosdywarch in the early hours. He could easily have heard a whisper at church – maybe people were even looking at him funny. And he'd've known it wasn't him who'd been there, so maybe he marched straight off to confront whoever it was?'

I sighed, remembering the emotions that had boiled in me when I discovered who had murdered Margaret Jones; the furious rage I had felt when I realised that I had left her in danger. I knew that if I had confronted her killer, I would not have been entirely responsible for my own actions.

Had Nathaniel Stockton confronted the man he believed to be responsible for Lizzie's death, and died himself as a result?

John

On the way to Rhosdywarch, I tried to picture Nattie Stockton going to Cilgerran to confront Lizzie's other man. Had there been a fight? It was possible – the bruising on Nattie's face and body showed he'd definitely taken some punches. But his knuckles hadn't been damaged, had they? So if there *had* been a fight, it'd been very one-sided.

Still, when we asked Mic Rees whether somebody'd been in bed with Lizzie on the night she died, I knew what Harry's next question'd be. *Is he from Cilgerran?*

When you thought about it, asking whether his daughter'd been courting in bed was about the most intimate question you could ask a father. But then, coroner's investigations put me and Harry in an odd position. For a short while we got to know a small number of people very well. We'd go back and forth to the same places again and again, asking questions, trying to get to the bottom of things. All the time inching closer and closer to the truth of what'd happened. And then, after the inquest, we just left. Like as not, we'd never see any of those people again.

It was the exact opposite of my job on the estate. At Glanteifi, I'd see the same people week in, week out, year after year, for the rest of my life. And I'd probably never get to know any of them as intimately as I knew the people we spoke to in our investigations after a single day. Was that something I needed to do? Really get to know the tenants, get them to trust me – not me, the agent for Glanteifi, but me, John Davies? Could I do that?

I didn't know. I was worried that people would keep me at a distance because of my job, but perhaps, if I went to talk to them, sat in their kitchens, I could show them that behind the title, I was just like them, that I knew how they thought, how they felt.

We splashed through the ford at the bottom of the hill below Rhosdywarch and I looked over at Harry. 'Are you going to try and have this conversation with Mic Rees privately?'

'I think we'd better, don't you? I don't imagine he'll tell us anything if we speak to him in front of his wife.'

—

I hadn't been inside the house at Rhosdywarch before, but there was nothing surprising in the kitchen. Esther Rees was a woman who liked to be in charge, and her house said as much. There was nothing of Mic in the kitchen at all. No tools propped in a corner waiting to be mended. No pipe sitting on the hearth. Even the cushion on the big chair next to the fire didn't have his arse-dent in it. It'd been shaken out, all its feathers fluffed up inside, as if it'd just been stuffed.

'We were hoping to have a word with your husband, Mrs Rees,' Harry said as we walked in.

Esther Rees was busy making butter in the cool draught between the open front door and the back window. 'He's not here,' she said, not so much as breaking her rhythm with the knocker. Up and down it went in the earthenware churn.

'When will he be back?' I asked.

'Sunday. He's gone down to Haverfordwest with the carrier to deliver cloth.'

'That's a long way from home.'

'Mic does good work. Takes it down to a tailor in the town this time of the year, every year, regular as clockwork.' She panted slightly as she spoke. It's strenuous work, making butter. And once you've started, you can't really leave off, so she wasn't being disrespectful, just practical. Most women would've asked if we minded if she carried on, but then Esther Rees wasn't most women.

'You probably won't have heard,' Harry said, 'but Nathaniel Stockton's body was pulled out of the river at Cilgerran on Monday.'

That stopped her. The knocker fell to the bottom of the churn and she stared at him. 'Dead?'

'Yes.'

'How?' She wasn't going to ask if he'd killed himself, like Sally Sips and her father.

'That's for the jury to decide. I'm holding the inquest on Monday. Can you ask your husband to attend, please?'

Esther grabbed the knocker's handle and got back to work. 'Why? Mic can't've had anything to do with it. He's been here all the time.'

'I'd like him to come, nonetheless. There are some questions I need to ask him, and as he's not here now, they'll have to be answered at the inquest.'

'Such as?' Esther Rees kept her eyes on the churn. She needed to keep beating the fat out of the buttermilk till it was just a lump sticking to the little wings of the knocker.

'Just ask him to attend, please. Ten o'clock on Monday at the Pendre Inn in Cilgerran.'

'Right. I'll tell him.' When Harry didn't reply, she looked up. She was waiting for us to leave.

But Harry wasn't finished. 'As I said, Mr Stockton's body was found in Cilgerran. Do you have any family there? Did Mic do business there?'

She didn't falter this time. Up and down. Up and down. She was a strong woman, Esther Rees, and the sound of the cream inside the churn was changing quickly. Squelching instead of splashing. Nearly done.

'No,' she said. 'My family's all over this way. Mic's from up by Llanybydder.'

'And he doesn't do business in Cilgerran? Doesn't take his cloth there?' Fair question – it was a hell of a lot closer than Haverfordwest. But then it was a lot smaller, too.

'No.'

'What about Lizzie? Did she know anybody in Cilgerran?'

'No.'

'You're sure?'

She didn't look at us, didn't hesitate. 'Sure as I can be.'

But knowing what we knew now about the night of Lizzie's death, that might not be as sure as she'd like to be.

–

It felt as if we were leaving Rhosdywarch with our tails between our legs, but it couldn't be helped. Mic was the only person who knew the name of the man who'd been with Lizzie Rees on her last night on earth, and he was on his way to Haverfordwest. It was time to get back home and deal with the living.

But Harry had other ideas. 'I think we should try and find out where Stockton went after he left the church on Sunday, and how he ended up in Cilgerran,' he said as we crossed back over the ford. 'You know – whether people saw him walking towards Rhosdywarch or towards Cilgerran straight away, whether there was anybody with him…'

'And who's going to tell us that?'

'Congregants at Eglwyswrw church.'

'He didn't stay for the service, remember? They'd all have been inside when he left – they wouldn't know where he'd gone or who with.'

'Latecomers, then. Or people who weren't at church who were about at that time.'

'Finding anybody who saw him would take too much time – we need to get back to Glanteifi. Or have you forgotten that it's Matthew Thomas's funeral tomorrow morning?'

The noise Harry made told me that yes, he had forgotten. And that he wasn't exactly pleased to be reminded. Well I didn't want to think about it either, come to that. Just saying the words had made me feel cold in the pit of my stomach.

'We have to be there, Harry. If you *really* think it's necessary, we can come back over here on Saturday. Or Sunday.' I had a sudden inspiration. 'Think about it – if we go to Eglwyswrw on Sunday morning, we're more likely to be able to talk to the right people, aren't we? The same people'll be late for church every week if it's the same as chapel. And the same people'll be hanging about in the street as well. They'll be there ready for us to talk to them.'

Harry gave one of those big sighs that meant he didn't want to agree with me but he knew I was right. 'Very well. Let's stop in Eglwyswrw on the way home for something to eat, and you can write a note for Caleb Richards. At least the magistrates won't be able to complain,' he added. 'They're keen that I should use the local constables, so let's see how much they like paying for the hire of a horse for a day while Richards rides over half of this side of the Preselis summoning witnesses.'

–

Whatever I said about going over to Eglwyswrw on Sunday, I had a pretty good idea that Harry'd want to go back earlier than that. But when we got home, Lydia Howell had news that put a stop to any thought of doing inquest business on Saturday.

We'd just finished telling her everything we'd discovered, and Harry'd announced that he was going to go and change for dinner, when Lydia said, 'Before you go, I've written to Mr and Mrs Saunders-James accepting their invitation to lunch on Saturday. I sent Twm over with the letter this morning and he brought a reply extending the invitation to John as well.'

Harry didn't reply straight away. If he was waiting for the words 'I hope that's all right?' he was going to have a long wait. Lydia Howell had done as she saw fit.

'I'm in the middle of an inquest, Lydia! I've only come back today so that I can attend Matthew Thomas's funeral tomorrow.'

'From what you've just told me, there's very little to be done before the inquest. There's no need for you to go back. Whereas given that Mr Saunders-James has explicitly invited the three of us because there's somebody he wants us to meet, I felt we risked offending him if we postponed our visit a second time.'

Harry's reaction was written all over his face. He wasn't pleased. But if he argued with her, he knew he'd just sound childish.

'Very well,' he said. 'I just hope that whoever he wants to introduce us to proves worth the sacrifice.'

As it happened, it turned out to be well worth the sacrifice. Because without that lunch, we might never have discovered the truth behind Lizzie Rees's death.

Harry

Had I been given the choice as to my occupation on the day after Matthew Thomas's funeral, I would not have chosen to take lunch with strangers. I felt that I had been quite sufficiently stared at and judged outside Treforgan chapel by the scores of mourners who had accompanied the old farmer on his final journey.

But just as my presence at the funeral had been a necessary act of atonement, so my attendance at the Plas Blaengwyn luncheon party was essential to my finding a tolerable place for myself in local society. Besides, I must confess to being just a little curious as to who it was that Anthony Saunders-James was so keen that I should meet, and why he had now invited John, too. Land agents, many of whom also practised as solicitors, were considered to be part of Teifi Valley society but Ormiston's resignation was not yet common knowledge; therefore, to society at large, John was still my under-steward and coroner's assistant.

So it was with a certain anticipation that on Saturday morning we bowled up to Plas Blaengwyn in the estate's workaday trap. Glanteifi's carriage was not only embarrassingly ancient, but uncomfortable; besides, after rain at Matthew Thomas's funeral, the weather today was fine, and the last days of summer were better enjoyed in the open air than from the dead-springed interior of a musty, brittle-curtained carriage.

Local opinion had taken an intense interest in recent developments at Plas Blaengwyn, and it was common knowledge that the interior had undergone a good deal of modernisation since Anthony Saunders had married Eleanor James and moved her widowed father into the dower house. I had not, however, been prepared for the magnitude of the transformation.

From the moment of our reception into the entrance hall, where panelling and portraits had been replaced by towering plants and a vertiginous wallpaper in green, black and gold, the house felt more like a wealthy London home than a Teifi Valley mansion.

The footman bore our coats away, but instead of leading us to the drawing room, Saunders-James (who must have been watching for our arrival like a swooning girl awaiting her lover, so quickly had he arrived to greet us) ushered us into the cloakroom, in the corner of which stood a newly painted door.

'Not too many of these locally,' he said, opening the door to reveal a water closet. Stepping in, he pulled a chain that caused water to rush loudly from an overhead cistern into the lavatory bowl below.

'No, indeed,' I said, somewhat surprised that he would begin the tour of his improvements before allowing his wife to welcome us as mistress of Plas Blaengwyn. However, there was more to come, and before we were escorted to the drawing room where she awaited us, we were treated to a tour of the kitchen, the billiard room and the music room – each with its own innovations as to wall covering, amenities and internal communications (gone was the hall boy, and in his place a series of bells).

Saunders-James seemed most pleased with the kitchen, which now boasted a huge modern range, a sink with taps for both hot and cold water, which he insisted on demonstrating, and, in the centre of the room, in place of the 'unhygienic' table on which the James' family's meals had undoubtedly been prepared for at least a hundred years, a long marble-topped item that would not have looked out of place supporting a reclining Roman statue. I wondered where the servants now ate.

Upstairs, more wallpaper obtruded itself upon our notice and plants seemed to stand sentinel at every turn. Fortunately, Saunders-James restrained himself from showing us the alterations he had made to the bedrooms, though I had been reliably informed that there was now a hip bath, commode and bidet in every dressing room, which must have left very little room for actually getting dressed.

In the drawing room, under a three-tiered crystal chandelier – imported, Saunders-James told us with an entirely unsuccessful attempt at nonchalance, from Venice – we were finally presented to his wife. Eleanor Saunders-James, who I remembered from my pre-Oxford days as a quiet and undistinguished young woman ideally suited to spinsterhood, seemed somewhat timid to be a lady in charge of her own household, though perhaps she simply lacked sparkle when set alongside her ebullient husband. Hoping to bolster her confidence, I thanked her fulsomely for our invitation before being presented to Mr Jeremiah Harborne and his engineer, a taciturn figure who, when introduced as Amos Bowen, simply bowed in our direction.

As there were no other guests, Harborne must be the person to whom Saunders-James was so keen to introduce me.

Lydia, perhaps taking pity on Mrs Saunders-James's hesitation as to how precisely a private secretary should be entertained, expressed a desire to know the names of the exotic plants that were ranged about the room, and the two of them moved off together.

'Now then,' Saunders-James said, 'I believe you, Mr Davies, have an interest in speaking to Mr Bowen about a potential engineer in our midst?'

I knew that John would be pleased to have the chance to advocate on behalf of Phoebe Gwatkyn's protégé, and I hoped that he would not, therefore, feel that he and Mr Bowen had been deliberately excluded from whatever exchange Anthony Saunders-James wished to broker between me and Jeremiah Harborne.

'Always excellent to be able to introduce men who may be of assistance to each other,' Saunders-James said as John and the engineer moved to one side. 'And I hope I may render you an equal service, Probert-Lloyd.'

He led us to a small table on which glasses had been set out.

'May I interest you in a cocktail, gentlemen?'

I sipped the sweetened sherry and wondered whether Saunders-James would succeed in changing the Teifi Valley's long-standing preference for punch.

'John tells me that your engineer only arrived this week, Mr Harborne,' I said. 'I must confess, I was surprised. I imagined that he would have been needed at a much earlier stage.'

Harborne put down his cocktail on the table. 'Oh, he was. All the drawings were completed more than a year ago and the machines are ready and waiting. They need only to be shipped. Even the waterwheel is almost done – the frame is being made at one of the Cardigan foundries and the wooden elements will be added on site. Amos has been working elsewhere for the last year.'

In my peripheral vision, I could see John and the engineer standing on the other side of the room; from what I could make out from his slender frame and dark hair, Amos Bowen was a young man.

'Has Mr Bowen done much of this kind of work before?' I asked.

'We worked for the same company in Newtown. He was apprenticed to one of the engineers there, but there was soon not much the man could teach him. Amos is something of a genius when it comes to machines.'

'Jeremiah is fortunate to have found an engineer who can adapt what's done elsewhere to the very specific situation in the Teifi Valley – converting steam-powered machines to run on water power and so forth,' Saunders-James said.

I wondered why he felt the need to act as Harborne's mouth-piece; John's account of the man had suggested that he would have no need of an advocate.

'Jeremiah has great plans for his factory,' Saunders-James went on, 'and indeed for the whole of the lower Teifi Valley.'

Harborne took this as his cue and leaned forward in his seat. 'This is the ideal time to develop the woollen industry here,' he assured me. 'It's going to make our fortune as iron and coal are making the fortune of Merthyr and Monmouthshire.' He pulled his chair closer to me, as if an increased physical proximity might make his words more persuasive.

'You see, it's all about getting our cloth from mill to market. I'm building my factory here – on Anthony's land – because of the plans afoot to improve transport links. But it's a race!' Now I heard in his voice the fervour that John had described. 'I assume you already know that a group of Manchester businessmen are planning a railway to Milford Haven – it's further west than Liverpool, so it would have a real advantage in transatlantic shipping. Their plan would be to make Milford Haven into a deep-water harbour.'

Though this was evidently old news to Saunders-James, who just made a sound of affirmation, I had heard nothing about a Manchester-to-Milford railway. It made me feel distressingly ill-informed.

'But,' Harborne went on, 'I'm investing *here*, not in Pembrokeshire, because there's an alternative proposal – one that the Admiralty already favours.' He paused, and I wondered how carefully he was watching my reaction. 'A deep-water harbour and port of refuge at *Cardigan*.'

I nodded. I had heard nothing about this plan, but I could see the logic behind it. In the whole sweep of Cardigan Bay – frequently battered by storms – there was no refuge for ships sailing from Liverpool to Bristol. Wrecks were common and the consequent loss of lives and cargo was diligently detailed in the press.

'The High Sheriff of Cardiganshire is behind the scheme,' Harborne went on, 'and he's being encouraged to stand for Parliament so he can present a bill to that effect.'

'Are you involved in any way, Mr Harborne?' To be such an advocate, surely he must have a stake in it.

'No, Mr Probert-Lloyd, all my energies are required here. But I make it my business to know what's in the offing so that I can plan accordingly.'

Lifting his cocktail to his lips, he sat back and crossed his legs, seemingly at ease, though his foot bounced restlessly up and down. 'If those promoting the railway line between Carmarthen and Cardigan can get it built in time to coincide with the opening of the new harbour, Cardiganshire will have a port capable of welcoming deep-draught ships *and* the means of getting goods there quickly and cheaply.' He spread his hands like a market trader protesting that he was giving his wares away at the price he was offering. 'In five years' time, my cloth will be steaming across the Atlantic and down to the coalfields in its thousands of yards, Mr Probert-Lloyd. There'll be stations all along the route from Cardigan to Carmarthen and on to the coalfields. Think of it – stations at Newcastle Emlyn, Llandysul, Pencader—'

'Isn't five years a little optimistic? It takes a long time to get a railway built.'

'On the contrary. The actual building progresses swiftly. It's getting all the estate owners to agree to sell the necessary land that takes the time.'

Was that why I had been invited? Was I to bolster the credibility of the parvenu Saunders-James in an attempt to persuade our fellow landowners to embrace Cardiganshire's own industrial revolution?

'Speaking of selling land, Probert-Lloyd,' Saunders-James slid back into the conversation, 'I wonder if we might talk about the land you own on the other side of the river – up on the hills?'

'Now?' I asked, my astonishment that he would introduce such a topic on our very first meeting doing battle with a slightly humiliating eagerness at the prospect of realising some much-needed capital.

'No, no, obviously not. I was just thinking we might make an appointment if you were amenable to discussing the matter.' It was neatly managed, but I could tell from his bluster that he had indeed been proposing that we discuss it now.

I knew the land he was referring to: two fairly extensive hill farms in an area separate from the rest of the estate. On a long-ago visit with my father, I had asked him why we had land up on the hills. 'It came into Glanteifi hands three generations ago in settlement of a gambling debt,' he had told me, his tone inviting no further conversation. My father had abhorred gambling. He would not even play whist for pennies in the evening, insisting that games should be played for their own sake. Perhaps that was why he had never seen investment in new companies as a viable way to shore up Glanteifi's fortunes.

'I'm happy to meet to discuss possibilities,' I said, trying to sound as if I had no views on the matter one way or the other, 'but what's your interest?' The farms under discussion had not been much improved over the years and contributed little to the estate's bank balance, nor did they seem likely to in future.

'As you'll know, I have land over there' – I winced inwardly at Saunders-James's use of the first person. In the Teifi Valley, squires did not own land, estates did – 'which I want to run as sporting ground. But at the moment, there's too little to make it worthwhile. If I could add yours to it, it might make a very worthwhile shoot.'

'I see.'

Evidently Anthony Saunders-James did not see himself as a farming squire. Unlike my father and the like-minded landowners he had persuaded to join him in forming the local agricultural society, Blaengwyn's new owner was not looking to improve his holdings, but simply to use them to entertain his business acquaintances. It was not a plan I imagined his father-in-law, Piers James, falling in with, but following the marriage that had united Anthony Saunders and Eleanor James as Mr and Mrs Saunders-James, presumably the old man had been forced to cede control. It was, after all, common knowledge that on their nuptials, Blaengwyn's extensive debts had all been settled.

'Very well,' I said. 'Let's meet in the next week or two, shall we?'

'Excellent. Perhaps we should include Harborne here in the meeting. I know he's looking for investors for his factory, and you'll be flush once you've sold the land to me.'

The habits of mind inculcated by one's youth are hard to break, and despite my years in London, I still found it distasteful to hear a man speak so openly about the acquisition of money. 'I'm not sure—' I began, intending to say that perhaps now wasn't quite the moment to discuss such things, but Harborne interrupted.

'If you're worried about investing in somebody with no track record,' he said, 'it might interest you to know that your London acquaintance Mr George Gelyot has taken a quarter-stake in the factory.'

The sudden introduction of somebody from my London life into the conversation threw me to such an extent that I could only ask, feebly, 'How do you know Mr Gelyot?'

'John Davies introduced us.'

John had not mentioned doing so to me. 'I see.'

'Mr Gelyot is a very forward-looking man. He can see that with plans as they are for the west coast, the mills of the Teifi Valley may begin to outstrip his in the north. And a canny businessman is always looking for the next new thing, Mr Probert-Lloyd. There's no standing still in business.'

I could hear Gus's father saying the same thing, and I must confess, the fact that Mr Gelyot felt confident enough in Harborne's venture to back him did pique my interest. Harborne obviously saw that and began outlining his plans for a series of factories that would in the fullness of time take raw wool and send it through each of the processes necessary to turn shorn fleeces into woollen cloth. And the more he talked, the more I began to see that, maladroit though Saunders-James's introduction of the topic might have been, Harborne's factories might be just the investment Glanteifi needed.

John

I was grateful that Jem Harborne's factory gave Harry something to talk about on the way home. I'd heard enough before we went over to Plas Blaengwyn about how we had to get back to Eglwyswrw as soon as possible in the morning. But when he mentioned Mr Gelyot senior's investment in the project, I felt as if somebody'd stuck a knife in my guts.

'Harborne tells me Gus's father has taken a quarter-share in the business,' he said. 'Your introduction made all the difference, apparently.'

'I didn't exactly *introduce* them. I just told the Gelyots about meeting him at the Exhibition. Mr Gelyot senior was interested, so I gave him Harborne's card.'

Of course, Mr Gelyot's investment made the whole factory proposal look a lot more attractive to Harry, and he spent the next mile or so giving me and Lydia all the details Jem had made him listen to. I hardly heard a word. I was too busy panicking at the thought of what people would say if they discovered that I'd been responsible for finding Harborne's biggest investor for him. How would the Glanteifi tenants who depended on weaving to make ends meet feel if they knew it was my fault Harborne was producing the cheap cloth that was undercutting them?

I'd just turned the trap towards Adpar hill and the three of us had got out to save the poor horse when Harry asked about Amos Bowen.

'What was your impression of him, John? Harborne described him as a genius with machines.'

I shrugged, stomach still churning. 'I'm not qualified to know a genius with machines from a molehill. But he knows how to *talk* about machines, that's for sure.'

Amos Bowen was a local boy, but he'd been surprisingly tight-lipped about his family circumstances to begin with. Eventually I'd managed to find out that he'd followed his cousin Jeremiah to the mills of Newtown to get away from the family farm. Or to be more accurate, to get away from his father. Reading between the lines, Mr Bowen senior'd been free enough with his fists and his boots to half-kill Amos on any given day of the week.

Mind, I could see why somebody like Amos Bowen would enrage a certain kind of man. He barely looked you in the eye, and when he wasn't talking about machines, he had a stutter that put you properly on edge. In the end, I'd found out why he didn't look at you properly – he only had reliable control of one eye. The left one looked off to one side.

When I told Harry that, his head whipped round. 'Amos Bowen has a squint?'

'Yes. Why?'

'The man who took the news of Lizzie Rees's death to her mother had a stutter, and what Dai Dolbannon referred to as a wandering eye. He was introduced as Barti, but that was obviously a nickname because he'd arrived at the farm wearing an eyepatch.'

'There can't be that many men with a squint and a stutter in the Teifi Valley,' I said. And on top of that, Jem had said his engineer'd been working away till that week. With Amos being from a farming family, he could easily have been working at Dolbannon rather than at another mill like I'd thought.

'David Jones said that Barti was always drawing,' Harry said. 'I assumed he was talking about pictures, but perhaps he meant machines.'

'Well, if it *was* Amos that was working over there,' I said, 'I don't like to think what kind of a time he had of it. He's not your usual farm servant.'

'Jones did tell me the other servants'd been a bit rough with him,' Harry admitted. 'Said his eyepatch hadn't lasted long.'

275

Something like that would've ended up in the midden or the privy after being thrown about like a football between the other lads. I could hear them laughing like fools while they did it. It doesn't pay to be different.

'Did Jem Harborne try and persuade you to put money into the factory?' I asked. 'Amos said he would.'

'Not directly. In fact he was a lot more discreet than Anthony Saunders-James. *He* as good as offered me cash on the spot for Moelfryn Uchaf and Isaf.'

In the corner of my eye I saw Lydia smiling. 'Not quite as comfortable in the drawing room as he is in the office, our Mr Saunders-James,' she said. 'Eleanor told me that before they got married, he employed somebody to coach him in the ways of the gentry.'

'Then his coach did a poor job,' Harry said. 'Even Gus Gelyot's father – who isn't exactly renowned for his drawing room manner – wouldn't have been so crass.'

'Are you going to sell the land to him?' I asked.

'Given our circumstances, it seems like too good an opportunity to pass up. Besides, those two farms have never felt like part of Glanteifi.'

'And what about investing in the factory?' A week ago I'd've been wary of asking, but if I was going to be Glanteifi's agent, then this was my business. 'I got the impression from Amos that the place is a bit of a risky venture,' I said. 'I don't know how much Mr Gelyot's invested, but Harborne still needs more, from what Amos said. Quite a lot more.'

'So why is Amos involved in the project – isn't it risky for him too?'

'They're cousins. And he feels beholden because Jem looked after him when they were in Newtown together.'

Harry said no more and the three of us used our breath for panting up the hill to the tollgate and the turn along the side of the hill to Glanteifi.

'Harborne was very persuasive,' Harry said when we'd all climbed thankfully back into the trap and I'd clucked the horse into a slow plod. 'He's obviously got a well-thought-out plan – getting his manufacturing capacity in place so that as soon as the railway and the port facilities are there he can take full advantage of them. And he's not a fool. He's starting with a simple weaving mill, and then as and when that's profitable, he'll move on to the other processes.'

He sounded impressed. 'You *are* thinking of putting money into it then?' I said.

'I'm not sure yet. But, if he genuinely could give us the kind of return on investment he's talking about, we'd have money to buy shares in the railway *and* the deep-water port scheme when they go on sale. And the income from those might well put Glanteifi on a very different financial footing.' He stopped, and I could see him looking at me in his side vision. 'It's going to take some thinking about.'

Not *What do you think, John?* Not *We'll need to discuss it, obviously.* No, Harry was going to think about it and Harry was going to make a decision. Well, if that was the way he wanted things, I was the wrong man to be his agent.

My heart started to race. 'I disagree. It's obvious what the right thing to do is. If we sell the land, we should pay off some of the mortgage. Invest in our own business, not speculate.'

'Oh, we should, should we?' He sounded half-amused, half-irritated.

'Yes.'

'We should be like all the other local landowners – scared of investing in something new?'

'Never mind what anybody else is doing! *We* should be doing what's right for Glanteifi. The mortgage is crippling us.'

'But if Harborne's returns are what he says they'll be—'

'Yes,' my voice rose to meet his, '*if*! From what you've told us – and from what I heard first-hand when we were sitting in Soyer's restaurant – there's an awful lot of ifs involved in Harborne's new venture. *If* he can get enough investors. *If* the railway line comes to Cardigan. *If* this deep-water port scheme happens.' Harry

277

stared straight ahead, chewing the inside of his lip. 'Your father wouldn't have invested in Harborne's factory,' I said. 'He'd have paid the mortgage off.'

He spun round to face me. 'How *dare* you tell me what my father would've done! You barely met the man!'

'I've been studying what he did with the estate for the last six months! Actions speak louder than words, and his actions were all for the benefit of Glanteifi!' I was almost sick with the beating of my heart in my throat, but I was damned if I was going to back down. Harry knew next to nothing about the running of the estate. He thought Mr Ormiston'd known what he was doing, for God's sake! He knew nothing about how his father had managed the place. Nothing!

'You think you know my father's mind better than me, do you?'

'About the estate? Yes.'

I felt something on my arm. I looked down and saw Lydia's hand. She was warning me not to go too far, not to say something there was no coming back from.

I took a deep breath. 'Perhaps now's not really the time...'

'Pull up,' Harry said.

'What?'

'Pull the horse up. I'm going to walk the rest of the way home. Because you're right. Now is very definitely not the time.'

Harry

Instead of walking straight home, I turned up the little Ceri valley and let my feet find the familiar way along the old parish road.

Lydia had offered to come with me, but I had sent her home with John. I was not in the mood for company, especially company that was likely to find fault.

Dammit, Lydia and John both wanted me to take more interest in the estate, but as soon as I *tried* to involve myself, to devise a plan that might extract us from the mire into which my father's policies had plunged us, I was challenged! I would not have expected Lydia to defend my position – not given what she had told me about John's lack of self-confidence – but the fact that she had not even attempted to mediate must mean that she thought I was in the wrong.

I marched recklessly along the little road, heedless of potholes and loose stones that might trip me up. My mind closed to intrusive thoughts, I refused to think about John's resistance and tried to let the warm air and the sound of bees in the last hedgerow flowers calm my mind. Bees were not plagued by doubt and criticism; they knew only a fixed, unalterable purpose and the instinct that drove them to it. Their tiny insect minds might never know joy, but neither would they know grief or despair, and just at that moment, I found such obliviousness profoundly to be envied.

–

An hour or so later, having returned home and slipped quietly upstairs to wash and change, I made my way down to the dining room. I had heard the clock in the hall chime the quarter-hour not long since, and I knew it would be easier to face John and Lydia if I was already at the table when they came in.

When I found Elsie lighting the candles on the chandelier, I berated myself for not having realised that somebody would be there making the room habitable for me.

'Beg pardon, sir,' she said. 'I thought I'd be finished before anybody came in.'

'It's my fault, Elsie. I'm early to dinner. Just carry on.'

After a minute or so that proved longer, I suspect, than either of us found ideal, Elsie fled, leaving me in the company of my own embarrassment. I could not have betrayed my failure to understand the workings of my own house more obviously if I had tried.

When the door eventually opened once more, John and Lydia came in together, as if one of them had waited for the other in the hall so that they could present a united front. How ironic. I had long wished for them to become better friends, but had not anticipated them allying themselves against me.

I rose as they came to the table. 'I apologise for my childish behaviour earlier. I can only plead the current trying circumstances in mitigation.'

'You're forgiven,' Lydia said, her pardon masking an ambivalent mumble from John.

We took our seats in an unwonted, and soon uncomfortably protracted, silence. Mercifully, before any of us resorted to platitudes, the soup arrived and we addressed our meal. What Ianto made of the oppressive atmosphere, I could not guess, and when he left the room to bear the soup plates away and bring the meat, I knew I must force myself to speak.

John, however, got there before me.

'Harry, if I'm going to be Glanteifi's agent, there's something I have to say.'

I held out a hand, giving him the floor.

'As assistant coroner I defer to you. You may not *think* I do,' he added, forestalling the objection I had been about to make, 'but putting a different point of view isn't the same as insisting on it. We've never given a jury advice based on what I think has happened. In the end, it's always your view that holds sway.'

'It's my responsibility. I'm coroner.'

'Yes, you are. And you're also the squire of Glanteifi.' I heard a click in his dry throat as he swallowed. 'But if I'm going to be your agent, I'm not prepared to have my views discounted. I want to have a say in how you spend the money you get from the sale of the Moelfryn farms.'

If he had leaned over and punched me I could not feasibly have been more shocked. 'What's this? "Do what I say or I won't be your agent"?'

'No.' His voice wavered, but he continued. 'I just want a proper discussion. Not only on this, but on everything. Otherwise I'm no more use to you than Mr Ormiston was.'

His words trapped my breath in my chest and turned my stomach into a cold fist, threatening to expel the soup I had just consumed. I stared into the whirlpool, John's face hovering just above the grey indistinctness, and failed utterly to identify an appropriate response.

'Harry...' Lydia put a hand on the tablecloth between us, as if she was laying claim to the space to speak.

'No.' I kept my gaze averted from her. 'This is between me and John.' I stared at the pale blur of his face. 'The job of an agent is to advise—'

'Yes! And the job of a squire is to *listen*! To listen and *take notice of what's said*. Not just to say, "That's very interesting but I'm still going to do what I was going to do before you opened your mouth"! That was Mr Ormiston's attitude when I tried to argue with him. And his attitude left Matthew Thomas *dead*.' In the silence created by his words, I could hear his agitated breathing. 'I know Jem Harborne's got a silver tongue on him – I heard enough of his plans in London. But he's only interested in how much money he can make and he doesn't care whose livelihood he destroys in the process. Do you *want* Glanteifi to be part of that?'

'At least Harborne *knows* how to make money, which is something most of the landowners in the Teifi Valley would give their eye teeth to learn!'

The simple fact was that land ownership was becoming more and more uneconomic as a way of making one's living. If John thought we could simply farm our way out of our financial difficulties, then our working relationship seemed doomed before it started.

'Is that what we're here for,' he demanded, 'to make money? When we first met, you told me that a landowner's first duty was to care for his tenants. When did that change, Harry?'

'When I saw that my father had mortgaged the estate almost to bankruptcy *caring for his tenants!*'

'Your father understood th—'

'*My father* treated the tenants like children who couldn't think for themselves.'

'If we can pay off some of the mortgage, we'll have a chance to start working *with* our tenants, instead of just seeing them as debtors whose payments service the interest on our loan.'

'And you think we'll be able to service the loan from rent income alone, do you? Because the figures say otherwise.'

'Obviously we need to start doing things differently. That's what I've been trying to tell Mr Ormiston. I've been looking at your father's diaries—'

'*What?*' I had had no idea that my father had kept a diary.

John hesitated. Did he look to Lydia for guidance? Did she give it? Not being able to see the movement of eyes had never been so infuriating. 'Your father's diaries.' His voice was not entirely steady. 'He kept notes on each of the tenancies each quarter, what he suggested to the tenant and what the tenant actually did. If you compare the ones who took his advice and the ones who didn't—'

'Where did you find these diaries?'

'In the pedestal of his desk when he—'

'What were you doing looking into his desk?'

'I wasn't *looking into his desk.* One day, while your father was still alive, Mrs Griffiths called me into the office – I mean his study

– and he was sitting there. He opened the drawer and showed me the books. He *wanted* me to read them.'

My father had shown John diaries whose existence I had been totally unaware of. Despite the fact that they would have been useless to me, that I would have been obliged to ask him to read them to me anyway, I felt somehow that in giving him those diaries, my father had passed the care of Glanteifi on to John rather than to me.

Suddenly the twilit gloom of the dining room seemed to close in around me until, the chandelier notwithstanding, I could hardly see.

In the silence, I was aware of the door opening and Ianto and Fred bringing in our dinner. They had obviously been waiting outside the door for a break in the argument into which they might insert themselves. I cringed inwardly at the thought of the two of them listening, the food going cold in its serving dishes. I put out a hand to my wine glass and felt it trembling.

'Leave it,' I said as Fred began to serve me. 'We'll serve ourselves. Come back in ten minutes.'

Did Fred look at Lydia for confirmation of my order? Whether he did or not, there was a perceptible delay before he murmured an acquiescence and retreated, Ianto with him.

'So, to summarise,' I said, ignoring the food, 'you believe that, having read my father's diaries, you know his plans for the estate and you consider them to be superior to any I might devise – is that broadly correct?'

'Harry.' Lydia could obviously contain herself no longer. 'Your father had been running the estate for fifty years. Can you not see how arrogant it is for you to imagine that you can come in and do it better in less than four months?'

'My father belonged to a different age! And Harborne's right – if local landowners don't seize the day and support new projects that'll bring modern industry to the west, we'll always be seen as the poor relations, country bumpkins who haven't realised that it's the nineteenth century. He's offering me – *us*, Glanteifi –

the chance to be part of something that's going to revolutionise Cardiganshire. We can be part of something bigger instead of sitting out here being ignored by Parliament and ridiculed by the national newspapers.'

'But what does that mean for the estate?' John asked.

'Money. Finances. Investment.'

'Machinery?'

'Yes. Why not?'

John stood up. 'You want Cardiganshire to be like England. Like London. Well I don't. Excuse me, Lydia.'

He left, and the next thing I heard was the front door being opened and thudding closed behind him.

John

The front door banged shut behind me, and I marched off down the lane, away from the mansion.

I needed to be out of the house, with other people. People I wasn't in the middle of an argument with.

The Drovers Inn; that was where I'd go. It was months since I'd been there – I hadn't been into town for a drink since I'd moved to Glanteifi. But I needed a drink now.

I left Seren in the stables. Didn't want to be a gentleman tonight. Trouble was, walking gave me time to fume, and instead of cooling down, I got more and more angry with Harry.

All that talk I'd had from him when we first met – about wanting me to be his equal and not wanting to be squire and how a few rich people shouldn't own all the land and expect everybody else to keep them in luxury – all that'd gone since his father had died. Just gone. And truth be told, I'd felt less equal to him since he'd made me under-steward than I had when I'd been just a solicitor's clerk he borrowed from time to time. I'd had nothing to lose if I argued with him then. Now, I had a whole life to lose.

Harry was out of his depth with Glanteifi. I think he knew that but couldn't admit it, so he'd just found ways to avoid his responsibilities. Ever since he'd been elected, he'd gone out to every sudden death that was brought to him, because being coroner gave him a cast-iron excuse not to think about being squire. If he was needed elsewhere, then he could leave everything to do with Glanteifi to his steward.

Or rather, to his steward and *me*.

When he first said he wanted me to be under-steward, I'd been pretty sure that what he really meant was that he wanted me to be always available as assistant coroner. Because the way Harry looked at it, if Mr Ormiston'd managed without help before, he could do it again while I rode off with him to conduct inquests.

But he'd forgotten the part of the deal that said Mr Ormiston would train me up for a year, then retire. I suppose, back in February, a year had seemed like a long time. But a twelvemonth wears out pretty quickly when you're always looking from one quarter-day to the next.

I stomped over the little humpbacked Ceri bridge, through the evening smell of honeysuckle in a cottage garden and followed the road up onto the slope above the Teifi. There was still some light in the sky behind me, but it was almost dark under the trees. I'd left the mansion in such a hurry that I hadn't thought to bring a lantern. But I'd be fine. It was only since moving to Glanteifi that I'd gone soft and had lanterns to light my way at night.

I jumped about a foot in the air as the sudden screech of a barn owl ripped terror through me like a red-hot wire.

Good job I didn't believe in omens, or I'd've been expecting bad news in town.

–

As it happened, it wasn't bad news I found in Newcastle Emlyn; it was Amos Bowen. As I walked over the bridge and up to the Drovers, I was beginning to worry a bit about the welcome I'd get. I hadn't been there for months, and I had a pretty good idea that I'd get some nonsense from the lads about thinking I was too good to go drinking with my old friends and that kind of thing. But I'd been busy since I moved out to Glanteifi, hadn't I? Studying for my exams, learning the ropes with Mr Ormiston, going out with Harry on investigations. I hadn't had time to come into town drinking.

I saw Amos as soon as I walked in. He was sitting by himself in the corner, well away from the card-players and the arm-wrestlers, with a sheet of paper on the table in front of him. But it wasn't him being by himself that made him stand out – it was the eyepatch he was wearing. I wondered where he'd got it – he hadn't been wearing it at Plas Blaengwyn earlier on. But wherever it had come from, to my mind that patch meant that Amos was definitely Barti Ddu from Dolbannon, so it might be worth having a word with him.

But I had something else to deal with first. The heckling had started.

Oh, here he is, lads, Gentleman John Davies!

Didn't think we'd see you in here again – too fine for the likes of us now you're living with the crachach!

Come to buy us all a drink, have you?

Dead body in here somewhere, is there?

There were some comments that were a bit sharper than that, too, but they came from people I wouldn't've given the time of day to back when I was here twice a week, so I took no notice and sat down with Dan James. These days he was a solicitor's clerk in town, but I'd known him since we were at Mr Davies's school in Adpar together.

'Well, well, well, come crawling back to us have you, John Davies?'

'I don't see any crawling going on, thank you very much! Just here for a quiet drink.'

I shut him up by ordering a round for everybody at the table. We chatted about this and that for a few minutes before I nodded in Amos's direction. 'Know him? The man with the eyepatch?'

Dan shook his head. 'No, who is he?'

'The engineer at the new factory in Llandyfriog.' The look on Dan's face told me that he thought he knew why I was here now. 'No, I didn't come into town to see him, but I could do with a word with him, as it happens.'

Dan nodded knowingly. 'Heard about the skirmish. The local carpenters and the ones up at the site. The man that got injured – died, has he?'

I stared at him. 'Hold on – what d'you mean, local carpenters? Is that who attacked the mill?' He'd thought I already knew, which meant that it was common gossip around town. 'Is it?' I pressed him.

Dan shrugged. 'That's what everybody's saying. Understand-able, anyway, isn't it? If Jeremiah Harborne wanted a mill built here, he should've paid local men to do it.'

He had a point. But as assistant coroner, I couldn't say anything that might be taken as mitigation of a crime. 'Last I heard, the man was still alive,' I said. 'We'll have to wait and see. But if you know who did this, Dan, you'd better tell me.'

He held his hands up. 'Whoa there, pony! I'm just telling you gossip. I don't know anything for sure.' He took a sup of his pint, looking at me over the mug. 'If it's not that, what d'you want to talk to him about? How d'you even know him?'

'Met him at Plas Blaengwyn earlier. He was there with Harborne and I was there with Harry.'

'*Harry*,' Dan scoffed. Couldn't get over me being on first-name terms with the squire.

I wasn't going to tell him I wanted to know whether Amos was also known as Barti Ddu, so to answer his other question, I fell back on a half-truth. 'There's a young lad I know who's keen to be apprenticed to him as an engineer.'

'Oh yes? Who's that, then?'

I opened my mouth to explain about Lleu, then shut it again. I was no better than Harborne, was I? He'd brought labour in from somewhere else, and here I was bringing a lad from Llanddewi Brefi to Amos instead of him finding an apprentice from town.

I tapped the side of my nose. 'Better say nothing till the deal's done, eh?' Solicitors' clerks know the value of confidentiality. We also know the value of knowing things nobody else knows yet, and Dan'd be bound to think I was keeping the secret for my own benefit.

'Suit yourself,' he said.

'Anyway…'

'Yes! Off you go for your little chat! 'Spect it'll be another six months before we see you in here again, will it?'

I grinned. 'To be honest with you, Dan, a man can have enough of wine.'

As I went over to Amos's corner, I beckoned to the pot boy. 'Evening,' I said.

Amos looked up, head down in his shoulders as if he expected a stick across his back, but his face broke out in a smile when he saw me, and he straightened up a bit.

I signalled to the pot boy to fill Amos's mug as well as mine.

'Oh, th–thank you.'

I grabbed a spare stool and sat down. 'Fetching eyepatch,' I grinned.

'M–Mr Jones the saddler said I c-could have it this evening if I c-came here to fetch it. I w-wanted to have it before ch-church tomorrow.'

'Church, is it?' I teased him some more. 'Too good for chapel now you're an engineer?'

He gazed at me earnestly for about a second and a half before looking away again. 'I used to g-go with m-my old *mistir* and his wife.'

Most likely he'd chosen to go to church with Dai Dolbannon instead of chapel with the other farm servants just to get away from them for a bit. The endless standing up and sitting down and muttering things in English from a prayer book would've been a small price to pay for a morning of not being treated like something in a freak show. Still, I wondered how he'd got on with all the solicitors and shopkeepers and chemists at Holy Trinity. It was quite a well-to-do crowd, the church's congregation here. Maybe he thought going to church would give him more of a place in society as the engineer to the factory.

He glanced up at me again from his beer. A lot more willing to look at me with his squint covered up, our Amos. He had eyes like a calf – big and brown, with lashes a girl would've been proud of.

'Heard something just now that Jem might be interested in,' I said.

He looked at me, but said nothing. I drank some beer. I'd almost forgotten what the Drovers' beer tasted like, and it brought back a flood of memories, not all of them very happy, to be honest. 'Did the police go and see the man Jem thought was responsible for wrecking the mill?' I asked, before I told him what Dan'd said. 'The weaver?'

Amos nodded. 'S-said it was n-nothing to do with him.'

'And maybe it wasn't.' In the end, it was only gossip, as Dan had pointed out, so I was careful what I said. 'I did hear that perhaps the mill wouldn't've been touched if Jem had employed carpenters from Newcastle Emlyn instead of bringing in a gang from Llandysul.'

Amos nodded. I could see that he understood what I meant. 'Y-you g-going to tell the police?' he asked.

'Not my business, is it? Not unless the carpenter who was injured dies. Then it'll be my business. Mine and Mr Probert-Lloyd's.'

'N-not Jem's fault.'

No, strictly speaking it wasn't Harborne's fault. And the wreckers must be praying that the man they'd whacked around the head – Jaco, the foreman had called him – would come round and still have all his wits. Because if he died, there'd be an inquest, and me and Harry'd be after them.

I looked at Amos. He was in the same decent suit he'd been wearing earlier at Plas Blaengwyn, and had neatly cut hair and a decent shave. Didn't look much like a farm servant. But he had to be Barti Ddu, didn't he?

I decided to use one of Harry's questioning methods and pretend I already knew the answer to the question I was going to ask. But I had to go in on the sly. 'When I was up at the factory site on Thursday,' I said, 'the foreman told me somebody'd gone up to Llandysul to fetch Jaco's family.'

Amos said nothing. To be fair, I hadn't actually asked a question, and his stutter meant he never spoke unless he had to.

'Did they come?'

'I d–don't know.'

I took a pull of my pint. 'Speaking of messengers going to fetch family, I hear you went on a similar errand the day Lizzie Rees died. While you were still working at Dolbannon.'

His head snapped up as if somebody'd caught him a swift punch under the chin, and his one good eye stared at me.

'It *was* you Dai Dolbannon picked to go over to Ffynone, wasn't it?'

He didn't answer, so I decided to give a bit of information in the hope of getting some back.

'Harry's holding an inquest for Lizzie Rees's sweetheart, Nathaniel Stockton, in Eglwyswrw on Monday. He's convinced his death and Lizzie's are related.'

'D-d–*dead*? N–Nattie Stockton's d–dead?'

There was no reason why he should know, was there? He'd been gone from Dolbannon by the time the body'd been identified.

'You knew him then, did you?' I asked.

Amos opened his mouth. But the stop-rush-stop of his speech couldn't seem to get to the rush bit this time. His neck was thrust forward with the effort of forcing a word out, and I could hear a noise coming from his throat, but nothing came from his mouth. Then he hit himself on his thigh, hard, and as if he'd released a jammed mechanism, a word spat out.

'Church.'

Small world. I'd have been willing to bet that neither of them was a churchgoer by his own inclination, but they'd both found their way to Eglwyswrw church for their own reasons.

'Coracle men at Cilgerran pulled him out of the river on Monday morning,' I said.

Amos blinked furiously.

'In case you're wondering, it wasn't suicide. Somebody killed him and threw him in the river.'

Later, I thought. They'd thrown him into the river *later*. Something about that started tickling at my brain, but I couldn't think about it because Amos was trying to get a question out.

'Wh-wh-*why*?'

'Why would anybody kill him? Good question. Got to be something to do with Lizzie Rees's death, though, hasn't it? People get suspicious.'

Amos looked at me, his face a shocked blank. 'D-D-Doctor Gwynne said n-natural causes.'

'I know. But Harry went there with the anatomist, Dr Reckitt, didn't he? That must've made people think he didn't believe Dr Gwynne.'

Reckitt'd found nothing, of course, but people hadn't heard that till later. Not till after he'd finished his testing of whatever had been in Lizzie's stomach. But by then, Nattie Stockton'd been dead.

'Wh-wh...' Amos hit his thigh again, 'when's the inquest?'

'Day after tomorrow.' And tomorrow, Harry'd want to go over to Eglwyswrw first thing.

I was dreading that ride.

Harry

The following morning, I rose early and, unable to face the stilted, avoidant conversations that awaited me over breakfast, made straight for Eglwyswrw.

Of course, the sensible course of action would have been to sit down and thrash the whole thing out with John, but I had been so derailed by his sudden rebellion that I had lost faith in my own judgement.

Leaving a note asking him to join me as soon as he was able, I headed for breakfast at the Sergeant's Inn.

-

Unsurprisingly, the inn was far from crowded when I arrived, and the landlord installed me on the settle next to the fireside. He fussed over me, insisting on speaking English and offering me coffee while I waited for my breakfast.

As I sat, allowing the coffee to warm and stir me, I could not help overhearing a conversation being carried on by the inn's only other Sunday-morning patrons. Either the two men concerned thought I would not understand what they said, or being overheard did not trouble them, for they took almost as little care to moderate their voices as Benton Reckitt.

I soon realised that they were anticipating Nathaniel Stockton's inquest the following day.

'Lizzie Rees's father'll have something to do with it, you mark my words,' one said. 'Mic y Porthmon. Always been a bit odd, that one.'

'Good weaver, mind,' his companion observed.

'Maybe, but I've never seen such a lazy mower. Don't know why Dai Dolbannon keeps him in the team.' He paused. 'Unless there's another reason.'

'What sort of reason?'

'Got an eye for a pretty girl, Dai Dolbannon has.'

'Lizzie, you mean? Never!'

'Come on – she was a beauty, wasn't she? Maybe Dai was keeping her father on so she'd bring his food to him while we were mowing.'

A silence suggested that his companion was giving this some consideration. Eventually he spoke. 'No. I don't believe it. Not with his wife sick at home.'

'That's the point, isn't it? Margaret Dolbannon won't see Christmas if I'm any judge.'

'Hah – hark at you! After Dewin Gwynne's job now, is it?'

'Common sense, man! You can see it plain as day. Yellow she is, poor dab. Dai'll be looking for the new Mrs Jones, you watch. Got little ones to look after, hasn't he?'

'So you're telling me he was courting Lizzie Rees? Properly, not just looking?' From a slight change in the sound of his voice, I could tell that the speaker had shifted his position, possibly so that he could look squarely into the face of his companion.

'Well, she was courting in bed the night she died.'

'*What?* Where'd you get that from?'

'My wife heard it from—'

'Tchah!' his companion interrupted. 'Women's gossip.'

'Don't you be so quick! There's something not right with Lizzie Rhosdywarch's death.'

'Don't talk nonsense. The coroner went there and spoke to everybody, *and* Esther Rees had the workhouse doctor to her. If there was something there, those two would've found it.'

They fell then to discussing who might be called to give evidence at 'the Englishman's' inquest, and I weighed up what I had just heard.

David Jones – Dai Dolbannon – had acknowledged that he knew Lizzie's father, and that his family bought cloth from Mic. Had that meant Jones visiting Rhosdywarch himself?

And if he was the other man that Lizzie had told Cadwgan Gwynne about, did that explain why Mic Rees had gone to Dolbannon for his messenger – so he could tell Jones that Gwynne had ruled her death accidental?

I ate my breakfast and waited for the tolling of the church bell to summon worshippers to morning prayer. As soon as it stopped, indicating that the service was about to begin, I would cross the road and wait in the churchyard in order to test John's theory about latecoming being habitual.

John. Would he do as I had asked and come as soon as he was able, or would he choose to find himself too busy and simply arrive in time for the inquest tomorrow? Our argument the previous evening had taken me completely by surprise, and following his abrupt departure, I had been forced to listen to advice I had not sought from Lydia.

'You have to decide who you are, Harry. Are you the autocrat squire who simply makes decisions and expects them to be carried out, or are you the egalitarian you've always claimed? If the latter, then you must see that John is right – you have to find a way of reaching a consensus on things.'

In truth, it had simply not occurred to me that the decision on whether to sell the land to Anthony Saunders-James might not be mine alone to make, but had it not been for John's reference to my father, I might have been able to discuss the matter sensibly. And Lydia had seen that. 'It was the diaries, wasn't it?' she had asked. 'The fact that your father gave them to John to read, not you.'

'Fat lot of good it would have done, giving them to me.'

Don't be fatuous, Harry. She didn't have to say it. But the alternative to retreating into fatuity was to face the truth: my father had not trusted me with his diaries. He might have shared them with me before John ever came to Glanteifi, before the strokes that eventually killed him had yet prevented him from speaking.

But why would he? I had given him ample evidence that I had no interest in the way he ran Glanteifi.

And now I had exacerbated things by running away. If John delayed in coming to Eglwyswrw, I would have to interview churchgoers and Sunday loiterers myself. To say I did not relish doing so without him at my side was an understatement.

–

Ten minutes later, I stood at the churchyard gate, nerving myself to accost any latecomers.

Yesterday's rain was gone, and the September sun smiled down on me as I waited, but today, apparently, the whole congregation had arrived in a timely fashion. Perhaps they had all been agog to hear any news of Lizzie Rees and Nathaniel Stockton. Two sudden deaths in the same week must surely be unprecedented in this small community.

Around the churchyard wall, at the side of the Cenarth road, a horse shifted, its harness jingling. Abandoning my post, I followed the sound and found a carriage and three traps, including, presumably, the one in which David Jones had conveyed his family and Amos Bowen to church the previous week.

A boy sat on the wall beside all the hobbled horses. 'Good morning,' I greeted him. 'Were you here watching the horses last week during the service?'

'Yes, sir.'

'Did you see anybody come out of the church and walk away – perhaps while people were still arriving? A young man, a little taller than me, with dark hair?'

He did not reply immediately, and being unable to tell whether this was due to effortful recall or the hope of payment, I took a small silver coin from my pocket – a threepenny piece as far as I could tell from its size.

It seemed to galvanise the child. 'There was somebody. Came running out.'

I held the coin in the palm of my hand, pretending to scrutinise it. 'Was there anybody with him?'

'No, sir.'

'Was there anyone else who might've seen him too? On the main street, perhaps?'

'Don't know, sir. Can't see much of the street from here, can you? And it would've been time for chapel, anyway.'

In other words, most Eglwyswrw folk would have been at Sunday worship burnishing their souls or maintaining the good opinion of their neighbours. I gave him the coin and was about to turn away when I remembered something else. 'The man who ran out of the church – did he go off towards Felindre or the other way, towards the Cilgerran road?'

'He didn't go either way. He went straight into the Sergeant's.'

'You saw him?'

'No. You can't see the Sergeant's from here, the stables're in the way. But I heard the door open and bang shut. There's a weight on it so it shuts by itself if you don't hold onto it – makes a heck of a noise.'

–

The landlord's response when I had established Nattie Stockton's movements on the previous Sunday was one of slightly affronted astonishment. 'That was the young fellow they dragged out of the river? Well, nobody told me that!'

'So,' I confirmed, 'he just drank a brandy and left – is that right?'

'Well, you know, we talked about poor Lizzie Rees. He'd only just heard.'

'What did he say?'

'Nothing much. Just how it'd been a shock hearing it like that when he'd come to church expecting to see her.'

'You hadn't met him before?'

'No.'

Could he be lying to me, trying not to get involved? Given the way news travelled, he must be aware that I was holding an inquest the following day in Cilgerran. I missed John and his skills of observation acutely, and I was becoming increasingly worried that he would not follow me this morning as I had requested. We had never found ourselves fundamentally opposed in this way before, and I was at a loss to know how to mend the rift.

'Have you heard much gossip in here about Lizzie Rees's death?' I asked the landlord, realising that I should have asked him before.

'You know how it is, Mr Probert-Lloyd, a publican hears all sorts, and if he's wise, he takes it all with a fistful of salt.'

I took this for what it was: a polite way of declining to comment. A publican with a loose tongue soon had no patrons.

'But,' he added, 'there was plenty of talk about that young man – the Englishman, I always heard him called. People would've taken Lizzie Rees dying like that a lot more easily if he hadn't been involved with her. Even sensible heads were saying he must've had something to do with it.'

Thanking him, I sat down again with a mug of beer to await the end of the service over the road.

So engrossed was I in my thoughts that I did not notice the door open behind me, and almost jumped out of my skin when John sat down opposite me and started speaking as if we had been in the middle of a conversation.

'Harry, what if Nathaniel Stockton never went to Cilgerran? What if whoever killed him just took his body there to throw it in the river?'

John

Harry looked as if he'd been shot when I sat down. Was he that surprised to see me? I knew we had things to sort out between us, and we would. But not today. Today was for finding out whatever we could about Nattie Stockton's death and we both knew that if we couldn't get what'd happened to him clear in our heads before the inquest, the whole thing'd be a shambles. I didn't want people from St Florence coming up here and saying we didn't know what we were doing.

'We've been assuming that because he was *found* in Cilgerran, he must've been killed there,' I said. 'But what if he wasn't?'

I sat back as the landlord came over with a jug of coffee and some cups on a tray. I hoped it'd be better than Reckitt's.

'Think about it,' I said when he'd gone. 'Reckitt says Nattie was probably killed late on Sunday morning or early Sunday afternoon, so he can't've gone far after leaving the church. More than likely he was killed somewhere near here.'

Harry chewed the inside of his lip. 'True. But why take the body to Cilgerran, then? It's a long way from here.'

'Not that far if you've got a horse or a cart.'

'After dark, presumably?'

'Probably. We know he was left somewhere after he'd been killed. Hidden somewhere small, with him being tucked up like he was.'

I wasn't going to admit it to Harry, but Nattie being killed here rather than in Cilgerran had been Dan James's idea.

After Amos'd left the Drovers, I'd sat down with Dan and another Newcastle Emlyn boy. Once they'd told me all the town gossip I'd missed, they'd tried to get me to talk about life at the mansion. In the end, the other lad had got fed up with me being discreet, and had left Dan and me on our own.

'Why are you really here?' Dan asked, keeping his voice low. 'It wasn't just because you fancied a pint, was it?'

I looked over the table at him. We'd been good friends at one time – even after we left Mr Davies's school to go to work – but I hadn't seen him, not to have a drink with, for months. Since Harry'd made me under-steward, I'd been living a completely different kind of life, but now, sitting here with Dan, I realised there were bits of my old life I missed.

'I needed to get out of the house,' I admitted. 'It gets a bit much sometimes.'

'What, living with the *crachach*, you mean?'

I grinned and supped my ale. Didn't want to be disloyal. 'Just feels like we're always talking about work. If it's not the estate, it's an inquest.'

'You're never telling me that it's *dull* being coroner's assistant?'

'No, it's not that...'

'What, then?'

I didn't want to tell him about the argument I'd had with Harry, so instead I told him about Nattie Stockton's death and the strange condition his corpse'd been in when Caleb Richards brought it to the Pendre.

'Compared to how we usually do things,' I said, 'we left it all a bit up in the air over there, to tell you the truth. We had to get back for Matthew Thomas's funeral yesterday, and we've been up at Plas Blaengwyn today.'

Daniel stroked his chin. It was something he used to do at school to make the rest of us laugh when our teacher said 'consider this, gentlemen', but I wasn't laughing now. 'If somebody threw him in the Teifi at Cilgerran,' he said, 'it was probably because they were hoping the tide'd wash him out to sea, right?'

That was what Caleb had thought too. Wouldn't have occurred to me, but then I didn't live by a tidal bit of the river. Neither did Dan, come to that, but he'd always been quick.

'So it doesn't necessarily follow that he was *killed* in Cilgerran, does it?' he said. 'That was just a convenient place to get rid of him. I reckon the killer's got to be whoever beat your Englishman up before.'

Which was the same conclusion Sally Sips'd jumped to. 'Why?'

'Well, if they thought he'd defied them, started seeing this Lizzie again – even got her courting in bed – they'd've been pretty bloody furious, wouldn't they?'

'Yes, I know. But what'd be the point of killing him after she'd died?'

'Punishment.'

'She died a natural death. And people knew that right from the off. Her father went for a doctor to certify the death before he even sent a messenger to tell her mother.'

'Maybe so. But what doctors *say* and what people *believe* are two different things, aren't they? What did everybody in Eglwyswrw *think*? That's the question. More to the point, what did the boys who gave your dead man his beating think?'

Dan leaned over the table, close enough for the acne scars on his forehead to show up in the light of the candle between us. 'They think this Nattie was courting in bed with this girl and while he was there she died, and now he's getting away with it. No inquest. No trial. No punishment. But they've lost the girl they were all chasing. They'd want him to pay, wouldn't they?'

I looked at Harry now. 'I think we should still talk to people after church – see if Nattie was seen going off with anybody. And then we should find out whether there are any ponds nearby.'

–

The Sergeant's landlord told us that the church service usually finished around half past eleven, so we walked out of the inn at a quarter past, just in case. It was a nice day. Waiting outside wasn't going to hurt us.

Opposite the inn, a boy I'd seen around the stables before was sitting outside, perched on a saddle horse.

'Not at chapel?' I said it with a smile, so he'd know I wasn't finding fault.

'Got to be here when they come for their horses,' he said, jerking his head backwards at the churchyard to let me know who 'they' were.

I stood where I could see him and keep an eye on the church-yard. Out of the corner of my eye I saw Harry quietly move out of sight. Good idea. Best if the child thought it was just me being nosy and the master'd gone on to wait for whoever we were here to see.

'Were you sitting out here last Sunday morning?' I asked.

The boy sucked snot back through his nose and spat. I waited, watching him. He'd be about eleven. His hair was too long and kept falling into his eyes. He pushed it away with dirty-nailed fingers, but it just fell straight back. Must drive him mad.

'Yes,' he said when he was good and ready.

'A man came over from the church, just around the time the service was starting,' I said. 'A young man. He went straight into the Sergeant's. Did you see him?'

The boy squinted up at me. 'What did he look like?'

I described the clothes Nattie Stockton'd been wearing when he died. 'About as tall as me,' I said, 'with dark hair.'

'Didn't see him go *in*. Must've still been seeing to the horses.'

'But you saw him come out, did you?'

He nodded.

'Think carefully, now. When he came out of the Sergeant's, was there anybody else about that you could see?'

He gave it some thought, glanced up and down the street, trying to remember. Then he chin-pointed up the road. 'Over there.'

'Who did you see?'

The boy started taking an interest in his fingernails, using the thumbnail of one hand to pick the dirt out from under the nails on the other.

'I won't tell anybody you told me,' I said. 'But I need to know. For the coroner.' It was a risk. Mentioning Harry could go either way – it might scare him into telling me, or scare him so much he clammed up altogether.

'Twm y Gof and his friends,' he said, without looking up. 'Having a smoke after chapel. Like always.' He was cleverer than he looked, this boy. If it always happened, it didn't need to have been him that'd told me, did it?

I looked behind me. The blacksmith's open-fronted workshop was barely twenty yards away, on the opposite side of the road. There was nobody there now. 'Chapel finish early last week, did it?' I asked. There weren't many chapels that let you out much before midday as a rule.

'Elders' meeting,' he said, wiping his nose with the side of a finger then rubbing the snot off on his trousers.

'When you saw the man come out of the Sergeant's, did they say anything to him, Twm and his friends?'

He shrugged, eyes down.

'What's your name?' I asked. He looked up then. I didn't suppose people usually asked. 'Gwilym.'

'Gwilym, I need to know what happened. It's really important, because somebody killed that man later that day.'

The boy's eyes widened, but then his face closed up. If the man he'd seen had been murdered, talking to me might be dangerous.

'Did Twm and his lot say anything to him?'

'Couldn't hear.'

'Did they follow him?'

A shake of the head, eyes down.

'So he just walked past them and they took no notice of him?'

A shrug.

'Gwilym, come on! Tell me what happened and then I'll go.'

The boy stared up at me, hoping I wasn't lying to him but worried that I was. 'He didn't walk past them. When he got to the coach house, he turned around and came back this way.'

I looked at the sight lines. Stockton wouldn't have been able to see the forge from the entrance to the Sergeant's – he'd only have seen Twm and his friends standing there when he drew level with the coach house.

'Then what?'

'He walked that way.' The boy nodded in the direction of the road to Cardigan.

I stared down the road. There was a lane that went off not far along.

'He went across the fields?'

Gwilym shrugged. If the man'd gone in the opposite direction from the one he'd take to go home, then at some point he was going to cut across the fields, wasn't he?

'And the men at the forge – they didn't follow him?'

The boy shook his head. 'They went off that way.' He nodded in the direction of Felindre Farchog. 'One of them lives along there.'

'Who?'

'Dai Blaengwndwn.'

'Was Wil Llain with them?'

He nodded.

'Anybody else?'

'No.'

Twm y Gof, Wil Llain and Dai Blaengwndwn. The three who'd been after Lizzie, according to Llwyo. If they'd also been the ones who'd given Nattie Stockton a beating, then no wonder he didn't want to walk past them. The question was, had they caught up with him somewhere on his way home?

By this time, a few people were standing in the churchyard and I could see the vicar by the door, talking to people as they came out. But now we knew when Nattie Stockton had last been seen and where he'd been going, there was no need to talk to the rest of the congregation.

I gave Gwilym a penny and went round the stables to tell Harry what I'd found out.

'Reckitt said somebody'd twisted Stockton's arm behind his back and forced his face into the water, right?' I said. 'But what if it wasn't just *one* somebody? These three names keep coming up whenever we talk about Lizzie Rees and Nattie Stockton – Twm y Gof, Wil Llain and Dai Blaengwndwn. So maybe all three of them were involved.' I could see him turning that over in his mind, working out if it fitted what we knew. 'Think about the bruising on his body,' I said. 'It's the kind of thing you'd expect if two people'd held him and a third had done the punching, right? So maybe once they'd finished punching him, they drowned him.'

Harry nodded, with that fixed look on his face that told me he was trying to see it all in his mind's eye; walk through it.

'If they intercepted him going over the fields, it does seem to add up.' He sounded cautious. 'If we can find a pond, and somewhere nearby where they might've hidden him, then I think it'd be worth calling the three of them to give evidence tomorrow.'

'We'd need to stop them getting together beforehand and coming up with a pack of lies.'

Just then, I saw Llwyo walking up to the stables and saying something to the boy. 'There's my prime informant,' I said. 'Let's go and ask him about ponds.'

—

Llwyo was not best pleased when he turned to see who was blocking the light and spotted the two of us standing in the doorway.

'I think you've mistaken me for the town crier. I've told you everything I know about Lizzie Rees.'

I watched him hanging his jacket on a nail. He must live in the village, because he'd already changed out of his Sunday best into his working clothes. 'It's not Lizzie Rees we're here to talk about,' I said. 'It's the Englishman. Nathaniel Stockton.'

He picked up a shovel and scooped up a pile of shit that a big grey gelding had just dropped. ''Scuse me.'

I followed him out to the midden and almost walked into a little pony trap that was standing in the small back yard.

'Mind that,' Llwyo said. 'Belongs to the Sergeant's and I don't want it scratched, all right?'

I stared at it. 'Is it left out here all the time?'

305

'No, mostly it's kept in the coach house, unless there's something paying to be in there.'

I could see that the trap'd be easy enough to wheel in and out without a horse between the shafts. It was a low little thing, obviously designed for a biggish pony, not a carriage horse. A man could easily stand between the shafts and pull it.

'High-class, mind,' I said. 'Lanterns and everything.'

'You know what it's like. Somebody takes it out in the morning, has a bit of a day somewhere, loses track of the time and ends up coming back in the dark.'

Very keen to talk about anything apart from Nattie Stockton, Llwyo was. Which suited me, seeing as he was telling me how three lads could easily have pulled this without a horse if they'd had to.

'Sunday night – was it out here?' I asked.

He sucked his teeth and thought. 'No, it would've been inside on a Sunday. Not much business— Oh, hold on, no. We had Mr and Mrs Esau staying at the Sergeant's that night. Horses in here, carriage in the coach house.'

Which meant the trap would have been here, nicely available. And the moon had been almost full on Sunday night – perfect conditions.

Llwyo was staring at me. 'That it? Can I get back to work now?'

'One more thing. Are there any ponds nearby?'

'Ponds?'

'Cattle ponds, duck ponds. Standing water generally.'

Eyes on me, he sucked a breath in. You could almost see the words 'What's this now?' floating above his head. 'There's what they call the drovers' pond. Just off the main road on Blaengwndwn land. 'Bout a quarter of a mile out of the village.'

Blaengwndwn. It had to be them.

Harry

I asked the landlord of the Sergeant's if we could borrow Llwyo for half an hour or so on coroner's business, and was granted as much time as I needed. 'My lazy toad of a son will have to shift himself if the next coach comes in before you get back,' he said. 'Won't do him any harm.'

Llwyo, however, obviously resented being press-ganged, and despite John's best efforts remained monosyllabic as we walked out of the village, a raggle-taggle of small children following us chattering and laughing. Two gentlemen walking along in the company of a groom obviously represented excellent entertainment.

Initially I humoured the children, turning around periodically and rushing a few steps towards them in mock fierceness, but when Llwyo came to a halt and pointed at a lane a few yards ahead of us, I decided that I had provided sufficient amusement. 'Enough now,' I said. 'Off home with you all. No more following us.'

I waited, but they did not turn around.

'Go on now, off you go!' I took a step towards them, my fierceness not false now, and waved my arms as if they were sheep.

They retreated, and one of the bigger ones turned around, inducing the others to follow suit. I watched them casting glances over their shoulders at us for a moment, then turned to Llwyo.

'The pond's just down there on the left,' he said, pointing once more.

'I'd like you to come with us, please.'

Without a word, he marched up the lane, John hard on his heels, with me following as fast as I could without running the risk of falling headlong. Once more I looked behind me. The children had returned and were advancing slowly towards us. 'Go! Go home now,' I shouted, 'or there'll be trouble!'

They stopped in their tracks, and one of the smaller ones burst into tears. Not wishing to induce any further wailing, I left them where they were and made as much haste as I could after John and Llwyo.

By the time I reached the pond, John was walking carefully around the edge. I stood back, so as not to trample on any evidence there might be, and watched his careful quartering of the ground.

At one point, he stooped as if to look more closely at something, then crouched down on his haunches. Though I was impatient to know what he had seen, I bit my tongue. He had evidently decided on a truce while we were on coroner's business, but it would not do to provoke him.

Fortunately my patience was not long in being rewarded. 'Llwyo,' he called, 'come here a minute, will you?'

As I picked my way carefully around the pond in the groom's wake, a lark burst into song above our heads, trilling notes falling from a single point in the air as the invisible bird hovered on fluttering wings. In an old reflex, I looked up, and immediately the sky was full of the flat grey nothingness of the whirlpool.

'See this?' I heard John say. 'There's been a scuffle here. Look – you can see where the grass has been torn and flattened. And just by the water, there? Prints made by boots, not hooves. And then there's these dents here.' He looked up from his squatting position. 'As if somebody's been kneeling down.'

'If you say so.' Llwyo sounded mutinously unimpressed.

'I do. And look here. Footprints. Two people, one each side of whoever was kneeling.'

Two people. One holding Nathaniel Stockton's arm hard enough that his shirt buttons bit into his wrist, the other pushing his face beneath the surface.

I could restrain myself no longer. 'How deep is the water just there?'

John pulled up his sleeve and thrust his hand in. 'Six inches or so.'

'And the bottom?'

'Mud with little stones in it,' he said, rising to his feet and shaking the mud and pond water off his fingers.

'Pond weed?' If the answer was no, then no amount of scuffling would convince a jury.

'Yes, all the way around the edge.'

He moved a yard or two to the left and squatted again to examine something.

'What can you see?' I asked.

'Some odd-looking prints. As if somebody'd been walking on their heels instead of with their whole foot.'

In my peripheral vision, Llwyo shoved his hands in his pockets as if he was bored. It was such an affectedly casual gesture that it instantly gave him away. 'Llwyo? You know something don't you?'

He shook his head. 'This is nothing to do with me.'

'Wrong. This is to do with anybody I see fit to question. Nathaniel Stockton was murdered. He had pond weed in his throat, which means he was drowned in a pond. If he was drowned in this one and you know something about those prints, you'd better tell me, or I'll have you up before the bench!'

I rarely made threats, and my time as a barrister had taught me never to make any that I was not prepared to carry out. Perhaps Llwyo saw that.

'Wil Llain's only got half of his right foot,' he said, reluctance in every word. 'Accident at the quarry.'

'So he has to walk on his heel?'

I could feel Llwyo's resentful gaze on me. 'Sam Cobs makes him a special half a boot.'

John's notion that the three friends might have conspired to kill Nathaniel Stockton made sense of the state of the corpse; he had been battered but had not landed a blow himself. Now, the evidence here also seemed to bear the theory out. Two men holding Stockton, one of them pushing his head under the water while the lame and less well-balanced Wil Llain stood by.

And Twm and Dai – leaving Wil at home to provide an alibi for them if necessary – could easily have pulled the trap from the Sergeant's to Cilgerran, with or without a pony. If anybody had looked into it in the dark, they would have seen nothing more than a man apparently curled up, sleeping off the effects of too much beer.

I turned and began walking back towards the road, the sun warm on my face. John and Llwyo fell into step with me. 'What's your real name?' I asked Llwyo. 'I need it for the records.'

'David Davies.'

'Very well, Mr Davies, I'm instructing you now, as coroner – which means as a magistrate – to say nothing about what you've seen and heard here to anybody. Particularly to Wil Llain, Dai Blaengwndwn and Twm y Gof. D'you understand?'

I caught an upward jerk of his chin.

'If I get the slightest inkling that you warned them that I know what happened here, I'll have you thrown in gaol, understood?'

'I'm not stupid,' Davies growled, made daring by my use of Welsh with him.

'Who's the *plwyfwas* in Eglwyswrw?' I asked. 'We'll need him to bring the three of them to the inquest and to make sure they don't cook up some story on the way.'

'You might have trouble there. Our *plwyfwas* is the blacksmith's brother. Twm's uncle.'

I heard a grunt from John. We both knew that the law came a very poor second to blood. But fortunately, I was not wholly reliant on the parish constable. Pembrokeshire might not have a uniformed police force as yet, but in each of the county's seven hundreds – the ancient administrative divisions – there were two salaried superintendent constables who oversaw all the parish officers. As soon as we got back to the inn, I would have John write a letter to the superintendents for Cemais. Twm's uncle could deliver them. We needed Wil and his friends to be brought to the inquest without having had any chance to agree a story beforehand.

As we all made our way back to the lane, something caught at the edge of my peripheral vision. Accustomed, by now, to analysing impressions that went unnoticed by the fully sighted, I stopped and angled my gaze over the rough ground to see better.

John turned to see what had stopped me. 'What's that over there?' I asked.

He followed my pointing finger up the shallow slope. 'Looks like a corn-drying kiln.'

Fieldside corn kilns were smallish stone-built structures usually dug into a bank. Used for drying grain before milling, a small one like this was unlikely to be in frequent use.

Which would make it an excellent temporary hiding place for a body.

John

The sun was shining as we rode up Cilgerran's main street, and people were enjoying the warm Sunday afternoon. Old people'd pulled chairs and stools outside their doors and were sitting talking to their neighbours while the women knitted or sewed and the men had their Sunday pipes. Little gangs of lads and girls were standing about, calling to one another and flirting, and children chased around like yapping puppies, playing the games little children play and laughing at things that stop being funny when your age goes into double figures.

Sitting on Seren's back, dressed like a gentleman, I caught some female eyes. I'd forgotten how pretty girls looked in their Sunday best. I smiled back at them, and that feeling I'd had the night before in the Drovers came to sit under my breastbone. A yearning for something I hadn't known I'd missed – people like me. Lads who'd grown up on farms, girls who'd been working at home or in service since they were eleven or twelve, ordinary people who didn't have to worry about law exams or inquests or running an estate. Especially not running an estate. All the worries I was trying to ignore – worries about how I was going to manage – rushed into my mind and I had to push them back out of sight before they could make me sick with fear. I fixed my thoughts on girls instead. It wasn't too difficult.

All the talk we'd heard about Nattie Stockton going to church to see Lizzie Rees had reminded me of why I used to go to chapel. And now, seeing the colourful Sunday shawls and the ribbons girls'd put in their hair and the smiles that only come when you're not rushing to get on with your work, I thought maybe I'd start going to chapel again.

On the ride over from Eglwyswrw, we hadn't talked about anything except the inquest, and it was the same now, when we sat down in the Pendre. I didn't want to start arguing again, and I didn't think Harry did either, and anyway, we had enough to think about. Like we always did before an inquest, we got on with planning the order we were going to call witnesses in and the questions we were going to ask. In particular, we talked about how to handle the three suspects.

Harry'd managed to badger quite a lot of information out of Llwyo about Wil, Twm and Dai. According to him, Wil and Dai had been thick as thieves since childhood – like brothers, he said – and Twm was Dai's cousin. That meant Dai owed loyalty to both the other two. Twm was the kind of man who didn't mind challenging strangers – we knew that because he'd come over to the churchyard when we were talking to Sally Sips to see if we were bothering her. So it looked like Wil was the one to go for. And it made sense for other reasons as well. Before the accident, his job at the quarry'd have meant that he was the one with money in his pocket, the one with good prospects. Now he'd be the lame one, the one who couldn't run properly, who'd always come off worse in a fight. The one who might not be so attractive to girls as he'd been before. He'd be the easiest to push into a confession.

'How do we handle him?' Harry asked. 'Sympathise with him about how hard it must've been to keep up with the other two, that we know all this can't have been his idea?'

I nodded as I swallowed a mouthful of beer. 'Yes. If we can convince him that if they're all tried, they'll all hang, under the doctrine of common enterprise, we'll have him. That'll be his chance to tell us which one of them actually pushed Nattie's head into the water. But we should bring him up to give evidence last, then we can use any of the lies the other two've told us to persuade him how much trouble he'll be in if he doesn't give us the truth.'

I'd learned a lot of tricks since becoming assistant coroner. Tricks I wasn't always proud of, if I'm honest.

Seeing as we were on the county's ticket, we stayed at the Pendre overnight instead of at Reckitt's freezing-cold house, and I got a decent night's sleep, which was a relief. With everything going on at Glanteifi, I hadn't been sleeping well at all.

The next morning, we were having breakfast in the landlord's parlour – which was a lot nicer than the taproom – when there was a knock on the door and a smartly dressed man walked in.

'Beg pardon, I'm Superintendent Constable Vaughan. Just thought you'd like to know that the witnesses you wanted bringing up from Eglwyswrw are here. Brought them all separately, like you asked.'

Harry stood up. 'Thank you. Where are they now?' He looked like a child next to Vaughan; the man was over six feet tall. Just as well to be big if you're going to frogmarch people around the countryside, I suppose.

'They're in the lock-up at the other end of the village. With the other superintendent and the *plwyfwas* we got in to help us.'

'Not the one from Eglwyswrw?'

'No, sir. Everything's been done exactly as you said in your letter. We'll bring them up here before you start – there's a room waiting for them, is that right?'

'Yes, upstairs. Have some breakfast before you go back, Mr Vaughan, and charge it to the coroner's account. In fact, send your colleagues up in turn. You must all have been up at the crack of dawn.'

'Well at least dawn's early enough, this time of year. It's when you've got to go marching about in the dark that it's hard on a man.'

Harry thanked him again and off he went to have his breakfast.

I wondered what the lock-up in Cilgerran would be like. It probably wasn't intended to hold five men at a time, so things could be quite cramped. Being roused at first light and marched up here would've told Wil, Twm and Dai that they were under suspicion, but at least they wouldn't've had any time to get their

314

story straight. Unless the children who'd followed us out to the pond had told them what we'd been up to. And that was a definite possibility. All it would've taken was one of them saying something at the evening service and our advantage would be gone.

Still, we'd done what we could.

–

The inquest was scheduled for ten, and people started drifting into the Pendre from nine onwards to get a good seat and catch all the gossip. The place had been properly scrubbed for the occasion – there was fresh sawdust on the floor, and the tables were clean and milky from limewash. It'd soon be back to normal, but at least the landlord'd made an effort for when people arrived.

From the snippets of conversation I heard, everybody seemed to know about Lizzie Rees giving Nattie the *coron fedw*, and the words 'courting in bed' came up quite a lot as well. That rumour'd gone around like butter in a hot skillet.

Harry and I were just working out where the witness chair would get the best light when Lydia Howell walked in. I'd wondered if she'd come, and to be honest, I was glad she'd be there to keep the peace on the way home.

She got some looks as she came over to us. She wasn't wearing a *betgwn* like a working woman, but she didn't exactly look like a lady, either. Her dress was plain, without all the frills and fancies you saw ladies wearing. But then if she'd been a lady, she wouldn't've come into the taproom. Especially not on her own.

Except she wasn't entirely on her own. Daniel 'Lleu' Williams was with her.

'What are you doing here?' I asked him.

'He arrived at Glanteifi yesterday,' Lydia said.

'I've left that school Miss Gwatkyn sent me to,' the boy piped up. 'It was no good to me. They wanted to teach me Latin and Greek and all that nonsense. I've got no use for that! I want to learn practical things.'

He'd been there a week.

'Miss Gwatkyn told me to try it, and I have,' he said, as if Phoebe Gwatkyn couldn't expect any more of him. 'It's not what I need. I need to go and see Mr Harborne and his engineer. See if they'll take me on.'

I turned to Lydia for advice, but all she did was raise her eyebrow. Did she think I was responsible for the boy running away?

'As it happens,' I told Lleu, 'I spoke to Mr Bowen – Mr Harborne's engineer – about you last week. His opinion is that you should go to school and learn mathematics and then go somewhere to study technical drawing. Don't they teach mathematics at the school Miss Gwatkyn sent you to?'

'Yes. But I'm wasting my time learning all that other stuff. Mr Bowen can teach me mathematics if I'm his apprentice.'

It was less than a fortnight since I'd seen him, but Lleu seemed to have grown. Then again, perhaps it was just his attitude that'd changed. He knew what he wanted now; he wasn't just the promising little boy who wanted to please his mistress. 'I'll take you over and introduce you tomorrow,' I said. 'But I'm warning you, I don't think there's much chance he's going to want to take on an apprentice. Especially one who doesn't know any mathematics.'

Lleu beamed. He obviously thought he'd have no trouble bringing Amos Bowen round to his way of thinking.

'I assume you've written to Phoebe Gwatkyn to tell her he's safe?' Harry asked Lydia. Miss Gwatkyn'd be beside herself if the school had told her that Lleu'd disappeared.

'Yes, though she's still in Italy at the moment, so she won't even know he's been gone until she gets back. More to the point, I've written to the school and told them he's here.' She gave Lleu a look that told him she didn't approve of him taking matters into his own hands, which coming from her was a bit rich, to be honest. Still, Lleu wasn't to know that.

We found somewhere for the pair of them to sit at the side of the room, out of the way of hecklers and drunkards. While they were getting settled, Harry spoke to Lydia. 'By all accounts, Nathaniel Stockton didn't speak Welsh, so I assume his parents won't either. Would you mind translating for them if it turns out to be necessary?'

'Of course. I'll help in any way I can. But speaking of the Stocktons, have you given any thought to how you're going to stop their son's inquest turning into a proxy hearing for Lizzie Rees?'

Harry didn't even blink. We'd both got used to Lydia not beating about the bush. 'Actually, I'm going to make sure it *is* a proxy hearing. As I see it, the first thing we have to do is quash the rumours about Nattie's involvement in Lizzie's death. He won't get a fair hearing for his own death otherwise.'

Lydia nodded thoughtfully. 'When you say "quash"…?'

'I'm going to force Mic Rees to name whoever was with his daughter on the night she died.'

Over Harry's shoulder I saw a couple come in and speak to the landlord. He pointed in our direction.

'Mr Probert-Lloyd?' Harry turned to see the couple coming towards him. 'I'm Edgar Stockton, and this is my wife.'

Nattie Stockton's parents were in their late forties or early fifties, both going grey, him a bit thicker round the middle than he'd have been when they courted, her tired-looking with lines on her face she probably hadn't had a week ago. Edgar Stockton was wearing a suit that was a cut above anything a village tailor could produce – what we'd been told about him owning his own farm must be true – and his wife was in a holly-green gown with lace trimmings. Didn't look like she had to turn her hand to farm work.

'Mr and Mrs Stockton, I'm so sorry to be making your acquaintance under such tragic circumstances,' Harry said. 'But rest assured, if it's within my power, I will see justice done for your son.'

'Do you know who did this to Nathaniel?' Mrs Stockton asked.

'I believe I do, yes. But it wouldn't be wise to name anybody yet. Not until the jury has heard all the evidence.'

'May I ask why you didn't conduct an inquest into the death of this young woman he was infatuated with?' her husband said. 'If you'd done so, if you'd ruled definitively that she died of natural causes, our son might still be alive.'

Wherever they'd stayed last night, the Stocktons'd obviously been given all the local gossip. Harry raised his chin a bit to take the criticism, but I knew he blamed himself just as much as Edgar Stockton did. 'At the time, there seemed to be no suspicious circumstances. Two doctors – including my usual medical witness, a man of unparalleled skill – concluded that no foul play had been involved.' He took a breath. 'I'm afraid the powers-that-be don't see inquests into natural deaths as being in the public interest.'

'But where suspicion lingers...'

'Unfortunately, I didn't discover the rumour that Lizzie Rees had been courting in bed on the night she died until after Nathaniel's body had been found. If I'd been aware of that, I assure you I would have held an inquest.'

The Stocktons looked at each other. Their son'd been murdered because of a rumour the coroner hadn't heard. But in truth, Harry would never have heard it in time to save Nattie Stockton. Nattie'd already been dead by Sunday afternoon, while we'd still been asking questions at Rhosdywarch.

Harry

At ten a.m. precisely, John and I walked from the crowded parlour where a few minutes before I had addressed the jury and I took my seat at the coroner's table.

I unstopped the ink bottle set ready for the purpose, dipped my pen and made an entirely unnecessary note of the date on the paper in front of me, something I did habitually, partly to calm my nerves and partly to remind both jury and spectators that though I might be 'the blind coroner', I still retained some sight. My wooden writing frame, constructed to my own design with a ratchet-wound ruler, enabled me to find the location of the last words I had written without obviously searching the page, and gave the impression that I wrote without difficulty. Anybody who had attempted to read the resultant scrawl knew how far that was from the truth, but nevertheless, I found it expedient to have paper and pen in front of me, not least so that I might communicate unobserved with John.

Sitting there waiting for the incoherent noise of dozens of overlapping conversations to die down, I was in the place where I felt most at home: the coroner's chair. I might never practise at the bar again, but for the duration of an inquest, I was both barrister and judge, the truth my only concern. It was so much clearer and more focused than my role as squire, which seemed to demand that I be simultaneously businessman, philanthropist, sage, archivist and patriarch.

Though my usual practice was to conduct my hearings in Welsh, offering translation as necessary for any monoglot English speakers, today I made my opening remarks in English out of deference to Nathaniel Stockton's parents.

'As the death of Mr Stockton seems inextricably linked with that of Miss Elizabeth Rees of Rhosdywarch in the parish of Meline, my intention at the outset of this hearing is to demonstrate that he played absolutely no part in Miss Rees's *natural* death. Once that has been established, we will hear from witnesses as to the circumstances of Mr Stockton's own death.'

Ignoring an outbreak of very audible interest and speculation, I called Dr Cadwgan Gwynne to give testimony. Once he had outlined his observations of Elizabeth Rees's body and confirmed that he had found no evidence of foul play, I asked him if he would cast his mind back to the previous time he had seen Lizzie, when she had been very much alive.

'What was the question Miss Rees had come to ask you, Dr Gwynne?' I asked after we had established the date of her visit.

This time Gwynne did not prevaricate with protestations of confidentiality. He knew the burden of my question and the necessity of its being answered.

'She wanted to ask me whether, having given the birch crown to Nathaniel Stockton, she might marry another man without the union being cursed.'

'In other words, Nathaniel had a rival for her affections?'

'Yes.'

I ignored the spectators' sudden chatter and forced them into quiet by simply continuing. 'Do you know who that man was?'

'No. She didn't tell me, and I had no reason to ask.'

I dismissed Dr Gwynne and called out to Caleb Richards over the great swell of speculation that arose instantly amongst the spectators. 'Mr Richards, be so good as to ask Dr Reckitt to come forward.'

John and I had briefed Reckitt the previous evening. 'I know you still have questions in the absence of a definitive cause of death,' I had told him, 'but we can't let those questions infect others. There can be no lingering doubts left in the minds of either jury or spectators. You *must* say that all your examinations showed that Lizzie's was a perfectly natural death.'

And to his credit, he did so with commendable, not to say unprecedented, brevity. I then turned to the rumours.

'Dr Reckitt, I have heard it suggested that Lizzie Rees was not alone when she died. That in fact she was courting in bed. Did you find any evidence to support that suggestion?'

'I found no *direct* evidence, no. However, there were indications that certain facts had been hidden from me. And indeed from Dr Gwynne.'

At my invitation, he explained – with as few details as I could confine him to – the body's tendency to void with the relaxation of muscles at death and the puzzling dryness of both Lizzie's petticoat and her mattress.

'When presented with this evidence, Mr Rees did in fact admit that he had allowed his daughter to sleep in the box bed rather than her own, and that he had changed her undergarments prior to Dr Gwynne's visit, did he not?'

'He did.'

'But he claimed that she had been alone and that giving up his own bed to her had been motivated only by a wish to have her recover from a cold more swiftly – is that correct?'

'It is.'

I turned to the jury. Before beginning the inquest, I had asked them whether they would require a translator, but all had claimed sufficient English to manage without. 'Do you have any questions for Dr Reckitt?'

One of the jurymen stood. 'Why do you think Mr Rees lied to you?'

Before Reckitt could respond, I held up a hand. 'You may ask Mr Rees himself that in due course. Do you have any *medical* questions to ask Dr Reckitt?'

The jury did not, and I asked Reckitt to step down but to remain on hand in order to give evidence as to his examination of Nathaniel Stockton's body. I then called Evan 'Cadi' Evans. Before he sat down, he made a small bow to the front row of spectators, where Stockton's parents were sitting. It was a gesture that I found both courteous and curiously moving, and spoke of his affection for the dead man.

Cadi's testimony as to Nattie's whereabouts on the night of Lizzie Rees's death having been laid before the jury, I asked if they would like to question him.

A figure rose to his feet. 'You say Mr Stockton wasn't with Elizabeth Rees on the night she died,' he said in the kind of well-modulated English that spoke of frequent use. 'But had he been courting in bed with her on previous occasions?'

'No.'

'You're quite certain?'

'Yes. As I said, three of us slept in the same loft. I'm quite certain.'

Another juror stood. 'Did Mr Stockton know that there was another man courting Lizzie Rees?' No doubt he was wondering, as John and I had, whether Nattie had come to Cilgerran to have it out with somebody and had picked a fight that had proved fatal.

'No, I don't think so. He was still talking about asking her to marry him when she got back from the south.'

There were no more questions, and I released Evans, pending his later testimony when we came to the inquest proper.

My heart beat a little more quickly as I turned once more to Caleb Richards. 'Bring Mic Rees in, if you'd be so good, Mr Richards.'

Now, finally, we would get to the truth.

As Rees came to the witness chair and sat down, I saw the inn's door open and a figure slide in, head bowed guiltily in acknowledgement of his lateness. There were always latecomers to any hearing, and I ignored him.

'Mr Rees,' I began, 'the members of the jury are keen to know why you tried to hide the fact that your daughter was courting in bed on the night she died. Would you like to tell us?'

Mic Rees's previous lies and half-truths had prepared me for reticence and hostility, but the question had hardly left my lips when his response came.

'I was trying to avoid exactly what happened to poor Nattie,' he said in heavily accented English. 'I knew there'd be trouble if people heard that Lizzie was courting somebody from outside the parish – a stranger. I thought the two of them should be left alone to see if they suited each other without people criticising and judging.'

'So just to be clear, Lizzie *was* courting in bed on the night she died?'

He hesitated, then nodded. 'Yes.'

I made a note in order to allow the spectators a moment to react. Some crowed, vindicated, while others speculated as to who this other man might have been. After half a minute or so, I signalled to Caleb Richards, who called for silence.

'Mr Rees,' I continued, once I could be heard, 'you allowed your daughter to stay at home when her mother and sisters went to the mansion at Ffynone to work for a few days. Am I to assume, therefore, that you knew what Lizzie was planning?'

'Yes.'

I held up a hand for quiet. 'Why did you and Lizzie conceal her intentions from your wife?'

Rees turned slightly towards the crowd. Was he looking at his wife? Was Esther Rees even here?

'Because she disapproved of any young man Lizzie became fond of.'

'Did she disapprove of this one in particular?'

Mic Rees sighed. 'She would have if she'd known. And I didn't want my daughter forced to run away and marry in secret, only to regret it later.'

Did that reveal something about his own courtship and marriage? Curious though I was, it was not a relevant question.

'Will you now tell us who this young man is?'

'No.'

The room erupted. This time, there was no quieting the outraged spectators with a raised hand, and I could only listen as a violent stream of invective was hurled at Mic Rees.

Eventually Caleb Richards' bellows of 'Silence!' prevailed and Rees was able to speak.

'What business is it of anybody here?' he demanded, facing the crowd and effectively turning his back on the jury; he knew it was not them he must convince. 'My Lizzie died a natural death. Why is that so difficult for people to understand? Two doctors – not one, *two* – have given *sworn testimony* that it was a natural death. We all know Dr Gwynne's abilities, and Dr Reckitt *cut her open…*' I thought for a horrified moment that he was about to weep, but he sucked in an audible breath and continued. 'He cut her open to be sure, to be *absolutely sure*, that there was nothing suspicious. And there *wasn't*! You've heard it wasn't poor Nattie with her the night she died; why should I give you another man's name? So you can blame him instead?'

Rees's defiance gave rise to a further outpouring of discontent in the crowded taproom, though I detected a diminution in the collective outrage after his impassioned plea.

I raised a hand for Caleb Richards to intervene, and in response to his bellowed orders, the crowd settled into a muttering that did duty for silence. 'Mr Rees, I'm afraid I'm going to have to insist that you tell this hearing who the young man concerned is. Your failure to be candid when I first visited you makes you a less than entirely reliable witness, and I would feel happier – as would everybody at this hearing, I'm sure – if I was able to receive the young man's own testimony.'

The drone of mumbled speculation fell away as every person waited to see whether Mic Rees would continue to refuse. The seconds ticked by. I was alert to John's posture, ready to insist once more if he leaned forward to indicate that I should press the witness. But he did not move. *Wait.*

'No,' Rees said finally. 'Cadi Evans has told you that Nattie wasn't there. That should be enough. I'm not going to put another young man at risk.'

As he was speaking, I saw movement in the crowd. A man was pushing his way towards me. I could not be sure, but from the downward tilt of his head, it looked like the latecomer.

Concerned that whoever this was meant to harm Rees, I beckoned for Caleb Richards, but then the man reached the front of the crowd and I saw his eyepatch.

'I-it was m-me. I w-w-was with Lizzie.'

Amos Bowen. Barti Ddu.

John

I stared at him. I couldn't believe it. *Amos Bowen?* With the pick of every unmarried man in the parish, why on earth would Lizzie Rees choose a stranger with a squint and a horrible stutter? I didn't know exactly what women looked for in a man, obviously, but Amos definitely wasn't who you'd expect to see with the prettiest girl in the parish on his arm.

As Mic Rees and Amos swapped places, I glanced around at the crowd. Everybody was staring at Amos and his eyepatch, and a few people – probably those who'd come up from Eglwyswrw and Felindre Farchog – seemed to know him.

He's the one from Dolbannon, I heard. *Soft in the head.*

He'd kept his good eye lowered all this time, but now he looked up at me and I gave him an encouraging smile. He wasn't getting friendly looks from anybody else. Even Mic Rees, at the front of the crowd, was staring at him with an expression I couldn't put a name to.

The to and fro of questions and answers between Amos and Harry was long and painful because of Amos's stutter. It seemed to take him five minutes to get a single sentence out, and I could tell he was trying to use as few words as possible to answer the questions. But that didn't suit Harry. Not at all. He wanted every detail, so he kept prompting Amos, over and over, then waiting patiently for him to answer. Prompt and wait. Prompt and wait. And while he was coaxing the story out, Harry leaned further and further over the table, as if he wanted to reach out and physically pull the words out of the poor man's throat.

All the while, the crowd stared at Amos like a freak in a show and heckled him with insults and mockery.

326

For the life of me, I couldn't work out why he'd come forward.

Anyway, in a nutshell, the story Harry dragged out of him went like this. Right at the end of his apprenticeship in Newtown, Amos had been working with his cousin, Jem Harborne, to adapt standard steam-powered machines to work off water power. Then, out of the blue, a letter had come from the chapel minister back home, telling him that his mother was very ill, and Amos'd left Newtown to go back to Llandysul.

His mother'd died not long after he got home, and, the day after her funeral, his father'd thrown Amos out of the house. He'd needed a job to keep body and soul together until Harborne was ready for him in Llandyfriog, which was how he'd ended up working for Dai Dolbannon.

Then, one day just after Christmas, Dai had sent him to pick up some cloth from Mic Rees, and he'd found Lizzie struggling with the wheel she and her mother used to spin their yarn. The mechanism'd jammed, and Amos had fixed it for her. Not just fixed it but made it work better than before, with some little adjustment or another. And that, believe it or not, had been that. They'd fallen for each other. That week, Amos'd started going to church instead of chapel, so that he could see Lizzie every Sunday.

'And nobody knew you were courting?'

'N-no.'

Amos had nobody to tell, and Lizzie'd kept it quiet because she knew her mother would throw a fit and forbid her to see him.

'Wh-when the factory'd b-been built, th-things would've been different,' Amos said. 'M-Mrs Rees would've s-seen that I could b-be a good p-provider then.'

I didn't doubt it. He'd've been rich quick-smart. Because Jem Harborne wasn't going to stop at one mill. As soon as he had his looms up and running, he'd be building a spinning mill, then one for carding. And each time there'd be more work for Amos. Designing, building, fixing, improving.

The more of the story that came out, and the more poor Amos stuttered, the louder the heckling got. From the shouts that came from the crowd, the thing that people couldn't understand – even more than Lizzie choosing Amos in the first place – was why she'd given the *coron fedw* to Nattie Stockton.

'Sh-she was m-m-making the crown for me,' Amos said when Harry asked him. 'At a ch-church outing. She was g-going to g-give it to me later. B-but the others s-started t-teasing her, going on and on about N-Nattie being s-sweet on her, how h-he'd come here f-for her. We-we-we didn't want anybody to know about us. So in the end, sh-she gave the c-crown to Nattie.'

God, life was unfair sometimes. I thought of all the lies and secrecy that'd surrounded Lizzie Rees's death, and wondered how the Stocktons would feel now that they knew their son was dead because he'd been open and honest and just worn his heart on his sleeve.

Harry

I found Amos Bowen's testimony about the night of Lizzie Rees's death excruciating. Quite apart from the glacial slowness with which his evidence emerged, his description of the dark interior of the box bed where he and Lizzie exchanged whispered confidences while wholly invisible to each other reminded me with painful vividness of my own courting days with Margaret Jones. The hayloft where she slept had wrapped us in a velvety, exclusive darkness that had induced us to say – and do – things we would never have contemplated in daylight.

I grew increasingly uncomfortable as I remembered the delights of intimate caresses, hands trembling as they stroked and searched, and I tried to focus only on Bowen's words. Fortunately I soon heard something that demanded my full attention.

'And th-then s-s-suddenly Lizzie s-seemed to g-go limp. And she m-made a noise.'

'What sort of noise?' I asked.

'L-l-like a l-little cough. Or a ch-choke.'

He had asked her if she was all right, and when he received no reply, he had put a hand to her face. But there had been no response. Becoming concerned, he had slid open the side of the bed and fetched a candle from the kitchen.

By its light, he had realised that Lizzie was not breathing, and had tried without success to revive her.

As he stuttered out this distressing testimony, I asked myself whether it could be true. Had Elizabeth Rees really simply expired during an exchange of mutual tenderness? How could such a thing happen? Even Reckitt could not explain it.

'Mr Bowen, please tell the inquest what happened next. Once you'd realised that you couldn't revive her.'

Bowen's vocal apparatus seemed determined to prevent him speaking of what had happened in the aftermath of Lizzie's death, so it was with the greatest difficulty, and much striking of thigh with fist, that he eventually outlined events as they had occurred.

Panic mounting, he had roused Mic Rees, but her father's attempts to revive Lizzie proved as unsuccessful as Bowen's own.

Subsequently, events had proceeded much as we had deduced.

Once he had managed an account of how he and Mic Rees had replaced Lizzie's wet nightgown – including, as John had suspected, the necessity of unpicking the row of stitches that divided its lower part – I asked Amos Bowen why Rees had done that before going to fetch Dr Gwynne. 'Wouldn't it have been better,' I suggested, 'for the doctor to see her as she was?'

Amos maintained, as Rees had himself, that Lizzie's father had been determined not to shame her. I nodded and made a note. *Shame*, I wrote, *because of (i) soiled nightgown (ii) birch crown given to NS but courting in bed with another man.*

At my side, John read my words and nodded deliberately so that I would see. *Any other reason?* I wrote. This time he spoke, his voice for my ears only. 'No.'

I looked up at Amos once more. 'And what about you? Didn't *you* think it might be a good idea to tell Dr Gwynne the truth?'

'Yes, what were you hiding?' shouted one of the spectators, loudly cheered and echoed by voices from all corners of the room.

'N-n-nothing,' Amos stuttered, audibly distressed. 'I was j-j-just afraid I'd g-get the blame.'

'A reasonable fear,' I said, addressing the crowd. 'If common gossip is to be believed, Mr Bowen was seen. But in the half-light, he was mistaken for Nathaniel Stockton.' I did not need to add that not much more than twenty-four hours later, Stockton had been dead. Amos's fear had been entirely justified.

Bowen turned towards Nattie's parents. 'I–I'm s-s-so s-s-sorry! I d–didn't know anybody'd s-seen me. If I had, I-I-I would've c-come forward. *But I didn't.*'

His genuine remorse would, I feared, be no comfort to Mr and Mrs Stockton. I wondered whether Nattie had had any inkling that he was not Lizzie's only suitor; that his pursuit of her – which must have seemed successful when she gave him the *coron fedw* – was destined ultimately to end in disappointment.

I hoped not. I hoped he had died still believing that his love was returned.

John

Now that everybody in the room knew what'd really happened to Lizzie Rees, Harry announced a quick break before we moved on to the inquest proper.

I looked around for Amos Bowen, but couldn't see him anywhere. 'Just nipping outside for a minute,' I told Harry. I needed to talk to Amos because something odd had happened just before the end of his testimony. Harry'd asked him if he had any further information about Lizzie's death, and instead of starting on his usual fight to get a word out, I saw Amos look across at Mic Rees and Mic give the smallest of head shakes. After that, Amos hadn't said anything more. Not even when I'd leaned forward to encourage Harry to press him and Harry'd reminded him that he was under oath.

I wanted to know what that head shake had been about; what Mic Rees didn't want Amos to say.

Outside, the sun was bright after the taproom and I squinted up and down the street. No sign of Amos. I trotted down to the livery stables, but they hadn't seen him there.

When I walked back up to the Pendre, Harry was standing outside with Lydia, Lleu and Reckitt. Quite a lot of other people'd come out for a spell in the sunshine as well. Some had brought a mug of beer with them; others were just standing about. But they were all so amazed about Amos and Lizzie that they seemed to've forgotten that what we were really here for was to find out how Nattie Stockton had died.

'Amos has made himself scarce,' I said.

Lydia looked up from her conversation with Lleu. 'Probably wise, in the circumstances.'

'Do we believe him?' I asked. 'About the way Lizzie died?'

'Everything he said was consistent with my findings,' Reckitt said. 'The young man's evidence may *sound* far-fetched, but I assure you, it is compatible with the physical evidence.'

'Fair enough,' I said, 'but there's still something we haven't got to the bottom of.' I told them about Mic Rees shaking his head at Amos. 'It was like he was telling him to keep quiet about something.'

Harry bit the inside of his lip. 'Rees has been keeping something from us right from the beginning. Each time we found him out in a lie, I thought we'd got to the bottom of it, but obviously there's something he's still not telling us.'

'However,' Lydia said, 'he's not obliged to tell you anything unless it has a bearing on his daughter's death or Nathaniel Stockton's.'

Harry sighed. He knew she was right. But in his own way, he was as bad as Reckitt for wanting to know things. 'Shall we go back in?' he said.

'If you don't mind, I'd just like a moment of John's time before you begin again.'

For a second or two, Harry just stood there with Reckitt and Lleu while they all looked at me and Lydia. Then he seemed to come to his senses and realise that she wanted to speak to me in private, so he ushered the other two back inside with him.

Lydia didn't waste time or breath, just lowered her voice so the people around us wouldn't hear. 'Your argument with Harry the other night – is it resolved?'

I shook my head.

'I suspected as much. I'm sorry to raise this in the middle of an inquest, but with the two of you at loggerheads, something needs to be done.'

My heart began to race. What kind of *something* did she have in mind? 'Go on.'

'You and I both know that Harry wasn't ready to be squire when his father died. He's struggling with it all. His fear of

Glanteifi going bankrupt means he isn't thinking logically and the estate's suffering.'

She could have added 'and people are dying' given what had happened to Matthew Nantyddwrgi, but that would have been a bit melodramatic for Lydia.

'At least he had the good sense to appoint you under-steward.'

'Yes, to make sure I was always available to go out to sudden deaths with him.' It came out more bitterly than I'd intended, and I could see that Lydia was taken aback.

'If it was just a matter of convenience, he could have found another assistant coroner, John. He made you under-steward because he could see that you're extremely capable.'

Extremely capable. Had Harry said that? I wasn't going to ask. 'Maybe,' I mumbled.

She took a deep breath. 'But if you're going to be Glanteifi's agent, it won't be easy for you to simply drop everything at a moment's notice and go off to look at suspicious deaths with him.'

My heart rate doubled. 'Are you telling me you've changed your mind? About being Harry's assistant?'

'No. It's not Harry who needs a new assistant. It's you.'

I stared at her. 'You want to be under-steward?'

'I'm not looking for another title. But you need to be able to go with him whenever he's called out as coroner. And that means that there needs to be somebody at Glanteifi who can carry out your instructions while you're away. Someone you and Harry can both trust.' She paused, eyes on me. 'It has to be your decision, obviously. As I say, I'm sorry to bring it up in the middle of an inquest, but at least you'll have time on the way home to mull it all over. Shall we talk about it tonight?'

I nodded. It made sense. Of course it did.

The question was, did I want somebody cleverer than me as my assistant?

Harry

I walked back into the Pendre, my mounting trepidation about what I was about to do pushing aside the questions raised by Lydia's sudden wish to speak confidentially with John. The county magistrates would disapprove if they knew how I was planning to conduct this inquest. They would contend that I was overstepping the bounds of my role.

And strictly speaking, of course, they would be right. Nowhere in Sewell's *Law of Coroner* did he claim that it was the coroner's duty to establish who was responsible for a homicide. The inquest jury's role was purely to decide how the deceased had come by their death; it then fell to the magistrates – or their proxies, the police – to investigate. However, in my experience, in the absence of eyewitnesses or compelling motives, such investigations tended to be at best perfunctory, at worst non-existent.

But my motive in this case was not simply to see justice done. I had a compelling personal reason for wishing to unmask Nathaniel Stockton's killer, because I could not shake the feeling that my visit to Rhosdywarch with Reckitt had raised suspicions about Lizzie Rees's death that had ultimately led to Stockton's murder.

While John was otherwise occupied, instead of taking my place at the coroner's table under the scrutiny of spectators whose eyes I could not meet, I made my way upstairs to the small room where the three men from Eglwyswrw were being held.

The burly superintendent constable who had reported to me earlier answered my knock, and I beckoned him out onto the tiny dark landing.

'Caleb Richards – the *plwyfwas* for Cilgerran – has been up to see you, I expect?'

'Yes, sir. Says he'll come up for them.'

'Good. One more thing – can you hear what's being said downstairs?'

'We can hear people talking, but not the words.'

I had assumed that would be the case, as the coroner's table was at the other end of the inn. 'Very well. We'll be starting again in a minute or two, so it won't be long now.'

The front door of the inn was closed when I came back downstairs. Presumably Lydia had concluded her business with John.

Apprehension plucked at me. What could be so urgent that she would wish to speak to him now? And why had she excluded me from the conversation? Did she have thoughts about the inquest that she had chosen to share with John rather than with me? Did she think I was mishandling things?

–

Following the usual inquest pattern, I first called on the coracle men, as the finders of the body, to give their evidence as to time and place. Then I asked Caleb Richards to come forward, and he testified that none of the innkeepers in Cilgerran had seen Nathaniel Stockton on the day he died – or indeed on any previous occasion – and that nobody had come forward to say that they had seen the young man in the village that day.

Reckitt took the witness chair next in order to present the jury with the facts of Nathaniel Stockton's death: that he had been beaten, as evidenced by the bruising on his torso and contusions on his face; that he had indeed been drowned, but not in the Teifi, as the river contained no pond weed; that his lifeless body had been hidden somewhere in a cramped seated position for at least ten hours, and subsequently transported to Cilgerran and consigned to the river, where it had been caught by the fishermen.

Cadi Evans was the second witness to be re-called.

After we had dispensed with his identification of the body and Nathaniel's time working with him at Gilfachwen, I broached the reason for the dead man's having come to the area.

'When I spoke to you a few days ago, you told me that it had been common knowledge that Nathaniel had come here specifically to court Elizabeth Rees, and that her favouring him caused a lot of resentment. That local lads didn't like it,' I added, in case Cadi's English did not stretch as far as 'resentment'.

'That's right.'

'And that he was warned off. Took a beating.'

'Yes.'

'Did he tell you who had beaten him?'

'He didn't know names. Just said that the lads who usually stood about outside the forge grabbed him as he was walking home one day and gave him a proper hiding.'

'The young men who were usually at the forge?' I said, suppressing a sudden excitement. 'You didn't mention them when you came to identify the body.'

'I didn't know. When I told Nye, the other servant who sleeps in the loft with us, what'd happened to Nattie, he said Nattie'd told him that he saw the same lads every Sunday when he was walking home from church. Said they always looked at him like a farm dog looks at a stranger on the yard.'

In other words, with their hackles up and teeth bared.

'Can you describe Mr Stockton's injuries after that beating?'

'He came home black and blue. Don't know how he got back, to be honest with you, because he couldn't hardly see out of either eye. Said two of them held him and the other one did the hitting.'

I turned to the front row of spectators. 'Dr Reckitt?' He stood. 'The recent injuries you described on Mr Stockton's body – the punches to face and torso – were they consistent with his having been restrained by one or more persons while he was beaten by another?'

'They were. Added to which, Mr Stockton's knuckles were undamaged, suggesting that though he'd been hit repeatedly, he had not landed any significant blows on his own behalf. In other words, he hadn't been in a fight, but had been beaten.'

My words of thanks were lost in the sudden muttering and murmuring of the crowd. Were the names of the three young men currently being held upstairs being whispered by spectators from Eglwyswrw? Whether they were or not, what mattered was that the similarity of the injuries inflicted on Stockton during the forge trio's assault and the beating he had taken prior to being drowned had been established. It was time to call a witness who could put names to Stockton's attackers.

'Mr Richards? Our young friend, if you please.' The previous afternoon, I had sought out Caleb Richards and given him instructions to ride over to Eglwyswrw this morning and bring back the stable boy John had spoken to.

While we waited for the lad to be brought in, I addressed the spectators.

'I'm going to interview my next witness in Welsh. Rather than translate question by question from the coroner's table, which would hold up proceedings, I'm going to ask my associate, Miss Lydia Howell, to translate for Mr and Mrs Stockton. If there is anybody else present who does not speak Welsh sufficiently, please come to the front and join them now.'

Nobody moved except Lydia, who took the seat that was courteously vacated for her.

'Gwilym,' I said, once I had established that the boy had not seen Nathaniel Stockton leaving the church but had seen him emerging from the Sergeant's Inn, 'can you tell us – was the service still going on in church when Mr Stockton came out of the inn?'

'Yes.' Gwilym's head was down, his answer directed into his lap.

'Did he come out a long time before it ended?' I wanted to know whether there was anybody apart from our suspects who might have followed him. Somebody leaving the church after the service was over was the most obvious candidate, but if Nattie had left the inn well before the service's conclusion, his having been followed by a congregant was unlikely.

'Yes, a long time before the end,' the boy said. 'They hadn't even finished the second hymn.' That confirmed the landlord's account of his short conversation with Stockton while he downed a tot of brandy.

'Did you see anybody else leaving the Sergeant's and following Mr Stockton?'

'No.'

'Where did you see Mr Stockton go?'

'He started off one way,' the boy told his lap, his index finger pointing to his left.

'Then what did he do?'

'Stopped and turned back. Went the other way.' His hand flipped over, his thumb extended to the right.

'When did he stop?'

'When he got to the coach house.' His voice was so quiet that even I could barely hear him.

'Speak up, boy,' one of the jurymen called gruffly. 'We can't hear you.'

The lad seemed to shrink into himself, and I held up a hand. 'No need. So you saw him stop when he got to the coach house next to the Sergeant's. What made him stop – do you know, Gwilym?'

The boy shrugged, head lowered.

'Do you think it was because he saw who was standing at the forge?'

Head still bowed, he remained mute, but the jury would take my point.

'You say he turned and went the other way – would he still have been able to make his way back to Gilfachwen if he went that way?' I asked, in case any of the jurymen were unfamiliar with Eglwyswrw's main street.

Gwilym seemed to curl in on himself even more at this question, as if he was afraid that even a glimpse of me would cause him to catch fire. He made no sound, but John gave a soft tap on the table. It was our code: one tap for 'witness indicates yes', two for 'no'; we had learned very early on that badgering reluctant witnesses to speak for my benefit rather than nod and shake their head had an unhelpfully repressive effect.

'Gwilym, some of the jury don't know Eglwyswrw,' I said. 'Can you tell us how Mr Stockton would have got back on the road towards Gilfachwen after going the wrong way?'

'Up the lane to Trewilym,' the child murmured. 'Then over the fields. Then back to the road.'

I repeated the information for the jury, then asked him who had been standing outside the forge. As Lydia quietly translated the question for the Stocktons, the boy turned his head to the crowd, presumably looking for the three men. He would not see them, of course, but given that Twm y Gof and his companions had been frogmarched out of their homes at first light, I suspected that he would see members of their families staring back at him.

'Gwilym?' I prompted. 'Don't forget you're under oath,' I added gently, hoping to reassure him that people would understand that he had no choice but to give up the names I wanted.

'Twm from the forge. Dai Blaengwndwn. And Wil Llain.'

If I had not already been familiar with the three men, his barely audible mumbling would have been unintelligible, so I repeated the names for the benefit of both spectators and jury. 'Do you know them well?'

He shrugged.

'I expect you see them about, do you?'

A smaller shrug and a tap on the table from John.

'Obviously Twm's at the forge all the time,' I said. 'But what about the others – are they there often?'

'Sometimes.'

'Particular days?'

A shrug.

'Sundays?' I prompted. 'After chapel?'

One tap. Yes.

'Not at any other time?'

'Evenings. Sometimes.'

'All three of them?'

There was a pause, during which John leaned back in his chair. *Wait*. 'Sometimes just Dai comes. Sometimes Dai and Wil.'

'Never just Wil?'

No audible answer came from the boy, but there were two taps on the table from John. No.

'Wil and Twm don't get on, then?' I was asking for my own benefit as much as for the jury's information, seeking a hole into which I might insert a lever so as to prise a rift in the trio.

The boy twitched a shrug so small that I would not have noticed had I not been watching him carefully over the whirlpool. Again, two soft taps made sure that I knew the answer.

'What did the three men do after Mr Stockton had turned round and gone the other way?' I asked.

'Nothing.'

'Nothing at all?'

Wait.

'They laughed,' Gwilym muttered.

'They laughed? Did the three of them stay at the forge long after that?' I asked.

'No.'

'Where did they go?'

Another shoulder twitch.

'Did you see which way they walked?'

'Towards Blaengwndwn.'

'Where Dai lives?'

One tap from John.

'That's the road towards Felindre Farchog?' I clarified.

One tap. The child was afraid to give voice to what he saw as a dangerous truth.

'So,' I said, for the benefit of the jury, 'it would have been easy enough for them to catch up with Nathaniel Stockton – the man who you saw coming out of the Sergeant's – if they'd gone up into the fields?'

Another single tap.

I turned to the jury and asked if they had any questions for the boy. One member stood.

'Did you ever see these three men talking to Nathaniel Stockton – the man you saw coming out of the Sergeant's – before that day?'

A nod, a tap.

'Often?'

'Only once.'

'What did they say?'

A shrug.

'You didn't hear?'

'Not my business.'

'Was it friendly?'

The boy hesitated. 'Not really.'

'Why?'

'He was laughing.'

'Who was – Nathaniel Stockton?'

One tap.

'Do you know why?'

'A word Twm said. An English word. It was the wrong one.'

So, not only had Nathaniel Stockton committed the cardinal sin of trying to woo a local girl, but he had mocked those who most objected to his doing so. Not a strategy calculated to win him friends in Eglwyswrw.

The juryman, apparently satisfied, sat down, and at my word, Gwilym fled. 'Ask David Davies to step in, if you'd be so good,' I called to Caleb. It was time for Llwyo to tell the jury what we had seen the previous day at the pond.

John

I was supposed to be making careful notes, but my mind kept snapping back to Lydia's suggestion. Did I want her as my assistant? It would probably be good for the estate, but would it be good for *me*? Arguments on both sides kept appearing in my head, as if there were two tiny people inside my skull shouting at each other. I knew there weren't, obviously – I'd seen the inside of more people's heads than I wanted to, thanks to Harry and Dr Reckitt – but the voices felt real, and I couldn't shut them up.

I don't know how I managed to record the things Llwyo said. Later, when I was reading my notes for the inquest report, I didn't have any memory of writing the words down. But there it all was – the evidence of what we'd seen when Llwyo took us out to the pond on Blaengwndwn land. The knee marks, the scuffling, the signs that Wil Llain and his half a foot had been there, that something'd been dragged through the mud and ashes in the corn kiln's flue.

'Dr Reckitt gave evidence that there was mud and pond weed in Mr Stockton's airways,' Harry said when Llwyo'd agreed that at least three people had been standing at the edge of the pond. 'Can you tell the jury whether there was pond weed in the water near to where the footprints were?'

'Yes. There was.' Llwyo flicked a glance at me, as if him having to give evidence was all my fault. Perhaps it was.

'You work at the Sergeant's Inn stables, which stand within sight of the forge in Eglwyswrw. That's right, isn't it?'

'Yes.'

'Did you ever see the three men the stable boy named –
Twm y Gof, Dai Blaengwndwn and Wil Llain – with Nathaniel
Stockton?'

Another glance at me. Regretted selling me those names now,
didn't he? 'No.'

'You never even saw them exchange the time of day as he
passed on his way home from church?'

'No.'

'So the incident Gwilym described, when Mr Stockton
appears to have mocked something Twm y Gof said – you didn't
see that?'

'No.'

He wasn't going to give us a jot more than he had to, Llwyo.
Didn't want anything getting back to Eglwyswrw about him
landing the three of them in the dock.

As soon as he left the witness chair, noise broke out everywhere again. Even the jurymen put their heads together and
started talking about what they'd just heard. Things were stacking
up, and in a different inquest – one with a coroner who wasn't
interested in doing anything more than he had to – they'd have
gone out now to decide on a verdict. The evidence of what we'd
seen at the pond and what Reckitt'd found in Nattie's throat was
easily enough to bring in a verdict of unlawful killing by person
or persons unknown. But that wasn't Harry's way. He wanted
Edgar and Beatrice Stockton to leave his inquest knowing who
was responsible for their son's murder. And he wanted to be able
to deliver the culprits to the local magistrate so they could be
arrested and kept in Cardigan gaol pending trial.

Caleb Richards had gone off to fetch the next witness, and
the pot boys were going round with their jugs. I watched them
making their way through the crowd, laughing with this person,
calling out to that one, but always keeping on the move, filling
pots and taking pennies.

Next to me, Harry was fiddling with his writing frame. 'What
did Lydia want?' he asked. 'Does she have views on my strategy

for the inquest?' I could tell he was trying to pretend he didn't care one way or the other.

'No, nothing like that. She had a suggestion about the estate. I'm sure we'll talk about it on the way home.' Better by far to talk about Lydia being my assistant than to go back to arguing with Harry about what to do with the money from the Moelfryn farms.

People in the front rows started craning their necks to see something behind us, and I swung round in my chair. Caleb Richards had come in with the man who'd called out to Sally Sips when Harry and I had been talking to her in the churchyard. Twm y Gof.

We'd decided to start with Twm because he seemed like the most likely ringleader of the forge gang. Meeting at his place would more or less put him in charge, so if we could get any information out of him, persuading the other two – especially Wil – to talk would be easy. That was what we'd thought, at any rate.

And when Twm came and sat in the chair in front of us, I had hopes that we were right. He might be stocky and muscular like you'd expect from a blacksmith's boy, but I could see he wasn't strong in the nerves department. Properly twitchy, he was – leg bouncing, fingers tapping on his knees, shifting in his chair every five seconds. I thought we'd be able to trip him up easily.

I was wrong.

Fair play, I don't think our strategy was a bad one. Instead of going through questions the jury already knew the answers to and letting him get settled, we'd decided to go straight in on the attack, throw him off balance. And we were doing it in Welsh – the Eglwyswrw boys'd be more on guard in English because they'd have to think carefully about the right words for every answer – so Lydia was still translating for the Stocktons.

Straight away, Harry told Twm that we knew the three of them had been competing for Lizzie Rees's affections. Told him we knew they'd all given love spoons to her, so an outsider coming in to sweep her off her feet must've been a very unwelcome shock.

And things seemed to be going to plan to start with. Twm was rattled – his knee was going up and down like a steam piston.

Then Harry told him we knew the three of them had tried to warn Nattie off, and that Nattie'd been seen trying to avoid them on the morning he was killed. 'He saw you, and straight away he turned back the way he'd come. But you weren't going to let him avoid you for long, because you'd heard the rumours about him being at Rhosdywarch, courting in bed with Lizzie, the night before, hadn't you? You thought he'd defied you. And now Lizzie was dead.' He sat there looking squarely at Twm and not seeing him at all.

'The thing is, Twm, earlier in this hearing, one of the Gilfachwen outdoor servants who shared a loft with Nathaniel Stockton gave sworn testimony that he didn't leave the loft that night.'

'Then he's lying!' Good. Twm was cracking.

'No. We know he's not lying, because both Lizzie's father and the man who *was* courting with her that night have given evidence. Amos Bowen was with Lizzie on the night she died, not Nathaniel Stockton.'

Twm was struck dumb for about five seconds. Then he shook his head as if he was clearing it. 'No. That's a lie. It was *him*. Stockton.'

'You don't go to Eglwyswrw church,' Harry ploughed on, 'so perhaps you don't know Amos Bowen. He works – or I should say *worked* – over at Dolbannon. You might have heard of him. He used to wear an eyepatch and he has a stutter.'

By that point, Twm was halfway out of his seat. 'What – Dolbannon's *twpsyn*? Don't talk nonsense, Lizzie would never—'

'In fact, Mr Bowen is far from weak-headed,' Harry said while Caleb Richards pushed Twm back down onto the chair. 'People often mistake a speech impediment for a slowness in thinking, but Lizzie Rees knew that wasn't true. She saw beyond the squint and the halting speech. She was in love with Amos Bowen.'

I thought we had him then. His face had gone a dirty grey. But shocked or not, he kept his mouth shut. And that was when our plan began to unravel.

'You and your two friends were seen walking along the Felindre Farchog road in the direction of Blaengwndwn on Sunday morning, a few minutes after you'd seen Mr Stockton,' Harry said. 'Mr Davies and I walked out to the Blaengwndwn land yesterday, and we found a pond. A pond where there were footprints – some of which could only have been made by your friend Wil Llain – and signs that somebody had been kneeling next to the water.'

My heart started to beat faster then. What would Twm say when presented with actual evidence that they'd all been there?

'Can you tell us what you were doing at the pond, Twm?'

'Yes.' Twm sounded as if somebody had their hands round his throat, squeezing it. He cleared it and tried again. 'Yes. We were drowning kittens.'

Shit. Those damned children must've told Twm and the other two that we'd been out to Blaengwndwn.

Mind, Harry didn't turn a hair. Barrister's training. 'Why would you take kittens all the way there from the farmhouse? Why wouldn't you just drown them in a bucket in the yard?'

Twm cleared his throat again. 'Dai's little sister. She's very soft-hearted. He didn't want her to see.'

If they all stuck to that story, we were sunk.

Twm had a bit of colour back in his face now, and he jiggled and jittered his way through the rest of Harry's questions.

Had they seen Nathaniel crossing the fields while they'd been at the pond?

No, they'd been too busy drowning kittens.

What had they put in the corn flue?

They hadn't put anything in there. A badger must've been in there looking for food.

What were the scuff marks at the edge of the pond, as if somebody'd been dragged there?

Wil Llain and Dai had tried to push him into the pond as a joke.

They'd got their story straight.

–

It was the same with Dai Blaengwndwn. He came up with more stuff about his little sister, and how she tried to persuade their father to let her keep each litter of kittens when there were more than enough cats on the farm already, but in the end, his story was exactly the same as Twm's, even down to him and Wil trying to push Twm into the pond for fun. They'd been there drowning kittens. They hadn't followed Nattie. They hadn't seen him in the fields. They hadn't killed him. They hadn't put him in the kiln.

I watched Dai while he was giving evidence. I could see that he might've been more attractive to Lizzie Rees than Twm. Twm was too twitchy. He'd be quick to fly off the handle, and no wife wants that. Mind, we hadn't got him to lose his rag and tell us the truth, had we, so perhaps he had more self-control than you'd've thought from looking at him. But either way, Dai was calmer, quicker to smile, especially when he was talking about his little sister.

Did the jury watch his face as carefully as I did? Did they see his reaction when Harry told him that it hadn't been Nattie courting in bed with Lizzie that night, or when he told him who it had been? He didn't go quite as grey as Twm, but something in his face changed, and I'd've been willing to bet anything you like that he suddenly felt cold and sick, the way you do when you suddenly realise that you've made a terrible, terrible mistake.

But that kind of reaction isn't evidence, is it? Not enough to convince a jury. Not with the kitten story to explain away the evidence. Especially when the dead man was a foreigner.

And anyway, half the jurymen were probably too busy watching Harry to notice Dai's face. He'd been doing this job nine months now, and he was good at it. Very good. He could

348

hold juries spellbound with his words in a way that witnesses with their ums and ahs and stops and starts just couldn't.

But whatever he said to Twm and Dai, whatever questions he asked or suggestions he made – *You wanted to punish him, didn't you, for Lizzie's death? Because who would, otherwise?* – neither one of them gave an inch. They just kept telling the same story. They hadn't seen Nattie Stockton. They'd gone to the pond to drown kittens. That was why their footprints were there, that was why there were kneel marks there.

And to be honest, maybe they were cleverer than we'd given them credit for. Maybe they *had* gone back and drowned kittens, so Dai's parents would back them up if they were questioned.

–

When Harry dismissed Dai and asked Caleb Richards to bring Wil Llain down, the crowd started milling around again and I saw Lydia get to her feet and excuse herself to the Stocktons. She came over to our table and leaned to speak into Harry's ear. I couldn't hear what she said over the noise in the room, but when she straightened up, Harry nodded, and she went back to her seat.

'New strategy,' he said. But there was no time for him to tell me what it was because Caleb was leading Wil Llain to the witness chair and the spectators were settling again.

Missing half a foot or not, Wil the quarryman was tall, upright in spite of his limp, and looked as if he had no nerves at all.

He was one of those slow people, Wil Llain. I don't mean he was stupid; he just took his time with everything. Deliberate. Even the expressions on his face didn't come and go like they do in most people. They lingered, as if it took a lot to make him feel something but then the feeling wasn't easily snuffed out.

He smiled when Harry asked him if he'd been sweet on Lizzie Rees. 'Every unmarried man in the parish was sweet on Lizzie. And some of the married ones as well, if you want the honest truth.' The smile was still on his long, beaky-nosed face when Harry swooped in with the next question.

'By Saturday afternoon, it was all around the parish that Nathaniel Stockton had been seen leaving Rhosdywarch at first light – that he and Lizzie had been courting in bed. Did you believe that?'

Clever. Asking whether he'd *heard* the rumour would've been as good as asking him if he'd had a motive to kill Nattie, so he'd've denied it. Asking whether he *believed* it suggested to the jury that Harry *knew* Wil had heard the gossip.

And Wil fell for it. 'She'd given him the *coron fedw*, so I reckoned it was probably true.'

'How did you feel when you heard she'd died?'

Wil looked straight at Harry and blinked a couple of times. 'It was a shock. Terrible. Being so sudden like that.'

'It was sudden,' Harry agreed. 'But not suspicious. Dr Gwynne had confirmed that before anybody heard a word about her death. Lizzie Rees died of *natural causes*.'

'So the doctors say,' Wil Llain said in his deliberate way. 'But they don't know everything, do they?'

Harry waited as a murmur of agreement went around the room. 'True,' he said, his blind gaze fixed on Wil to make him feel uncomfortable. 'But the fact is, if a doctor says that somebody's died a natural death, there's no inquest, is there?'

Wil Llain stared at Harry for a long time but gave no answer. In truth, he didn't need to. Harry was just making a point.

'And if foul play goes undetected and there's no inquest,' Harry went on, laying out his words in that careful way that meant he was thinking while he spoke, 'then somebody gets away with murder.' He sighed. 'A year ago,' he continued slowly, 'I found myself in that position. I knew somebody'd got away with murder, and I had to decide what to do.' He was still looking in Wil's direction and nodding a little bit as if he was agreeing with himself – or with Wil. 'Somebody I cared about, somebody I loved – a young woman very much like Lizzie Rees – had been killed and I knew I couldn't just let the man responsible get away with it. I had to do something.'

No response from Wil except in his eyes. They narrowed just a tiny bit. He was wary, Wil Llain.

People in the crowd leaned to their neighbours, whispering, wondering why Harry was telling him all this.

'In the end, I couldn't bring the killer to justice,' Harry said. 'He was beyond my reach. But at least I knew the *truth*.' His fist came down on the table with a quiet thud that sounded louder than it was in the sudden hush.

'And that was what *you* wanted, wasn't it, Wil? The truth.'

Wil stared at him. I couldn't have named the expression on his face, but his hands'd clenched into fists. I wondered if the jury would notice. Probably not; they were all watching Harry too.

'It must've felt as if fate was taking a hand that morning, when Nathaniel Stockton came out of the Sergeant's and almost walked right into you. When he turned round and walked the other way, you must've known at that moment that he couldn't face you because of what he'd done.' Harry paused for a second or two, eyes on Wil. 'I know what that feels like, Wil. The man who murdered the woman I loved fled too. All the way to America.'

By now, the room was completely silent, but it was an uneasy silence. *What's the coroner doing?*

'You saw Nattie Stockton walk off the other way and you knew he'd be going up the lane so he could cut back across the fields. It was perfect, wasn't it? Just as if it was *meant*. Dai had already been trying to talk the two of you into coming with him to get rid of some kittens, so after a few minutes, you said the word and off you all went.'

You said the word. Harry was telling Wil that, half a foot or not, he knew that he was the strong one of the three, the leader. Was that what Lydia'd whispered to him, or had it been her idea for him to talk about Margaret Jones?

'It must've been easy to spot Nathaniel Stockton in the fields,' Harry continued. 'Did he run away when he saw you? Didn't matter, though, did it, because Dai and Twm brought him back to you. And they held him while you tried to make him admit what he'd done to Lizzie. Because you knew – you *knew* in your heart – that he'd hurt her, didn't you?'

I swear, half the people in the room were holding their breath now. You could almost feel the stillness of the air.

'But he just wouldn't give in, would he? Wouldn't tell you the truth. He kept lying, saying he hadn't been there. However hard you worked on him, *he kept lying.*'

Harry wasn't asking questions, he was telling a story, and Wil Llain just sat there listening to him. And it seemed to me that his fists were a bit less tightly clenched.

'I understand what you were doing, Wil. You wanted to take him to the magistrates with a confession, didn't you?' Harry didn't wait for an answer. 'I know how that feels – to hear that you were right, that what you knew all along was *right* and those who said it couldn't be true, that you should just let it go, were wrong.

'So you decided to frighten him. You could see that a beating wasn't going to do the trick. And why would it? You'd tried that before, but he'd still defied you, still gone to Lizzie that night.

'The pond was right there, waiting to give Nattie Stockton the fright of his life and show him you were serious, that he had to tell you the truth.'

Wil's face hadn't moved. He was just watching Harry, listening with no expression.

'Twm and Dai held his arms behind him and forced his head down into the pond. With his face under the water, he could still hear you telling him he had to tell the truth.'

And now *I* was holding my breath, thinking about Nathaniel Stockton's face being shoved down into the water and the weed and the mud.

'How many times did Twm and Dai let him come up so you could ask him the same question – *What did you do to her?* Twice, three times?'

Harry waited, eyes on Wil. It was as if they were alone in the room, just the two of them, with Harry offering Wil a way out, a way for him to make people understand.

'You didn't *mean* to kill him. Of course you didn't.' Harry's words were gentle, almost kind, and Wil was shaking his head, just tiny little movements from side to side as if he hardly dared move, eyes fixed as if he was still watching Twm and Dai holding Nattie face-down in the pond.

'You only wanted him to tell you what he'd done. But he *wouldn't*,' Harry said. 'He'd killed Lizzie and he *wouldn't confess*!'

I waited for Wil to deny it, to drag out the story of the kittens but things'd gone too far for that and he said nothing, just stared at Harry, moving his head in that small, small way.

'He couldn't confess, Wil,' Harry said, 'because he didn't do it. He wasn't with Lizzie that night. She was courting in bed with another man.'

'*Liar!*'

Wil was halfway to Harry in one stride, fist drawn back ready, but Caleb Richards had his other arm up behind his back before he could move another inch. A couple of men surged forward out of the crowd to help him.

'You're a liar just like him! He killed her! I knew what he'd done, but he thought he'd got away with it. Thought all he had to do was *keep saying no*!' Spit flew out of Wil Llain's mouth as he shouted, and the three men who had hold of him only just managed to stop him coming at Harry.

Harry was on his feet too. Whether he wanted to defend himself or to try and assert some authority, I don't know, but the spell in the room broke as Caleb and the other two men wrestled Wil to the ground and Caleb handcuffed him. Suddenly you couldn't hear yourself think for all the shouts and questions and accusations.

I saw Lydia comforting Mrs Stockton, who had covered her face with her hands and was sobbing.

Harry turned away from the noise and spoke to the jury. 'Gentlemen, unless you have any questions or you'd like to hear from any other witnesses, you should discuss your verdict.'

As the foreman turned to the rest of them, I took my watch out.

It took them less than two minutes to decide on their verdict, and the three men who'd drowned Nattie Stockton by accident because they wanted a confession and justice for Lizzie Rees were taken away.

Harry

John and I were in the habit of discussing our inquests as we made our way home, and the presence of Lydia and young Lleu with us on our journey home from Cilgerran proved no barrier to such a discussion, especially given the need to recognise Lydia's invaluable advice as to a change of direction.

However, satisfactory though it was to have laid bare the truth behind Nathaniel Stockton's death, I found myself oppressed by a sense of futility that John seemed to feel too.

'You know,' he said, 'for once I agree with Dr Reckitt – people should pay attention to science. If Wil and the others'd listened to what Cadwgan Gwynne and Reckitt said, they wouldn't've gone near Nattie Stockton. But no, they decided that the doctors didn't know what they were talking about, because they *wanted* to believe Nattie'd killed Lizzie. Because he was a foreigner and he'd gone one better than them with her.'

But it was not only his killers' preference for their own view of the world that had been responsible for Nattie Stockton's death; secrets had killed him as surely as prejudice. If Lizzie had not hidden her feelings for Amos out of fear of her mother's reaction, Amos would not have been mistaken for Nattie when he had been seen leaving Rhosdywarch on the morning of her death.

And Lizzie had not been the only one keeping secrets. There was something that both Mic Rees and Amos Bowen knew that Mic did not wish to be made public. It was not my job to discover what they were hiding, and yet I knew that unless I did, I would be no more satisfied that I had resolved the truth of Lizzie Rees's death than Reckitt was.

We were more than halfway home, and had been travelling in a slightly melancholy silence for a little while, when John reined Seren in, causing our little cavalcade to slow from a trot to a walk. 'Perhaps now's not the time, but then I don't know when the time might be,' he said, sounding uncomfortable. 'There's something we need to discuss, Harry. Lydia has suggested that when I'm out on inquest business with you, Harry, she should stand in for me on the estate.'

Though he had managed to deliver the news without prevaricating, he sounded guarded, uncertain. Did he expect me to object? Perhaps he *wanted* me to object, having found himself unable to say no to her. Lydia could be formidable when she chose, and her ideas, as I knew to my recent advantage, were rarely other than sound, which made them hard to reject.

The lady herself, seated next to Lleu, whom she had allowed to drive, said nothing.

'Well,' I said cautiously, 'I have no objection, but it must be your decision, John.'

An uncomfortable silence developed, during which Lleu began, unaccountably, to whistle. Finally John spoke up. 'I think we should try it. See how it goes.'

'I'm not suggesting that I step into John's shoes as understeward,' Lydia said. 'Just that I would be available to carry out his instructions and, if necessary, to make minor decisions on his – and your – behalf.'

If she granted herself the same latitude in carrying out his instructions that she laid claim to when acting for me as private secretary, John would be well advised to apply a firm hand to the reins from the outset. Accepting the Saunders-Jameses' lunch invitation without consulting me was hardly the only occasion on which she had acted on her own initiative.

'In Lydia's capacity as occasional assistant,' I asked cautiously, 'would you anticipate her being a party to discussing such things as investments and the sale of land?'

The silence that greeted my question was palpable. Lleu's whistling ceased, and even the children shouting in a nearby field seemed to have fallen silent, leaving only the birds in the hedgerows on either side of us to sing and chirp as if we did not exist. When John said nothing, Lydia spoke up, and I wondered whether she did so at his silent direction. 'I must confess, I'd find it strange if we felt we couldn't discuss things like that as freely as we discuss politics or philosophy.'

Her words conjured a vision in my mind's eye: the three of us sitting in the library after dinner, deep in conversation. Perhaps consideration of the estate's future did not need to consist only of the sense of leaden responsibility that I dreaded.

'Miss Howell should definitely be a party to those discussions,' John declared. 'You and I don't always find the right solution. Look how her intervention just changed the course of the inquest.'

'Shall we discuss this further at another time?' I asked, directing my blind gaze at Lleu, as if it were his presence that was responsible for my reluctance to continue the discussion rather than the disturbing notion, provoked by John's words, that my performance as squire might frequently require Lydia to step in and proffer advice when my own ideas proved inadequate.

–

'Mr Probert-Lloyd! Mr Probert-Lloyd!' Wil-Sam, our hall boy, burst out of the house as soon as he heard us coming up the drive.

'What is it?' I asked, smiling at his excitement. 'Is the Queen here?'

'There's a visitor! From London! Mr *Augustus Gelyot*.' He pronounced Gus's name as if it were a summoning spell.

I told the boy to take the horses round to the stables, and asked Lleu to follow him with the trap. 'And Wil-Sam?' He spun around. 'Then you can take Lleu Williams here to the kitchen and ask Mrs Elias to give the pair of you something to eat.' That would keep our would-be engineer occupied until I decided whether he should eat dinner with us or with the servants.

As John, Lydia and I trooped into the house, I wondered what on earth had brought Gus to Cardiganshire. He had not written to announce his intention to visit, so either he had very bad news to impart, or he had come on a whim.

'Did he mention anything about coming down when you saw him the other week?' I asked John.

'Not a word.'

We discovered Gus sitting at the library's open French windows, reading a newspaper in the late-afternoon light.

He sprang up as we came in. 'Ah, the prodigals return!'

'If there's a prodigal here, Augustus, it's you,' I said, shaking his hand and grinning like an idiot before I remembered my manners and introduced Lydia.

'Ah, the famous Miss Lydia Howell. So pleased to finally make your acquaintance, Miss Howell.'

'Likewise, Mr Gelyot.'

'What on earth has possessed you to quit civilisation, Gus?' I asked.

'I needed an excuse to get out of London. You know the city's intolerable in summer. Only the Exhibition has made it bearable. But even that has paled now.'

It amused Gus to affect a louche persona who disdained gainful employment, but he had become a barrister with the express intention of honing his wit for Parliament, and he stood up in court relatively frequently.

'And what excuse did you find?' I asked, crossing to the drinks cabinet. Though I actually wished for nothing so much as a cup of tea, I did not want Gus to start teasing me about becoming a dull provincial just yet.

'Brandy?' I held the decanter up.

'Dear God, P-L, do you *still* have no sherry? Even if you can't muster a cobbler, you might at least give me something that won't have me drunk before dinner.'

I remembered the sherry cocktail Anthony Saunders-James had served us at his boastful luncheon, and vowed that sherry would never have a place in Glanteifi. 'Afraid not, old pal. Brandy or tea. Or claret, obviously.'

'Then perhaps we should settle for tea. I don't want either of us to be befuddled when I tell you why I've come.'

–

'The thing is,' Gus said once we had been provided with tea and given notice that, if we pleased, dinner would be served in an hour, 'my dear pa is a wary old specimen. As you know, he's fond of saying that he hasn't made his money by being a credulous fool but—'

'By taking nobody at his word,' I chorused with him. We had both heard Mr Gelyot's guiding principal often enough.

'Exactly so. And though he found your man Harborne's plans for a wool factory commendable – not to say refreshingly ambitious for Cardiganshire – he wasn't inclined to take them at face value. Not when there was a proposed twenty-five per cent stake in the business to consider.'

'Harborne led me to believe that he'd already invested,' I said.

Gus raised his teacup to his lips. 'He has not.'

As he put his cup back in its saucer with an audible clink, it struck me how very infrequently I had seen him drinking tea. But then the nature of our friendship had hardly been domestic; we had spent our time in taverns and dining houses and London's new nightclubs, chiefly Laurent's Casino, where one might dance all night if one had both the leisure and the stamina. Pushing aside such painfully exquisite memories, I waited for Gus to continue.

'Before making any significant investment, my father makes it his business to seek advice from those best suited to providing it. Having done so in this case, he made some interesting discoveries. That for instance the Carmarthen to Cardigan railway is likely to proceed in short order. Apparently there's no shortage of pledges from eager investors.'

'That's what I'd understood too.' I might not match George Gelyot's mistrustful diligence, but I had heard nothing but enthusiasm for the railway.

'The deep-water port, on the other hand, is currently no more than a castle in the air. And if it doesn't become a good deal more substantial, the impetus to get the railway built all the way to Cardigan will decline considerably.'

Gus finished his tea and twisted around to put the cup and saucer on the table behind him. His movements possessed a feline fluidity that I had always envied, and the difference between us would be all the more marked now that my own movements were so carefully deliberate.

'But the information that ultimately led to his decision not to invest in Harborne's factory was learned in Newtown.'

'Your father went there?' John asked.

'No, Mr Davies. He sent people there. And their discreet enquiries revealed that Harborne had left his employment in Newtown under something of a cloud. There was talk of orders for which he had been responsible mysteriously going astray. The suspicion was that he was diverting them into his own business and blaming the inefficiency of suppliers.'

'Suspicion? It wasn't proved, then?' Though Gus's news must be music to John's ears, as it meant that I would have to think again about investing in Harborne's mill, it did him credit that he wanted the facts absolutely clear.

'The mill owner concerned decided to cut his losses and simply dismiss Harborne. My father didn't say as much, but I imagine the man didn't want his own affairs looked into too closely either.'

The sun had set by now, and the east-facing windows of the library had dimmed, leaving the room in half-light and shadows. With dinner imminent, the servants would not disturb us to light the lamps, but I suddenly felt the gloom acutely.

'So Harborne's a potential crook and your father's not investing. Couldn't you have put that in a letter?'

'Of course I could.' Gus's easy tone ignored my own sharpness. 'But I had a yearning to see you, P-L.' He was teasing me, but behind the levity, I detected something else. Had John or Lydia written to him to tell him that I was failing to manage the estate properly, that I was in danger of bankrupting us? 'Besides,' he added. 'I wanted to see that shower bath I sent you for your birthday in action.'

Unwilling to discuss the as yet unused shower bath, I stood up. 'Speaking of ablutions, perhaps we should all go and change for dinner.'

I needed time to think.

John

When I came downstairs the following morning, Lleu was eating breakfast with Lydia.

Harry'd had him in the dining room at dinner with us the night before, so I wasn't surprised to see him. He'd come up in the world, Lleu. Just like me.

'What time are we going over to see Mr Harborne this morning?' he asked once I'd sat down. It was on the tip of my tongue to tell him that we weren't going at all, that I didn't want him anywhere near Jem Harborne's mill. But when my brain caught up with my mouth, I realised that I'd be safe taking him over there – the likelihood of Amos wanting an apprentice was approaching none at all, and even if he did agree to take the boy on, Harry'd persuade Miss Gwatkyn that it wasn't a good idea. And anyway, I wanted to know about the injured man, Jaco. If he died, I'd have an inquest to organise.

I cracked the shell of a boiled egg and started peeling it. 'We'll go over first thing after breakfast.' The sooner we could pack Lleu back off to Alltybela, the better.

The boy had finished his breakfast, so while I got on with eating, he started gibbering on about something he'd been very taken with at the Great Exhibition – the velocipede. It was an odd-looking, four-wheeled contraption where the rider sat in amongst the wheels and worked treadles to make them go round. It'd looked uncomfortable and impractical to me, but Lleu'd been thrilled with it. 'You could adapt this to make a hansom cab drawn by a man instead of a horse!' he'd said to me. 'Think about the money that'd save! No stabling or food for the horse. And look at all the shit horses scatter about the city – it's everywhere! If you had velocipede carriages instead, the streets'd be clean.'

Now I took a mouthful of bread and butter and boiled egg and listened to him telling Lydia how man-powered carriages would clear London's streets of what he politely called horse manure and make the city stink less. Was that what it was like to be an engineer – always looking at things around you as problems to be solved? I was beginning to suspect that the likes of Amos Bowen wouldn't rest until they'd made the whole country into one gigantic Crystal Palace, full of inventions and improvements. Machines everywhere, doing our work for us. And the work of horses, too, if these velocipedes were going to catch on. I couldn't imagine it – didn't want to, truth be told.

'Lleu,' Lydia sad when the boy paused for breath, 'before you go out to Llandyfriog with Mr Davies, you might like to go and ask Mrs Griffiths if she can lay her hands on some of Mr Probert-Lloyd's old britches and boots, so you can ride. Melchior will need a rest today after pulling the trap all the way to Cilgerran and back yesterday.'

The boy was canny enough to know he'd been given an instruction, and off he went like a lamb. I waited. Lydia obviously had something she wanted to say to me.

'I thought we should clear the air about my offer of help,' she said.

I looked up in surprise. 'Clear the air? What d'you mean?'

She looked me in the eye. 'Yesterday, when you told Harry what I'd suggested, you didn't sound too pleased. I was afraid you felt I was forcing you into something.'

I took a swig of tea. 'No. Not at all. I just wasn't sure how to tell him. Or even if I had to. I mean, if I was going to be a normal agent – if I didn't live in the house as part of the furniture, so to speak – I could take on whatever assistant I wanted, couldn't I? I wouldn't need to ask Harry's permission. But I live here, and... well, I didn't exactly want to *ask* him, but I had to tell him what we'd been talking about. He'd be offended if you just started working for me without so much as a by-your-leave.' Always assuming he still wanted me to be his agent, of course. We hadn't shaken hands on anything yet, still less signed a contract.

She breathed in and out again quickly, as if she was clearing something from her windpipe. 'Good. If that's all it is.' She put her hands palm down in her lap, ready to get up and get on. 'Right then, is there anything you'd like me to do this morning while you're over in Llandyfriog? I think Mr Gelyot's going to keep Harry occupied.'

—

By the time we rode away from the mansion – with Lleu in britches that were a bit big for him and old riding boots that somebody'd polished in a hurry – the rain that'd come lashing in overnight had lost its spiteful edge and was just falling quietly in a sort of drenching drizzle. It wasn't often I wished for a rubberised Mackintosh coat like Harry's, but by the time we got to Llandyfriog, the water running off the brim of my hat had come right through the shoulders of my coat, and my knees were wet and cold above my boots. Lleu didn't have gloves, and his hands must've been freezing, but in his excitement, I don't think he noticed.

We clattered over the wooden bridge to the factory site and Lleu stood in the stirrups to look about – first at the men who were replacing the sluice gate in the repaired dam, then down the muddy slope to the buildings. I saw things through his eyes and thought how modern and exciting the mill seemed in comparison to all the other buildings in the little valley. They were all made from the turf and stone that came out of the ground beneath them, and looked as if they'd grown there instead of being built by men's hands.

But to me, the mill looked foreign, as if it didn't belong. Would the Teifi Valley really be full of buildings like this before the decade was out? Jem Harborne certainly thought so. And if it was full of spinning and weaving machines, would other machines come in as well – farm machines? Amos Bowen had adapted the engines he'd seen in Newtown to run on water power in the little valley above Llandyfriog. If he could do that, what was to stop other engineers adapting the mechanical implements we'd seen at the Great Exhibition so they could be used in our hilly little fields?

I thought of the mowing teams that went from farm to farm in strict rotation, cutting hay according to the orders of the farmer in charge, and tried to imagine machines doing it instead. No scythes rhythmically swinging as the men sang mowing songs, no indoor servants coming out to the fields with drinks and something to eat, no games going on amongst the young people of the farm. Would girls wear the harvest green any more and lie down in the mown hay with young men? No, not if machines were going up and down everywhere, doing everything three times as quickly as it was done by hand.

But even if other estates went in for machines, Glanteifi couldn't afford them. Not now and not for the foreseeable future, unless things changed. And that'd be up to me, wouldn't it? Everything on the estate'd be up to me.

'John Davies!' Amos walked over from where he'd been helping with the replacement sluice gate. He was in his element here, and he looked straight at me with his uncovered eye. 'J-Jem's not here. I don't kn-know when he'll be back.'

I grinned at him. 'Don't worry, it's you we've come to see.'

But he *was* worrying – I could see that in his face. He must've thought I was here to carry on badgering him about whatever it was Mic Rees didn't want us to know. 'It's nothing to do with the inquest,' I reassured him. 'Remember me telling you about a young man who wanted to be an engineer?' I jerked my thumb in Lleu's direction. 'Well, this is him.'

There didn't seem any point me doing any more talking when Lleu could speak perfectly well for himself, so I left them to it and went down the slope to talk to the carpenters. I had to be careful not to slip on the wet grass and mud – my riding boots were so slick on the bottom, it was like walking on ice.

Jem Harborne's team had done a huge amount of work since I'd been there last – so much that I wondered whether he'd taken the advice I'd given Amos and paid local boys to work with the carpenters he'd brought in. All the damage'd been repaired, there were new upper floors in place and the roof was already being fitted with wooden tiles. That surprised me, because everybody seemed to be using slate these days, but then the wooden frame was going to have enough weight to support with the power looms and the machines to run them without adding a heavy roof.

I found the foreman I'd talked to before and he grinned his gap-toothed grin when he recognised me. 'By yourself? No newspapermen this time, then?'

'Can't live an exciting life all the time, can I?' I grinned back. 'No, I had to bring the lad to talk to Mr Bowen,' I tilted my head back up the hill towards the two of them, 'and I thought I'd come and ask after the man who was injured in the attack.'

'Jaco? Back in the land of the living,' the foreman said. 'But come and talk to Mattie-Siôn. He's Jaco's brother. He can tell you properly.'

He whistled to get the men's attention, then called out for Mattie-Siôn, who came down a ladder with the nimbleness of a monkey.

I explained who I was and why I was there.

'Oh, don't you worry about Jaco. Head as thick as a ram, that one,' he said, following me out of the building and down onto the churned-up mud and grass.

'Glad to hear it. We heard he was still out cold when they took him home,' I said, once we were outside, away from the din of saws and mallets.

'True enough. But he's right as rain now. Coming back in a day or two, when he can get a ride with somebody. Too idle to walk, Jaco.'

Mattie-Siôn glanced over his shoulder, and when he saw that the foreman wasn't watching him, he nodded towards a pile of timbers a little way off and took out his pipe and a tobacco pouch. 'Sit down for a minute?'

I nodded. Mattie-Siôn didn't seem to mind getting the seat of his trousers wet, but I stayed standing while he filled his pipe and took out a box of matches. I was surprised. Matches were expensive, and you didn't see them much locally. Harborne must be paying well.

'They were lucky, the boys who came here to wreck the place,' he said in between sucking and puffing his pipe into life. 'If Jaco hadn't got a clout round the head to knock him out like that, they'd've burned the place down, I reckon. And Mr Harborne wouldn't've let 'em off then.' He blew out a mouthful of smoke.

'They'd've been up in front of the beak and breaking rock in Cardigan gaol, not getting taken on to help us here.'

So I'd been right.

Mattie-Siôn looked at me through the smoke from his pipe. 'Mind, they were lucky in another way, too.'

'Oh yes?' I wasn't really listening, too busy watching Amos and Lleu and hoping Amos was managing to persuade the boy that he needed to go back to school.

'Yes,' Mattie-Siôn said. 'If they'd hit our cousin Benji instead of Jaco, it might've been a different story.'

He was obviously waiting for me to ask, so I turned to him, thinking he was going to make some kind of joke. 'Why's that then?'

He raised his eyebrows. 'There's a family curse on that side.'

All right then, not a joke. 'Family curse?'

'Yes. Affects the side of the family up in Llanybydder, it does. Me and Jaco are all right because we're only cousins by marriage, not by blood, but it's a terrible thing. Jaco'd have been a goner, sure to be, if he'd been one of my uncle's wife's lot.'

I eventually got the whole story out of him. Names, places, history. And at last I knew how Lizzie Rees had died.

Harry

Though I had succeeded in persuading Gus that it would not be appropriate for him to accompany John and me to Rhosdywarch, he was with me nevertheless as we rode over to speak to Mic Rees; I simply could not put the conversation we'd had the previous evening out of my mind.

After first Lydia and then John had retired, Gus and I sat by the fire in the library until both brandy decanter and coal scuttle were empty, and I explained my predicament in a way I had never managed in my letters to him.

'You know my views on birth and position and merit,' I told him, 'but ever since I came back here, the idea that I might treat anybody except other men of means as my equal has been greeted like some kind of certifiable medical delusion. And now, despite my best efforts to create a household in which I might feel that I am among friends, I find myself sitting on a squirely throne! In making John my agent, I find I've placed him beneath me, and now, damn him, he has decided to accept Lydia's offer of assistance, putting *her* beneath *him*! We've become a hierarchy. It's intolerable!'

'Then do something about it. Disrupt the status quo.'

'How?'

'You're a lawyer. Resort to the law.'

–

On the other side of the river, the weather seemed to turn, and as we climbed upwards out of the wooded little Cych valley and on to a higher, more windswept stretch of road, the Frenni hills were completely invisible beneath a low bank of cloud that extended mistily into the air around us. The greyness dampened our spirits and beaded the mares' coats and our own with moisture.

By the time we arrived at the Reeses' smallholding, we were both thoroughly damp. I hoped that a cup of tea might be offered to warm us, but the nature of our visit meant that such hospitality could not be guaranteed.

At the sound of our horses' hooves, the cottage's front door swung open to reveal Esther Rees.

'Good day, gentlemen.'

I dismounted. 'Good day, Mrs Rees. Is your husband at home?'

'He's weaving. You'd better come in.' She made to turn and go back inside, but I forestalled her. 'Is there room to put our horses in the byre?' I had no wish to ride home on a sodden saddle.

The horses seen to, we trooped into the kitchen.

Both Rees daughters were sitting on the bench, one knitting, the other doing something to a shirt or petticoat.

'Gwen, go and fetch your father,' Esther instructed, swinging the kettle over the fire on its chain.

John and I stood in the middle of the room until Esther indicated the chairs that had been pushed back to one side of the fire. 'Please, sit.' As we did so, Gwen reappeared with Mic, and suddenly the kitchen seemed crowded.

'Mrs Rees, if you wouldn't mind, we'd like to speak to your husband alone.'

This was Lydia's recommendation. 'If Mic Rees has been hiding things, best you talk to him by himself,' she'd said after John had finished telling us the carpenter's story the previous day. 'It's not your business to tell his wife secrets he's been keeping from her.'

Esther Rees did not respond immediately, but went over to the fire and poked it into brighter life. I watched her in my peripheral vision, braced for the argument I feared was coming, but she merely said, 'Just let me make you your tea, then the girls and I will go and get on with our work in the weaving shed.'

'Thank you.'

Mic stood at the side of the box bed, where kitchen met bedroom, as if he was loath to hear what had brought us back to his house. Nobody spoke while Esther laid out teacups and milk, and the smell of damp tweed began to flavour the air.

I jumped when Mic spoke suddenly. 'Gwen, Ann – take your work into the weaving shed like your mother said.'

The girls obeyed as their mother poured boiling water into the teapot and straightened up. 'Right,' she said, 'my husband can see to the rest. I'll leave you in peace.' She strode towards the corner of the room, then turned. 'I'm sorry, there's no sugar. After the inquest, my custom isn't wanted at the shop.'

I was surprised that her pride allowed her to admit such a thing, but then Mic spoke. 'Esther...'

She ignored him, sweeping past him and out of the kitchen, her barb having found its mark. The shopkeeper's refusal to serve her had no doubt been a reaction to the news that Lizzie had been courting not one, but two men from outside the area; that she'd given the *coron fedw* to Nathaniel Stockton while she had secretly been intending to marry somebody else. With her father's connivance. Esther would not easily forgive her husband for going behind her back.

Mic Rees had been forced to step sideways out of his wife's path but made no attempt to leave his corner.

I rose from his chair. 'Mr Rees, please, come and sit down.'

He hesitated, then drew closer, but refused to displace me. 'No, you sit there. I'll have the stool when I've done this.'

He bent to the hearth to pour the tea, and I resumed my seat, feeling my damp britches cold against my legs.

I accepted the cup he proffered and put it on the floor to cool down. 'Mr Rees, I believe you told Dr Reckitt and me when we first met that you were from near Llanybydder, is that correct?'

'Yes.' The word seemed to lodge in Rees's throat, precluding the uttering of any more.

'Do you have a cousin called Benji from up that way?'

'Benji Rees of Cwmcille,' John reminded me.

'Yes, Benji Rees, Cwmcille. Which was still in your grand-father's hands when you left to go droving, I believe?'

'Who told you?' Rees sounded defeated, as if a long struggle was over.

'Mattie-Siôn the carpenter,' John said. 'He and a whole load of people you'd have known once upon a time are working on a new wool factory the other side of Newcastle Emlyn.'

'Wool factory?' Rees asked, momentarily distracted by the confusing term.

'A man called Jem Harborne is building a mill for power looms over there,' John said.

I did not want Rees distracted. 'Mr Davies recently had reason to speak to Mattie-Siôn about one of the other carpenters, who'd been injured in an attack on the mill building.'

'Who was it?' Rees asked, clearly suspecting that this was another of his family. 'Is he badly injured?'

'Name of Jaco,' John supplied, 'brother of Mattie-Siôn.'

I saw Rees nod. 'He's making a good recovery,' I said, keeping my voice low, despite the fact that we had heard the door to the weaving shed close. 'But Mattie-Siôn told Mr Davies that it was a good job Jaco wasn't from the other side of the family, or the family curse might've got him.' I paused, but Rees said nothing. 'I think you'd better tell us about it, don't you, Mr Rees?'

John

As soon as Benji's name was mentioned, Mic Rees knew the game was up. I could see it in his face.

'I dare say Mattie-Siôn and Benji between them have told you everything there is to know,' he said. 'I'm not sure what you want from me.'

'The truth,' Harry said. 'Keeping secrets killed Nattie Stockton.'

Mic's head drooped at the mention of Nattie's name. 'You'd've done no different if you'd lived with what I've had to live with,' he said. 'You'd have kept it a secret too.'

'Benji Rees hasn't.'

'Benji's a fool who loves to hear the sound of his own voice. And *his* sister didn't die.'

'Tell us about your sister, Mic,' Harry said gently, when Mic just sat there looking like he was fighting back tears.

At first I thought he wasn't going to say anything. Harry had no authority over him now, did he? But I was wrong.

'Susan. That was my sister's name.' He gave a deep sigh, as if he'd just put a heavy load down. 'She grew up terrified,' he said. 'All our lives, me and her, we'd been told about the family curse. Our grandfather'd died of it when our father was small, and our father's brother – an uncle we'd never known.'

He stopped, and I watched his face, wondering what it must be like talking about something you'd run away from and tried to forget for twenty-odd years. I thought of what Benji Rees had told me when I'd asked Mattie-Siôn if I could have a word with him.

'They didn't fall ill then die,' he'd said. 'They had no weakness or pain or any of that. They just upped and died. One minute they were fine, the next minute they were gone.'

According to Benji, the family curse went back generations, and each death was remembered in stark detail. Every memory passed down. Some had died in their sleep after going to bed perfectly well. One or two had died when doing heavy work. Others laughing and dancing. 'That's the worst of it,' he'd told me. 'It's not just that you go through life not knowing if you'll wake up in the morning. The worst thing is that you can't do what everybody else does – you're always afraid of working too hard, you never really let yourself properly enjoy anything in case it brings it on and that's the end of you.'

'When did your sister die?' Harry asked Mic quietly.

'Just before I went droving. But it wasn't the curse that killed her. Well, it was and it wasn't.'

Harry drank his tea and waited.

'It was too much for her,' Mic said, eyes on Harry. 'Every day she woke up and thought – is it today? Will I die today? She'd never play with the other girls for fear of laughing too much. She'd lie awake at night, terrified of going to sleep in case she didn't wake up again. She prayed and prayed for a sign that the curse wouldn't touch her, but it never came. So she went through her days like a ghost, only half living, to try and keep the curse away.' He stopped, searching Harry's face for understanding. 'It affected her. Mind and body. She started dwindling away. Got thinner and thinner as the fear gnawed at her.' He dropped his head into his hands and his voice was muffled after that, so we had to lean closer to catch what he was saying. 'In the end, she couldn't stand it. It was a living hell, a life of nothing but fear.'

I had a pretty good idea what was coming next.

'She drowned herself in the river. My parents told everybody that she must've fallen in and been too weak to save herself. But I knew that was a lie. She just saw her chance and took it. She'd already told me that hell couldn't be any worse than the life she was living.'

I looked at Harry, waiting for him to speak, but I don't think he knew what to say any more than I did.

'Things take us all differently, don't they?' Mic said. 'Maybe because Susan was so afraid, I took the other road and just decided to live as if there was no curse. Because there are other things that can kill you just as unexpectedly, aren't there? And we don't spend our lives fearing them.'

True enough. Jaco the carpenter could easily have died from the blow to his head, and I don't suppose he'd got up on the morning of the attack on the mill worried that he wouldn't see another day.

'But you can see why I didn't tell Esther or the girls, can't you, Mr Probert-Lloyd?' Mic pleaded. 'I wanted to spare them the fear that killed my sister. I wanted them to grow up with hopes of marriage and children instead of the dread of sudden death.'

It seemed a fair point. But Harry had another question. 'Do you think it was fair not to tell your wife what you might be passing on to the children you'd have together?'

'Might, Mr Probert-Lloyd. *Might*. Would it have been right to cast a dark shadow over her life? To plant a fear inside her that she'd feel every time she looked at our children? There've been people in every generation of our family who've lived long lives. I hoped and prayed that I didn't have the bad blood; that I wouldn't pass it on.'

We sat there just drinking our tea for a minute or so, then Harry said, 'So can you tell us now what actually happened on the night your daughter died?'

Mic shook his head. 'There's nothing to tell. You heard it all at the inquest. Everything apart from Amos almost going mad because he thought it was his fault and me having to tell him that it was the curse. I had to, in the end,' he said, his head sagging again. 'The boy would've done himself a mischief otherwise.'

So that was what the head shake had been about. Amos'd wanted to know whether he should tell the inquest about the curse.

374

'Why did you go to Dolbannon for a messenger?' Harry asked. 'You must've known there was a chance David Jones would send Amos.'

'That's why I went there,' Mic said. 'I knew Dai would call Amos from the harvesting. Everybody knew he hated working in the field gang – even Dai Dolbannon, and he doesn't generally care for anybody but himself.'

Harry frowned. 'Wasn't it cruel to send Amos with the news?'

'No. When I sent him back to Dolbannon before he was missed, he was still jittering about it being his fault and getting hanged for it. I told him I'd get Dewin Gwynne over to certify the death. He'd see it was natural. I had to tell him what the doctor had said.'

'Dr Gwynne told us that you asked him to tell you whether your daughter'd been cursed,' I said.

Mic Rees hung his head and sat there shaking it slowly. 'I wanted to see if he could tell what'd killed Lizzie. Wanted him to explain it to me, tell me how I could know whether my little girls are cursed too. But he couldn't see anything. Said no, it was just natural death. And I couldn't tell him the truth. I just couldn't.'

'What if he'd been suspicious, said he wasn't sure that it was a natural death, would you have told him then?' Harry asked.

'Yes. I wouldn't've put Amos at risk of being arrested.'

He'd put Nattie Stockton at risk, even if he hadn't realised that. But it wasn't his fault Amos'd been seen leaving Rhosdywarch and that Amos and Nattie were both average-sized, dark-haired lads, was it?

'Please, don't tell anybody. It won't help Nattie's parents, and if my wife and daughters find out, it'll ruin their lives. I don't want Annie and Gwen to suffer like my sister.'

Harry took a deep breath, his eyes on Mic's midriff so he could see as much of his face as he was going to, and nodded. In his inquests, he kept the *whole* truth quiet often enough when it would do nothing but cause distress.

Mic Rees's keeping quiet might indirectly have caused Nattie Stockton's death, and he'd have to live with that. But I wasn't sure I'd've done differently.

Epilogue

John

One evening three weeks or so later, I got back from a day out and about on the estate to find Lydia by herself in the library.

'Where's Harry?'

'He got Twm Davies to take him into town in the trap. He was quite evasive about what he was doing, but I'm pretty sure he's gone to see Llewelyn Kerr.'

I sat down by the fire, my spirits suddenly lower than they had been ten seconds ago. If Harry'd gone to see the estate's solicitor, it must've been about the sale of the Moelfryn farms. We'd had several arguments about the whole business – not so much about whether he should sell the land to Anthony Saunders-James but about what to do with the proceeds. He still thought we should invest the money, though at least he wasn't talking about investing in Harborne's mill any more. Now that Mr Gelyot senior wasn't taking his quarter-share, the mill's future was in doubt, and work on it had stopped for now.

'Are you all right, John?'

I looked up. 'Just thinking about wool factories. Even if Harborne's doesn't get built, do you think that's the future here?'

'Yes. Possibly not this year or next. But in ten years, I'm sure there'll be factories like that here. You can't stop progress.'

Just then I heard the sound of the trap coming up the drive.

'Here he is,' Lydia said, looking out of the library window at Twm pulling up for Harry to get out at the front door. 'Now we'll find out what he's been up to.'

We listened to the sounds of Harry coming into the house and chatting to Elsie as she took his coat and hat before he joined us in the library. As usual, at the first hint of dusk, Lydia had the place blazing with candles and lamps for Harry's benefit.

'Afternoon,' I said, standing up, 'or is it good evening already?'

Harry gave a half-smile but didn't reply. He was carrying some documents, which he put down carefully on the table. I thought I saw his hand trembling, and my heart started beating faster. If Harry was nervous, he'd done something serious.

'Been to the solicitor's?' I asked. Better to know the worst as soon as possible.

'Let him sit down before you start questioning him, John!'

But Harry didn't sit down, just stood at the table with one hand still on the documents as if they might fly away if he stopped holding them down.

'Come on then,' I said. 'Tell us what you've got there.'

Harry chewed the inside of his lip and said nothing. I looked at Lydia and she moved to his side. 'Would you like me to read it?' she asked.

'No. I know exactly what it says. I dictated it myself last week, and Llewelyn Kerr read it to me word for word less than an hour ago. And then he tried to persuade me to rip it up.'

'Why?' I asked. 'What is it?'

'A deed of sale.'

'For the Moelfryn farms?'

Harry trained his eyes somewhere to my side, trying to see me in his peripheral vision. 'No. For Glanteifi.'

I felt as if the ground had given way under me. '*What?*'

Lydia moved past Harry and took my arm. Did she think I was going to faint? Perhaps she was right. My brain was whirring, but I couldn't seem to think. Sell Glanteifi? How long had he been thinking about this? What was I supposed to do now? Could I really earn my living as a solicitor? Would Llewelyn Kerr give me a job? And what about Lydia?

All these questions poured through my head in half a second, but I couldn't answer any of them.

'Harry, come and sit down and explain,' Lydia said. 'You too, John.'

Just then, Elsie arrived with tea. Lydia took the tray and told the girl that she could go. Then she gave me a cup with three chunks of sugar in the saucer. I knew what that was for. Shock.

'You didn't mention that you were thinking of selling,' she said. How could she sound so calm? Hadn't her future just fallen around her ears as well?

Harry unclamped his jaw. 'No. I had to be sure in my own mind before speaking to you two.' When he took the cup she passed him, it rattled in its saucer. His hands were shaking. 'But I knew I had to do something, because the current situation is intolerable. I never wanted to be squire. I don't have the temperament.'

'So our lives get turned upside down because you don't like being squire?' I knew I sounded upset. I *was* upset.

'I hope your lives aren't going to be turned upside down,' he said. 'I hope this will be good for you.'

I leapt to my feet, tea sloshing into my saucer. 'How can selling Glanteifi be good for us?'

'Because it's you I'm selling to.'

I stared at him. Had he gone off his head? He knew I was looking at him, and he just lifted his cup and took a sip of tea, as if he hadn't just said something completely ridiculous.

'Harry,' Lydia said. 'Please explain.'

Had she known about this? 'Did you know—'

She shook her head and held up a hand. *Let him speak.*

'While I own Glanteifi and you both work for me, we can't be equals,' Harry said. 'And I wish above all things to live amongst my equals. I'm not like my father. He saw his position as squire as part of the natural order. I don't. I want you to be able to tell me when I'm making bad decisions without being afraid that I'll sack you. I want you to be able to tell me your opinions without holding back because you're *just servants.*' He pointed his eyes in Lydia's direction when he said that, so that was obviously a conversation they'd had. 'I don't want you to have to think before you speak lest you upset my delicate sensibilities. I lived my whole life before I came back here – school, Oxford, the bar – amongst my peers: arguing, fighting, discussing, debating, sometimes winning, sometimes losing. But *always* on equal terms.'

I glanced at Lydia. From the look on her face she didn't know anything more about this than I did.

'This deed of sale,' Harry said, putting a hand on the document on his lap, 'effectively divides the ownership of Glanteifi into three equal shares. I will retain one share, and I am proposing that you each buy one of the two remaining shares. Then we'll be equal. I'll no longer be squire. We'll *all* be responsible for the running of Glanteifi. For all decisions equally.'

'That's all very well,' I said, trying to sound calm, 'but there's one small problem.'

'Money isn't going to stop us doing this, John. The sale price for your shares is a shilling. Just one shilling.'

Lydia stared at him, blinking. 'You're not selling us shares,' she said, 'you're making us partners. The payment is just a legal fiction.'

'Yes. I'm making you equal partners. That's the only way in which I can conceive of us all continuing to live and work together. So... What do you say?'

Historical notes

Courting in bed

Unlikely though it seems, I didn't make up the whole concept of courting in bed for the purposes of my plot; for exactly the reasons Harry mentions in the book, it was a custom widely practised in Wales in the mid nineteenth century. The practice died out as the century progressed, partly as a reaction to the opprobrium heaped on it by the infamous Report on the State of Education in Wales, 1847, and partly as a response to the creeping anglicisation of culture and mores that took place in Wales during the Victorian era.

Interestingly, it was not unique to Wales but was also practised in other parts of the UK and in the Netherlands, making its way to America with emigrants where it was practised in some areas throughout the nineteenth century and is rumoured to be sanctioned, still, in some Amish communities.

The Teifi Valley Woollen Industry

I've taken the liberty of bringing forward the start of the industry in the Teifi Valley by a few years in a way which is wholly plausible in terms of contemporary economics, based on all the infrastructure plans that Jem Harborne mentions in the book.

Harborne's statement that there was only one spinning mill in the Teifi Valley in 1851 is true and the kind of development he is proposing didn't really come into being until a decade later, in the early 1860s. The epicentre of the industry was further up the Teifi Valley in Dre-fach which later came to be known by the suffix Felindre – mill town. But, by the 1880s and 1890s there were woollen mills of varying sizes all over the lower Teifi valley and the valleys of its tributaries. Some survive today.

You can visit the National Wool Museum in Dre-fach Felindre, right in the heart of Harry's jurisdiction, between Newcastle Emlyn and Llandysul. And, if you'd like an idea of what woollen mills were like in Harry and John's day, you can visit Melin Tregwynt, a small, whitewashed mill in a remote wooded valley in Pembrokeshire. Both the museum and Melin Tregwynt still make woollen textiles, though not the flannel for clothing that Jem Harborne was intending to produce.

To see pictures of the sort of mill Harborne was planning, have a look at Elvet Woollen Milll's website. The history detailed there is very typical of the kind of resourcefulness seen in Teifi Valley entrepreneurs as they repurposed buildings for a new and different industry.

Deep Water Port of Refuge in Cardigan

There was, indeed, a plan to create a deep water harbour of refuge at Cardigan and Mr John Lloyd-Davies, mentioned in the book as a future Cardiganshire MP, spoke in favour of it in the House of Commons in February, 1856. Sadly for the local economy then and ever since, it did not come to pass.

And it's all *plus ça change plus c'est la même chose* because, in writing about Harborne's enterprising plan to make use of infrastructure that was still on the drawing board, I was inspired by the case of an entrepreneur in London who acquired land and built up a business to take advantage of the new Crossrail line in London, only to go bankrupt as a result of endless delays in the line's completion.

The Carmarthen and Cardigan Railway

The Carmarthen and Cardigan railway was planned as an extension of the South Wales Railway to link the two ports and it seemed likely to improve economic conditions locally, especially when combined with the plans to expand Cardigan's port facilities mentioned above. However, failure to raise enough finance for the scheme meant that it was delayed and, from the opening of the first section to Cynwyl Elfed in 1860, the railway was loss making. It was extended as far as Llandysul by 1864 but the line to Newcastle Emlyn wasn't completed until 1895, well after the Carmarthen and Cardigan Railway had been absorbed by the Great Western Railway. The final stretch from Newcastle Emlyn to Cardigan was never completed, with a 'charabanc' or bus service linking the two towns instead.

Cilgerran slate

Cilgerran slate quarries were part of the wider slate quarrying industry that ran in a band through Pembrokeshire and parts of Carmarthenshire and included more than a hundred quarries. In Cilgerran, most quarrying was carried out on the south or Pembrokeshire side of the Teifi though there was some work on the other bank. The slate was then transported down-river to Cardigan. Some of the slate was used for buildings locally but much was exported directly by railway for use within Britain with the remainder being exported by sea.

As mentioned in the book, legal action was taken against those quarrymasters who allowed the river Teifi to become fouled with debris which posed a danger to the ships that came up on the tide to load.

Though there were almost a dozen quarries in the Cilgerran area, some of which survived into the early decades of the twentieth century, nothing remains of this important industry and, now that nature has done what nature does and reclaimed the workings and spoil heaps, visitors to the area might find it difficult to believe that it ever existed.

If Dr Cadwgan Gwynne struck you, dear reader, as being a little fanciful, believe me when I say that he's quite vanilla when compared with the real-life nineteenth century father and son who inspired him. John and Henry Harris – known as 'the wizards of Cwrt Y Cadno' – came from the Cothi Valley in Carmarthenshire and they plied their trade, very much as Dr Gwynne is described doing, until Henry's death in 1849. If you'd like to know more about them, do look up the paper by Richard C. Allen entitled 'Wizards or Charlatans, Doctors or Herbalists? An Appraisal of the 'Cunning Men' of Cwrt Y Cadno, Carmarthenshire'. It's available as a pdf online.

But in case you were wondering, the people of Wales were not unique in hedging their bets between modern medicine and what might be called traditional practice. Wikipedia has an excellent, thoroughly-researched article on 'Cunning Folk in Great Britain' which is well worth a read in this context.

Meigan Fair

Harry's reminiscences of Meigan Fair are based in reality as it was one of the major social events of the lower Teifi Valley. *Ffair Feigan* was a cattle-selling fair that took place in Eglwyswrw every year on the first Monday after All Souls' Day (2nd November, though St Meigan's Day is actually on the 1st of November).

By the way, Meigan Fair shouldn't be confused with the rock festivals known as Meigan Fayres which took place in the village between 1973 and 1975 in a time when the lower Teifi Valley played host to many young people trying to escape the rat race and live a more 'alternative' lifestyle. (Universally known locally, when I was growing up there, as 'the hippies'.) Incidentally, if you look at the Meigan Fayres' website it will tell you that Meigan Fair took place in the summer. I can find no evidence for this – Welsh newspapers of the 1840s mention it taking place in November and Kelly's Directory for South Wales lists it as occurring on the date above in 1910. But then, outdoor rock festivals wouldn't be as attractive in November.

Buildings

The Sergeant's Arms inn still exists on Eglwyswrw's main street, though it's now a private house, and the building which was once the inn's stables – otherwise known as the Armoury – stands opposite.

The eighteenth century Pendre Inn in Cilgerran is still there, serving the refreshment needs of locals and visitors alike.

Felindre Farchog still boasts the little college building mentioned in the book as being near Dr Gwynne's house. It is a 17th-century building founded by Sir George Owen and modernised in 1852 in the Gothic style to house the Court of the Lordship of Cemais.

I must confess to playing fast and loose with the location of Eglwyswrw's forge as I needed it to be where I've placed it for obvious plot reasons. Apologies to descendants of Eglwyswrw's blacksmiths for taking the liberty!

Acknowledgements

As always, I'm going to kick off by thanking the one person in the world without whom none of my books would be written a) because I'd probably be too fed up and b) because I would definitely be too busy scrabbling together a living instead of just contributing a part-time salary to the family finances. Edwina, you keep me sane, keep a smile on my face, keep all the paperwork in order, stop me polishing the skirting boards and make our garden one of the places I love most in the world. Thank you, my love, for everything.

2020 was a strange year for writers. We couldn't get out and about – no crime fiction festivals to attend, no bookshop signings to do, no readers groups to speak to. It was all very dispiriting. A lot of writers, me among them, missed those opportunities to meet our friends and readers acutely, and it was brought home to us how important a part those opportunities to get out and talk to people play in our writing lives. Thank goodness (and all their organisers!) for all the online opportunities writers were given this year. I'd like to say a particular thank you to the inimitable Jacky Collins whose online interviews have been such a lifeline for me and many other authors this year.

As we could only see family and friends online, suddenly we were all Zoom officionados. (That's my next acknowledgement – give a very big medal to the team who developed Zoom because, without it, I'm not sure how any of us would have coped during the Covid pandemic.) But I was luckier than most. Our son, Rob, and his then-fiancée-now-wife Floriane abandoned home-working in their little London flat and came to live with us for the duration. Thank goodness for the luxury of a house big enough for us all to work in separate rooms and the luxury – for me at least – of working in the garden. (See paradise, above…) Thank you, guys, for being here with us – having you to spend time with was wonderful.

Our other son, Sam, was also a lifeline of sanity during the writing of the early parts of *Not One Of Us*, not least in suggesting and organising weekly family quizzes during those months when it was impossible to see each other. Sam, those quiz evenings, and being able to spend virtual time with everybody, were one of the saving graces of lockdown and I'm not going to forget winning the identify-the-chocolate-bar-cross-sections round in a hurry. (Signs of a chocolate-gobbling youth – Lion Bar anybody?)

Just before the pandemic hit, my previous publisher, Dome Press, was taken over by Canelo and I blanched at the thought of how lockdown was going to affect getting new editions of the series printed, shipped and into bookshops. But Canelo managed it all with incredible aplomb and the new editions were in bookshops more quickly than anybody could have anticipated – huge thanks, Michael Bhaskar and Iain Millar, for your herculean efforts on that front. And to Iain for making my day, my week and my month by comparing the Teifi Valley Coroner books to Phil Rickman's Merrily Watkins series – you couldn't have made a comparison that pleased me more, Iain!

Canelo have also been very accommodating in the matter of editors and have allowed me to work with author and freelance editor, Russel Maclean, who has now edited all but one of the Teifi Valley Coroner books. Russel, it's been such a joy working with you again. Not only do you 'get' my books you also make me up my game and keep me from my own worst excesses. I hope we have many more books to work on together.

While we're on the subject of editors, I'd also like to thank the eagle-eyed Jane Selley for the marvellous job she did in copy-editing *Not One Of Us*. Jane, you made it a pleasure to read through my proofs!

Bookshops are an author's life-support as readers are their life's blood, so thanks to Emma at Book-ish bookshop in Crickhowell who, while I was writing *Not One Of Us*, asked me to do an online launch event with Book-ish for my previous book. That event allowed me to believe that perhaps 2020 wouldn't be a year totally devoid of sales due to lockdown after all. And thanks also to all the brilliant bookshop owners who have been such stalwart supporters on social media this year – particularly Matt at Chepstow Books, Karen and Nikki at Gwisgo Bookworm in Aberaeron, Bethan at Victoria Books in Haverfordwest and Tim at Cover to Cover in Mumbles. I'm enormously grateful to you and to all the other bookshop owners who have been supportive online this year.

Writers depend on the support of their peers and I'm lucky enough to have two amazing groups of writing friends who have been more vital even than usual in the weird year during which *Not One Of Us* made its way into the world. Thanks so much to the Macmillan New Writing crew – we may not have been able to occupy our usual table in Browns for more than a year, now, but you've been there for me and, for that, I'm enormously grateful. And to the gang at Crime Cymru, the Welsh crime writers' collective, I'd just like to say that you are all awesome and thank you so much for your support and for keeping the faith with me.

Thanks to all the book-bloggers who've been so supportive and who have written such lovely reviews of my books – those reviews make all the difference in spreading the word to a wider readership. Particular thanks to Karen at Bookertalk who has been so supportive of me and of Crime Cymru as a whole. I do hope you all like *Not One Of Us*!

Heartfelt thanks, as always, go to David Headley because, without him, the Teifi Valley Coroner books wouldn't have seen the light of day and I would never have found myself on the wonderful roller-coaster that writing books about Wales is proving to be. Thank you, David, for believing in Harry and John.

And finally, thanks to you, my readers. I feel I've got to know some of you on Twitter and Facebook and I thank you from the bottom of my heart for all the emails, tweets and Facebook messages you've sent. I literally couldn't do this without you.